Imposters of Patriotism

ISBN-10: 1499175884
ISBN-13: 9781499175882

To Beth,
always,
and to
Meredith and Margot

Acknowledgments

First and foremost, to my wife, Beth, thank you for all of your support and patience as I made my way through the journey that resulted in my first novel. You were a tireless champion and I couldn't have done it without you. And to my editing team, the Rubin sisters, Michele and Dina, your expertise and enthusiasm for this project were greatly appreciated.

For his generous assistance, a special thanks to Hugh Golson, a true southern gentleman and a source of priceless information related to the magical city of Savannah, Georgia.

I would also like to express my gratitude to the early supporters of this book, Steve Skillman, Scott Humphrey, and Abner Oakes. And a special thanks to the many friends who offered their kind support throughout this endeavor.

For their generous assistance in the research of this book, I would like to acknowledge the kind folks at the Owens-Thomas House for granting me access to archival materials related to the Marquis de Lafayette's visit to Savannah in 1825, and to the Bull Street Library for giving me a behind the scenes tour of their impressive building.

Imposters of Patriotism

A Novel

Ted Richardson

Guard against the impostures of pretended patriotism.
— George Washington

1

Present Day

Savannah, GA

D ays like this made Matt Hawkins miss living in New England. It was barely ten o'clock in the morning and the bank's outdoor digital display was already cruelly flashing ninety degrees. He rolled down both windows on his vintage Chevy C-10 pickup in a futile attempt to stay cool. Factory-installed air-conditioning was offered on the '66 half-ton model, but evidently the original owner didn't live in the South or had been too cheap to install it. Even the truck's old drum brakes didn't bite like they used to, and Matt had gotten pretty good at rolling stops. On a day like today, avoiding a complete stop meant avoiding instant sweat and suffocating heat. The air was thick with humidity as he sat and waited for the red light to flip to green.

The interior of the truck was a classic 1960's minimalist vision—a bare-metal dash and a simple instrument panel that could be read without having a PhD. The enormous steering wheel looked like it belonged on the old Boston Whaler he and his father used to go fishing in along the north shore of Massachusetts. And on hot days like this, the steel-gray vinyl bench seat would stick to his skin and rip the hair from the back of his legs if he got out of the cab too fast. But the old Chevy had been love at first sight for Matt. It had great lines and an eye-catching, graceful body. He had passed by it one day, sitting in a drugstore parking lot with a For Sale sign in the windshield. On impulse, he did a U-turn and an hour later had written a check for it. That was like him. He definitely leaned to the impulsive side of the personality curve. It was a trait that had mostly worked out for him over the years. Mostly; but not all of the time.

That had been eight years ago. Right after what some would call an irrational change of careers. He had acquired a large antiques business smack-dab in the middle of the historic district of Savannah, Georgia. He shook his head in disbelief at how a Yankee kid from Boston ended up in the heart of the South, and at the strange turn of events that had landed him there. A sudden horn blast from the car behind him interrupted these musings, as the traffic light mercifully changed to green. A couple of blocks later, just south of Forsyth Park, he pulled into a small parking lot outside of the Bull Street Library. To his pleasant surprise, he found an empty space in the usually full lot.

As he made his way up the stately marble steps of the oldest library in Savannah, he couldn't help but be impressed by the beauty of its neoclassical architecture. Built in 1916, Bull Street was Matt's favorite library in town. Its design was impressive, but what he really loved was the Robin Hood mural that covered the entire south wall of the children's section, just to the right of the main entrance. The mural had been painted during the mid-1930s as part of the government-funded WPA program. He had developed a real fondness for WPA-era paintings—not only because he admired Roosevelt's program that had put thousands of unemployed craftsman, artists, musicians, and other trades-people back to work—but because of the social realism the art captured.

"Hey, Doug," Matt called out, upon reaching the second floor office of the branch director.

Doug Stone looked up from his computer, "Hey, Matt, what's going on? I haven't seen you since our last book sale."

Matt had met Doug shortly after he had acquired his antiques store. He had approached him with the idea of purchasing out-of-circulation books that the library had neither the need nor room for any longer. Over the years, their relationship had grown, and now Doug would always call Matt a few days before the announced start of the library's periodic sales, giving him first dibs on books before the sale opened to the public.

"I know, I'm sorry, but I've been crazy busy with the store. Let's try to grab a Sand Gnats game before the end of the season," Matt offered.

The Savannah Sand Gnats were a Single A minor league team affiliated with the New York Mets that played in a cozy stadium just a few miles southeast of the library. Both men had played ball in college and had taken in a few games together over the years. In fact, it was through Doug that Matt had come to discover the fascinating and rich history of baseball in Savannah, where players like Shoeless Joe Jackson, Babe Ruth, and Hank Aaron, all household names, had played at one time or another.

"I'll take you up on that game; let me know a night that works for you," Doug replied. "Come on, let's head down to the basement. I've got a few boxes set aside to check out."

He guided Matt through a locked door and down a narrow back staircase that led to the basement level of the library. As they snaked their way down two levels, Matt marveled at the ingenious design of the black wrought iron book stacks. Constructed so that they ran floor to ceiling from the basement all the way to the top level of the library, they served the dual function of load-bearing wall as well as secure storage for thousands of books.

Reaching the basement level, Doug pointed to a half dozen corrugated boxes. They were filled with early twentieth-century books that the staff had discovered while cleaning out a long-forgotten storage space under the basement stairwell. "Take a look through these and see if there's anything of interest to you."

Matt squeezed past Doug, knelt down, and began sifting through the old books. He separated them into two piles and, after he was done, the "yes" pile contained a stack of oversize atlases dating from the 1890s through the 1920s. Matt had always been fascinated with old maps, loving their unique and unbiased window into the past. Nice old atlases, particularly with colorfully drawn maps, sold pretty well in his store. People in Savannah loved their history, and a vintage atlas gave them a chance to look smart to their visiting houseguests. And it didn't hurt that such a book also looked great on a coffee table.

"I'll make you an offer on these," Matt said.

After some minor haggling he left the building, loaded down with two heavy boxes. He hoisted them into the back of his truck and made his way back toward his shop on Monterey Square.

———

Savannah had a total of twenty-four squares, and each square had its unique character and symmetrical beauty. James Oglethorpe, who had founded the city in 1733, is credited with developing the original master plan that laid out the city in a grid-like fashion around four open squares, originally intended to provide the colonists with space for military exercises. Fate had a hand in preserving that beauty when, in December 1864, the city was spared destruction by General William Tecumseh Sherman during the Union army's devastating March to the Sea. Sherman, charmed by the city, made Savannah his Christmas gift to President Abraham Lincoln.

When Matt and his now ex-wife had first visited the city twelve years earlier, Savannah's beauty and history had also captivated him. But so much had changed in his life since then. He had been married and now he was single. He had been a successful trader on Wall Street in Manhattan and now he owned an antiques shop in Georgia. He had been a lifelong northerner and now he resided in a small southern town. And it had all started with that first visit to Savannah to attend the wedding of a college friend.

The best word to describe Matt back then was driven. He was competitive, focused, knew what he wanted, and usually got it. He had been born and raised in a disciplined, but close-knit family on the north shore of Boston. His father had owned a machine shop and his mother had waited tables to help make ends meet. He was the youngest and brightest of the four Hawkins kids. His grades had earned him an academic scholarship to the Ivy League—Brown University in Rhode Island. At Brown, he had excelled in both academics and sports, and had even been offered a small contract to play minor league baseball in the Cleveland Indians farm system. Instead, he had accepted a job at Goldman Sachs in New York City and eventually became a trader on the bond desk. It was during this time that he had met his wife, who had been raised in the New York area and worked in the fashion industry.

By any measure, Matt had been successful, but he had always felt there was something missing from his life. The honest workingman's values of honesty and integrity, which had been instilled in him by his father, were hard to find on Wall Street. And the sense of community and family on which he been reared was lost amid the hustle and grime of New York City.

Maybe it was the timing that had made the difference. He had already grown disenchanted with Wall Street, and his marriage was suffering. He had proposed after a brief whirlwind romance, and they had eloped. But the honeymoon was short-lived and their personalities began to clash almost immediately after moving in together. Despite being a highly compensated bond trader, Matt wasn't caught up in the materialism that Wall Street success breeds. She was. He recalled how, during that trip twelve years ago, he had taken a long walk around Savannah's historic district when something inside him just clicked. He needed to make a change. With his usual decisiveness, he had quickly set in motion a series of events that would alter his life forever.

Somehow, he convinced his wife to move to Savannah where he found a job as a financial advisor in a boutique financial services firm. He would be making only a fraction of his Wall Street income, but he didn't care. His friends thought he was nuts, but he took to his new life right away. Unfortunately, his wife didn't. It took less than a year for her to leave their new southern home, and their divorce was final in less than two. Chalk the failed marriage up to one of those times when Matt's impulsiveness had backfired.

Even though his competitiveness, charm, and brains had paved his way to Wall Street, his real love was history. A childhood field trip to Old Sturbridge Village in Massachusetts, a living history museum depicting early New England life, with historians in costume and period buildings, had planted a seed in Matt at an early age that he had never nurtured. Now he had the chance to pursue that childhood passion. After the divorce was finalized, he made a clean break from his past. He quit the world of finance for good and used his last Wall Street bonus to purchase a somewhat dilapidated 6,800 square foot mansion on Monterey Square. The previous owner had been running it as an antiques business for close to thirty years.

Matt bought the building and the inventory in it, and never looked back. He converted the third floor of the 1850s-era mansion into a living space for himself and continued running the antiques business out of the lower floors. He was a quick learner and parlayed his love of history into his career. His ability to make connections and close a sale—skills he had honed on Wall Street—helped him build a steady clientele.

The building, which had been marketed to him as the "last unrestored grand mansion in Savannah," had fallen into considerable disrepair over the years. By the time he had purchased it, paint was peeling in sheets from the walls and there were gaps, shaped like Paleozoic continents, clearly visible in the crumbling plaster ceilings. But Matt could see that the old place had good bones. He saw it in the marble fireplaces, original bronze and crystal chandeliers, and floor-to-ceiling windows. He felt it when his hand ran over the smooth, varnished surface of the sturdy mahogany staircase banister that snaked its way elegantly up to the third floor. All these things hinted at what the house had been, and Matt hoped, could be again one day. Unfortunately, at the time, the house paralleled the state of his personal life: both required a considerable amount of repair. Eight years later, he had put enough plaster and paint into the old place that it was now more chic than shabby. His personal life, however, continued to be a work in progress.

He pulled the truck into the driveway behind his store, unloaded the boxes of atlases, and lugged them through the ground floor entryway, above which hung a small black metal sign that read HAWKINS ANTIQUES in white stenciled lettering. It was still early and there appeared to be no customers, none that Matt could see anyway. But this didn't mean there weren't any in the store.

With three floors chock-full of eclectic antique furniture, paintings, mirrors, books, statuary, and countless smaller decorative items, there was really no way for Matt to tell if someone was roaming around in the place or not. Every room had its own unique cross-section of treasures that customers were left on their own to discover. As if excavating through the layers of the earth, from the crust to the mantle to the core, one room might contain a pair of Empire chairs perched precariously atop a Victorian-era sideboard, with a sixteenth-century Persian rug underneath. Store policy was to let customers wander and, if they had a question, to simply holler for help. Not the most sophisticated of customer service models, but nobody seemed to mind. Exploring was part of the shopping experience and it worked.

Christina was behind the counter when Matt entered. She had just hung up the phone and, in her usual flippant way, said, "So let me guess, you picked up a first edition *Moby-Dick* for a buck because the pinheads at Bull Street didn't know what they had."

Christina had graduated from Savannah College of Art and Design, also known as SCAD, a couple of years before, but still needed to work for Matt because she couldn't sell enough of her somewhat bizarre abstract paintings to pay her bills. She was a good kid and a dependable worker with a good eye for the eclectic, so Matt tolerated her sarcasm and occasional rants against the injustices of society.

He threw her a sideways glance and, with a half-smile, said, "No, smart-ass, just some early twentieth-century atlases."

"How thrilling," she answered, with mock enthusiasm. "Pretty soon we can open a library of our own. I swear, Matt, you need to stop buying books from that old library until we sell the ones you bought like three years ago."

"Oh, come on, Christina, it's not that bad. Books make good filler for the store. And besides, we sell a few of them every month."

"Whatever."

"Speaking of which, did you sell anything today?" he volleyed back, keeping the good-natured but never-ending banter going between them.

"No, because that would require having an actual customer walk in the door. Seriously, the only person in here this morning was old Mrs. Higgins. She's poking around upstairs somewhere, assuming she hasn't keeled over. Not that it would matter. She never buys anything anyway."

Business was never as bad as Christina made it out to be. In fact, revenues had increased steadily over the years. She just loved to bust Matt's balls whenever the opportunity presented itself. But beneath her crass exterior, she had great affection for him, even though it rarely surfaced. This had a lot to do with the long list of men in her life, starting with her father, who had treated her like shit. So she was still learning how to behave toward someone like Matt, who genuinely had her best interests in mind.

"Be nice. She's a sweet old lady with lots of great stories. You have to get over the fact that 'just looking' is part of the antiques business," he said. "The next nine people through that door could all be tire-kickers, but the tenth one might be the whale that makes our month."

"First of all, I'm always nice to Mrs. Higgins and I do listen to her boring stories, with a plastic smile pasted on my face, even though I've heard them all before. Second, you haven't landed a whale since your Wall Street days. And third, I still think we should charge an entrance fee to keep the tire-kickers away. Remember that magazine article I e-mailed you? There's that store in California that charges shoppers five bucks to shop in their store. If you buy something, the money gets applied to the sale, but if you don't buy anything, we keep the deposit."

"Remind me again why I should take business advice from a woman who changes the color of her hair from pink to blue on a regular basis and who has a tattoo on her arm that reads 'Rage Against the Machine'?" he said with a smirk. "Never mind, I'm going to go price these atlases. Try to sell something, will you."

He made his way out of the room to find a quieter place to take a closer look at his cache of books.

2

February 1778

Valley Forge, PA

*I*t was the lowest point of the Revolutionary War for George Washington. Never before, in the almost three-year-old fight for independence, had the commander in chief of the Continental Army been more anxious. If his men weren't dying from disease, they were deserting by the dozens; close to three hundred officers alone had resigned since the past summer. What was once an army of more than 11,000 soldiers had been reduced to a force of less than 5,000 starving, desperate men huddled around campfires. Floggings had been stepped up in recent weeks out of necessity to maintain discipline and stave off mutiny. And additional sentries had been placed along the perimeter of the camp, in a futile attempt to stem the tide of daily desertions. Washington wrote to Congress warning that an all-out collapse of his army was a real possibility.

For two months, the Continental Army had been waging a losing battle against winter's fury, encamped on the high ground above the Schuylkill River, twenty miles northwest of Philadelphia. The men had worked relentlessly through the month of January to build close to two thousand fourteen-by-sixteen-foot wooden cabins, designed to sleep twelve enlisted men apiece, using timber harvested from nearby forests. A makeshift village had now been completed, but the orderly rows of small, drafty wooden huts with leaky *roofs provided little more than the most basic form of shelter. Provisions continued to be scarce, and the men were forced to survive on rations of flour, living for days, sometimes weeks, without any meat whatsoever. In stark contrast, the British Army, under the command of General William Howe, was ensconced in the relative comfort of the city of Philadelphia, less than a day's march away.*

These were some of the thoughts that consumed Washington, as he and his devoted wife, Martha, hosted a modest dinner for two of Washington's top generals, Nathanael Greene and Henry Knox, and their wives Caty and Lucy, respectively, at Washington's cramped but tidy stone farmhouse. The farmhouse served as Washington's temporary home and military headquarters while at Valley Forge. The simple dinner that had consisted of pork stew, assorted breads, and pudding had come to an end, and the servants had begun to clear the table.

"George, are you listening?" Martha looked with some concern at her husband, who was clearly distracted and not paying attention to the conversation at hand. "Caty just asked if there was any news from Congress regarding your request for additional provisions. But you seem to be somewhere else."

Nathanael Greene jumped in to rescue his superior, "It's quite all right, Martha. My wife surely understands that the general has many responsibilities that keep him preoccupied."

"No, no, Nathanael, Martha is right. My sincerest apologies, Caty. My mind does seem to be filled with many matters at the moment," replied Washington. "But unfortunately, I have little in the way of good news to share from our esteemed congressional assembly, currently holed up in York. My urgent requests for more provisions have fallen on deaf ears. They seem more inclined to spend their time making foolish plans with Gates and his new Board of War, rather than focusing on our plight here."

There had been no love lost between Washington and General Horatio Gates during the almost three-year struggle for independence. Gates, who in his own opinion, was unjustly passed over for the position that Washington now held, had been working political back channels to lobby for a supervisory role over the man whose job he coveted. The prior November, shortly after Washington's successive defeats at the battles of Brandywine and Germantown, Gates had gotten his wish. Congress created the Board of War, inserting essentially a new layer of command between themselves and the man serving as the commander in chief of the Continental Army. General Gates, the hero of the recent American victory at the Battle of Saratoga, was appointed president of this new executive agency. Now, all military strategy decisions had to go through the Gates-led Board of War.

"But how can they be so blind to the atrocious conditions here?" asked Caty incredulously. "Do they not care that these poor men are half-naked and literally freezing to death every day?"

Catharine Littlefield Greene, known as Caty, had been friends with George and Martha Washington since her husband, Nathanael Greene, was first summoned to Boston after the outbreak of the revolution in 1775. Caty was younger than her husband by more than a decade and was blessed with uncommon beauty and an equally uncommon, especially among women of her time, willingness to express her opinion. But rather than suppress his wife's inquisitiveness and candor, Greene reveled in it. And her natural beauty and disdain for playing the part of a genteel wife of a general had made her a favorite of Washington's over the past few years.

"Ah, but my dear Caty, if only I could dispatch you to York to prevail upon our noble assembly, I have no doubt that our camp would be overflowing with ample provisions!" declared Washington, to good-natured laughter from his guests.

Henry Knox interjected, "Unfortunately, in addition to conducting a war against the British, we must also wage political battles with our own Congress, let alone the Board of War's preposterous plans for attacking the British in Canada. At least the British are clear with their hostile intentions, whereas our enemies in Congress operate behind the veil of politics to usurp our commander's authority."

The first major decision of the new board was to send a force of more than two thousand troops north of the border on an ill-conceived mission to invade Canada. In a clear slap in the face of Washington, Gates chose the

Marquis de Lafayette to lead the incursion, effectively separating Washington from one of his fiercest supporters and protégés, the young Lafayette. Washington had met the wealthy nineteen-year-old French aristocrat the year before and it hadn't taken long before he developed a fatherly bond with the young nobleman. The tall and slim Lafayette was an intelligent and exceedingly passionate revolutionary. And although lacking battlefield experience, he proved to be a fast study and quickly became a member of Washington's inner circle of trusted confidants.

"Gentlemen, let us retire to the privacy of the next room, to spare our wives of such depressing talk. Ladies, as always, time with you offers such a welcome diversion from this dreary place. Please forgive me, for I must borrow your husbands for a short while," Washington said. And with that, the three men pushed back from the table and made their way to the adjoining room that served as Washington's office, to continue their conversation by the warmth of a small stone fireplace.

After the three generals were safely out of earshot of their wives in the other room, Washington spoke directly to his longtime friend and comrade-in-arms, Nathanael Greene, "Nathanael, what is the current state of the troops?" He winced from a sharp pain in his mouth caused by his crudely constructed dentures that rubbed against a sensitive section of his lower gums. A constant reminder of how few of his own teeth remained.

Major General Nathanael Greene stood at just under six feet tall, and possessed a firm but even disposition that had made him one of Washington's most dependable officers. Greene was considered a gifted military strategist and Washington valued his counsel perhaps more than any other. "Well, sir, the situation is quite bleak. The food crisis has gone from bad to worse. With last week's blizzard making normal routes impassable, the few meager supplies we were getting have now ceased altogether. The men have not had meat in more than a week and are subsisting on nothing more than fire cakes at this time. Twenty men, maybe more, are dying each day from disease, made worse by the lack of food. Morale has plummeted and desertions continue to rise," replied Greene evenly.

"*What about the foraging parties sent out to secure cattle and provisions from local farmers?*" *Washington asked.*

"*Unfortunately, they have had very little success, primarily due to the fact that the farmers are more likely to sell to the British forces because they pay in solid pounds sterling, which far outweighs the depreciated value of our own Continental currency,*" *said Greene.*

"*Dammit, don't these people understand we are fighting for their independence, too?*" *scoffed Washington, as he tossed a small log onto the waning fire. Incredulous, he continued his questioning of Greene:* "*Of the 10,000 men who entered Valley Forge, what's your best estimate of the number fit for service today?*"

"*We've lost close to 2,500 to death, desertion, and resignation since December. Of the remaining 7,500 men, I believe that another third or more are unfit for duty due to weakness from dysentery, typhus, influenza, and other maladies,*" *Greene said.*

Washington grimly did the tally in his head, "*My God, that leaves us with a fighting force of less than 5,000 able-bodied men!*" *Turning again to Greene, Washington asked,* "*And how many British troops do we believe General Howe now has encamped in Philadelphia?*"

"*Our spies believe there are between 10,000 and 12,000, but there are rumors that massive reinforcements have been requested that could push the number of British troops to 17,000 or more,*" *replied Greene.*

Washington turned to Henry Knox, his rotund chief of artillery, who was refilling his tankard of wine. He asked, "*Henry, what about the horses?*"

Prior to the war, Henry Knox had been a Boston bookstore owner with a love of history and a special interest in artillery. Washington and Knox had formed a bond of friendship in the early days of the fight for independence that had only gotten stronger over the years. Knox had subsequently been promoted to brigadier general, serving as Washington's chief of artillery. In that role at Valley Forge, he was responsible for establishing a perimeter defense to safeguard the winter encampment.

"*More than five hundred horses have perished and most of the rest are too weak from starvation to be of any use to us. If attacked tomorrow, we would not be able to deploy our artillery effectively for battle. Nor would we be able to take our cannons with us if we are forced to retreat to a new location across the river," replied Knox. He shifted uncomfortably in the stiff wooden Windsor chair. The finely turned spindles crackled loudly under the stress of his considerable girth.*

With the flickering flames of the fire casting eerie shadows across his face, Washington said, "With all the spies and double agents about, let alone the scores of deserting soldiers making their way to Philadelphia, it is inconceivable that General Howe remains ignorant to our dire situation. And if these rumors regarding a request for more troops are true, then perhaps the British are readying for a winter attack to take advantage of our current vulnerability."

"It is exactly what we would do if the situation were reversed," exclaimed Knox. "May I ask if there is any news on the proposed alliance with France that Mr. Franklin is attempting to secure?"

The Continental Congress had previously dispatched diplomats Benjamin Franklin and Silas Deane to France with the intent of securing a treaty that would both recognize American independence and commit the French to a military alliance with the upstart American nation. While such an alliance would significantly enhance the American chances of victory, there had been no word of progress from the distinguished American emissaries.

"I'm afraid we cannot put our confidence in a foreign power at this point. Even if an agreement were to be signed today, it would be months before troops or provisions would reach our shores. No, gentlemen, we are on our own. Not only can we not count on the French; we do not even have the support of many in our own Congress. And I'll be damned if I will put my army's fate in the hands of that corrupt agency headed by Horatio Gates," Washington said.

After a long silence, with the only sound coming from the ticking of the walnut case clock in the corner of the room, Washington continued, "I think we can all agree, gentlemen, that given the current state of our troops bivouacked here on this frozen ground, an imminent attack by Howe's army

*would have catastrophic consequences for our cause. I think the time has
come for us to rethink our options. Carefully but quickly, for all my instincts
are telling me that Howe is indeed meditating a stroke against our army here
at Valley Forge."*

*After a brief pause, he continued, "Almost 25 years ago, I found myself
in a predicament that I care not to repeat. Ironically enough, at the time I was
a major serving in the British Colonial Militia during the French and Indian
Wars, at Fort Necessity. As you know, we were defeated because we were
outgunned, outmanned, and undersupplied. It was either negotiate surrender or
face a certain bloodbath. But we waited too long and had no leverage with which
to negotiate. It was only by the grace of God that our troops were allowed to
safely return to Virginia, in return for surrendering the fort."*

*"But, Your Excellency, if you mean reconciliation, you must remember
Congress' failed negotiations with Howe a year ago last September. The talks
failed because the British refused to recognize our independence," replied
Greene, surprised that his commander had raised the topic of surrender.*

*"We are not the same army we were then, Nathanael," Washington
said, his voice rising ever so slightly. "We may have to open the door to
negotiations with General Howe on terms that may not be as favorable as
we would ideally like. If we don't take decisive action now, we may soon be
completely out of options."*

*"But, sir, Congress would never allow opening discussions with Howe
without their consent. And our enemy Mr. Gates would most assuredly
manipulate the situation at the expense of your reputation," countered
Greene.*

*"You're quite right, and that's why we will need to act independently
of Congress. We need to communicate directly with Howe, via courier, to
understand his current terms for a negotiated surrender. At a minimum, by
taking this route, we may delay or even postpone indefinitely an attack by
the British," argued Washington, who appeared more anxious than either
general had ever seen their commander in chief.*

*After some thought, Greene said, "I agree that with every passing day
our position weakens, and that we cannot sit idly by waiting for an inevitable*

attack from Howe. But to open the door to surrender is a decision that cannot be undone, sir."

"I understand that all too well, my friend," Washington stated solemnly. He then turned to Knox and asked, "Henry, where do you stand?"

"As I said earlier, if I were Howe, I would not hesitate to take advantage of my strength in numbers and strike a final, decisive blow against my weakened enemy. So I cannot disagree that the advantages of opening negotiations outweigh the risks at the moment." Knox replied.

"The hour is getting late, gentlemen. As always, I thank you for your invaluable counsel. Let us sleep on it and we'll speak again in the morning. I trust you will keep a conversation of this import in the strictest of confidence," Washington said. He stiffly rose from his chair by the fire, signaling that their meeting had come to a close.

———

Washington awoke earlier than usual the next morning. He made his way quietly downstairs, from the second-floor bedroom used by him and Mrs. Washington to his office on the first floor, where the flurry of daily activity had yet to begin. In the quiet chill of the predawn hour, he sat at his Queen Anne desk and put on his oval-lens spectacles. After a few last moments of indecision, he thrust his favorite quill pen in ink. By the light of a single candle, he began to draft a secret letter to General William Howe, commander in chief of the British Army.

Later that same morning, Washington summoned General Greene to his headquarters. Upon his arrival, Washington directed Greene back outside into the cold, gray morning so they could have a private discussion. Once outside, Washington reached into his overcoat and discreetly handed the letter over to Greene, which had been secured with his personal wax seal. "Nathanael, there is only one man I trust with delivering this letter. I cannot stress the severe consequences for us all if it were to fall into the wrong hands," he said, his condensed breath bridging the frigid divide between the two men.

Greene, shivered as much from the cold as from the recognition that
the letter he now held in his hands was the secret surrender letter they had
discussed the prior evening. "Am I to understand this is the surrender letter
to General Howe?" he asked.

"It is. And I want you to leave immediately, with a military escort, of
course, to personally deliver it to Howe in Philadelphia. You are to return
without delay with his reply. Do you understand?" Washington asked.

"I do, sir. I will make preparations to leave within the hour," Greene
said dutifully. He was shocked that Washington had made his decision so
quickly, but as always, he would honor his commander's orders and deliver
the letter as instructed.

It was late in the day by the time Greene and his personal escort
reached Philadelphia. Once there, however, they discovered through their
local spy network that General Howe had departed unexpectedly that
very morning for New York and would be gone at least a week. Greene
turned straightaway back to Valley Forge with the undelivered letter in
hand.

His traveling party, however, did not have enough daylight left to make
it back before nightfall, so they decided to make camp for the night en route.
Sitting alone by a small campfire late that evening, doubt began to overtake
Greene. He trusted Washington implicitly, but wondered why the general
had acted in such haste and chosen not to share the final wording of the letter
with him or Knox. In the dim light of the waning fire, he anxiously turned
the letter over and over in his hands and wrestled with the questions that
had been weighing on his mind throughout the day. What was the current
state of mind of his commander and friend? Just how far did he go with
his offer of a negotiated surrender? Should his loyalty be to Washington
or to the country for which he was ready to sacrifice his life in the name of
independence? He stared at the wax seal, the only barrier between him and
the answers to these vexing questions.

And then, in a moment of clarity, he made up his mind. Duty to country must outweigh loyalty to his commander. His decision had been made, so
he broke Washington's official seal and read the letter.

Greene knew that by breaking the seal he had violated Washington's confidence and that he could never return the letter to him without the broken seal being discovered. Instead, he decided to concoct a story of spotting British patrols upon his return trip, which had forced him to make the prudent decision to burn the letter rather than run the risk of letting it fall into unwanted hands. But the truth was that he never did burn the letter. Upon his return to Valley Forge the next morning, Washington accepted his explanation, after which Greene returned to his quarters that he shared with his wife, Caty, and stowed the letter in his brown, tooled-leather portmanteau personal effects trunk. Whether or not he intended to destroy the letter and simply forgot about it, or whether he had other motives for keeping it, nobody would ever know—because Greene never spoke of it again.

In the weeks and months that followed, a series of significant events occurred that changed the tide of the war for the American cause. The flow of provisions increased significantly and Washington's troops began drilling daily under the tutelage of a Prussian officer, Baron von Steuben, who arrived unexpectedly at Valley Forge in late February. As a result, the Continental Army's discipline, health, and morale improved dramatically. More importantly, a treaty with France was signed that secured the promise of French allied troops, muskets, and provisions.

Washington never again revisited talk of surrender.

3

Present Day

Central Texas

The central Texas heat didn't bother the blackbuck antelope. They grazed during the day no matter how hot the temperature. And unlike most exotic game introduced into Texas, they remained wary and alert. They would flee at the first sign of danger. Once they started to run, you could forget about bagging one. Blackbuck could reach top speeds of fifty miles per hour. Big Bill Emerson, however, was bothered by the heat and was sweating profusely as he looked through his field binoculars. His sights were set on the cluster of pin oaks ahead in the distance, his eyes scanning for the small herd of blackbucks they had been tracking for the better part of the afternoon.

They had driven to a remote section on Emerson's sprawling 2,000-acre ranch, near the border of San Saba County. Located in the region of Texas known as Hill Country, it was famed for its rugged hills and granite plateaus. For the last thirty minutes, they had carefully traversed the rocky, cactus-laden terrain by foot, looking for any sign of movement. Finally, they worked their way to within shooting range of the nomadic herd that was foraging amid some tall grasses. Bill had what looked to be an eighty pounder in his sights and was just about to pull the trigger when he heard a shot ring out from his left. His trophy antelope had just been dropped with a single shot by Chuck Conrad.

"Goddammit, Chuck!" Bill yelled.

"Sorry, boss, you were just a little slow on the uptake again," replied Chuck, with a slow smile. He was Emerson's oldest friend and current campaign manager, directing Big Bill's run for president of the United States.

"Son of a bitch. That big buck was mine. Those horns were more than twenty-five inches," Bill said. The blackbuck antelope was not indigenous to Texas but had been brought there from India a half century earlier. Swift and elusive, it had thrived in the rugged Texas landscape. Even so, the males' distinctive black-and-white hide and V-shaped horns, which corkscrewed twenty-five inches or more from their head, made them a popular exotic species with hunters.

"Tell you what," Chuck said, as they walked toward the kill, "if they measure more than twenty-five inches, then you can have them."

"It's my goddamn ranch Chuck, I'll keep them either way," Bill said, still miffed at Conrad for bagging his prize. According to the tape, the spiral horns measured exactly twenty-three inches. Bill had once again come up short in a friendly competition with his friend. "Come on, you pain in the ass, let's head back to the lodge. I need a drink."

As they made their way back to the Jeep for the twenty-minute ride back to Emerson's massive ranch house, Conrad slung his arm around his bigger friend and said, "Mr. Future President, if you're buying, then I'm drinking."

Even though they had grown up on different sides of the tracks in their small East Texas town, Chuck Conrad had been friends with Bill Emerson since grade school, and he loved him like a brother. It was true that when it came to sports and grades,

Chuck had always bested Bill. Not that Bill was dumb. Chuck just had head-of-the-class smarts. But nobody could compete with Big Bill's larger-than-life personality. He might have had average looks and second-string athletic ability, but his outgoing personality and easy charm had always landed him the best-looking girls. As the son of a moderately wealthy oilman, he also had the best parties and the best cars. That moderate wealth had eventually turned into obscene wealth when one of the largest oil fields found since the 1940s was discovered on an obscure tract of land that had been in the Emerson family for generations.

Bill had attended the University of Texas at Austin, where he majored in partying, primarily, even though the degree said Business. Arriving on campus, Bill had picked up right where he left off in high school. By the time he graduated six years later, he had become a legend for his epic parties and equally epic antics. His excesses put an extra forty pounds on his already large frame, and he acquired the handle Big Bill. Upon graduation, however, the party was over. His father had put young Bill to work straightaway in the family's oil business.

To his credit, Bill worked as hard as he had once partied. He leveraged his natural charm to negotiate contracts, close deals, and grow the business. He was so successful that, when the Emerson's finally sold their independent company to a large multinational, Big Bill had walked away with a tidy $150 million. That had been ten years ago.

Shortly after the sale, when a six-term U.S. senator from Texas, and close friend of Bill's father, decided to retire, Big Bill was hand-picked as his replacement. Although Big Bill had very little interest in politics, his father thought it would be a good idea to have his son in Congress protecting the family's substantial financial holdings and investments. And that was that. The campaign had been financed with $50 million of family money and Big Bill was elected to the Senate in a landslide. He had served just one term before his father talked him into entering the race for president. With the election now just a couple of months away, fifty-two-year-old William Washington Emerson found himself in a dead heat with his Democratic opponent.

Sitting on the large wraparound porch of the main lodge of the ranch complex, Bill and Chuck were enjoying their second round of bourbons. It was a gorgeous evening and, from their vantage point, they could see for more than forty miles as the sun began to set on the western horizon. When Big Bill had made his fortune, one of the first things he did was to design and build Blackjack Ranch, a sprawling complex of buildings and structures that took up a full seven acres of his two-thousand-acre property. The complex consisted of a main lodge constructed out of massive cedar logs, thirty-foot ceilings, and three enormous rock fireplaces that cost $60,000 each to build. There was also a working saloon, two kitchens, an enormous pool, and enough beds to sleep fourteen people. For entertainment, in addition to hunting exotic game, the ranch was equipped with a tennis court, a three-hole golf course, a fifteen-acre pond stocked with bass, and a lighted shooting range for skeet and trap.

"You are a lucky son of a bitch, you know that, Bill," Chuck said, gazing out over Big Bill's central Texas kingdom.

"Yeah, well this is the first day I've had away from the campaign trail in over two months. So I'm not sure I'd call it a charmed existence," he replied.

"I know partner, but we're in the home stretch now, so we can't let up. After you recharge your batteries today and tomorrow, it's back on the road again. We've got Atlanta on Tuesday, Charlotte on Wednesday, and Richmond on Thursday."

"Well, at least we'll be in friendly territory." The southeastern states had voted solidly Republican in the last few elections.

"Enjoy it while it lasts, my friend, because after that it's off to the Midwest swing states to duke it out for the rest of the campaign. By the time this November rolls around, you're going to be on a first name basis with every blue-collar Joe in Ohio and Pennsylvania."

"Speaking of getting back on the road, do you think we're going overboard with the whole Washington connection? I mean, we've even got the campaign bus wrapped with a picture of his ugly mug," Bill asked.

Emerson had gained notoriety during his stint as a U.S. senator when Ancestry.com had anointed him as the most direct descendant of George Washington. It had gone so far as to claim that if there were a monarchy in America, Big Bill would be next in line for the crown. At Chuck's direction, the Emerson campaign had leveraged this connection to the hilt, hoping to use the patriotic imagery of Washington to further Big Bill's chances in November.

"Our polling shows that your family's link to the most famous Founding Father is helping your 'trust' ratings, so we're sticking with it. In fact, we're going to start running those commercials next week. You know, the one with you shaking hands with the group of old broads from the Daughters of the American Revolution in front of the Washington Monument, with that song 'Proud to Be an American' playing in the background?"

"Yeah, I like that commercial. For once I don't look so goddamned fat," Big Bill lamented.

"Pretty amazing what the camera can do, huh?" Chuck said, laughing.

"Fuck you."

"Come on, stop being so sensitive. Besides, that's what the American public loves about you. You're human. Hell, ninety percent of the country is overweight, for God's sake. Besides, have you seen the latest polls? We've gone from eight points behind, when this thing started, to pretty much even. And a lot of it is due to the fact that the American public relates to *you* and not that wooden, liberal prick from Massachusetts."

"Still, I should lose a few pounds."

"Bill, you've got to stay focused on the big prize. We're so close to achieving our goal."

"Sometimes I think you and my father want this more than I do."

Chuck thought to himself, *you're damn right.* He never had it easy like Bill. It was true that he had been blessed with brains, but he had had to scrape and claw for everything he had achieved in life. He had put up with the elitist pricks at the Ivy League college he had attended—the kind who looked down their noses at the scholarship kid from east Texas. Their disdain had only stiffened his resolve to succeed. And his success as one of the top litigators at the prestigious Dallas law firm where he had worked had provided some validation. But he still felt as though he didn't fit in and that people looked at him with doubt and mistrust.

For Chuck, only one thing could prove his naysayers wrong, and that was getting Big Bill elected president of the United States. He believed that three things had gotten William Washington Emerson this far: his daddy's money, his famous middle name, and Conrad's guidance. He also knew that even though Emerson could be the one sitting in the Oval Office one day soon, he would be the chief of staff running the White House. But he needed to tread carefully and continue to prop up his friend. Big Bill was his golden ticket to 1600 Pennsylvania Avenue and to all the power and prestige that came with that address.

So he said, "Bill, we're all in this together. Your father and I only have your best interests in mind. Do you realize the things we're going to do together when we get you elected? This country has been held hostage for too long by liberals, environmentalists, and accountants. The American public is ready to clean house, and you're their guy."

"I know, you're my best friend and I trust you, it's just that sometimes I think I'm in way over my head."

"It's natural for you to feel that way. But I've got your back, so you've got nothing to worry about." After draining the last of his bourbon, he continued, "Speaking of having your back, we need to spend most of the day tomorrow getting you prepped for the debate in a couple of weeks."

"I guess that means we're not taking the ATVs out to the skeet range tomorrow," Big Bill said.

Chuck looked over with raised eyebrows, but before he could remark, Bill held up his hand and said, "I'm kidding, you just give me the words, and I'll make them sing. You know I can charm the pants off a preacher's wife."

"That's my boy!"

4

1790

Mulberry Grove Plantation

Savannah, GA

*T*he usually vivacious Caty Greene sat quietly crying by the bank of the Savannah River in front of her large plantation home. Her precise features and pristine complexion that had enchanted so many men over the years were hidden from view, buried in her hands. Spread out in front of her was an elaborate system of irrigation works—levees, ditches, culverts, floodgates, and drains—used to control the flow of water from the river to and from the rice fields currently under cultivation at Mulberry Grove. It was getting late in the growing season and the brute force of scores of slaves was on display, as hundreds of acres of river swamp were being prepared for harvest. The late summer sun shone off of her dark brown hair, but fatigue rimmed her usually brilliant violet eyes with red. The enormity of her situation had simply become too much for her to bear. At only thirty-five years old, with five children to raise, a sprawling plantation to run, and mounting sums of money owed to friends, the irrepressible Caty had reached her breaking point.

It had been more than four years since Caty's husband, Revolutionary War hero General Nathanael Greene, had died suddenly from complications *due to sunstroke, at the premature age of forty-four. Shortly before his death, out of financial necessity, Greene had been forced to relocate his family from their home in Rhode Island to a rundown rice plantation located on the west bank of the Savannah River, about fifteen miles north of Savannah, Georgia. The Greene's had not planned on uprooting their young family from their quaint New England home, but their dire financial situation had left them no choice. The vast but overgrown estate, called Mulberry Grove, had been awarded to Nathanael Greene by the Georgia legislature at the conclusion of the Revolutionary War, in appreciation for his role in "saving the South." The plantation had been confiscated years before, from British loyalist Lieutenant Governor John Graham, and had sat untended for years, leading to its current state of deterioration.*

Since his death, Caty had been engaged in an endless quest to petition Congress to indemnify her husband from his wartime debts. While serving as quartermaster general in the Continental Army, Greene had failed to keep any official receipts of his transactions with merchants. As a result, Congress held that he was personally responsible for the promissory notes he had signed, despite the fact that they were for the purchase of clothing and other provisions to keep his army properly supplied. To make matters worse, Greene's investments in various stocks and shipping concerns had all gone bad. In order to make good on his promise to pay back the merchants, Greene had been forced to borrow money from his wealthy friends, which had put him heavily in debt. These debts had only accumulated since his death. For even though he had left his widow with land assets consisting of several thousand acres, only a few hundred acres were currently being cultivated at Mulberry Grove, so Caty had no choice but to continue to borrow from friends to support herself and her five young children.

About a hundred yards behind where she sat crying in the late afternoon sun, sheltered by a stand of mulberry trees, was the spacious, two-story Federal-style house that her family had called home for the past five years. Her children, aged eight through fifteen, had been born in rapid succession during the war years. But Caty had not seen her oldest child, George Washington Greene, in more than three years, which only added to her current gloom.

Young George had been sent away to Paris for schooling under the supervision of the Marquis de Lafayette, the French revolutionary and dear friend of Caty's, who had insisted on helping pay for young George's education.

Her next-oldest child, Martha Washington Greene, now fourteen, helped her mother around the house by attending to her three younger siblings, who were all currently being tutored by a young, Connecticut-born and Yale-educated tutor from Rhode Island, named Phineas Miller. In addition to schooling the children, Miller was responsible for helping Caty manage the day-to-day operations of Mulberry Grove. Unfortunately, the plantation had yet to produce enough income to cover her considerable expenses. So to provide much-needed income, she had been forced to sell most of her most prized possessions. But even this wasn't enough to satisfy her debts, and soon the creditors had moved in and, like crows picking at a carcass, had steadily stripped Caty's home of all the furnishings that had held any value.

Despite her responsibilities as a mother and plantation owner, she somehow found the time, over the past couple of years, to gather affidavits, documents, and eyewitness testimonies to support her petition to Congress for indemnification from her husband's debts, as well as reimbursement for the personal fortune he had risked for the cause of independence. She had been a woman on a mission, shuttling back and forth between Savannah, New York, and Philadelphia, to meet with the likes of Secretary of the Treasury Alexander Hamilton, Secretary of War Henry Knox, and even newly elected President George Washington, to solicit help in her fight with Congress. Unfortunately, she had little to show for her substantial efforts. She still had not been granted permission to present her petition to Congress, and with financial ruin inching ever closer, Caty's steadfast resolve had morphed into a desperate fear for her future.

She wiped the tears from her face, slowly lifted her small frame off the ground, and headed toward the house. Halfway up the bluff from the river, she diverted from her path home and, on impulse, decided to take a walk around the grounds. She hoped the exercise would relieve the terrifying tension that had taken hold of her body. She made her way past the house, beyond several outhouses including the kitchen, smokehouse, coach house, stables, and poultry barn. She silently moved through the forest of spreading live oaks, their branches dripping with Spanish moss. These trees had once held such enchantment for her, but now only reminded her of the weight upon her own shoulders.

Finally, she made her way past the slave cabins that ringed the area near the main house, and back around to the large vegetable garden. The beauty and serenity of the garden had always been calming to her, so when a mockingbird sang out from a nearby flowering shrub and a mild breeze nudged a stray strand of hair from her face, Caty's spirits were lifted. Her heavy mood lightened ever so slightly, she made her way up the stately central brick staircase and crossed the threshold into the house, resigned to make one last attempt to have her case presented before Congress.

———

Two things had been working in Caty's favor. First, she had always been a voracious reader, and this skill had been put to good use these last couple of years, as she had to pour through hundreds of letters, legal documents, and affidavits. Second, she had always enjoyed the company of men over women, and had held her own in political discussions with her husband and his comrades-in-arms during the war. It was in these politically charged discussions, with the naturally flirtatious Caty at the center of attention, that she had gained valuable experience in formulating and presenting an argument.

Caty, her head a bit clearer, was in the downstairs parlor of the main house, looking out the wide glass panels that offered an unobstructed view to the Savannah River and beyond. She was in the middle of jotting down her thoughts in a small journal she had been keeping for the last couple of years. The journal had been given to her by Henry and Lucy Knox, from General Knox's own bookstore in Boston, shortly after the conclusion of the war. It had an expensive calfskin leather cover and was imprinted with an intricate gold leaf rose design. She kept the journal partly to help remember events that could prove useful in building her case, and partly for cathartic reasons. Writing in her journal helped alleviate the loneliness of being a widow, and gave her an opportunity to keep fresh those harrowing but incredibly exciting days of the revolution. She documented some of her most memorable experiences from the war, and also recorded the noteworthy events of her current life, to help organize her thoughts as she prepared her case for Congress.

Her writing was interrupted when one of her house slaves entered the room to bring her a locked box that had just been found in a far corner of the third-floor attic. Evidently the box had been stowed inside her husband's leather travel case that he had carried with him during the war. Unable to disengage the rusted locking mechanism after many attempts, she became increasingly curious to find out what sort of treasures the box might hold.

Desperately hoping that it might contain something of financial value, Caty finally got help from a slave who handled carpentry on the plantation to pry open the box. But after loosening the strong hinges from their casings, her heart sank when she found nothing inside but a stack of old wartime correspondence. Dejected, she began to halfheartedly sort through the stack of old letters. She had all but lost interest when suddenly, at the very bottom of the box, she came across a letter with an official-looking seal that had long ago been broken. Pulling the letter out, she carefully flattened the creased folds in her lap, and to her surprise, discovered that it was in the hand of General George Washington, dated February 1778, Valley Forge. This got her attention. But it was to whom the letter was addressed that caused her sharp intake of breath—General William Howe, commander in chief of the British Army.

Her pulse began to quicken as she finished reading and the reality sunk in that she held in her hands what appeared to be a surrender letter written by George Washington!

After the initial shock subsided, Caty sat on her sofa in the fading light of day, baffled as to how her husband came to possess the letter, and why it had apparently never made it to General Howe. Her thoughts eventually returned to her current fight for her family's survival. She was no political novice, and she knew that her time before Congress was drawing near and that there was a good chance that her reimbursement request could be denied. So her mind instinctively began to ponder the possible leverage the discovery of this explosive letter could provide in her fight for the money she believed was rightfully hers.

To date, her dear friend, newly elected President George Washington, had offered her advice on her congressional petition, but had been hesitant to get personally involved in resolving the matter. She was keenly aware that the Republic was still in its infancy, and that the revelation of a letter of surrender from Washington could increase the distrust that some in the government felt toward him, and fan the flames of conspiracy theories that had been circulating recently in newspapers throughout the country. Several factions had raised concerns that Washington and his former generals had secured too many positions of power in the newly formed government. The fear was that these men would stage a military coup and undermine the newly formed Democracy.

But Caty had more immediate problems of her own. Foremost in her mind was that if she didn't secure reimbursement from Congress, she would be destroyed financially and unable to provide for her young family. In this regard, the timing of the discovery of the letter was fortuitous, because it had just been announced that, the following spring, General Washington would be making a presidential tour of the South, and was scheduled to make a personal visit to her at Mulberry Grove.

With a renewed sense of purpose, Caty dutifully recorded in her journal the account of her shocking discovery.

5

Present Day

Savannah, GA

Matt let Christina leave early. She had to prepare for an art show that a funky uptown eatery held each month to help support struggling young artists. Admittedly, Christina had talent, but her style was way too dark and macabre for Matt's tastes. Creepy bloody dolls and black raven kind of grim. She was a sweet kid, but she had some deep-seated shit she'd have to deal with someday. If only she'd lighten up a bit, he thought, maybe she'd actually sell something. But he could never figure out a good way to tell her without hurting her, or worse yet, pissing her off. So he always just let it go. As he was closing up the register and reconciling the sales receipts for the day, it occurred to him that he had never gone through the box of books he had purchased that morning from the Bull Street Library.

Two Yuenglings later, with his feet up on the kitchen table, he grabbed the last book from the bottom of the box. It was an atlas of South Carolina published in 1922. His mother would roll over in her grave if she knew what her son had paid for the vintage red Formica kitchen table upon which his feet now rested. He had come from a family of modest means, and his parents had furnished their home with cast-off furniture from the 1950s and 1960s. Not because they preferred the style, but rather because it was cheap. Now, however, that same furniture had a name—"mid-century"—and had become highly desirable.

Matt's upstairs apartment took up the entire third floor of the mansion that served as both his business and his home. Over the years, most of the renovations he had done on the building had gone into updating his upstairs living quarters. As he looked around his apartment, it struck him that he had probably decorated it the way he had to try to achieve the same comfortable, lived-in feel of his childhood home. Although he knew that, without the sounds of the raucous Hawkins clan, his bachelor pad would never come close. A pang of loneliness crept into his psyche, as it oftentimes did, but he quickly shook it off.

He returned to the final atlas. The only reason Matt had purchased this particular book was because its subject matter was relatively local, as South Carolina was Georgia's neighbor to the north. He cracked it open and started to flip through its oversize pages. Unfortunately, the maps inside weren't very well decorated. He began to think this one was a total bust. But before he put it down, he flipped to the middle of the book and saw something remarkable.

He snapped to attention, swinging his feet off the table and almost knocking over what was left of his beer. He removed the atlas from his lap and laid it flat on the smooth Formica tabletop. He pushed his chair back and stood up hesitantly. Apparently, someone had cut away what appeared to be about a ten-inch-square opening in the middle pages of the atlas. They had purposely left the last few pages intact to conceal the opening from the back of the book. But more astonishing was what lay inside the carved-out cavity—a small book that appeared very old.

His first thought was that his buddy Doug, from the Bull Street Library, had played a joke on him. But something about the way the pages were cut gave him pause. It was clear that whoever had carved out this clever little hiding place had done so a very long time ago.

The sun had mercifully set, but it was still hot. It had suddenly become quite still in the stuffy top floor of the old mansion. Matt walked over to the large window overlooking the park. It had been stuck in a slightly open position for years. Undeterred, he tried one more time to open it wider. It wouldn't budge. Someday he'd have to get that fixed, he thought to himself. He switched on the ceiling fan to get some air circulating. The kitchen table was bathed in the bright white glare from a solitary light hovering above. Finally, Matt reached into the atlas and, like a surgeon removing a vital organ, carefully extracted the little book from inside the cavity.

The brown leather cover was worn smooth. There were traces of a gold inlay design of some kind. But it had long since faded and cracked to the point where the original motif was no longer legible. Matt thought that it must have been an expensive book to make back in the day. He gently pulled back the front cover to take a look inside. The binding crackled audibly and was loose to the touch, but the book itself seemed to be intact and in fairly good condition. He wondered if the cool, dry climate of the library basement had helped preserve it all these years.

He stopped and wiped his perspiring hands on his pants legs before handling the more than two-hundred-year-old pages. The inside front cover was inscribed in flowing cursive with the words *Journal of Caty Greene*. The name Greene, spelled with an *e* at the end, looked vaguely familiar to him, but didn't immediately ring any bells. His heart began to race, however, when he turned to the first page of writing and saw the date at the top of the page: *March 1787*.

Shocked and excited, a flood of thoughts rushed into Matt's mind all at once. *Holy shit! Who the hell is Caty Greene? How did an*

eighteenth-century book end up inside a twentieth-century atlas? I told you
these books were worth it, Christina! I need another beer.

To calm his nerves, Matt walked a few short steps and freed
another bottle from the confines of the refrigerator. He retrieved
his laptop from his study and searched the Internet for Caty
Greene. To his surprise, there were dozens of references. He
spent thirty minutes getting to know Catharine Littlefield Greene.
He read about her experiences during the Revolutionary War as
well as her life after the war. He discovered that she had spent
time living on a plantation called Mulberry Grove, located just a
few miles north of Savannah. He also discovered why the name
Greene seemed familiar to him. There was a fifty-foot-tall monument to her husband, Nathanael Greene, planted in the middle
of Johnson Square less than a mile from Matt's house. When
he discovered that Caty had been married to a Revolutionary
War hero, and had been friends with George Washington and a
slew of other revolutionary icons, he nearly sprinted back to the
journal.

He spent the next hour flipping through the pages, very carefully so as not to damage them. Suddenly, he came upon an entry
that was so inflammatory he had to read it again to make sure he
hadn't misinterpreted it. Caty Greene had alleged that during the
Continental Army's dismal winter encampment at Valley Forge,
America's most famous Founding Father, George Washington,
had written a surrender letter to British general William Howe!

Matt's excitement quickly turned to apprehension. He knew
that he had to think through his next steps very carefully, because
he held in his hands an incredible story that, if true, would literally rewrite history. A car horn blared on the street three stories
below his window and he jerked so hard he almost fell over backward in his chair. He took a deep breath to force himself to calm
down, but the uneasiness in his gut told him that he was in way
over his head. He quickly made up his mind to find an expert

and get an informed opinion as to the authenticity of the book, and more importantly, the validity of the seditious claim inside.

He thought for a moment about whom he could consult. Then he remembered reading an article recently, in the *Savannah Morning News*, about a local historian. He recalled that she had just published a book about the southern campaign of the Revolutionary War. She could probably provide additional background on Caty Greene and perhaps even authenticate the journal. He searched the Internet again until he found the online version of the article. Her name was Sarah Gordon: born, raised, and still living in Savannah. And the rather attractive accompanying picture of Miss Gordon did not go unnoticed by Matt. In fact, if he were honest with himself, it was probably the reason he had recalled the article in the first place.

He made the decision that if she agreed to meet with him, he would not reveal the passages related to the surrender letter, unless he felt he could trust her. He had learned to rely on his instincts over the years because, most of the time, they had proven to be correct. When he looked at his watch, however, he realized that it had gotten very late.

He would have to make the call first thing in the morning.

6

May 1791
Mulberry Grove Plantation
Savannah, GA

*I*t *was mid-morning and Mulberry Grove Plantation was humming with activity in preparation for President George Washington's visit later that day. Caty Greene was nervous, not only because the president was about to pay her a personal visit for an early afternoon dinner at her home, but also because she expected their conversation might not be a pleasant one.*

She entered the outbuilding that served as the plantation house's kitchen, to check on the preparation of the dinner meal. Directly in front of her was the kitchen's large hearth with its massive wrought iron crane swing arm, on which multiple iron pots were hung for the purpose of cooking over an open fire below. The slave who ran the kitchen was busy preparing for the midday meal, cutting up vegetables from the garden and adding them to one of the larger kettles. Some of the kettles weighed over thirty pounds empty, but the heavyset kitchen slave hoisted them aloft as easily as if she were lifting a basket of cut flowers. The fire burning in the Dutch oven, on the far wall, was already throwing off enough heat that Caty could feel its warmth from ten feet away.

She left the warmth of the kitchen and made her way back to the main house and into the dining room. She checked inside the simple pine corner hutch for the creamware tea set that would be brought out after dinner, and took note that the table was laid out with her surviving fine set of eastern porcelain china, given to her and Nathanael on their wedding day. Somehow the creditors had overlooked the sentimentally priceless china. She looked around her modest dining room, thinking that given the large entourage traveling with President Washington, it would be a tight fit. But at least she was comforted by the fact that the preparation for the affair seemed to be under control. She did wonder, however, with all these people around, how she would find time alone with Washington to have the private conversation that she had been anticipating for many months.

Word soon came downriver that the president had left Purysburg, South Carolina, just a few miles north of Mulberry Grove, and would be landing in less than an hour. Caty and her family, including her four youngest children and their tutor, hurried to assemble down at the plantation's boat dock. Her oldest child, George Washington Greene, was not present due to the fact that he was being schooled in Paris, courtesy of her dear friend and wartime acquaintance, the wealthy Marquis de Lafayette. The president would be disappointed not to see his namesake, but he had wholeheartedly endorsed the idea of Lafayette's offer to pay for the boy's schooling when Caty had consulted him on the matter three years earlier, prior to agreeing to the arrangement. Finally, around the far bend in the river came a large boat carrying the president and his traveling staff. The rest of the flotilla, comprised of several smaller vessels, oars slapping against the choppy water, carried an assortment of dignitaries and military escorts.

It was not until after dinner that Caty seized her opportunity to gain a private audience with the president. "Your Excellency, might I ask you to accompany me on a stroll around the grounds?" Caty asked Washington, a bit nervously. "I believe some air will do us good after such a large meal."

"I would be delighted. Gentlemen, please excuse me while I steal away with this lovely woman for a breath of fresh air," replied Washington. And with that, he took Caty's arm and led her outside and down the steep brick front steps of the main house. It was a lovely Georgia spring day, with only the slightest hint of a breeze rippling the waters of the Savannah River. The

late afternoon sun had dropped lower on the horizon, but still packed plenty of warmth so that Caty did not require a shawl around her shoulders.

They walked slowly along the packed sand drive in a direction away from the house. The large oak trees lined either side of the drive and provided a natural canopy from the sun. Caty, who had been anticipating this conversation ever since she discovered the surrender letter, could not wait a moment longer, so she dived right in and said, "General, I must tell you that I found something of yours among Nathanael's personal effects."

"Something of mine?" asked Washington, surprised. He was dressed practically, in fitted buckskin riding breeches and a high-waist, double-breasted coat with broad lapels that fell away in the back to a long-tailed skirt. About three inches or so of vest showed from under his buttoned-up coat.

"Yes, well, more to the point, a letter. A letter you wrote, during the war, that I don't think you intended for Nathanael to possess," stuttered Caty, who now looked a shade paler than when she had exited the house just moments ago.

Washington noticed the change in her pallor and, with fatherly concern, said reassuringly, "Caty, I wrote hundreds of letters during the war, so the fact that your husband has one is not really that surprising. If this is what you wished to talk with me about in private, I can assure you that you needn't be so anxious."

Suddenly, as if exorcising a demon that had taken control of her soul, she blurted out, "But the letter was addressed to General William Howe, commander in chief of the British Army." The words came out louder than she had intended, as if she had raised her voice to be heard above the music, and the instruments had stopped playing.

Washington stopped walking and slowly turned his head toward her, but did not say anything. To fill the uncomfortable silence, Caty continued, "In the letter, apparently written during that dreadful time at Valley Forge, you extend an offer of surrender to the British."

After the shocking revelation of a letter he thought had long ago been destroyed, Washington struggled to regain his composure. He turned away and began to walk again. Casting a furtive glance around to ensure their privacy, he began to speak, "That winter at Valley Forge was indeed a very dark period for the Continental Army. You were there, Caty. You remember the conditions my men were suffering through—no food, half naked, dying from any number of diseases. We were barely surviving on that windswept plateau. And our spies in Philadelphia were convinced that Howe had sent to New York for reinforcements to prepare for a midwinter attack. An attack, I might add, that with our reduced numbers and overall weakened state, we would not have survived."

Washington vividly remembered the morning he wrote the letter to General Howe. He recalled how torn he was to even be broaching the subject of a negotiated surrender with the British, as well as the tremendous sense of relief he had felt when Greene returned to camp without delivering the letter. And until Caty's unsettling revelation, he had thought that dark chapter in his life was long lost to history.

He continued, "So after discussions with Nathanael and Henry Knox, I made the decision to explore the possibility of a negotiated surrender with the British. I dispatched Nathanael to Philadelphia to personally deliver the letter, but upon his arrival, he discovered that General Howe had been summoned to New York that very morning. He reported this to me upon his return to Valley Forge, and he also told me that he had burned the letter to prevent it from falling into the wrong hands. What I cannot understand is why Nathanael kept it all these years."

Caty, having had a moment to regain her own composure while listening to Washington's explanation, said, "I have no idea why Nathanael chose to keep the letter. He never spoke of it to me. I only stumbled upon it, quite by chance, when searching through his personal effects while compiling my indemnification petition to Congress."

Washington's mind was still spinning and he asked Caty pointedly, "So what do you intend to do now?"

"Absolutely nothing; you know I would never betray your confidence, especially given our history together. My loyalty is to you, unequivocally." She waited a beat to see if Washington would inquire as to the whereabouts of the letter, or would ask Caty to destroy it, but to his credit, he did neither.

Sensing her opportunity, she quickly changed the subject to her case before Congress. "Speaking of my petition, George, you know I am having the devil of a time getting Congress to grant me permission to present my case. And if I don't get indemnified from Nathanael's debts, accumulated in the service of his country, I might add, I will be financially ruined and in a most desperate state."

Her not-so-subtle quid pro quo message, that loyalty goes both ways, was not lost on Washington. He smiled imperceptibly, even with a hint of pride, because Caty had always been shrewder and more politically savvy than many of his former generals. In fact, it was exactly this spirited personality that endeared her to him in the first place. So he retook her arm in his own and said, "Caty, I can assure you, I will do everything in my power to ensure that does not happen." With their unspoken understanding reached, Caty and the president made their way back to the house, walking arm in arm, like the two dear friends that they were, and would always be.

Later that year, Caty sailed from Savannah to Philadelphia, the nation's new capitol, to present her case to the government. She brought with her the trunk load of affidavits and other supporting documents that she would reference when she appeared before Alexander Hamilton and the Treasury Department. She successfully presented her petition, doing an extraordinary job of piecing together a very convincing case that all of her husband's actions, including his financial dealings, had been in support of the men under his command. Particularly compelling were the affidavits that she read aloud from Revolutionary War notables Anthony Wayne and Benjamin Lincoln, and an especially impassioned endorsement from General Henry Knox, who currently served as Washington's secretary of War, and who also happened to be the only other person alive with knowledge of the surrender letter.

So it came to be that, less than a year after his private meeting with Caty Greene at Mulberry Grove Plantation, and after receiving approval from Congress, President George Washington signed her petition for indemnification and monetary reimbursement. As a result, Alexander Hamilton, the secretary of the Treasury, was duly authorized to issue a government *check for $23,500 and a promissory note for another $23,500, payable by Congress within three years. Caty finally received the vindication she had worked so hard to achieve, after more than five years of personal struggle. More than that, the small fortune gave her the financial security she so coveted, allowing her to return to Mulberry Grove with the means to begin the next chapter in her life.*

7

Present Day

Savannah, GA

Matt woke up with a sore neck and a pounding in his cerebellum. He had slept like crap due to some crazy dreams and woke up with his skull wedged up against the headboard. He couldn't remember exactly what he had dreamt about, but vaguely recollected a huge black raven and a disembodied Mrs. Higgins. He silently cursed Christina. After a hot shower and an even hotter cup of black coffee, he felt human again. He picked up the phone and called Sarah Gordon.

A few hours later he was sitting in an alternative lunch joint across the street from the Bull Street Library. He wasn't sure why he chose that location, maybe he thought that its proximity to the library would somehow lend credibility to his story.

She was late. About twenty minutes after their agreed upon meeting time, Sarah Gordon walked through the propped-open front door. Matt waved to her from a back table facing the large front windows. As she walked toward him, he realized that the online picture hadn't done her justice.

He noted that she was taller than average and had the lithe build of a dancer. Her auburn hair was swept back from her face and fell in waves that gathered naturally at the tops of her shoulders. She had a slightly olive complexion and impossibly full lips. As she gripped his hand in a firm handshake, Matt's eyes were drawn to the tiny flecks of gold encircling her irises that gave intensity to her gaze and commanded his full attention.

"Sorry I'm late," Sarah said apologetically.

"Not a problem. I'm just glad you could make it on such short notice," he said. "I hope you don't mind, but I went ahead and ordered. I didn't have any breakfast, so I'm starved. I got the house special, peanut butter with bananas, honey, and bacon on rye toast. I just couldn't pass up that combination. Do you want me to order you something?"

"Thanks, but I'm fine. So you said on the phone that you had an extraordinary revolutionary-era book you wanted me to look at?" she said, getting right down to business. "I have to say, you made me more than intrigued when you wouldn't reveal the name of the author."

Matt knew he had to pique Sarah's interest somehow, so that she would agree to meet with him so quickly. So when he had called her that morning, he had purposely used phrases like "revolutionary era" and "surprising historical references." He wanted to remain just vague enough so that she would want to see the book for herself. Apparently it worked.

"Sorry for being so cagey. But if this book is authentic, it's quite a find," he said, while pulling the oversize atlas from his backpack.

Sarah's brow wrinkled in confusion as she watched Matt pull out a twentieth-century atlas. She was expecting an eighteenth-century journal. Her look said it all—this trip had been a monumental waste of time. But before she could gather her things to leave, he held up his hand and said, "Don't worry, I just wanted you to get the full picture."

Sarah looked even more confused. "I'm sorry, but I'm not following you. If this is some kind of joke, then I'm not getting it."

"Just open it, please," he said, and slid it across the table.

Sarah reluctantly played along. She rotated the atlas around so that it was facing her, and opened it slowly. It was almost as if she expected it to be booby-trapped. After flipping through the first few pages and still seeing nothing unusual, her patience was almost up.

"Now open it up to the middle of the book," Matt said calmly, with a trace of a smile.

She tentatively flipped to the middle pages. Matt enjoyed watching her eyes light up when the little book inside the cavity was finally revealed to her.

"Pretty cool, huh?" he was smiling more broadly now.

Sarah looked across the table. Matt's boyish grin seemed to soften his steel-gray eyes to a lighter shade of blue. And his slightly unkempt mop of sandy blond hair made him appear more innocent than he probably was. But, she thought, it was the confident, easy smile that must have broken a few girls' hearts along the way. She smiled back, but then asked seriously, "Are you going to explain why there's a book inside another book?"

He proceeded to tell her the story of how he had purchased the book from the library across the street. He recounted his discovery of the mysterious journal inside and everything he knew about Caty Greene from his Internet search the night before. He told her about Caty's Revolutionary War experiences and her home at nearby Mulberry Grove, where she had evidently authored the journal. He stopped short, however, of telling her about Washington's surrender letter.

Matt could see the mesmerizing effect the journal had had on Sarah. "So, do you think it's authentic?" he said.

She opened the leather cover and saw the words *Journal of Caty Greene* written on the inside front cover, just as Matt had described. She was astonished and had to remind herself to breathe.

"I'm a historian Matt, not a book authenticator, but it certainly looks real to me. And, if it is, it's an incredible find. Do you realize what you could have here? My God, an authentic eighteenth-century journal that offers a firsthand account of events from the founding of this country?!" she spoke rapidly. "I mean, Caty Greene was a remarkable woman in her own right, but her acquaintances are a Who's Who of the American Revolution. And she also just happened to be married to Nathanael Greene, who has a monument erected to him right here in Savannah for his role in saving the South." She suddenly realized how animated she had become. "Sorry, I talk with my hands when I get excited."

Matt laughed. "It's OK, you should have seen me last night, pacing around my house like a mad man. So you're familiar with Caty Greene?"

"Very much so—outside of my father, probably more than anyone else alive," she said.

"Now it's my turn to be confused."

"Oh, I thought you knew. My ancestors bought Mulberry Grove in the 1850s and it remained in my family for almost 125 years until it was sold in 1975. The stories that my father used to tell me about the old plantation, when I was a little girl, are how I got interested in history in the first place. I thought that was one of the reasons you called me."

"No, I had no idea, but I guess I picked the right person."

Matt wasn't a big believer in destiny, but when she had shared her family's personal connection to Mulberry Grove, he thought the hand of fate had to have been involved somehow. And there was something about her genuine enthusiasm for his discovery that made him trust her even more. He knew it was irrational and that his impulsiveness had gotten him into trouble in the past, but he had also learned to trust his instincts. So in that instant, he made the decision to share the rest of the story with Sarah Gordon.

"There's something else you need to know," he said. "There are some things written in the journal that are inflammatory, to say the least. And when I say inflammatory, I mean the kind of information that, if true, will rewrite the history books."

Sarah looked at him skeptically.

Sensing her doubt, he volunteered, "Here, let me read you a few passages." He came around the table and leaned over her shoulder to find the pages he was looking for.

When he had finished, Sarah took hold of the journal again. This time though, it was as if she were handling a newborn kitten. She was deep in thought, trying to absorb everything Matt had just read to her.

She exhaled and put the book back down on the table. "Oh my God, I see what you mean."

"So what do you think we should do?" he asked.

"We?" she said, quickly placing the journal back inside the atlas, as if it were suddenly cursed.

"Sarah, I called you because I need your help. I'm not asking you to commit to anything here, I just need some advice," he said, with a hint of desperation.

Her posture relaxed. What was the harm in giving a little advice, she thought. "Well, like I said, I'm not an authenticator, but if I were you, I'd have an expert confirm that the book is of the period, or at least old enough to be real. By examining the cover, the binding, the paper, and the ink, they should be able to tell you if the book dates to the right time period. Then, with regard to the journal entries themselves," she paused, as if debating continuing, "well, you might want to get my father's opinion. He's an expert on anything and everything related to Savannah, especially anything related to Mulberry Grove."

"Thank you," he said. Then, figuring he had nothing to lose, asked, "So do you know any good authenticators?"

"As a matter of fact, I do," she replied. "She's an old friend of my father's, and she works over at the Harper Fowlkes House, which is owned and run by a nonprofit group out of Washington, D.C., called the Society of the Cincinnati. I can give her a call and see if I can get you a meeting."

Matt raised his eyebrows. "The Society of the Cincinnati? It sounds like one of those cloak-and-dagger secret societies," he joked.

"Well, it is the oldest private military society still in existence today and it was even associated with some controversy back in the day," Sarah said. She went on to explain that the society had been around since just after the revolution and that George Washington had been its very first president. It had originally been formed as a hereditary organization with membership open only to male descendants of Revolutionary War officers. This had evidently caused quite a stir back in the 1780s, when some prominent public figures accused the society of plotting a military conspiracy against the newly formed government.

Matt just assumed he had not heard of it before because his ancestors were more likely to have been army regulars, not officer material. "If you think this society can help, then let's give it a shot," he said. "But Sarah, I'm a bit out of my league here, assuming your friend will take the meeting, would you mind coming with me?"

While it was true that he needed her expertise, Matt also knew that part of the reason he asked her to tag along was because he simply wanted to see her again.

"Well, it's not often you come across a find of this significance," she replied tentatively.

Sensing her indecision, he said, "Come on, it will be fun. Just one meeting and you'll be done with me forever."

He flashed an easy smile and, to her surprise, she found the thought of being done with him forever an unpleasant one. So she dug her cell phone out of her handbag and said, "Why not, it's just one meeting, right?"

8

Winter 1792

Philadelphia, PA

*I*n *the almost ten years since the end of the Revolutionary War, former general Henry Knox had not gotten any smaller. A large man then, he was now immense, and after being named secretary of War in Washington's first cabinet, he had acquired immense authority to match. In his short tenure as secretary, Knox had formed the fledgling country's first permanent navy, a national militia, and was executing a plan to fortify key strategic points along the nation's coastline with additional artillery to discourage attacks from foreign aggressors. He was a man who commanded respect for a number of reasons, not the least of which was his close personal friendship with President Washington. Knox had met Washington in the early days of the revolution in Boston, and had impressed him with his knowledge of artillery and, more importantly, his ability to put that knowledge into tactical action. It was his love of history and military tactics, especially as they pertained to the deployment of artillery, that would set the path for his life and, ultimately, result in the ascension to his present position of secretary of War.*

Knox was busy at his desk applying his signature to a pile of requisition orders pertaining to the coastline artillery installation effort, but his mind was on another matter altogether. He had summoned Richard Clough

Anderson for a meeting that morning and was waiting for his arrival. He had gotten to know and trust Anderson when both men were encamped at Valley Forge during the dismal winter of 1778. Anderson had been a captain, and eventually a colonel, in the Virginia Continental Line who had fought valiantly in most of the critical battles of the conflict. Anderson had been shot in both thighs during the war but never lost his zeal for the fight for independence. Knox had always admired Anderson's tough defiance and passionate patriotism, which was the reason he had summoned him.

He wanted to discuss a mission of sorts that he hoped would appeal to Anderson's patriotic principles. And even though the private meeting took place in Knox's War office, the subject was unrelated to any government matter, at least directly. Rather, the topic was a matter of concern for another organization of which both men were charter members, an organization called the Society of the Cincinnati.

Knox had helped found the society, primarily to protect the interests of the officers who had served in the Continental Army, but more specifically to lobby Congress for back pay and military pensions. George Washington had been elected the society's first president, and continued to serve in that capacity even after he became president of the United States. The Society had come under attack almost immediately after its inception for a particularly concerning "hereditary" provision in its founding charter. The provision in question related to the fact that membership was only open to officers of the American army, and that membership could be passed down through the oldest son. Some critics, both inside and outside the government, including such notable public figures as Benjamin Franklin and John Adams, saw the society as a veiled attempt to establish aristocratic nobility in America, akin to the British system of privilege. Still others charged that due to the placement of many of their members in positions of government authority, the society was readily capable of staging a military coup and takeover of the newly formed Democracy. George Washington, well aware of the controversy swirling around the society, had politically distanced himself from the organization, especially after becoming president of the United States.

Upon *Anderson's arrival, Knox stood and closed the door to his office, to ensure their conversation would remain private. He directed Anderson to a nearby seat and then manipulated his girth behind his enormous desk, landing heavily on the worn red leather seat of his sturdy Sheraton chair. Once settled in his seat, he said, "It's good to see you again, Richard. How is your Kentucky plantation faring these days?"*

Anderson had removed his double-breasted riding coat upon entering, and held his hat in his lap. He filled Knox in on the state of his Kentucky home and family, and then asked with a curious smile, "So, to what do I owe the honor of a meeting with the secretary of War?" His smile faded, however, when he noticed the look of concern on the secretary's face.

"We have a problem," Knox replied. "Or should I say a potential problem. And to be clear, what I am about to tell you cannot be repeated to anyone outside of this room, understood?" Anderson sat up a bit straighter in his chair.

"Understood, sir," Anderson said. Without realizing it, he had reverted back to the military protocol of address for his superior ranking officer.

Knox continued, "What I'm about to share with you is known by only three people alive—me, President Washington, and Nathanael Greene's widow, Caty Greene, whom I'm sure you remember from Valley Forge."

He proceeded to recount the story of the surrender letter written by Washington while encamped at Valley Forge and the details of its failed delivery. He then dropped the bombshell that, earlier that year, Washington had confided to him the details of his meeting with Caty Greene. And her shocking disclosure that her husband, the long since deceased Nathanael Greene, had not destroyed the letter and, more to the issue at hand, she still had it in her possession.

Anderson's fashionably tailored breeches that fit tight to his thighs now made him feel slightly claustrophobic. After a slight pause, he replied, "I see the cause of your worry. If this letter were to be revealed publically it would be very embarrassing, to say the least."

Knox had not been a witness to the exact wording of the final draft of Washington's letter, so he was unsure of just how damaging the letter would be if it were to come to light. Still, he said animatedly, "No matter what the exact wording of the letter, there is no doubt in my mind that if the public were to find out that Washington had proposed surrender of any kind, regardless of the dire circumstances, and regardless that the letter was never delivered, it would be more than embarrassing. It could deal a crippling blow to his reputation, perhaps even to the stability of our new Democracy."

Anderson interjected, "Not to mention the repercussions for the Society of the Cincinnati. Washington is, after all, president of the society in addition to being the president of the United States."

"Exactly. And as you know, the society already has enough enemies spreading conspiracy theories about our activities, and the many positions of power our members hold in the government, myself included. Imagine how they would manipulate a discovery such as this to serve their own political agendas!" he said, his face reddening.

Shifting uncomfortably in his chair, with a feeling that he knew the answer to his next question before it was asked, Anderson said, "So what is it you want me to do?"

Knox met Anderson's even gaze and replied with grim seriousness, "I want you to go to Savannah and pay a visit to Caty Greene on her Mulberry Grove Plantation, find the letter, and bring it directly back to me, with or without her permission." Anderson nodded his assent, confirming the acceptance of his orders from the secretary of War. "Oh, and one more thing. This is to be done without the knowledge of His Excellency, General Washington. I think we both know that he would never approve of this, but we also know that what we are about to do is in General Washington's, and the country's, best interest."

———

It was the spring of 1793 by the time Anderson made the trip south to Savannah from his home in Kentucky to confront Caty about the letter.

*When approached by Anderson, Caty brushed him off. She claimed igno-
rance to the existence of the letter, and further maintained that she would
never betray General Washington, even if such a letter did exist. Anderson
waited patiently for more than a week, and when Caty finally took a short
trip away from the plantation to visit friends in town, he thoroughly searched
the house, outbuildings, and grounds of Mulberry Grove, under the all-too-
believable disguise of a creditor looking for payment.*

*Even though most of Caty's debts had all been settled at that point,
he knew that the presence of another creditor seeking remuneration would
not raise suspicion. Anderson failed, however, to find any trace of the letter
and became discouraged. But after more than ten days away from the affairs
of his own plantation, he decided that his obligation to Knox had been
fulfilled and that it was time to go. Before leaving, he sent a couriered note
to Philadelphia to inform the secretary of War of his unsuccessful mission,
and then he headed out of Savannah on the sandy road leading northwest
toward his Kentucky home.*

*Anderson's knowledge of and intense interest in Washington's letter
had left Caty extremely unsettled, even a bit fearful. Many questions had
run through her mind after his departure, like who had sent him; was he
acting on Washington's behalf; who else might pay her a visit; should she be
concerned for her safety? She knew that the time had come for her to come
up with a more permanent solution for the letter. After all, it had already
served its purpose for her.*

*She had won her case and received the money she felt was rightfully hers,
and more than that, she believed with certainty that Washington had held
true to his word and had helped her cause. Given all of this, the right thing
to do now was to destroy the letter. Deep down, however, she knew that she
could never do that. She understood that part of the reason she could not
destroy the letter was pragmatic, in the event that one day she might have
use for it again. But what really prevented her from destroying the letter was
her unassailable belief that she simply did not have the right to do so. Her
husband had been compelled to save the letter and, for that reason alone, she
could never bring herself to destroy it.*

To help sort through these conflicting thoughts, Caty removed her personal journal from its hiding place under a loose floorboard in her upstairs bedroom, sat down at her desk, and began to write. And, as with all the significant events in her life, she dutifully recorded the unsettling visit from the mysterious Richard Clough Anderson and her decision, for now, to hold on to the letter.

9

Present Day

Savannah, GA

Matt pulled into the narrow driveway behind the gray clapboard cottage rented by Sarah Gordon. It was a modest home but in a great location, overlooking Forsyth Park. Forsyth was a thirty-acre gem of a park located on the southern end of Savannah's historic district. It had become famous over the years for its large fountain that ran green during Savannah's annual Saint Patrick's Day celebration. It was also a great place to run, which Matt had often done, or to take in the occasional concert at the band shell located near the center of the park.

He had insisted on picking up Sarah that morning so they could drive together to meet with the book authenticator. Matt had already been up for hours, anxious to find out if the little journal he had discovered was the real deal. Instead of adhering to his normal workday dress code, shorts and a T-shirt, he had put on a clean pair of khakis and a button-down shirt. He tried convincing himself that it was because he had a meeting to attend. But the truth was he wanted to look good for Sarah. And that bothered him.

Sarah answered the knock on the back door, looking freshly scrubbed herself. She was dressed in professional business attire, save for the hot-pink cat bowl in her hand, and bare feet.

"Come on in. I've just got to feed the cat and then I'll be ready to go," she said, walking back across the hardwood kitchen floor. "You want some coffee?"

"No, I'm good, thanks. Great place you've got here." He took a look around and felt immediately at home. The house had a warm, lived-in feeling. And it smelled nice, too. Her voice snapped him out of his reverie.

"Yeah, if you can tolerate the occasional park crazies, but I guess it's a lot better than it used to be. The city has really made an effort to clean it up over the past few years," she said.

"I run in the park sometimes, and I've never had a problem," he said. "So how long have you lived in this house?"

"Almost six years, ever since I got out of grad school. My dad knew a guy who knew a guy, and I got a good deal on the rent. I think he just wanted me to be close to him since he only lives a few blocks from here. The landlord's been great, but my guess is that with park properties appreciating in value, he'll want to sell soon," she said. "OK, I'm ready."

They climbed into Matt's Chevy and headed toward the north end of town. "Nice truck, love the color," she said.

"Yeah, I guess you could say it was my midlife crisis purchase."

"You look too young to have had a midlife crisis."

"I am too young. I've still got a couple of years to go before I hit forty, so let's call it a pre-midlife crisis," Matt said, grinning. "Seriously, though, I got divorced about eight years ago and one of the first things I did was to buy this truck. It just seemed like the thing to do, but then again, I tend to be impulsive." Then he thought to himself, *Why am I sharing all of this with her?*

"So is that how you ended up in Savannah?"

"How are you so sure I'm not from here originally?" he asked, in sarcastic indignation.

"Well, let's see, the accent is Yankee all the way, the pants aren't seersucker, and you didn't open the door for me when I got in the truck."

"Guilty as charged. I was born and raised just north of Boston, so I can't stand the Yankees either, at least the pinstriped kind. You'll never see a stitch of seersucker on this sucker, and where I come from the women open the doors for the men," Matt kidded, an even larger grin spreading across his face.

"I'll have to remember that. By the way, I hate when guys open the car door for me," she countered.

"I'll have to remember *that*," he said. "OK, here's the real story. I moved here nine years ago from Manhattan because I was tired of my job, tired of big city living, and Savannah was love at first sight for me. I thought it was a great idea, but my wife hated it and she probably hated me, too, by that point. But that's another story." He looked her way to see if he was sharing too much. She simply nodded.

"She moved back to Manhattan in less than a year, we were divorced a year later, and she was remarried a year after that. Me, I bought an antiques store off Monterey Square, got my truck, and never looked back. That's about it," Matt concluded, still wondering why he had shared so much personal information. Slow down, he thought, you hardly know this girl.

At the time, the divorce had been devastating for Matt, mostly because he was not used to failing at anything. He blamed himself and questioned everything, especially his ability to have a meaningful relationship again. Even though down deep, he realized that his wife and he had probably never been right for each other, that hadn't prevented him from keeping his guard up. He had learned to keep the few women he had dated since the divorce at a safe distance, finding creative ways to push them away if they attempted to break through his protective veneer. And it had worked—so well that he had begun to resign himself to a life of bachelorhood.

He quickly diverted the spotlight back to her, asking, "So what's your story?"

"Pretty boring compared to yours. I'm the local girl who never left," she said. "At least if you don't count the four years I spent at the University of South Carolina. I spent another four plus years at UNC Chapel Hill earning my master's in history and not quite earning my PhD, before returning home to Savannah. I spent the last few years, as you know, writing a book on the Revolutionary War."

"No tragic love stories? Come on, I shared," he prodded.

She looked at him with raised eyebrows, debating how much she should share. But something about his genuine honesty made her feel comfortable opening up.

"Well, the short answer is, I never found the right guy. I thought I did once; I was engaged a few years ago but luckily called it off. He ended up being a real jerk; it just took me longer than everyone else to realize it. Since then, nothing really that serious. I guess I've just been too busy with school and writing. Pretty boring, right?"

"Really boring," he said with a straight face, before cracking up. Humor was Matt's best defense when conversations got too personal. One of the many defenses he used to keep people at a safe distance. Although for some reason, he was finding it hard to do that with Sarah.

"Hey!" she said. But try as she might, she couldn't keep the smile from her face. The truth was she had led a pretty boring life lately. Maybe it was time for a little adventure, she thought.

"I'm kidding. I mean, who am I to talk about boring? I own an antiques store for chrissakes!"

They parked in front of the Harper Fowlkes House and made their way up the stately front steps of the grand Greek Revival mansion overlooking Orleans Square. The Harper Fowlkes House was so named because a woman named Alida Harper had left her home to the Society of the Cincinnati when she passed away. Evidently both her brother and father had been members of the society. Since then, the 1842 house had served as a functioning museum, as well as the headquarters for the Georgia Chapter of the society.

Sarah and Matt were led inside. They were ushered past a tour group gawking skyward at an ocular-shaped staircase in the middle of the front hallway. In addition to its aesthetic beauty, Matt overheard the tour guide saying, it also had a functional purpose when it was built in the nineteenth century. During the oppressively warm summer months, louvered panels on the top floor of the home would be opened so that the sauna-like hot air could be drawn upward, creating a cooling draft throughout the home. They must not be working today, Matt thought to himself. They finally arrived at the administrative offices toward the rear of the house. There, they found Sissy Hightower, resident archivist and part-time administrator for the museum.

"Sarah! How are you?" Sissy shouted. She sprang up from behind her desk and wrapped Sarah in a warm embrace. "I haven't seen you in ages. Congratulations on the book, by the way. Your daddy must be very proud."

"Sissy, it's so good to see you." Turning quickly to introduce Matt, she said, "This is Matt Hawkins, he's the one who found the book I told you about. Matt owns an antiques store here in town, on Monterey Square."

"Nice to meet you," he said, and held out his hand.

Sissy ignored his outstretched hand and surprised Matt with a big hug. "I think I've been inside your store before, although it's been years. It's an old mansion isn't it?"

"Yes, it is, and probably just as shabby chic as you remember it, but I'm making progress," he said, awkwardly disengaging himself from her unanticipated embrace.

"Come on in, I'm excited to see what you've brought me today. Evidently something very mysterious, based on what Sarah told me over the phone," she said, clapping her hands together loudly, with a look of anticipation on her face. It reminded Matt of a little girl getting ready to open her birthday presents.

He had to smile at her enthusiasm, however. She was one of those people you could just tell enjoyed life and had no time for anyone with negative energy. She was petite in stature but had a personality that filled up the room. He liked her immediately. If he had to guess, he'd put her somewhere in her mid-sixties, but her youthful exuberance made it hard to pinpoint her age. Her dress could best be described as "abstract preppy," splashed with pinks and greens. And the entire ensemble was topped off with a red headband planted firmly in her bob of white hair, like the cherry on top of a sundae. It occurred to him that Sissy probably never went unnoticed when she walked into a room.

He reached into his backpack and pulled out the little journal, without the atlas this time, and placed it on the desk in front of Sissy. He told her the story of how he had found it and how it appears to have been written by Caty Greene in the late eighteenth century.

Sissy listened to Matt while examining the book. When he had finished filling her in, she said, "Hmm, this appears to be an octavo size book, which measures approximately five by eight and a half inches. The cover is definitely calfskin and, at one time, there was a decorative design that would have been stamped or imprinted into the leather with a heated tool. Most likely it would have been gold leaf, but it has flaked away so much that it's hard to tell. With some further testing I could tell you definitively."

"So it was an expensive book to make then?" Matt asked.

"Oh yes, you've got to remember that in the late eighteenth century books weren't cheap. Primarily because making a quality book involved more than thirty steps. And it took an apprentice many years to become a highly skilled binder. Books were definitely an indulgence that only the upper class could afford," she explained. "Now let's open her up. The paper is definitely of the period because the toning is very natural. Let's see, the hand stitching is right. There is very little foxing. Those are the brown stains or spots you sometimes see on old documents," she shared. "Foxing is usually caused by the book's exposure to dampness or by the chemical content of the paper itself.

"What's this?" she asked, taking a closer look. "It looks like someone added their initials here on the first page. Looks to be the letters *T. M.* but it doesn't appear to be in Caty's hand. My guess is these initials were added much later because lead pencils didn't become commonplace in America until the latter part of the nineteenth century. Perhaps these are the initials of the person who possessed the journal before it was stowed in the library," she conjectured. "Speaking of the library, clearly the fact that this book was stored for years in a cool, dry basement has certainly helped its condition. And the fact that the paper was made from a combination of cotton and rags, commonly referred to as rag paper, also helped its condition, because that particular type of paper has very little acid content."

After a few anxious moments, Sarah spoke up, "So Sissy, what do you think?"

"Well, I'd like to spend a little more time with it, but in my opinion I'd say you've got yourself an authentic eighteenth-century journal!" she said enthusiastically, as if announcing the sex of a child to the expectant parents.

She was caught off guard, however, when she noticed Sarah and Matt exchanging a somewhat furtive glance. "Sorry kids, but did I miss something? I just confirmed that your book is the real deal. I thought you'd be jumping up and down by now."

Matt looked anxiously over at Sarah. She nodded back at him with a look that said, *you can trust her.* He turned back to Sissy and began tentatively, "Sissy, there are some things written in the journal that are controversial, to say the least." After a brief pause and a deep breath he launched into the story about Caty Greene's claims pertaining to the existence of a surrender letter from Washington. "So you see, while we're thrilled to have an authentic historical book, we're not sure if the writings inside are the musings of a desperate widow or a legitimate accounting of actual events."

Sarah added, "Matt feels like we should do a bit of research before going public with this, to try to find anything that might corroborate Caty's claims. This is George Washington we're talking about here, so we have to tread carefully, for the sake of his reputation as well as our own." Matt couldn't help noticing Sarah's use of the word *we*, which brought a smile to his face. Apparently the authentication of the little book had awakened her curiosity.

"I understand your caution. Is there anything I can do to help?" Sissy asked.

Matt looked at Sarah again for guidance. She thought for a moment, then brightened and said, "Maybe there is. When I was writing my book on the revolution, I became aware that the Society of the Cincinnati had a pretty extensive manuscript collection in its national headquarters. It supposedly dates back to the revolutionary time period. Evidently it contains some pretty rare and personal materials bequeathed by its members over the years, including letters, journals, and memoirs from Washington, Knox, and other prominent generals. It just occurred to me," she explained, "that considering Washington's connection to the society, these archives might be a good place to begin an investigation into Caty's surrender claims. Unfortunately, from what I was told, the collection is only available for viewing by special appointment. Do you think you could help get us in to see these materials for ourselves?" She looked across the desk at Sissy.

"Oh, I'm sure that I could," she replied without hesitation. Then she snapped her fingers as an idea popped into her head. "There may be a way to shortcut your investigation."

She explained, "You see, the society's archives are pretty vast and it would take weeks to pour through the thousands of manuscripts and documents in the collection. But the good news is that the staff has spent the last two years scanning and digitizing the entire collection so that every word in every document now resides on a huge computer database. Specific queries can be run that would expedite your search considerably." She paused before continuing. "Of course, I'd have to confide in the society's head research librarian as to the nature of your search, but he'll understand the confidentiality of the subject."

"As long as he can run his database queries discreetly, then it sounds like the best way to cover a lot of ground quickly. I'm in favor," Matt said. Then he turned to Sarah for agreement, as if to confirm their partnership. "What do you think?"

"I can't see the harm, and it may save us a long trip up to D.C."

"Consider it done then," Sissy said excitedly. "Keep in mind it may take a few days before he can fit the search into his schedule."

10

March 1901

Savannah, GA

*L*arz Anderson was a member of the Society of the Cincinnati by virtue of being the great-grandson of Revolutionary War officer Colonel Richard Clough Anderson of Virginia. Larz had been born into a wealthy family and had attended prestigious Phillips Exeter Academy in New Hampshire before enrolling in Harvard College in Cambridge Massachusetts. After college, Anderson entered the diplomatic corps with the help of fellow Harvard alum and fraternity brother Robert Todd Lincoln, son of President Abraham Lincoln, then serving as U.S. minister in London. It was while serving at the consulate in Rome in 1894 that Larz met his future wife, Isabel Weld Perkins, whose own fortune made Anderson's wealth look paltry in comparison. When Isabel was only five years old, she had inherited seventeen million dollars from her grandfather William Fletcher Weld, at the time making her the wealthiest woman in America.

By the year 1901, Anderson had hired the architectural firm of Arthur Little and Herbert Browne of Boston to design for him and his wife a palatial fifty-room estate, complete with a tennis court and three-story carriage house and stable. The house, to be located in the heart of Washington, D.C., was to be the winter residence for the Andersons and was intended to be used for entertaining fellow diplomats and foreign dignitaries.

Money and membership into the society weren't the only things that Larz had received from his distinguished ancestors. He had also inherited an ardent patriotism and fascination with history, especially related to the Revolutionary War era. Many stories had been passed down to him through the years from his famous forbearers. But one intriguing story had always stuck with Larz, ever since it was told to him when he was just a boy. The story, believed by his father to be more fable than factual, held that Washington had allegedly written a letter of surrender to British general Howe during the winter encampment at Valley Forge. The letter was never delivered, but had somehow survived the war in the possession of Revolutionary War hero General Nathanael Greene. The story told to Larz was that his great-grandfather, Richard Clough Anderson, was dispatched to retrieve the letter from the late Nathanael Greene's plantation in Georgia but had been unable to do so. Evidently he had been sent to Savannah by ex-Revolutionary War general Henry Knox, who was afraid of what the letter might do not only to the reputation of Washington but also the society, which at the time was being accused of conspiracies against the government.

The surrender letter story had resurfaced in Larz's memory recently when he had met a gentleman by the name of Colonel Asa Bird Gardiner, who was president of the Rhode Island Chapter of the Society of the Cincinnati, whose most famous member was one Nathanael Greene. Anderson and Gardiner had met at a recent society meeting, where Greene's name had unexpectedly come up in conversation.

"You mean to say someone stole Greene's remains?" asked Anderson disbelievingly.

"No, more like nobody is quite sure where they put old Nat's body in the first place. Evidently he died with enormous debts and couldn't afford a marker for his grave. They know he was interred in the Colonial Cemetery in Savannah, they're just not sure exactly where," replied Gardiner in his gravelly baritone voice.

Bird was a force of nature. A lawyer by trade, by the time Anderson met him, Gardiner had turned his considerable energies, even at age sixty-two, to the affairs of the society. And his latest project, it turned out, was to find the remains of Nathanael Greene, which according to Gardiner had been missing for more than a hundred years, and to have them returned to his home state.

"So now you want to go to Savannah to find his bones? What are you going to do, start digging up all the unmarked graves in the Colonial Cemetery?" Anderson said, while he stroked his prominent handlebar mustache, of which he was quite proud.

"Not exactly, son. We've done our research and we've narrowed down the location quite considerably. In fact, we're pretty sure Greene's remains were interred in a vault that originally belonged to the Graham family. You see, John Graham had been lieutenant governor, loyal to the British, but when the war started, the state of Georgia confiscated his plantation, called Mulberry Grove. Nathanael Greene was awarded the estate for his revolutionary service and the Graham family vault in the Colonial Cemetery came with the estate. The vault subsequently passed into the possession of the Mossman family. There was gossip over the years that the Mossman family had the body secretly removed, but that's probably nonsense. If we're correct, we'll find Nathanael Greene's remains right where they were originally interred," finished Gardiner, sounding very much like he had just rested the prosecution's case.

As Anderson listened to the story, he suddenly had a preposterous idea. And one that made the hair on the back of his neck stand on end. Due to his family's history, he was very familiar with Mulberry Grove and the circumstances surrounding Nathanael Greene's death. He also knew something that Professor Gardiner, as his friends called him, did not. He knew the story of Caty Greene and the existence of the infamous surrender letter written by Washington. Could Caty have somehow buried the letter with her husband in the Graham vault? Admittedly, the timing of that did not add up, since, according to the story, Caty claimed to have had the letter in her possession long after her husband's death. But then another, more plausible thought occurred to him. He remembered being told that Caty's oldest son, George, named after Washington himself, had died right after Anderson's great-grandfather's visit to Mulberry Grove, and was subsequently buried in the same vault alongside his father. Perhaps that was the moment Caty chose to rid herself of the letter by placing it in the vault. As far-fetched an idea as it was, Anderson knew that he could not pass up an opportunity to solve a century-old family mystery.

All these thoughts ran through Anderson's mind in a matter of seconds, so it was only after a slight pause that he replied, "I'd like to come with you to Savannah. My great-grandfather was a friend of Nathanael Greene's and it would be an honor for me to help you find Greene's remains and return them to their rightful home in Rhode Island." To further seal the deal, Anderson added, "And of course I would like to contribute the funds necessary to offset the cost of the search."

"Splendid. Consider yourself a member of the expedition," replied Gardiner, happy to have the trip financed. Unbeknownst to Gardiner, however, Anderson's motivations had nothing to do with finding a missing corpse.

———

Two months later, in March 1901, the two-person expedition team, consisting of Asa Gardiner and Larz Anderson made their way to Savannah. Gardiner hired out some local workmen to break open the vault. Using pickaxes, they broke through the bricked seal on the old Mossman family tomb, and the men, armed with lanterns, made their way slowly down into the vault, at times crawling on all fours through the dingy, dank abyss. Inching their way past the most recent addition to the vault, a coffin interred just prior to the Civil War, the men eventually made their way to a second tomb toward the back. There they came upon a pile of bones. According to descriptions and paintings of Greene, he had been quite tall with a pronounced forehead. The skull they found amid the pile of bones fit that description. Gardiner and Anderson, looking in from just outside the vault, received this bit of news with great anticipation. The next discovery, however, solved the mystery with finality, for amid the brittle remains of a rib cage, the men found a badly corroded silver coffin plate. When handed outside, Gardiner wiped the plate, rubbing it with a handkerchief moistened with spit, and barely made out the inscription:

NATHANAEL GREENE
Died June 19, 1786
Age 44 years

Much to the surprise of Gardiner, once the remains had been positively identified, Anderson abruptly entered the vault. He scrambled his way back through the darkness to where the workmen were and asked for a moment alone. Relieved for the chance to be free of the claustrophobic vault, the men gladly handed over one of their lanterns and left him alone. Anderson knelt down and began to respectfully but thoroughly sift through the sand beneath the old bones. It became clear that there were actually two sets of bones, the second of which no doubt belonged to Nathanael's son George. Anderson shook his head in the darkness of the crypt, suddenly feeling very foolish for having come all this way to dig through an old tomb searching for a letter that had probably long since disappeared, if it existed at all. But those feelings of apprehension quickly turned to expectation when something clattered audibly against his small trowel. Thinking he might have hit upon a container of some kind, Anderson's heart began to pound. However, it soon became apparent it was way too small a thing to have held a letter. And upon further inspection, Anderson discovered merely a handful of metal buttons with the faint outline of an eagle, common among the dress of an officer during the time of the revolution. He was crestfallen, not because these buttons offered further proof that they had indeed found the remains of Nathanael Greene, but because there was simply no trace of Washington's alleged letter.

Over the next year, Rhode Island and Georgia battled over which state should claim Greene's remains. Finally, Greene's descendants decided that his bones should remain in the city where he had spent the final years of his life and where he had originally been laid to rest. So in the summer of 1902, Greene's remains and those of his eldest son were reburied beside the fifty-foot tall obelisk monument that had been erected in his honor, years *before in Johnson Square. The cornerstone for the monument in Greene's honor had actually been placed at a groundbreaking ceremony, way back in 1825, by his dear friend and comrade-in-arms, the Marquis de Lafayette, during Lafayette's famous and triumphant tour of the Unites States. The obelisk monument was finished in 1830, but would not truly be completed until Greene's remains were finally reburied beside it more than seventy years later, thanks to the efforts of the Society of the Cincinnati.*

One mystery was laid to rest, yet another lived on.

11

Present Day

Washington, D.C.

The sonic boom of thunder shook the building and alerted him to the storm that had descended like Armageddon upon Washington's historic Dupont Circle neighborhood. The typically hot and humid late summer afternoon had turned black with clouds over the past hour. But Todd Spencer was unaware of this or any other development in the outside world. That's because Spencer's windowless office was located on the basement level of the Society of the Cincinnati's palatial office-mansion, known as Anderson House. The Beaux Arts mansion had been donated to the society by Isabel Anderson in 1938, shortly after her husband's death.

Spencer was the head of the research library, located on the lower floor of Anderson House and open to the public by appointment only. The library's main purpose was to collect and preserve printed and manuscript materials relating to the military history of the eighteenth and early nineteenth centuries. Given the society's roots in the American Revolution, its collection focused on the people and events of America's war for independence. It was comprised of thousands of rare military documents and personal manuscripts donated from the archives of many of its own members.

Spencer's backlog of requests for research materials was exacerbated when he lost his library cataloger to maternity leave two weeks earlier. Finally, the library's director assigned a summer intern from Baylor University to help Spencer for the next two weeks. Stu, the summer intern, was more than happy to help out. Even though his internship was focused on curatorial research, he figured it couldn't hurt to learn how a research library operated. He had been working with Spencer for less than a week and had already made a sizable dent in the backlog.

"Thank God you came when you did, Stu. At the rate I was falling behind, it would have been Halloween before I got my head above water," Spencer said.

"No problem, Mr. Spencer, glad I can help. I've just finished up with the request for the manuscripts related to the War of 1812, so I've got some bandwidth to take on the next project." Stu was a clean-cut young man with a face that looked too young to be attached to someone in graduate school.

"Great, let's see what we've got. Oh shit, I forgot all about this one. You better run this query next," Spencer stated. He had just stumbled across the somewhat odd request from Sissy Hightower buried beneath some folders on his desk. "I got this one in a few days ago from the Georgia Chapter of the society, located in Savannah. Sissy's a friend and she asked me to handle this one personally. But as you can see, I just don't have the time, and clearly, you're more than capable." He handed over his handwritten notes that he had jotted down during his telephone conversation with Sissy.

The air-conditioning didn't work very well in the basement level so Todd's office was more stuffy than usual. Today's humidity only made it worse.

"Evidently an antique store owner in Savannah found an eighteenth-century diary of some kind hidden inside a twentieth-century atlas," Todd conveyed, before draining the last of his water bottle.

"That's pretty cool," Stu said, flopping down in the chair next to Spencer's desk.

"I know; very mysterious, right? Well, it gets better. Sissy didn't go into great detail, but evidently the author of the journal, a woman named Caty Greene, alleges that Washington wrote a letter of *surrender* while at Valley Forge to General William Howe, commander of the British Army. Fortunately for us, it never got delivered, or we'd be enjoying tea and crumpets right about now," he joked. "Anyway, somehow the letter ended up in her husband's possession after the war. Sissy asked me if I'd run a database query to see if there was anything that could corroborate Mrs. Greene's claim. I highly doubt you'll find anything, but that, Mr. Baylor University Intern, is your next assignment."

"Sounds interesting. I'll get on it right away. Anything else?" Stu got up to leave.

"I wrote down some suggested key words to query, so why don't you start with those. If those don't work, I'm sure you'll think of more. You should begin your search with the revolutionary era collection and then branch out from there if you don't get any hits," he said, before dismissing the eager-to-prove-himself intern.

Stu grabbed a quick cup of coffee and found his way to a secure terminal in the back of the library to conduct his query. After logging onto the password protected computer database, he began his search. Just as Spencer had predicted, every search Stu initiated came back with the words *No Entries Found* blinking on the screen. He had been at it for over an hour and had covered the entire collection of manuscripts and printed materials from the revolutionary era. Nothing had turned up.

As a last resort, he opened a separate database that contained the digitized personal collections of documents and manuscripts donated by the society's members. He again typed in the words *surrender*, *Valley Forge*, and *General Howe* and hit Run Search. He leaned back in his chair, stretched his neck and shoulders, and rubbed his eyes. When he glanced back at the screen he was more than a little surprised to see the words *Matches Found* blinking on his screen. Underneath the words was a single entry, but Stu felt a jolt of adrenaline nonetheless. The surge of energy intensified when he saw the name on the source document referenced—*Larz Anderson Journals, Volume Five.*

Larz and Isabel Anderson had led an adventurous, globe-trotting life, and Larz had dutifully recorded everything in his journals, from his life in the Diplomatic Corps, serving stints in the United Kingdom, Italy, and Japan, to his acquaintances with the Astors, Vanderbilts, and other prominent families of the newly industrialized twentieth-century America. The thirty-eight typed volumes spanned a half century of personal experiences and firsthand accounts of world events, from the Spanish-American War to the Great Depression. But the only entry Stu cared about at the moment was a single one from *Volume Five.*

He took a deep breath, clicked on the link, and was brought directly to the entry in question. He surely would have missed it, if not for the wonder of digital scanners that had made an obscure search like this one possible. Fascinated, Stu read Larz Anderson's account of a trip he took to Savannah, Georgia, in 1901 under the guise of exhuming the bones of Nathanael Greene from their resting place in the Colonial Cemetery. Anderson revealed that the real reason he had made the trip was to solve a century-old family mystery. Evidently the mystery surrounded the existence of a surrender letter written by Washington during the Revolutionary War. Stu could not believe what he was reading. Anderson was looking for the same letter that Caty Greene had claimed to possess, which meant that the journal discovered in Savannah was telling the truth. If this wasn't corroboration of the existence of a surrender letter from Washington, then Stu didn't know what could be. Excited to share his unexpected find, he picked up the phone and dialed Todd Spencer's extension.

Spencer joined him a few minutes later. Stu brought him up to speed on the details of the database search and where the reference had been discovered in the archives. Spencer was still shaking his head in disbelief when Stu asked, "The one thing I can't figure out is why this hasn't been discovered before?"

Spencer thought for a moment and then offered up an explanation, "You've got to remember that this collection of journals had been in a private collection since the 1930s. They were only gifted to the society four years ago by the descendants of Larz Anderson's first cousin. And the last two volumes didn't arrive here until just last year. So, when you consider that the collection was out of public view until very recently, coupled with the fact that we are talking about thousands of pages spread across thirty-eight leather-bound volumes, it really isn't all that surprising that a single entry pertaining to a surrender letter from Washington could be missed. And besides, we only just finished digitizing the collection a few months ago, which is the only way this needle-in-a-haystack search was even possible."

"Makes sense. But still, pretty incredible don't you think?" Stu said. The fluorescent lights hummed loudly above his head.

"It is, and before we do anything else, I'll need to inform Director Fox of this find, especially since it came from the personal journal of Larz Anderson." Executive Director James Fox ran the day-to-day operations of the Society of the Cincinnati. Spencer liked the man but hadn't spent enough time during Fox's tenure to get to know him very well.

He continued speaking as he got up to leave, "Before I get back to my Savannah contact, I need to find out how Director

Fox would like us to proceed. And," he added with seriousness, "given the nature of this discovery, I expect you to keep all of this confidential."

"Of course, Mr. Spencer, I won't say anything."

Spencer was halfway to Director Fox's office when he happened to spot the front section of the *New York Times* sitting on a desk inside an empty cubicle. The front page headline read, "Emerson Closes the Gap" in bold letters. A subhead exclaimed, "Washington Connection Apparently Helping." He took a few more steps, then hesitated and returned to the deserted cubicle. He picked up the paper and began to read. The article talked about how the Emerson campaign's use of its candidate's link to Washington had been playing favorably with the American public. Evidently when surveyed, people perceived that Emerson's connection to the Founding Father made him more trustworthy and more qualified to be a leader.

After a quick scan of the article, it suddenly dawned on him that the revelation of Washington's surrender letter might not be the best thing for the Emerson campaign. He wondered to himself, would voters be influenced if they knew about Washington's alleged treason? Would the society's image be hurt by this revelation? He decided that he'd share these concerns with Director Fox and let him decide the best course of action. These types of decisions were way above his pay grade.

12

Present Day

"J. J., it's me," the voice said, after he picked up on the second ring.

J. J. Stanton, a former marine who had served in the first Gulf War, had been in the private investigation and security business for the past fifteen years. The man on the phone had done business with Stanton's Dallas-based security firm a number of times over the years. He had used their services to dig up dirt on organizations or competitors who threatened his interests. Stanton's tactics were not always legal and included phone taps, hidden wires, and even strong-arm intimidation in extreme cases. As a result, whenever the man had hired them in the past, it had always been "off the books," with funds from an alias account. He had not wanted a paper trail then and he certainly didn't want one for the job for which he was about to hire Stanton.

"It's been a few years," J. J. said matter-of-factly. "You've been busy."

"Things have definitely been headed in the right direction lately and I'd like to keep it that way. That's why I called," the man replied.

"Understood. So what is it you need this time?"

"I need you to go to Savannah, Georgia, and find the identities of some people who are in possession of something that could hurt my interests." He proceeded to outline the details of Caty Greene's journal and the potentially damaging claims made against Washington. Once he was able to find the identities of the people who possessed the journal, J. J. was instructed to follow them and keep him posted on their activities until further notice.

He also reminded him that, as always, this assignment was to be off the books; *way* off the books.

13

Spring 1793
Savannah, GA

S *ince she had won her case before Congress the year before, Caty's life had taken a marked turn for the better. Not only had her newly acquired fortune provided financial freedom for her family, but her oldest son, George, had at long last returned home from France, after five years abroad. George had left home a boy and had returned a young man, full of stories from his time spent in France. Earlier in the year the French Revolution had heated up and, fearing for her son's safety, Caty had written to the Marquis de Lafayette, who had sponsored her son's education, to request that he send George home immediately. Lafayette had secured passage for George on a ship home to America, with George just barely managing to escape the escalating violence. His host was not so fortunate. Lafayette had been captured and imprisoned after he had fled France into Belgium with fifty-three officers loyal to the king. With George safely home, for the first time in a very long time, Caty was surrounded by all of her children, and she could not have been happier.*

She had also acquired a quite unexpected, but nevertheless welcome, houseguest the previous fall, with the arrival of the recent Yale graduate, Eli Whitney. Whitney had landed at Mulberry Grove quite by chance when, upon arriving in Savannah, he discovered that the tutoring job he had come to Georgia to take paid only half of what he had been promised. Caty and Whitney had sailed from New York to Savannah on the same ship and had struck up an immediate friendship. So when Whitney's job fell through, Caty had insisted upon his staying at her plantation until he figured out what to do next.

Almost immediately after his arrival on the plantation, Whitney had learned of the very difficult and labor intensive process of ginning cotton, that is, the process for removing the seeds from the soft, fibrous substance. The mechanically inclined Whitney had shown an extraordinary knack for problem solving and entrepreneurship starting at a very young age. As a thirteen-year-old boy, during the revolution, he had convinced his father to begin producing nails in their forge, as they were in great demand from the Continental Army. And after the war he continued to produce tools, farm implements, and even hatpins for bonnets, all the while tinkering away at his father's forge. He also had an innate thirst for learning, which eventually earned him acceptance into Yale.

So, to earn his keep during his stay at Mulberry Grove, he helped Caty by fixing things around the house. It was because of these abilities that she decided to approach him with an unusual request. Caty confronted Whitney one afternoon, as he worked in one of the outbuildings that had been converted into a makeshift workshop. He had been hard at work on a full-scale model of the cotton gin machine that he hoped could be powered by a single man and a horse.

"Eli, can I bother you for a moment? I'd like to discuss something," she said.

"Of course," he said. He put down the try plane that he had been using to straighten an edge on the housing for the cotton gin's large cylinder. "Is that barn door that I repaired sticking again?"

"No, it's working just fine," she replied. "Actually, I have a different kind of job for you."

Having witnessed Whitney's mechanical genius on more than one occasion, Caty had decided to approach him about designing a receptacle to hold and protect Washington's letter. "I'd like to take advantage of that clever mind of yours to have you build me a container of sorts, that is durable enough to stand the test of time and elements."

"And how big does this mysterious container need to be?" he asked, his interest piqued at the somewhat ambiguous nature of the request.

Caty had held her hands out in front of her, about twelve inches apart. "About this long and not even as big around as a rolling pin. It just has to be large enough to hold a document." She did not elaborate on the nature of the document that Whitney's creation would ultimately hold. Nor did she speak of the recent unsettling visit of Richard Anderson to Mulberry Grove, whose ominous presence had precipitated her request. After she had answered some additional design-related questions that he had, she excused herself and left her resident genius to do his work.

Whitney applied his considerable talents like never before and, in just over a month, he had completed an invention that was decades ahead of its time. With very little to guide him, knowing only that his design had to be large enough to contain a valuable personal document, he eventually constructed an impenetrable metal container. Similar in dimension to an oversize cigar tube and just large enough to conceal a rolled-up document, when properly fitted together, Whitney's cylindrical engineering marvel provided an airtight seal.

The device had far exceeded Caty's expectations and she was comforted by the fact that Washington's letter would henceforth be thoroughly protected. Now all she had to do was pick a safe place to hide the document from those who might wish to acquire it. Later that day, as she wrote in her journal about Whitney's container, Caty could not believe her good fortune at having the clearly brilliant young man as a guest in her home.

———

Her happiness, however, was short-lived. Just a few weeks after the completion of the cleverly designed container, the son she had just welcomed home after five long years away, died in an accidental drowning in the Savannah River. George, who was only seventeen years old, had been paddling with *a friend when their canoe capsized. He had tragically never resurfaced and his body did not wash up on the shoreline of Mulberry Grove until the next morning. Caty was heartbroken and entered into a deep depression, knowing she would never fully recover from the loss of her firstborn. She was numb the next day, when her son's lifeless body was taken downriver by boat, just as her husband's had been seven years before. After a somber ceremony, young George's body was placed in the same vault as his father in the Colonial Cemetery in Savannah. With her world crashing in on her, Caty was barely able to function in the following weeks and months. Things that had once held importance ceased to matter. And this applied especially to Washington's letter. Those confounded words written on a single piece of rag paper, that once held such significance for her, now seemed terribly trivial.*

And so, the surrender letter was forgotten, safely encased in Whitney's metal tube, where it would lie untouched in the third-floor attic at Mulberry Grove for the next seven years.

14

Present Day

Savannah, GA

"You two are going about this all wrong," Hank Gordon said. He was talking to Sarah and Matt, sitting across from him. They were in the library of his completely restored home in Savannah's Victorian District. Hank had bought the property fifteen years earlier and had painstakingly returned the stately home to better than its original condition. He decorated the home in 1870's high-style New York, with neo-Grec period furniture that he had diligently acquired over the years from local antique stores, European travels, and eBay auctions. The latter being an addiction he couldn't quite kick.

Sarah had received Matt's permission to drop off the journal with her father the night before. Hank had subsequently spent hours reading and rereading Caty's captivating stories, while taking copious notes. There was nobody's opinion Sarah trusted more than her father's. They had always been close but had grown even closer since breast cancer had taken the life of her mother more than a decade earlier. That was shortly after Sarah had finished college at the University of South Carolina. She had chosen South Carolina because it was her father's alma mater, and she had further followed in his footsteps by pursuing a career in the field of American history.

"What do you mean, Dad?" Sarah asked.

Hank Gordon had taught high school history in the Savannah public school system for close to thirty years. He was one of those rare beloved teachers former students kept in touch with as they moved through their own adulthood. Mr. Gordon's AP history field trips were the stuff of legend. Hank had always said, "Why read about it in a book when you can see it with your own eyes." And, like the pied piper, he would lead his kids to places of historical significance in and around Savannah, so that they could see, feel, and smell for themselves the places where history had been made. But he had retired close to a decade ago, after his wife's death and the school's liability policies had dimmed his spirits, like a three-way lightbulb permanently stuck at the fifty-watt level. Time and support from his daughter, however, had eventually helped him reclaim his natural enthusiasm for life, despite the irreplaceable loss of the only woman he had ever loved.

"I mean, you shouldn't be wasting your time trying to corroborate Caty's claims. You should be looking for the surrender letter itself."

"What?" Sarah replied, in disbelief.

Matt jumped in excitedly and said, "You really think the letter could still exist, I mean, if it ever existed?"

"Of course it existed, my boy. Why would Caty Greene go to such lengths to concoct a story about a fictitious surrender letter? And if she did concoct the story, why would she write about it in a journal that she didn't intend for anybody else to read?" Hank reasoned.

"Dad, even if the letter was written as she claims it was, it couldn't have survived for more than 200 years."

"Sarah, my dear historian daughter, you know better than that," he challenged his skeptical offspring. "Historical documents have turned up in the strangest places over the years. Don't you remember, when you were just a little girl, a first printing of the Declaration of Independence was found in a four-dollar picture frame? I think it was later sold at auction for a million dollars. And are you forgetting the diary Matt just found? That survived, didn't it? So why not Washington's surrender letter?"

"OK," she relented, "I'll grant you that it is not beyond the realm of possibility. But you must admit that it's *highly* unlikely. A bound book with a leather cover is one thing, but a single sheet of eighteenth century rag paper?"

"But that's exactly why it could have survived. Paper in the eighteenth century was made from cotton and linen rags and had very little, if any, acid content. That is why documents that have survived from back then are in better condition today than last week's *Savannah Morning News*. But you're forgetting something even more important than the paper that Washington wrote on," Hank said.

Sarah looked at him with confusion, waiting for her father to answer his own riddle.

"Whitney's invention," Matt interjected, as if on cue.

Hank slapped his knee and pointed at him. "Exactly, my boy."

Matt picked up the journal and said, "The way Caty described it in her journal...let me find the passage. Here it is, 'Mr. Whiney built me an impenetrable cylindrical metal container.' It sounds pretty solid to me."

"And don't forget, this is Eli Whitney we're talking about, not some uneducated farmhand," replied Hank. "This is the guy who invented the cotton gin and who would later experiment with the use of interchangeable parts to make weapons for the government, as well as a host of other inventions. The man was a mechanical genius. Now I'm not saying this thing still couldn't have ended up lost to history on the bottom of the ocean or buried in a ditch somewhere, I'm just reminding you of the fact that Washington's letter was housed in a metal cylinder, designed by Eli Whitney, that was clearly built to last," Hank said, resting his case.

Matt and Sarah were lost in their own thoughts, pondering the persuasive argument that Hank had just posited. Finally, Matt looked up with a lopsided grin and said, "So Hank, if you were an impenetrable cylindrical metal container, where would you be hiding after two hundred years?"

Hank returned the smile and replied, "Now that's a very good question, and I believe I know just the place to start looking." He turned to his daughter and raised his eyebrows. "And I think you do, too."

Sarah looked like she had just sat down in the dentist's chair for a root canal. "No way, Dad, no. You know I hate snakes, and the only thing I hate more than snakes is alligators." She shook her head from side to side, but all she got in return was her father's distinctive chuckle, which sounded like a small engine sputtering to a stop.

"Sorry, but I'm lost; can someone fill me in on the joke?" Matt said.

"My crazy, lawbreaking father wants to take us on one of his famous field trips."

"You know what I always say, honey, why read about it in a book..." But he didn't get to finish.

"When you can see it with your own eyes," she finished for him. "But seriously, Dad, you almost got arrested the last time you went out to the old Mulberry Grove property."

"Wait a minute. You guys are talking about going to see Mulberry Grove? Count me in!" Matt said excitedly.

"Hold on a minute, I've got three good reasons we shouldn't go on this little field trip," Sarah said, resorting to reason. "I already mentioned the snakes and alligators. Then there's the fact that the property is now owned by the Georgia Ports Authority, who has erected fences with large Do Not Trespass signs on them to keep hunters away, and the occasional crazy historian out of their hair."

"That's only two reasons," prodded Matt.

"The third reason is that, as my grandfather used to say, 'it's hotter than a Billy goat in a pepper patch' outside today, and I'm hardly dressed for a walk in the woods!"

"So it's settled then. Shall we get going?" Hank said, putting an affectionate arm around his daughter's shoulder while tossing a wink Matt's way.

Sixty minutes later they were standing on the overgrown grounds of Mulberry Grove Plantation. They had driven north on the old Augusta Road for about twenty miles. Then they continued by foot, led by the surprisingly nimble Hank, who did not look or act seventy years old, save for his white beard and mustache. They made their way through swampy, chigger-filled woods right on past the well-marked Do Not Trespass signs. When they finally stopped walking, they were standing in front of the ruins of the original brick steps that had once led up to the front door of the Federal-style plantation home of Nathanael and Caty Greene.

Matt felt as if he were on sacred ground. As he looked to his right he could see the outline of the final stretch of the two-mile-long hard-packed sand drive. It was still lined with the large oaks, ladened with Spanish moss, that George Washington and Caty Greene had once traversed. Off to his left, not more than fifty yards away, was the west bank of the meandering Savannah River. While the view was mostly blocked now by twisted oaks and underbrush, Matt could still picture the expansive view Caty once had of the majestic Savannah River as it snaked its way past her home.

"See that far bend in the river," Hank said, pointing to the north, "that's where Caty and her family would have first spotted

Washington and his flotilla rowing hard toward Mulberry Grove. My guess is he would have disembarked right down there, which is where the plantation's dock would have been back in 1791." He pointed to a spot down a muddy fifteen-foot embankment just to the left of where they were standing.

"And according to Caty's journal, down that way," Sarah said, pointing toward the drive, "is where she would have dropped the bombshell on Washington about the survival of his surrender letter from Valley Forge."

"This is incredible, Hank. And you're right, there's no substitute for seeing it with your own eyes. Thanks for bringing us here. It's pretty remarkable to think that we're walking on the same ground as Eli Whitney, Nathanael Greene, and George Washington," Matt said, in genuine awe.

"My pleasure, Matt, it's really a treat for me, too. You know, I used to roam these grounds as a kid, fishing the river and getting into all kinds of mischief during the day and night. We'd hunt raccoons in the pitch dark by shining a flashlight right up in those trees over there. The reflection off their eyes would give them away," Hank said, pointing into the dense woods, with a faraway look. "It's always been a magical place for me, and now it's even more so with your discovery. So I should be thanking *you* for giving me another excuse to sneak onto the grounds. Obviously I didn't bring you here to search for the letter, but I did think it would be helpful to get a firsthand perspective of the old plantation, because words on a page just don't do it justice."

"I've read a little bit about Caty's time here at Mulberry Grove and how she had to sell the place around 1800 due to financial problems. What happened to her after she left here?" Matt asked, while picking up one of the bricks from the staircase and turning it over in his hands.

Sarah spoke up, "She and her second husband, Phineas Miller, built a new home on Cumberland Island, about a hundred miles south of here, and named it Dungeness. Cumberland Island is one of the barrier islands off the coast of Georgia and only accessible by ferry. At one time it was a privately owned island, but now it's been designated as protected national seashore and is run by the National Parks Service."

"Is there a chance the letter could be there?" Matt asked hopefully, as the three of them walked to the edge of the bank to get a better look at the Savannah River. To their left they could make out a rotting tree stand, long since abandoned, that hunters had once used to wait out their prey.

"I doubt it. Dungeness isn't in much better condition today than Mulberry Grove," Sarah said. "If I recall correctly, Caty's Dungeness home burned to the ground in the 1860s. Andrew Carnegie eventually purchased the land and built a new and much bigger home in the 1880s, which he also called Dungeness. But that too burned to the ground, sometime in the 1950s, so all that's left are some old ruins." She was glancing nervously over her shoulder, making sure no critters were sneaking up from behind.

"But don't forget, Caty *is* buried on Cumberland," noted Hank, stating the facts while purposely stirring the pot.

"What are you saying? Do you think there's a chance she was buried with the letter?" Matt asked, clearly energized by the prospect of uncovering a lead on the whereabouts of the letter. Hank simply shrugged as if to say, don't eliminate the possibility.

"Hey guys, can we discuss your theories about the letter back in Savannah? I'm getting eaten alive by these mosquitoes and I think the alligators are drawing up an attack plan," Sarah declared, as she began to move away from the water's edge.

"Good idea, I could use a cold beer anyway," Hank offered.

"I like your style, Hank, I do some of my best thinking over beer," Matt said. Soon they were retracing their trespassing steps out of the woods to their car, which they had left parked by the side of the road, a good mile away.

———

An hour later, they sat comfortably at a booth in the Crystal Beer Parlor, located just a little off the beaten path. At the corner of West Jones and Jefferson Streets, it was far from the bustling River Street tourist destinations further to the north. The Crystal, as it was known to the locals, had been an institution since the Great Depression. Legend had it that the original owners operated a speakeasy in the basement during Prohibition. Even though you couldn't buy a ten-cent draft anymore, the Crystal still had its welcoming bar, classic red leather tufted booths, and menu stocked with comfort food. All in all, the place had remained remarkably true to its unpretentious roots.

They were famished from their field trip, and began devouring a dinner of creamy crab stew, burgers, and homemade fries while discussing how best to approach their search for Washington's surrender letter.

"I must say, Matt, that I like your choice of venues. The Crystal is an old favorite of mine. My daddy used to sit me on his knee right over there," Hank pointed to the recently expanded mahogany bar that now stretched the full length of the room. "He'd feed me spoonfuls of beer when I was just a lad. And my granddaddy used to tell me stories of playing cards and drinking moonshine in the basement during Prohibition," he finished, with a conspiratorial wink.

"And don't forget about the ghosts, Daddy," Sarah reminded.

"Oh yes, there have been lots of tales about paranormal activity in this restaurant. That's why it's a popular stop on some of those ghost tours Savannah is so famous for," he said.

"Well, if I were ever to come back as a ghost, a bar wouldn't be the worst place to be stuck for eternity," Matt joked.

"Can you believe that blowhard?" Sarah said, changing the subject abruptly. She motioned with a nod of her head toward the flat screen television behind the bar. It was showing a clip from a Republican campaign rally.

"Oh, Emerson's just a harmless good old boy from Texas. I have to admit, though, it is a bit scary that a guy named Big Bill could be our next president," Matt said with a smile.

The television was turned to CNN. The twenty-four-hour news station had been covering Emerson as he canvassed the country promoting his hard-line platform, as the handpicked conservative candidate for president of the United States.

"He's a spoiled frat boy who only made it through college because his daddy donated a new building to the school. And now he's this close to becoming the leader of the free world," Sarah said, her thumb and index finger an inch apart.

"He's definitely swimming in the deep end of the pool, but I kind of feel sorry for the guy. I mean, you know he'd rather be riding his ATV around his ranch than campaigning for president. But his overbearing father didn't give the poor bastard a choice. If he wins the election, it's not Big Bill we'll have to worry about, it's his power-hungry father," Matt said.

"And don't forget about the right-wing wackos who pull the strings behind the scenes. It drives me crazy how they try to wrap their conservatism in patriotic rhetoric so it can be digested more easily by the American public," Hank said with disgust.

They returned to discussing possible locations for the surrender letter. Sarah suddenly looked at her watch, and when she saw how much time had gone by began to collect her things. "Well, it's getting late, guys, and I've got an early morning. So I'll leave you two to finish your beers. Dad, don't have too many, you know they give you a headache the next day," she warned.

"Oh don't be silly, I'm sober as a Mormon preacher on Sunday morning," Hank said, and proceeded to take an exaggerated swig.

Sarah shook her head, with a look on her face that said, *boys will be boys*. "Matt, I'll call you if I hear anything from Sissy."

"I hope her contact at the society comes up with something, because otherwise finding Washington's letter will be like trying to find a black cat in a coal cellar," Hank noted. He got up and hugged his daughter good-bye.

"Let me walk you out," Matt offered, feeling surprisingly deflated that Sarah had decided to leave.

They made their way outside the restaurant. "Your dad is really an amazing guy. I can see why you two are so close."

"He's definitely a character. And, hey, thanks for sticking around and having another beer with him. As jolly as he may seem, he gets lonely knocking around that big house by himself, so I know he's enjoying a night out."

"Are you kidding? He's great. I'll stay all night as long as he keeps telling me interesting stories and buying me beers," he said, smiling at Sarah.

"Is that all it takes?" She looked up into Matt's piercing blue eyes, suddenly wondering why she had decided to leave.

"What can I say, I'm a cheap date," he laughed. "Speaking of which, are you free Friday night? I'd like to treat you to dinner at one of my favorite restaurants in town."

This guy is certainly direct, she thought to herself, but somehow he pulls it off without being pushy. And she had to admit that she did like being around him. What the hell, she thought, time to stop being boring. "I'd like that," she said, feeling a flush rise in her cheeks.

"Great, I'll pick you up at seven."

"I'll try to be ready this time. And thanks again for keeping my dad company," she stood on her tiptoes and gave Matt a peck on the cheek. Feeling embarrassed, she turned quickly to leave.

Caught off guard, Matt was momentarily silenced. But he gathered himself in time to shout out teasingly, "Watch out for alligators, I heard there's one on the loose near Forsyth Park!"

Sarah gave him a quick wave without turning around and kept on walking.

He watched her walk away until she disappeared around the corner, then he made his way back inside to find Hank.

He hadn't noticed the black Cadillac Escalade with tinted windows parked across the street.

15

Present Day

Atlanta, GA

The crowd had been worked into a frenzy. The chants of "Em-er-son! Em-er-son!" slowly began to transition into "U-S-A!"—led by some carefully placed staffers among the crowd. Bill Emerson held his hands up theatrically, in a half-hearted attempt to quiet the enthusiastic southern crowd. It had little effect. The campaign was on its final southern swing before heading north to do battle against its Democratic counterpart in the five remaining undecided swing states. The trip through the South had been painstakingly orchestrated to build momentum before entering the hotly contested rust belt. Emerson would spend the remaining six weeks of the campaign crisscrossing Ohio, Indiana, Pennsylvania, and other key midwestern states, trolling for precious votes.

Big Bill's speech was drawing to a close. "Today I urge you to choose a new path for our country, because the current adminis-tration has driven us so far off course that we've lost our way as a nation. We've lost our way fiscally. We've lost our way interna-tionally. And we've lost our way morally."

Emerson paused as the predominantly white southern Baptist crowd cheered loudly. "And we keep getting more and more off course, to the point where we are in danger of never finding our way back; unless we change directions." The crowd responded with thunderous applause. He paused to let it subside before speaking again. He knew the secret to a great speech was momentum and flow—and today he had both.

He was dressed in a crisply pressed blue suit, white shirt, and red tie. He removed his jacket after taking the stage and rolled his sleeves up to his elbows—a choreographed move. Nothing on the campaign was left to chance.

"The Democrats' socialist policies spend money we don't have. Then they wring their hands when their failed policies fail to generate any growth. As my forbearer, George Washington, once said, 'Worry is the interest paid by those who borrow trouble.' Well my friends, we've let the Democrats borrow trouble for far too long. It's time to stop borrowing from our future; it's time to stop worrying about being lost; it's time to chart a new course!"

Like the master public speaker he was, Emerson coaxed the crowd toward a final crescendo. "Give me the chance to get our country back on the right path! Give me the chance to restore the patriotic values this country was founded on! Give me the chance to fill this country with pride again! We shouldn't be apologizing for being Americans; we should be proud to be Americans!

"Are you proud to be an American?!" Emerson began his well-practiced final repartee with his enraptured supporters.

"Hell yes!" yelled the crowd in anticipated unison.

"I said, are you proud to be an American?!"

"Hell yes!" they roared, even louder this time.

"Are you ready to take back our country?!"

"Hell yes!"

"Are we going to win in November?!"

"Hell yes!" The crowd continued to chant the final refrain, "Hell yes!" over and over as Big Bill waded into the crowd, smiling and shaking hands like the apostle of patriotism he had become.

Chuck Conrad stood just off the main stage and looked on in wonderment. Say what you want about his politics, there was no denying that Bill Emerson could deliver a passionate speech. At stop after stop, he was like an evangelical preacher proselytizing before his congregation. And it had worked. They had gone from eight points down back to dead even. But Conrad knew all too well that things could change in a heartbeat, especially when it came to dealing with his unpredictable candidate.

There was the time a few years earlier, when Emerson was running for the open U.S. Senate seat in Texas. The press had gotten wind of a party that Emerson staffers threw after it had become apparent that the election was in the bag. Accusations surfaced immediately that a very intoxicated senator-to-be had slept with a campaign volunteer the night of the party. There were two problems with this development: The first was that Bill happened to be very married at the time and the father of two teenage girls. The second was that the alleged tryst was with a girl who was only seventeen, just a couple of years older than his elder daughter. And more importantly, she was young enough for Bill to be charged with statutory rape. Conrad remembered when he had confronted him; instead of a denial, the only thing Big Bill could muster was, "She said she was twenty."

When the shit hit the fan, Emerson had been distraught enough to contemplate quitting the race. That's when Conrad stepped in and set him straight. He demanded that Bill give him a week to work his connections in the Texas legal and law enforcement back channels, and that he'd take care of everything. In the meantime, he told Bill to keep his mouth shut and his pecker in his pants. Rumors of the incident disappeared as quickly as they had arisen. New rumors surfaced, of payoffs to both the girl and certain members of the Texas state police. But in time, these too disappeared, when no proof could ever be found. Conrad had worked his black magic, and rather than the illegal tryst costing Emerson the election, it had only cost him some hush money, the largest sum paid to keep his wife quiet. She subsequently became his ex-wife after filing for divorce shortly after Bill was elected to the U.S. Senate.

Conrad shook his head in an attempt to push these unpleasant thoughts from his mind. He turned and looked back at the podium. Emerson was posing with a man and his wife who had donned Washington wigs and were mugging for the cameras. The campaign had borrowed heavily from the patriotic image of the Sage of Mount Vernon. It had incorporated Washington's quotes into speeches, used his image in campaign collateral, and consistently referenced Emerson's legacy in press releases and other public relations materials. Conrad had to smile. Even he was amazed at how well the strategy had worked.

16

Present Day

Savannah, GA

J. J. Stanton hated surveillance. It was an incredibly tedious, albeit necessary, part of the job, and not nearly as exciting as Hollywood made it out to be. At the end of the day, most people, he had come to learn through experience, led predictable and boring lives. And today was no exception. He had been watching Hawkins Antiques for the better part of four hours. And while a dozen or so customers had come and gone, Matt Hawkins had yet to emerge. Stanton carried on his observation from a parked car on the opposite side of Monterey Square. From his vantage point, he had an unobstructed view of the front of the store.

The lengthy surveillance had given him plenty of time to get acquainted with the various points of ingress and egress around the somewhat dilapidated old mansion. A final bit of simple recon told him that if Hawkins did have an alarm system installed in his residence, he probably was not in the habit of enabling it. He could see through his binoculars that a large casement window had been left open about six inches. Past experience told him that people who leave windows open generally don't enable alarms. The window in question was also conveniently located at the top of a black wrought iron fire escape. Bingo, he had his entry point. All that was missing was a big neon sign that said "Enter Here."

He yawned as he watched two squirrels chase one another, nimbly jumping from one oak tree to the next in the shade of Monterey Square. He became wide awake, however, when his eyes shifted back to the store. Hawkins had emerged from the building and was heading for his vintage pickup truck. He was wearing khakis and a button-down shirt and he didn't have anything in his hands. That meant he had left the journal inside his apartment. Stanton breathed a sigh of relief.

He decided to sit tight until he was sure Hawkins was gone for good. He knew couldn't afford any slipups on this job, especially given the reputation of the man who had hired him. If he did, he would surely regret it. He glanced down at his watch; it was just before seven thirty in the evening.

About thirty minutes later, after dusk had darkened completely into night, he made his move. He was out of the car, across the street, and up the fire escape in less than five minutes. He carefully lifted up on the old casement window that had been left ajar. It didn't budge. He tried again, but quickly realized Savannah's summer humidity had swelled it so that it wouldn't move. "Damn," he swore under his breath. With a quick look down toward the street to make sure nobody was within earshot, he reached up and gave two quick but firm raps on either side of the oversized window. Other than dislodging some loose glazing from the sun-beaten mullions, it still wouldn't give. He banged a little harder. Finally, it loosened, just enough so that he could slip his large frame through the opening.

After about twenty minutes of searching, he spotted the corner of an atlas sticking out from underneath a stack of file folders on top of an antique-looking desk. He pulled out the atlas and quickly opened it. To his enormous relief, nestled inside a hidden cutaway cavity sat the journal. He quickly removed it and flipped the atlas aside.

He spent a little more time tossing Matt's apartment so that it would appear more like a random robbery than a targeted theft of the journal. To complete the ruse, he stuffed a pair of silver candlesticks and a few other small valuables into his coat pockets. Then he squeezed back through the window and began to descend the fire escape.

Halfway down the zigzag metal rungs, an English-accented voice called out, "Young man, what the devil are you doing up there!"

J. J. looked toward the alleyway behind the house. The voice belonged to an old geezer who had spotted him while walking his two little yappy dogs. After hearing their master call out, the Yorkshire terriers decided to start a barking contest. If Stanton wasn't so rushed, he thought, he'd shoot the little bastards. Instead he kept his head hidden in the shadow of his baseball cap and scampered down the last ten rungs. He leapt off the iron structure and hit the ground running.

———

Matt and Sarah had finished their drinks at a favorite rooftop bar in town. But instead of going straight to dinner, they made a quick detour to Monterey Square. Sarah wanted to see Matt's store, so they headed in that direction.

Most of the homes in historic Savannah had rear-facing garages accessible via small alleyways that ran behind the home. As Matt pulled in, he saw his neighbor, old Mr. Hussey, yelling at someone in the alley between the old mansion and the building next door. Mr. Hussey and his wife of more than fifty years had moved to Savannah just a few months before, from England.

Matt hopped out of the truck. "What's going on, Mr. Hussey? Who are you yelling at?"

"Oh, hello, Matthew," the diminutive old Brit said excitedly. "There's a man on your fire escape. I thought it was you at first, but when I called out..."

Matt was already running in the direction of the alley. Turning the corner, he saw the dark shape of a man on the far side of the building. He had just hopped over a small fence and was heading toward Monterey Square. Matt sprinted in that direction and was up and over the same fence in a matter of seconds. Back in his college days, he was the leading base stealer on the baseball team and, thanks to his frequent runs in the park, he hadn't lost a step.

He had already cut the distance between himself and the intruder in half. As his legs churned, he glanced down and saw what appeared to be the candlesticks from his kitchen table. They had been discarded in a bed of annuals that surrounded the monument honoring General Casimir Pulaski in the center of the square. Evidently the fleeing perpetrator had been forced to drop some of his cache in order to lighten his load.

Matt had closed the gap to less than fifty feet when the man abruptly stopped and pivoted. He aimed a large handgun directly at Matt in a manner that left no doubt that he was well practiced at this kind of thing. Matt had no time to think, only to react. He dove to his left just as the first shot rang out.

He felt a whooshing sensation as the bullet hurdled by his left ear. He landed hard and scrambled on all fours to get behind the closest cover. Unfortunately, the only obstruction available was a slat-back wooden park bench, one of many scattered throughout the green spaces of Savannah's famous squares. While it didn't offer much cover, it was better than being completely exposed. Another round ripped through a wooden slat just above Matt's head. He lay as flat as he could and kept his head low. Splinters rained down around him. His mind spun through potential options, but failed to come up with any viable solutions. He was trapped.

Surprisingly, however, no more shots came. And after a few moments of silence, Matt slowly lifted his head. Seconds later, a squeal of rubber on asphalt about a block away confirmed that his assailant had decided to flee. Matt stood up quickly but could only make out the silhouette of a large SUV as it disappeared around a far corner. As he brushed himself off he realized he was shaking.

Sarah hurried through the gate at the far entrance to the square. "Matt, are you all right?" she yelled. "I thought I heard gunshots."

"You did," he said, anger slowly overtaking his fear. He turned to look over his shoulder one last time, but the man was long gone.

She looked down and saw blood stains on his pants, "Oh my God, are you hurt?"

"I'm OK, just a couple of scraped knees. Guess I'll need a new pair of pants, huh?" he smiled weakly, in spite of everything that had just happened.

"Let's get you cleaned up and call the police," she said.

They made their way back to the mansion and up the stairs to Matt's apartment. He unlocked the door and looked inside. The place was a mess. Drawers had been rifled and left open. Items were strewn all over the apartment. Whatever the thief hadn't wanted had simply been tossed to the floor. He walked slowly across the room and returned the candlesticks to their rightful place on the kitchen table, as if to restore order to the chaotic scene around him.

Sarah walked over, put her arms around him, and gave him a consoling hug. "I'm so sorry," she said. There were tears in her eyes. He hugged her back, but his mind was elsewhere. Something was gnawing at him. Then he had an idea.

He broke away and hurried into his study. When he returned, he had the atlas in his hand and a defeated look on his face.

Sarah looked at him in confusion. He opened the book and showed her the empty cavity. The journal was gone. "Matt, we need to let the police know what's going on," she said, and took a few steps toward the phone.

"Wait," he said quickly. "I'm not sure that's a good idea right now." Sarah stopped and turned with a questioning look on her face.

He held up the neutered atlas and said, "Look Sarah, somebody wanted this journal badly enough to steal it; so badly that they took a couple of shots at me down there in the square. Believe me, I don't like being shot at, but there's clearly something bigger happening here than we know. And until we figure out what that is, I don't think we should get the police involved. I just don't want that journal slipping out of our hands for good."

"But the police have detectives whose job is to figure stuff like this out," she pleaded.

"Come on, Sarah. Mr. Hussey was too far away to get a good look, and I'm not sure I could even identify the guy who shot at me." Matt wasn't being totally truthful because, in fact, he had noticed a distinctive scar running down the man's left cheek.

"And besides, it's not like in the movies where detectives dust for fingerprints or anything. They'll just ask a lot of questions, file a report, and that will be the end of it. Trust me, my store has been ripped off a couple of times in the past and that's exactly what happened. I say we do some digging on our own first."

Matt had been raised in a rough-and-tumble blue-collar neighborhood. Grudges were held and scores were settled, especially when it involved someone's home or family. Police were called in only as a last resort. He had been in a few fights over the years and knew how to take care of himself, even if he didn't have a particularly violent personality. The only "weapon" he owned was his lucky aluminum baseball bat from his college days. Even so, a part of him still hoped to have the opportunity to meet the guy from the fire escape, face-to-face.

"Somebody just shot at you!" she said, as if he had somehow forgotten what had just happened outside.

"I know that, Sarah," he acknowledged, trying to force calm into his voice. "It's just that my gut is telling me that we're better off trying to figure it out on our own, at least for now. I'm not saying we won't call the police eventually, just not yet."

She shook her head in frustration and sat down on the over-stuffed couch.

He walked across the room and stuck his head out the semi-open window. He tried to picture the route the perpetrator had taken. A shiver clawed its way down his spine as he looked toward Monterey Square and thought about how long the thief must have watched his apartment, just waiting for him to leave.

"Matt, you're scaring me," she said, noticing the concern in his normally easygoing face.

"There's nothing to be scared about; he's long gone," but his voice lacked conviction.

After a few moments of silence, Sarah spoke up again, "Why would someone want to steal the journal anyway?" She opened and closed the atlas, as if by doing so, the journal would somehow magically reappear.

"What's bothering me is not why but who. Besides me, you, and your dad, nobody else even knows the journal exists. Oh yeah, there's also Sissy Hightower."

Sarah said, "Matt, Sissy is an old friend who I trust completely, so if you're thinking that she was somehow involved in this…"

He held up his hands and protested, "No, of course not. I don't think Sissy would ever be involved in something like this,

I'm just thinking out loud. But the facts are that those are the only people who know about the journal."

"So what do you want to do? If we're not going to the police, where do we start?"

"There's only one place to start. We talk with Sissy and find out who else she told about the journal."

17

Present Day

Savannah, GA

Matt and Sarah arrived at the Harper Fowlkes House first thing in the morning. They were there to pay an unannounced visit to Sissy Hightower. After being escorted back to the administrative offices by one of the volunteer tour guides, Sissy seemed pleasantly surprised to see them.

"Well, hello, you two. What an unexpected treat," she said, popping out of her chair to greet her guests. She was dressed head-to-toe in pink, accented only by oversized white orb costume earrings and strawberry-red lipstick. When she noticed the serious looks on their faces, she quickly added, "I'm so sorry but I haven't heard anything back yet from my contact in Washington, which is odd, come to think of it. He promised he'd have something to me within a few days." Sissy motioned for them to have a seat. There were two simple folding chairs that barely fit in her cramped office.

"Sissy, who exactly is your contact at the society's headquarters in Washington?" Sarah asked, not making a move to sit down.

"Like I said the other day dear, he's the head research librarian. He owes me a favor, which evidently he's forgotten about. I'm sorry, I should have followed up with him yesterday but it was the anniversary of my husband's death, so it's been a bit of a rough week," she replied, while also remaining standing.

"Oh, I'm so sorry," Sarah said, her tone softening.

"Sissy," Matt stepped forward and asked with more directness then he had intended, "did you tell anyone else about the journal?"

Sissy was clearly startled by Matt's abruptness. She responded, "Why no, dear, is something wrong? You two seem very upset." A mix of concern and confusion, which could not have been faked, showed on her face.

Sarah glanced over at Matt and then back at Sissy again. She sat down with a sigh. "Sorry for coming on so strong. It's just that the journal was stolen from Matt's house last night."

"Oh my heavens," Sissy reflexively put her hand to her mouth. "That's awful. Now who would do a thing like that?"

Matt could see that Sissy's reaction had been genuine. Any scintilla of doubt that had remained regarding her potential involvement in the theft immediately dissipated. He sat down heavily.

The edge was gone from his voice when he said, "That's exactly why we're here. You see, only the three of us, and Sarah's father, know of the journal's existence. But the person who stole it from my place last night clearly knew we had it. He must have waited for me to leave and then took it. We don't know why, but we have a feeling it was a coordinated effort. We think he may have been following us for the last couple of days, just waiting for the right opportunity to make his move." He purposely left out the part about being shot at in Monterey Square. He didn't want to upset Sissy any more than was necessary.

Sarah continued, "We need your help, Sissy. Are you sure there was no one else you told about the journal?"

"I swear; the only person I talked to about it was Todd Spencer, the head librarian at the society."

"Well, we need to have a chat with Mr. Spencer then," Matt said. He was clearly pissed off, not only because the journal had been stolen, but also because someone had threatened his life.

"Hang on a second, Matt; that might scare him off. Maybe we should approach someone higher up in the food chain first. Spencer may be more apt to talk to his boss than a couple of strangers from Savannah, especially if he was involved somehow," Sarah asserted. Her clear-headed thinking was on display yet again.

"You're probably right," Matt agreed. "Sissy, do you have any suggestions on whom we could talk to?"

"Well, the person who runs the day-to-day operations up there is the executive director of the society—a man by the name of James Fox," she said, eager to help in any way she could.

"Do you think you can arrange a conference call with Mr. Fox?" Matt asked, leaning carefully forward in his wobbly folding chair. He was worried that the thing could snap shut around him like a mousetrap, at any minute.

"Well, I can sure give it a try. Hang on a sec and let me find the society's internal telephone directory." Sissy rummaged through her desk with a flurry, noisily opening and closing drawers. Matt was baffled at how she could know where anything was in that office.

"Ah, here it is," she said, and without missing a beat, picked up the phone and started dialing.

Matt was impressed with Sissy's spunk when she told Fox's assistant that there had been a "security breach." She refused to elaborate any further until the director called her back personally. He made a mental note not to get on Sissy's bad side. Ten minutes later, the phone rang. It was the director on the line. She put him on speaker and introduced Matt and Sarah.

Sissy proceeded to fill Director Fox in on the discovery of the journal and the query she had subsequently requested from Todd Spencer. Matt then spent the next ten minutes filling him in on the details surrounding the theft of the journal. Finally, he shared the fact that the only person to know about the book, outside of the four of them in Savannah, was Fox's head research librarian. The accusation hung in the air like a bad odor.

Like Sarah, Fox was a historian and author himself. Ironically, he had recently published a book on the presidency of George Washington. According to Sissy, he was known as a straight shooter and was respected by his peers.

"First of all, what an incredible piece of history to find; I would have loved to have read the journal myself. And I'm truly sorry about the theft. Of course I'll do everything in my power to help in any way I can. But I have a hard time believing that Todd Spencer had anything to do with the crime you describe. Todd is a family man with a wife and two kids; it just doesn't fit what I know of him."

"Will you at least talk to him about this?" asked Sarah, gently.

There was a lengthy pause on the other end of the line before Fox spoke again. "I already have."

"Excuse me?" said Sarah.

"What?" Matt said simultaneously.

"Look, the reason Spencer hasn't gotten back to Sissy with the results of the query she asked him to perform is because I told him to wait," Fox explained. "I had to check with our legal counsel before I could release the results of the search, which I just received late yesterday afternoon."

Matt, barely able to contain himself, nearly shouted at the phone, "Results of the search? You mean you actually found something?!" Both Sissy and Sarah inched closer to the speaker, as if their proximity would hasten Fox's explanation.

"The database did come back with a hit; a *single* hit. And the reference came from the personal journal of a very prominent deceased member of the society. Larz Anderson," he said.

"Larz Anderson; as in the guy who built Anderson House?" Sissy asked incredulously.

"Yes, as in the man whose former home now serves as the headquarters for the Society of the Cincinnati," Fox confirmed. "Evidently Larz and Isabel Anderson led a very adventurous life traveling around the world, and Larz recorded many of these experiences in a series of journals. They filled thirty-eight typed volumes, to be exact."

He took a deep breath and continued, "The journals had been in a private collection since the 1930s and were only gifted to the society four years ago by the family of Larz's first cousin. Anyway, it was in one of these volumes, from the year 1901, that we found a reference to a surrender letter from Washington. Evidently it was a reference to the same letter that you folks found in Caty Greene's journal." Fox then clarified, "Todd briefed me on your discovery after he found the entry in Larz Anderson's journal."

"Oh my God, are you telling us that Anderson corroborates Caty's claims? The surrender letter she described in her journal is real?" asked Sarah.

"Not exactly, what I'm telling you is that evidently Larz Anderson's ancestors *believed* the letter existed. In fact, according to Larz, Richard Clough Anderson, who was his great-grandfather, was dispatched to Mulberry Grove Plantation in early 1793 to retrieve it."

"Dispatched by whom?" Matt said. "Caty wrote about Richard Anderson's visit in her journal. But she didn't know who had sent him. But clearly the visit spooked her."

"According to Anderson's journal entry, it was General Henry Knox, who had served under Washington. As you may know, Knox was also one of the founders of the society. He asked Richard Anderson to go find the letter and bring it back, presumably to protect Washington's reputation," he said.

Sarah interjected, "And perhaps to protect the reputation of the society as well." There was silence on the other end of the line, so she finished her thought. "Remember, Washington was the society's president, too. And there were lots of conspiracy theories flying around back then concerning the intentions of your organization." Sarah had studied the history of the society as part of her research for her book on the revolution.

Fox countered, "You may be right, Sarah, but most of those theories were proven to be unfounded."

"Still, I find it very interesting that General Henry Knox, who was you organization's founder, had such a keen interest in the letter," Matt broke in. He made no attempt to disguise his skepticism.

"Guys, let's debate the intentions of the society later," Sissy said. "I'm more interested in what Anderson wrote about the letter in his 1901 journal."

"Well, here's where it gets a bit interesting," Fox continued. He went on to tell the story of Larz Anderson's trip to Savannah, as part of the Rhode Island Chapter's efforts to recover the missing bones of Nathanael Greene. He also shared with them that Larz had a separate covert mission—to look for the alleged letter from Washington, which he had hoped might have been stowed in Greene's burial vault, after the drowning death of Caty's oldest son in 1793.

"Well I'll be damned," Sissy said.

"So now we've got another source claiming the existence of a surrender letter from Washington," said Sarah.

"Yeah, but unfortunately one of them has been stolen, quite conveniently by the way, right after Sissy's conversation with

Spencer. Forgive me, Mr. Fox, but the Society of the Cincinnati seems to always be at the center of the action when it comes to Washington's letter, first in 1793, then in 1901, and now again today," Matt pointed out, accusingly.

"Matt, as I told you before, Todd Spencer is as squeaky clean as they come. I enjoy a juicy conspiracy, too, but the society is just not the cloak-and-dagger organization that you've painted us out to be. We're a nonprofit organization devoted to promoting the patriotic principles that this country was founded on. There's simply no hidden agenda and never has been," Fox replied, defensively.

"All I know is that Sissy made a call to you guys and now the journal is gone," Matt added, with increasing agitation. "I'm sorry, but I don't believe in coincidences, and I sure as hell don't enjoy strange men tossing my apartment."

It was time to call a truce. So in an attempt to calm the emotions that had started to run a little high, Sarah said, "Mr. Fox, we appreciate everything you've told us today. You didn't have to tell us all that you did, so thank you for sharing what you found in your archives. You seem to be very forthright and I believe you when you say you trust Mr. Spencer. But let me ask you this, could anyone else in your organization have been privy to the results of the query?"

Her softer approach seemed to work. Director Fox said, "Thank you for trusting me, Sarah, and please, call me James, by the way. You raise a valid question and one that frankly I didn't have cause to ask Todd when he initially brought the issue to my attention. If you'll hang on a second, though, I'll give him a call and ask him right now."

While they were on hold, Matt said, "I don't trust this guy, I mean the Society of the Cincinnati has been looking for this letter for a hell of a lot longer than we have. You heard him yourself, Sarah, the man whose house now serves as their headquarters was looking for the letter over a hundred years ago, for crying out loud. Then we show up with a journal that makes claims regarding the same letter. And a few days after notifying the society, it disappears. If they aren't the prime suspect, then I don't know who is."

"I agree it's pretty coincidental, but I don't know, I just don't feel like Fox is lying to us. He seems sincere. And besides, why would he share with us the story of Larz Anderson's search if he were trying to hide something? It just doesn't add up," she said.

"We're going to have to agree to disagree on this one," Matt said. He was convinced that the society and maybe even Director Fox were behind the theft.

Fox came back on the line and said, "OK, I just got off the phone with Todd. There was someone else with knowledge of the query, but he's not even an employee. He's just an unpaid intern from Baylor University working here for the summer. And Todd specifically told him to keep the results of the search confidential. But that's it, nobody else on this end knew of the journal's existence. Just Todd and the intern. Are you sure there's nobody else in Savannah who might have somehow found out about it?" he countered.

The question sounded more like an accusation. And that irked Matt. But before he could open his mouth, Sarah jumped in quickly to head off another heated confrontation. "We're pretty sure, James, but we'll keep thinking about it, and thanks for following up with Todd for us," she added diplomatically.

"My pleasure, Sarah, and thank you for calling, Sissy. I apologize for not getting back to you guys sooner with regard to your original query. I certainly wish you all the best in finding the journal. It would be a travesty for something of its historical significance to disappear forever. And as I said earlier, if there's anything else I can do, please don't hesitate to ask."

"Thanks for all your help, James," Sissy said.

But Matt remained conspicuously silent, deep in thought.

18

Present Day

Savannah, GA

They were back at Matt's favorite watering hole, the Crystal Beer Parlor. It had been a whirlwind twenty-four hours, and his head was still spinning. Sarah sat to his left and her father, Hank, to his right. They were the only people at the forty-foot-long bar, save for the texting waitress planted on a wooden stool near the kitchen. It was just before four o'clock in the afternoon, which accounted for why they had the place to themselves. Matt's head felt like a pinball machine. The flippers kept rattling thoughts around his head like a steel ball banging against his cranium. He was almost on tilt. He had called their little gathering to try to make some sense of the events of the past twenty-four hours. And as always, he thought better with a cold beer in his hands.

"Well, you two had yourself quite an evening," Hank said with a smile, reaching for his beer.

"Not a bad first date, eh Sarah?" Matt said. His trademark grin reappeared for the first time that day.

"Yeah, you really pulled out all the stops," she said, smiling in return.

"I like to start things off with an armed robbery. Then throw in a little conspiracy just to spice things up," he said, sarcastically.

"Well, at least you haven't lost your sense of humor," Hank said, chuckling.

"If I wasn't laughing I'd be crying, believe me," Matt replied. "So what do you make of all of this?"

"Well, like you, I think it's a little too coincidental that all of this occurred right after you notified the Society of the Cincinnati in Washington. But from what Sarah told me, that Director Fox fellow seemed to be very forthright and willing to share everything he knew. So it doesn't appear as if he's trying to hide anything."

"I know he sounded sincere, but the society had to be involved somehow. The timing is too convenient. Their ties to George Washington go back more than two hundred years. Maybe all of this has to do with protecting their reputation. Maybe they don't want Washington's name slandered by the surrender letter claim. After all, he was their first president, too. So by protecting him they're protecting themselves," Matt postulated.

"I'm not sure they'd go to all that trouble...," Sarah started to speak, but Matt cut her off.

"Or maybe Larz Anderson did find the letter back in 1901 and his journal was just a cover-up to throw people off the trail. Or maybe the society had the letter all along and they just didn't want anybody to find out about it because it would disparage their hero," he said, continuing to throw out hypotheses, no matter how far-fetched.

"Matt, stop. You're not making any sense. If Larz Anderson had found the letter, he would have destroyed it or hidden it somewhere. He certainly wouldn't have written about it. What he wrote in his journal was the truth; he searched but didn't find the letter. Nobody else even knew about it, so he wasn't trying to throw anybody off any trail," she said rationally.

"All right, I'll admit I'm a little frustrated." Matt knew his emotions had probably gotten the better of his judgment. "But I still don't trust the society, no matter how sincere Fox sounds. My gut tells me they're connected to the theft somehow."

The back door of the bar opened and they all turned that way. They had grown accustomed to the darkened bar, so the shaft of light assaulted their eyes. A nattily dressed old man with a trimmed gray goatee made his way to one of the back booths. He sat down, removed the newspaper from under his arm, and immediately turned to the crossword puzzle. The first regular of the day had arrived.

"I know you're frustrated, Matt, but I have to agree with Sarah on this point. I just don't buy into your conspiracy theory regarding the society. The members I know here in town are nice enough people, and very civic-minded and dedicated to preserving and promoting Savannah's rich history. They're not part of some shadowy organization that runs around breaking into people's homes. It just doesn't fit," Hank said. He paused to wipe a smudge from his eyeglasses. "They're nothing more than a harmless group of old blue bloods who get together once or twice a year to reminisce about the good old days and swap old war stories. I think it's time to open up a new line of thinking."

"So why *would* someone want to steal the journal?" Sarah asked. "Logic would say that there can only be two potential motivations for taking it. Either they stole it to help *find* the letter, thinking the journal contained clues to the letter's whereabouts, or they stole it to *prevent* the letter from ever being found," she concluded, with scholarly reasoning.

"I like that rationale, Sarah," her father said. "Perhaps we should think about all the people who would *want* to find the letter and all the people who would *not* want the letter to be found, for whatever reason."

"Well, the obvious reason for wanting to find the letter would be money; the surrender letter would be very valuable, even priceless to some. And greed is a powerful motivator, powerful enough to make someone resort to stealing the journal. Especially if they thought that important clues to its location could be found inside," Sarah said. She was in her problem-solving comfort zone.

Matt chimed in, "OK, I'll play along with you guys. I think the suspect is someone who did *not* want the letter to come to light. So, leaving the society aside for the moment, who else would be hurt by the revelation of Washington's decision to surrender to the British?" His stomach had started to growl, so he reached for a menu left on top of the bar.

"All right, let's pursue that angle," Sarah said. "The logical place to start would be with an organization whose reputation is or was linked to the Founding Father."

"Well, there are lots of institutions named for the first president. There's George Washington University, Washington and Lee, Washington University in St. Louis, just to name a few. There are countless organizations, monuments, bridges, and other edifices in his name. And there are plenty of towns named after him," Hank added, clearly enjoying the analytical exchange.

Matt wasn't sure this was getting them anywhere. He turned to the television mounted behind the bar. It was the middle of the afternoon and no games were on. The TV was tuned to CNN, but with the sound turned down. He was about to turn away when CNN cut to a live speech being given by William Emerson, currently campaigning in Richmond, Virginia. The camera panned to the crowd and back again to Big Bill, who was in the middle of one of his patriotic speeches.

There were images of George Washington everywhere the camera panned: on the podium, on banners, on T-shirts, and on buttons. The staff had even passed out those little wooden paddles with the Founding Father's picture affixed to the ends of them, so people could put them over their faces. Matt had always felt that the Emerson campaign had gone a bit overboard with the whole Washington association. But he had to admit, the sea of Washington paper faces that stared back at Emerson delivered exactly the patriotic symbolism the campaign had no doubt been after. And the well-orchestrated photo op was being beamed LIVE across the country in high-definition.

"Now there's a guy who would be pissed off by the discovery of a surrender letter from Washington," Matt smiled and pointed with his long-necked beer toward the television.

Sarah and Hank looked over to see where he was pointing. "You're right about that," Hank said with a chuckle. "It always did seem a bit ironic to me that this bombastic Texan could be George Washington's closest living kin anyway. I always thought he was dumber than a bag of hammers." They turned away from the television laughing.

Suddenly, Sarah sat bolt upright on her bar stool. "Wait a minute," she said, "what did you just say, Dad?"

"Emerson's dumber than a bag of hammers?"

"No, no, the part about him being a Texan." She turned away from her father and looked at Matt with a sudden intensity. "And you're absolutely right; he would be hurt by the revelation of the surrender letter. In fact, he is the *one* person in this country with the most riding on the Founding Father's reputation, because he borrows from that reputation on a daily basis." She pointed emphatically at the television, which was still broadcasting his patriotic speech, to emphasize her point.

"Sure, Sarah, but what are you suggesting? That the Republican nominee for president is behind the theft of the journal? And you guys thought I had some wacky conspiracy theories," Matt scoffed.

"Sarah, honey, how could Emerson even know about the journal?" Hank said, swiveling in his stool to face his daughter.

"It just clicked when you said that he's from Texas. Matt, do you remember today when we were talking to James Fox; he said that another person had been aware of the search. The intern, remember?"

"Of course I remember, Sarah, but he was just a kid intern from...," and then the realization struck him, "holy shit, the intern was from Baylor University!"

"Right. And where is Baylor University located?"

"I believe it's in the great state of Texas!" Matt shouted, which garnered an annoyed look from Mr. Crossword Puzzle.

"Is somebody going to fill me in?" Hank said, looking back and forth between his high-fiving bar mates.

"Sorry, Dad," said Sarah excitedly. "The other person who was involved in the search at the society was a summer intern from Baylor University. He's the only one not accounted for, so it has to be him. Don't you see; he had to be the one that leaked the results of the search!"

She was quite animated now, and the rush of making a critical link made her talk even faster. She said, "Director Fox said that he trusted his head research librarian implicitly, and I believed him. So that only leaves the intern. And the Texas connection fits—maybe he worked on the campaign or has a friend who did."

"Your daughter's a genius, Hank," Matt said, reaching over and squeezing Sarah's hand.

"The apple doesn't fall too far from the tree, I guess," Hank said with a wink. "So what's our next move?"

"We need to get Director Fox back on the phone right away, and find out more about this intern. Sarah, do you think you can get his number from Sissy?" asked Matt.

"I'm already on it." She pulled her phone from her oversized handbag and began dialing Sissy Hightower.

Five minutes later, after securing his number from Sissy, Matt dialed James Fox in Washington. When Fox didn't pick up, Matt left an urgent message to call his cell phone as soon as possible.

He motioned to the bartender for another round for himself and Hank. Sarah was still nursing her first one. He gave Hank a concerned look and said, "You know, if Sarah's right and that intern was the leak, then this just became a whole different ball game. Because that means someone in the Emerson campaign authorized the burglary of my apartment."

"That thought had crossed my mind," Hank admitted. "I think you two need to be very careful from here on out."

"You guys are scaring me again," Sarah said, and began to pick nervously at the damp bar napkin under her beer.

"Well, it's the truth; you need to be careful," her father replied. "Matt's right, if your theory turns out to be true then this *is* a whole new ball game. If these people will steal to get the journal, then what else are they capable of doing in order to get their hands on the letter?"

"We'll be careful Hank, I promise," Matt said, trying not to freak Sarah out too much. "Let's just take it one step at a time. We'll talk to Fox and go from there. Besides, like you said, they've already stolen the journal so they've probably forgotten about us by now."

But deep down, Matt knew that was wishful thinking.

19

Present Day

Savannah, GA

Matt awoke to his alarm going off. But as he opened one eye and registered his clock flashing 7:13 a.m., he realized that it didn't sound like an alarm. It sounded more like a phone. Now close to fully awake it finally dawned on him that his cell phone was ringing. It could be James Fox calling him back from Washington!

By the third ring he was up and out of bed, trying to locate his phone. But it wasn't on his bedside table where he normally put it. It rang again and Matt noticed his pants in a heap, at the foot of the bed. The phone was sticking out of the back pocket. He was so tired by the time he got home the prior evening that he had stripped down and literally fallen into bed. The fourth ring chimed and Matt took a quick step toward it. That's when his big toe caught on the corner of the bed.

"Ow! Shit, son of a bitch," he yelled out, as he collapsed in pain on the floor. Ring number five sounded out and it was about to go to voice mail. With one hand grabbing at his foot, he reached out with the other and hit the answer button. He stifled a final curse before saying a strained, "Hello."

"Uh, hello, I'm looking for Matt Hawkins, this is James Fox calling."

"Yeah, James, this is Matt, hang on a second." He rolled over, got up and sat on the bed. His toe hurt like hell but it wasn't bleeding. He took a deep breath and put the phone to his ear. "Sorry, James, I was in the middle of something when you called. I see you got my messages."

"I did. Sorry I didn't get back to you yesterday, but I had a meeting in Reston, Virginia, and never made it back to the office. Most people call my cell, so I didn't even think to check for messages on my office phone until I saw the light flashing when I walked in this morning. Anyway, it sounded urgent, what can I do for you?"

Matt ran his hand through his disheveled hair while he collected his thoughts. "I called to talk to you about that intern, the one from Baylor University? We think that maybe he was the one that leaked the information about the journal."

"The intern? Why would he do that?" Fox said, clearly confused.

"Listen, it's a long story and maybe a little far-fetched, but it's the only theory we have as to why the journal was stolen. But before I go any further, I have to know that I can trust you, James. Sarah says that I should, but I'll be honest with you, I'm still not entirely convinced that the society is not involved someway in all of this."

"Look, Matt, I'm just a historian and author who for the past three years have served as executive director of the Society of the Cincinnati. As much as you'd like to believe that we're running some kind of covert operation here, nothing could be further from the truth," Fox said.

"Well, at the moment, I really don't have much of a choice but to trust what you say, because I need your help. But you need to know that what I'm about to tell you changes the, uh, scope, I guess you could say, of everything."

"I don't know what else I can say to earn your trust. I'd like to help you, but ultimately it's your choice."

After a momentary pause, Matt said, "Sorry, James, you've done nothing to make me distrust you. I'm just a little bit paranoid right now, especially after being shot at the other night."

"Shot at?" Fox gasped.

"Yes, I didn't mention it to you on the phone yesterday because I didn't want to upset Sissy, but the man who robbed my apartment had a gun and took a couple of shots at me when I tried to chase after him."

"Oh my God, Matt, I'm sorry, I had no idea. I guess you've earned your paranoia."

"You could say that. But after you hear our theory, maybe you'll understand why my paranoia has gone up a few more notches since then."

"Uh-oh," Fox said nervously.

"Uh-oh is right. So here goes, I'm going to start by telling you who we think is behind the theft of the journal and then work backward from there. You ready?" Matt asked.

"Why do I feel like I'm going to regret saying this, but yes, I'm ready."

"William Emerson."

After a long pause, Fox said, "As in the William Emerson running for president?"

"One and the same. And before you call the paddy wagon, let me lay it out for you. We were brainstorming yesterday when Sarah raised the point that Emerson has staked his election on the reputation of George Washington. They have become inextricably linked together, not only because of their ancestral connection, but also because of Emerson's own campaign strategy. I'm sure you've noticed how shamelessly the Republican Party has used Washington's image to prop up their candidate's integrity and patriotic values. And I think you'd agree that if it were to be revealed that Washington offered to surrender to the British, that his image would be forever tarnished. So if there's anyone in this country who doesn't want the surrender claim to be revealed, it's Emerson," Matt argued.

"I'll admit that politically he could have a lot to lose if Washington's image is tarnished, but I'm still not following how you think he is connected to the theft of Caty Greene's journal."

"That's where your intern comes in," Matt said excitedly. "You told us he was a graduate student from Baylor University. Well, Baylor University is located in Waco, Texas, which just happens to be a stone's throw up the road from Emerson's campaign headquarters in Austin," Matt paused to give Fox a chance to digest the information. He was still sitting on the edge of his bed in his boxers, rubbing his big toe, where a nasty red welt had begun to take shape.

"Well, I agree with you on one thing, that your theory is a little far-fetched. I mean, come on, Matt, Texas is a big state. Just because he's a student at Baylor doesn't connect him to Emerson," Fox said.

"I know that, but he is the only person unaccounted for who knew about the journal. I can vouch for everyone on this end, and you said yourself that you trust Todd Spencer unequivocally. So that leaves the intern." He let the accusation hang in the air before adding, "How well do you know this kid anyway?"

"Beyond meeting him briefly a couple of times, I don't know him very well at all. But he's like most graduate interns we get here: clean cut, polite, focused, and, of course, smart."

Matt cradled the phone between his neck and shoulder while pulling on his jeans. "James, this is our best lead; frankly, it's our only lead at this point. So would you be willing to at least do a little digging into his background? You must have a personnel file or something that can tell us if he has any connection to Emerson."

"I'll pull his resume and I'll give Todd a call to see what he can tell me, but I don't want to give you false hope, Matt, I think this is a long shot."

"That's all I can ask," Matt said as his phone buzzed, alerting him to another call coming in. He could see by the caller ID that it was Hank Gordon. "James, I've got another call coming in. Will you call me later and let me know what you find out?"

"Of course. I'll let you know if I find anything of interest."

"OK, and thanks for your help." Matt quickly hit the answer button on his phone to see what Hank wanted so early in the morning. "Hey, Hank, what's up?"

"Good morning, Matthew, I wasn't sure I was going to get you. Sorry for calling so early."

"No problem, I was already awake. What's up?"

"Well, I don't know why I didn't think of this before now, but I believe there's someone here in Savannah who may be able to help us in our search for the letter."

Matt noticed Hank's use of the words *us* and *our*, and although he was more than happy to have the help of Hank Gordon, he said, "I thought you said it would be dangerous to pursue the letter, and now you're offering up leads. Why the change of heart?"

"When they stole your journal, they stole a piece of history," he said. "And as a historian, that just doesn't sit well with me. So if there is any chance that letter may still exist, we owe it to ourselves and the world to try to find it. And if we do, we should display it for all to see. That's my job as a historian, to study history and learn from it. So what if Washington wrote a surrender letter? Many other leaders of men might have done the same thing, given the dire circumstances that they were suffering through during that winter at Valley Forge. If it tarnishes the deified image that's been created of him, then so be it. We are all just men, Matt, there are no gods."

"I can see why your students loved you, Hank. So who is this person you want me to meet?"

"Her name is Martha Sampson and she is the daughter of a man named Toby Morton, who just happened to be one of the last slaves ever born on Mulberry Grove Plantation in 1864. I actually met Toby a few times when I used to roam the old plantation hunting and fishing, when I was just a boy. Old Toby had reached the ripe old age of ninety-four when he passed away in 1957," Hank explained.

"You actually talked to a man born into slavery during the Civil War era? That's pretty cool, Hank," Matt said, wishing he could have been around to share in that experience.

"Cool indeed. Toby used to regale me with tales of plantation living that had been passed down to him by his ancestors, who had preceded him as slaves on Mulberry Grove. He was the one who first told me that Washington had once walked the grounds there, and he showed me where the big plantation home once stood and where the rice fields used to be. Back then, some of the slave quarters were still standing and he showed me those as well. As you can imagine, it was a fantastical place for a young boy's imagination," Hank said with a touch of melancholy.

"It's no wonder you became a historian."

"There's probably some truth to that. Anyway, an idea struck me when I remembered seeing that notation on the first page of Caty's journal. Do you remember those initials, written in pencil, that Sissy told you had probably been entered at a much later date? Well, a lightbulb went off in my head, and it occurred to me that T. M. could stand for Toby Morton. It makes sense when you consider the similarities between some of the stories I heard Toby tell and those described in the journal. When I made that connection, it naturally led me to think of Toby's daughter, Martha," Hank said. "I don't know why I didn't think of all of this sooner. Maybe at my age the synapses aren't firing as fast as they used to, but I thought that maybe there's a chance that Toby passed on some stories to Martha that might be worth hearing. You have to remember that since most slaves were uneducated, they developed an incredibly rich oral tradition, and some stories passed down today date back literally hundreds of years. So you never know what Martha may have heard from her father, perhaps even something related to the letter. What do you think? Am I a crazy old man, or is it worth seeing if Martha has any tales to tell?"

"No, I don't think you're crazy at all. Why couldn't T. M. stand for Toby Morton? It's certainly worth a shot, but do you think she will be up for talking with us? She's got to be quite old herself by now."

"She's probably close to ninety, maybe older. I believe Toby, the old polecat, was in his early sixties when he fathered her. It's been awhile since I last spoke to her, but she's an old family friend and I'm sure she'd welcome our visit."

"I think it's a great idea, Hank. I'd love to talk to her either way. I'm sure she's a fascinating woman," Matt said enthusiastically.

20

Present Day

Savannah, GA

Matt and Hank arrived in front of Martha's modest but well-kept home in the Southover section of town. They received more than a few stares when they emerged from Matt's truck. Two white males tended to stick out in the predominantly African American neighborhood. If they had been driving a sedan and wearing neckties, they might have been mistaken for a couple of detectives. As it was, Matt could feel the suspicious gaze of Martha's neighbors as he and Hank made their way up to her home. But Martha greeted Hank so warmly that anyone who might have been concerned returned to his own business.

Martha was a solidly built woman with a broad smile and a twinkle in her eye. She had perfectly aligned, bright white teeth and a youthful appearance that belied her age. The only clue to her advanced years was large, thick-lens glasses covering the top half of her face.

When her unexpected guests had arrived, Martha insisted on fixing up a batch of her special homemade lemonade. She returned a few minutes later and they politely sipped from their glasses on Martha's tidy front porch.

"My goodness, Hank Gordon, it's been a long time. When did you get so old and gray?!" she said with a hearty chuckle.

"A long time ago I'm afraid, Martha," he replied. "But you look exactly the same. How do you stay looking so young?"

"Never drank nor smoked, so the good Lord saw fit to keep me in good health. That and my exercise bike inside," she said and laughed at her own joke. She had never been on an exercise bike in her life.

"Young man," she said turning to Matt, "you said you in the antique business?"

"Yes, ma'am, I own a shop in the historic district. It's in an old mansion that I'm slowly renovating. You ought to stop by and I'll give you the grand tour."

"Thank you, child, you're very sweet, but I don't leave the neighborhood much no more; I tire easily. But I'm sure your shop is lovely." She turned back to Hank and continued, "So what brings you out this way to pay a visit to old Martha? If I know you, Hank, you probably up to something; you always was." Turning back to Matt she said, "He tell you what a high-spirited boy he was? He done run around that old overgrown plantation stirring up all kind of mischief." Again, her easy laughter bubbled over.

"Now don't exaggerate, Martha, I was just a curious young lad," Hank said with a conspiratorial wink. "But as a matter of fact, we have come to talk to you about Mulberry Grove. In particular, those stories your father used to share with me about the plantation's early days."

"Oh, Daddy have lots of stories, that's for sure true. Now, separatin' out the truth in them stories, that's the tricky part," she said with a sly grin.

"Your father used to love talking about Washington's visit to Mulberry Grove. I can remember him telling me to kneel down and put my hands flat on the sandy drive that led out to the plantation. He'd tell me that I was touching the same ground that George Washington had walked upon. You can imagine how thrilling that was for a young boy to hear."

"Oh yes sir, he like his George Washington stories. Had a bunch of them, he did. Daddy know how to tell a story," she said and nodded, looking over Hank's shoulder at a fat robin cleaning her wings in a puddle left over from the prior evening's thunderstorm. "And he didn't need much proddin' to tell them neither."

"Well, Martha, if you don't mind, the story we're interested in talking to you about today involves George Washington. We were hoping that, if it sounded familiar, you might be able to fill in some additional details that your father may have shared with you," Hank said.

"Well, I'm game to try, Hank. Just what kind of details you looking for?"

"I'm going to let Matt take it from here," said Hank, and he gestured for Matt to begin.

Matt cleared his throat and said, "Martha, remember how I told you that I own an antiques store? Well, I recently acquired an old atlas from the Bull Street Library. They sell me books occasionally, and then I resell them at my store. Anyway, inside the atlas I made a remarkable discovery. A secret cavity had been cut out of the oversized pages, and inside the opening was an eighteenth-century journal—and not just any journal. It was Caty Greene's journal from when she lived at Mulberry Grove." Matt paused for a moment. Martha's face was, for the first time that day, devoid of any emotion. Surprised by the stony look, he glanced over at Hank, who motioned for him to continue.

"The journal contained some incredible accounts of Caty's life at Mulberry Grove. As well as her experiences during the Revolutionary War with her husband General Nathanael Greene," he went on. "There is one story in particular that is,

well, I guess you could say controversial." Martha stared off into
the distance beyond Matt's left shoulder.

"Are you all right, dear?" Hank interrupted, with a look of
concern on his face. A barely perceptible nod from Martha signaled Matt to go on.

He picked up where he had left off. "In her journal, Caty
wrote that George Washington, when he was the commander in
chief of the Continental Army at Valley Forge, wrote a letter to
General William Howe, commander of the British Army. The
two had corresponded quite often during the course of the war.
But this letter was different," he said, and paused briefly before
continuing. "In this letter, Washington offered to negotiate terms
of surrender with the British. The surrender letter, however, was
never delivered. And Nathanael Greene, for reasons that are
unclear, held on to it. It subsequently ended up in the possession of Caty Greene after her husband's premature death. Some
years later, Caty asked Eli Whitney, who was staying with her at
Mulberry Grove at the time, to make her a metal canister to store
the letter for safekeeping." Matt paused for a minute, hoping he
wasn't confusing her.

Hank interjected, "We know this may sound a bit crazy,
Martha, but we think there's a possibility Washington's surrender
letter may have survived. We're trying to find it, which is why we
came here today. On the outside chance that your father told you
stories related to the canister that could potentially lead us to its
current whereabouts."

"Is any of this sounding familiar to you?" Matt gently prodded, sensitive to the fact that they had just dumped a lot of information on a ninety-year-old woman.

Martha replied quietly, as if a wave of fatigue had suddenly
come over her, "Now why'd you think a story like this would
sound familiar to *me*?"

"Well, there's something else, Martha. We also discovered some initials written on the inside front cover of the journal—the initials T. M.—and it made me think of a man I knew a very long time ago with those same initials. Toby Morton," Hank said, "your father."

At the mention of her father's name, Martha's eyes became moist and she said, "Can I see this journal?"

The two men looked awkwardly at one another. Matt finally said, with some embarrassment, "Actually, we don't have it anymore; someone stole it from my home shortly after we discovered it."

It had become quite still and uncomfortably warm on the front porch. Matt could feel his shirt beginning to stick to the sweat on his back. No one spoke. Martha seemed to be lost in a different place and time. Finally, a breath of air mercifully stirred. A tinkling sound came from a homemade glass wind chime hanging near the front door. That seemed to break the spell that had taken hold of Martha.

At long last, she spoke. "You know, I never had no children of my own. I wanted to, but the good Lord had other plans for me. Most of my friends and family is long dead, and I don't have very much time left here on God's green earth. But I do know some things." Martha paused again before finally making up her mind to continue. "I got stories. But I don't have nobody left to tell them to," she said, and hesitated one final time before she concluded, "so maybe God sent you two here today to hear them stories."

Clarity returned to Martha's eyes, as if a hypnotist snapped his fingers and released her from a trance. She stated simply, "I know all about Miss Caty Greene's journal."

The two men sat, mouths agape, stunned at Martha's admission. Even though Hank had come up with the theory regarding the initials T. M. belonging to Toby Morton, deep down he hadn't really expected it to be true. All he had hoped for was that

Martha could share some details from her father's many stories that might help them in their search for the letter.

Hank finally recovered and said in disbelief, "You do?"

"Yes sir, I surely do. And the story I'm gonna tell you ain't never been told to no one outside the family. But since you found that journal, I suspect its God's way of telling me that you should hear the Morton family secret."

She shifted in her chair and took a small sip of lemonade. She gathered herself and started to speak. "The initials T. M. do stand for my daddy, Toby Morton. I didn't know he wrote them in there because I was only a little girl the last time I laid eyes on Miss Caty's journal. But I'll come back to that in a minute. To understand how my people, the Morton's, came to be in possession of the journal, you have to go much farther back than my father. In fact, you need to go all the way back to the year 1800. Right before Miss Caty sell Mulberry Grove and move herself out to Cumberland Island," she noted.

She looked ten years younger than just moments before, and the twinkle in her eye had returned. "Toby's great-grandmother, my great-great-grandmother, Mary Morton, found the journal in an old floorboard while sweeping up the house one day. It wouldn't of meant nothin' to most slaves, because most of them couldn't read a lick. But Mary could read jus' fine," Martha boasted, a measure of pride in her voice.

"You see, she was born a house slave, so Mary was raised up in the big house with Caty Greene's little ones, at least when she was still a little girl. She ate with the Greene children, played with them, and slept in the same room with them. And, for a short time, she was even homeschooled with them. Which's how she learn to read. So when she found that journal, she could read every word Caty had written. Over time, you can see how she might have become quite attached to it. Those stories took her to places she ain't never dreamed of going herself. She came to own it because Miss Caty toss it out one day, and Mary went and pulled it from the burn pile. From that day on, the journal became the property of the Morton family," she said.

"So how long did your family have the journal?" Hank asked, feeling very much like the history student, not the teacher.

"Mary passed the journal on down to her daughter, Sally, who passed it down to her grandson and my daddy, Toby," she said.

"So how did it end up in the Bull Street Library?" Matt asked.

"Until jus' now, the whereabouts of that old journal been a mystery to us. You see, when I was just a little girl, my father took a job as a weekend janitor at the Bull Street Library. He got it in his head that the library would be a safer place to keep the journal than in the little wooden shack on Mulberry that we lived in. So he took his pocketknife and carved out the middle pages of an atlas he found. Then he put the journal inside and hid it in some out-of-the-way bookshelf. It worked fine for a time. It was in a safe and clean place and Daddy could access it whenever he please.

"Then, sometime in the '30s, it must have been, he gone to work one day and found out that some renovations had begun. They was adding a new wing or some such thing to the library. He come to find out the atlas had been moved as part of the demolition. Daddy searched everywhere, but could never find it again. Over time he gave up hope and we all just figured the journal had been thrown out or destroyed somewhere along the way. So you can imagine my surprise when you show up here today and said you gone and found it," she said. "My heart almost stopped." She reached for her glass once again to wet her dry throat. She wasn't used to talking so much.

"Sorry to have surprised you, Martha, we had no idea. And I'm also sorry we lost the journal. I wish you could have seen it again," Matt said with genuine disappointment.

"Don't you be sorry, child; you made an old woman very happy today. I thought that old book was gone and lost forever, and now I know it's not. My father surely would be pleased to know it survived; he never did forgive himself for losing it," she said. She brightened suddenly and said, "But I haven't answered your question yet."

"Sorry, ma'am?" Matt looked confused.

"The letter, you asked if I had any details having to do with the whereabouts of Washington's letter," she said matter-of-factly.

"Oh yes, of course, the letter. Sorry, I got so wrapped up in the story about your family's history with the journal that I forgot all about the letter," he said, feeling like an idiot.

Martha sat patiently, smiling at his embarrassment, waiting for Matt to catch on to her meaning. He finally caught on and asked, "Wait, you mean you know something about the letter's whereabouts?"

"I do indeed," she announced.

For the second time that afternoon, the two men were stunned into silence.

"Martha, you can be assured, you have our undivided attention," Hank said with a smile. "Please continue."

"Remember I told you my great-grandmother Mary pulled the journal from that burn pile? Well, 'round that time she also seen Miss Caty put the canister that Mr. Whitney had built into a wooden shipping crate. She recognized the canister because Miss Caty had described it in her journal. And the box was addressed to a man in Paris, France." She was on a roll now. It was clear that she was enjoying leading the two men slowly down the path of discovery.

Hank could tell Martha was having fun and said, "Now you're teasing us, Martha. Did this man have a name?"

"That he did. Quite a famous one as a matter of fact," she hinted, but went no further.

"Martha!" Hank cried in exasperation.

"Oh, Hank, you need to let an old woman have her fun. All right. Ya'll ready for this? The name on the box was the Marquis de Lafayette."

"Holy shit," slipped Matt. He received a stern look from Martha and quickly said, "Sorry ma'am." He looked over at Hank and asked him, "But why would Caty want to send Washington's surrender letter to the Marquis de Lafayette all the way over in France?"

"First she throws away the journal, and then she ships the letter out of the country. Maybe she felt guilty about the whole thing. Or maybe the letter made her sad because it reminded her of her dead husband," Hank hypothesized, trying to piece together a plausible explanation on the fly. "We'll probably never know. But clearly Caty was ready to move on with her life without it. She was friends with Lafayette from the war days, and maybe she trusted him more than anyone else."

"That visit from Richard Anderson had scared her into creating the canister in the first place," Matt said. "So maybe you're right, maybe she wanted to send it as far away as possible to keep it out of the wrong hands."

Hank added, "And you couldn't get much farther away than Paris, France."

21

Early 1800

La Grange, France

*A*fter *being imprisoned and exiled for almost eight years outside his be-loved country, as a consequence of his being on the wrong side of the radical faction in the French Revolution, Gilbert du Motier, Marquis de Lafayette had finally been allowed to return to his homeland. Although he still clung to the hope that he would one day be called into service to help establish a democracy in France, for now Lafayette was simply grateful to be home. When he had been forced to flee France eight years earlier, he had been commander in chief of the National Guard, a national hero, and a man of considerable wealth. Much of that fortune, however, had disappeared during his extended absence, as he had lost title to the productive large tracts of land he had owned and managed. Even La Grange, his once grand chateau, was in such disrepair that Lafayette had spent most of his time in early 1800 supervising reconstruction of the home and grounds, in quiet seclusion.*

His vision was to re-create Mount Vernon, in honor of his hero, the late George Washington. And the news of his adopted father's passing earlier in the year had only increased his resolve to restore his home to its former glory. It was late summer and the reconstruction of La Grange was in full swing. An architect was busy drawing up plans to renovate the chateau.

It was during this time that a mounted courier arrived at La Grange. He was carrying a package and an accompanying hand-sealed letter from a dear friend in America, Caty Greene. Lafayette had first met Caty in the early years of the revolution. He had come to admire and appreciate her intelligence and considerable charm, especially during their encampment together at Valley Forge. Caty's youth and unbridled optimism had provided a glimmer of hope in a dismal situation. And for that, she would always hold a special place in his heart.

To his surprise, however, the personal note he had just received from her was more grave than gay. And the lighthearted personality that Lafayette had recalled so fondly was nowhere to be found. After reading the ominous yet somewhat vague note, Lafayette turned his attention to the shipping box. Inside was a strangely shaped cylinder, wrapped very carefully.

He was surprised when he felt his hands tremble—and so much—that when he separated the two ends of the cylinder, a letter tumbled out onto the stone floor. A bit flustered, he bent down, uncurled the single sheet of paper, and began to read. What he found was something he would never have guessed in a thousand guesses. It was a letter from George Washington, written while at Valley Forge. And the letter was addressed, incredibly, to General William Howe, commander in chief of the British Army. Lafayette read the letter for a second time, but the second reading did nothing to dissipate his shock and disbelief. Finding himself uncharacteristically drained, he sat down on a nearby wooden bench.

The instructions in Caty's note were very direct. Only he was to decide what to do with Washington's surrender letter. And her other stipulation was also quite plain, that she never wished to speak of it again. It had become too much of a burden for her to bear, but as she explained, she still could not bring herself to destroy it. And the fact that she had gone to such extraordinary lengths to send it all the way to Paris, made clear to Lafayette that she had placed a great amount of importance on Washington's letter. And on who should determine its fate.

He read the letter for the third time and slowly began to understand why. As the initial shock and confusion wore off, he found something very powerful and oddly comforting in his commander in chief's words written during the darkest days of the revolution. They revealed a man Lafayette knew well. A man burdened with the weight of a country on his shoulders, torn with a difficult decision. Clearly not the omniscient God that people made him out to be.

Lafayette sat unmoving on the bench for close to an hour. The realization slowly sank in that he now bore the same burden of possessing the letter that Caty had so desperately wished to be freed from. And he found himself stuck in the same predicament: with a certainty that publicizing the letter would wrong the man he so respected and potentially harm the country he fought so hard to liberate, but with an equal unease about destroying the letter outright. He finally made the decision to hold on to the letter until time or fate revealed the proper course for him to take.

Little could he know, however, that day would not come for another twenty-five years.

22

Present Day

Savannah, GA

The hot, humid air had worked its unseen magic on their lemonade glasses. Condensed water had accumulated in thick rings on the Plexiglas table. Matt and Hank had been sitting on Martha's front porch for over an hour. She had provided them with more information than they could ever have hoped to gain. They never would have made the Lafayette connection without Martha's story about her great-great-grandmother. But they had already taken up a lot of her time and they didn't want to overstay their welcome.

"Martha, we can't thank you enough for sharing your family's history with us. We are honored that you chose to tell us your story today. I felt like I was back in class, and that's about as good as it gets for an old history buff like me," Hank said.

Matt pushed up from his chair to leave, and echoed the sentiment, "Thank you, Martha, and if we ever recover Caty's journal, we promise to come back and share it with you."

"Where do you two think you're going?" she remarked, surprised that they were leaving. "I haven't finished telling my story."

The two men exchanged befuddled looks, but remained standing. Martha waved her hand, "Go on now, and sit your fannies back down." So they did.

"There's more?" Matt said.

"Oh yes, the best part, in fact. 'Specially as it pertain to the surrender letter you're looking for."

"Martha, I do believe you've been holding out on us," Hank said, smiling. And he wagged his finger at her, as if scolding a child.

"Hank, you of all people should know that a good story isn't rushed. If there's one thing my Daddy taught me about storytelling is that a good one unfolds slow." She folded her hands in her lap and continued, "You got to remember, in the old days stories was about the only entertainment we colored folks had. So believe me, storytellin' was savored, never hurried."

She waited patiently until the two men settled back down in their chairs. "Now where was I? Oh yes, the Marquis de Lafayette. To understand the next part of the story, we need to move ahead twenty-five years. That's when the marquis made his big tour of the United States. I know you're familiar with that, Hank, you being the history professor and all."

"Of course," Hank interjected, "Lafayette was asked by President James Monroe to return to America in 1825 to celebrate the fiftieth anniversary of our country's independence. He was originally expected to stay only a few months. But his visit was lengthened to well over a year so that he could visit every state in the Union, due to the overwhelming response of the American public. And Savannah was one of the stops added to his itinerary. One of the reasons he came to Savannah was to lay the cornerstone for Nathanael Greene's monument in Johnson Square." He enjoyed showing off his immense knowledge of history whenever given the chance.

"That's right, and it just so happens that my great-grandmother Sally Morton was a house slave for a woman named Mrs. Maxwell. She ran the boardinghouse where Mr. Lafayette stay durin' his two-night visit to Savannah. Oh Lord, my memory going. What's that boardinghouse called now, Hank?" she said.

"You mean to tell me your great-grandmother was at the Owens-Thomas House during Lafayette's stay? I must say, Martha, your family certainly was in the right places at the right times. But please continue; you were talking about Lafayette's visit."

"Yes, like I was saying, my great-grandmother Sally was a slave working for Mrs. Maxwell when, one evening, in walks the Marquis de Lafayette. Now mind you, she heard his name many times before from her mama's stories, and from Miss Caty's journal. So she was real excited to see the famous man in person," she said.

"Remarkable," Hank muttered, shaking his head in wonder.

"And when he arrived, he didn't disappoint. He was dressed in his finest clothes and arrive on a fancy carriage, trailed by hundreds of cheering town folk," Martha continued.

"It must have been an incredible sight to see," Hank said, still marveling at the thought.

"I imagine it was," Martha agreed, "but Sally saw something even more incredible when she visited Mr. Lafayette's room later that evenin'. Evidently she went to his room to see if he needed anything. He had his back to her when she come up to his open bedroom door. He had just taken something out his luggage at that exact moment. And when Sally saw what he had in his hands, she jus' about fainted."

Martha paused momentarily before she said, "Because there it was, Mr. Whitney's canister, exactly as Miss Caty had described in her journal."

It took a moment for the enormity of Martha's words to sink in. The two men looked at one another in utter astonishment, unsure of how to react to the news that Lafayette had brought the letter back to America!

Finally, Matt spoke up. "I'll be damned," he said, "the surrender letter had returned home." And with his trademark lopsided grin perhaps a bit larger than usual, he added, "I've got to tell you, Martha, you tell one hell of a story."

To which Martha responded, "I come from a long line of storyteller's son, a long, long line."

23

Spring 1825
Savannah, GA

*T*he Marquis de Lafayette's four-month tour celebrating the United States' fiftieth anniversary had now stretched into its eighth month. Crowds in Boston, New York, and Philadelphia had numbered in the tens of thousands with each city trying to outdo the other's celebration in both scale and pageantry. Neither Lafayette nor President James Monroe had anticipated the American public's incredible outpouring of affection when Monroe had extended the invitation to Lafayette the year before. The response to his return to the country for which he had fought so valiantly had been so overwhelming that a southern and western swing had to be added to the original itinerary. The triumphant processional was now scheduled to make a stop in every one of the country's twenty-four states.

Along his journey, Lafayette traveled by all means of transportation including stagecoach, horseback, canal barge, and steamboat. The bumpy early nineteenth-century roads had often left the sixty-seven-year-old man quite exhausted, so that by the time he disembarked from his steamboat on March 19, Lafayette was looking forward to spending the next two days in the relative calm and beauty of Savannah, Georgia. He was also glad to have arrived in Savannah for another reason. It was in this city that he had finally determined to find a permanent resting place for Washington's surrender letter, composed nearly fifty years before.

For Lafayette, this was his first time back in the United States since receiving the mysterious package from Caty Greene twenty-five years earlier. But there would be no emotional reunion, as she had succumbed to a summer fever more than a decade before. Lafayette brought the cylinder and hidden surrender letter with him on the trip, with the hope that he would find the appropriate place to permanently stow it. When he was told that, while in Savannah, he would be laying the cornerstone for a monument to be constructed in honor of Nathanael Greene, he knew that he had at last found its eternal home. And with the knowledge that Washington's letter would not be leaving Savannah with him when he departed in two days time, Lafayette felt his spirits lifted. It was as if ballast had been removed from the hold of his body, making his entire being more buoyant.

Upon his arrival in Savannah, Lafayette made his way through the throngs of adoring citizens. He stopped to shake hands and reminisce briefly with a few revolutionary war veterans, now well into their seventies. His traveling entourage, including his son as well as the governor of Georgia, finally made its way to a boardinghouse. There, they would spend the next two nights.

Mary Maxwell's boarding house stood proudly on the northeast corner of Oglethorpe Square, the sixth and final square in Oglethorpe's original grid-like vision. The house was notable for two reasons. The first was that it had a large cistern installed on the roof that provided running water for the house—the only house in Savannah that offered such a modern convenience. The second was that it had an elaborate cast iron veranda, held in place by four green acanthus scroll supports. The ornate porch was located just outside Lafayette's first-floor master bedroom. And it provided the podium from which he was forced to conduct an impromptu address for the adoring citizens of Savannah later that evening. They had gathered outside his window and simply would not let him sleep until he had spoken a few words to them.

After arriving at Maxwell's boardinghouse, Lafayette was shown to his room and his bags were brought to him separately, save one. He had *insisted on personally carrying a small, well-traveled leather satchel without assistance. Sally Morton, one of the boardinghouse's slaves, had been about to knock on his door, which had been left ajar, to see if the marquis needed anything. Through the half-open door, she saw Lafayette remove an odd-looking cylindrical metal container from his satchel and place it carefully on top of his large oak dresser. It took just one glimpse of the distinctive metal container for Sally's mind to race back in time to stories that her mother, Mary, had told her, from when she had been a house slave at Mulberry Grove Plantation.*

She had read Miss Caty's journal so many times after it had been passed down to her that she could recite all the stories from memory. She knew the events surrounding the surrender letter from Washington and Eli Whitney's invention of the peculiar metal container as if she had lived them herself.

But the most important secret she knew came directly from her mother's mouth, the knowledge that the Marquis de Lafayette had been the recipient, some twenty-five years earlier, of a package from Caty Greene—a package that contained the surrender letter from George Washington. Sally had laid eyes on the cylinder for only a few seconds before Lafayette returned it to his satchel. But she knew with absolute certainty that the container he had just unpacked, and Whitney's clever invention described so vividly in Miss Caty's journal, were one and the same.

Sally Morton never recorded her sighting of Lafayette with the metal container in any journal. But she did tell the story to her daughter, who in turn told it to her son. And so, it was recorded orally over the next two centuries by the descendants of Mary and Sally Morton.

24

Present Day

Savannah, GA

The men had to shout to be heard over the 327-cubic-inch, V-8 engine under the hood of Matt's 1966 Chevy pickup. The fact that the vintage truck had no AC forced them to roll down both front windows, which only added to the noise level. But they were so excited after their incredible meeting with Martha Sampson that they probably would have been shouting anyway.

"There's only one place the letter can be, right!?" Matt said. He had to make a concerted effort to control his adrenaline to keep from speeding.

"Absolutely. If Lafayette were going to put it anywhere, it would have to be in the monument dedicated to Greene in Johnson Square," Hank replied, feeling like one of his students on the field trip of a lifetime.

"It *has* to be," shouted Matt, slapping his hand on the steering wheel. "It's so perfect— Nathanael Greene is the guy who originally hijacks the letter. So who better to end up with it, right?"

"It was an elegant solution. The cornerstone-laying ceremony for the monument to Greene gave Lafayette the perfect opportunity to rid himself of the infamous letter," Hank agreed, with admiration for Lafayette's choice. "He could fulfill Caty's request to do the honorable thing, without destroying Washington's reputation in the process. There is a certain symmetry to the fact that the final resting place for the letter is with General Greene."

"You mean the final resting place, *until now*," Matt added.

"Hold on a minute, Matt. First of all, we don't know *for certain* that Lafayette put the cylinder inside the monument. And even if he did, how would we get it out?"

"Oh, we're getting that cylinder out, Hank. Come on, you mean to tell me that you could walk by that monument for the rest of your life knowing there is a letter, a *surrender* letter no less, written by the father of our country, buried inside?"

"No, I guess not, but we need to take a deep breath and come up with a game plan. In the short time that I've known you, I think you'd just about drive this truck into the monument to get to that letter," he said with a smile.

"Funny you should say that, because I'm headed to Johnson Square right now," Matt replied evenly.

"Matt, I was joking, you're not seriously considering..."

"Calm down, Hank," he laughed, "I'm not going to knock down the monument. I just want to take a look at it, and, as you said, try to come up with a plan. Speaking of a plan, can you call Sarah and have her meet us there so we can bring her up to speed?"

They sat on a wooden park bench in Johnson Square, directly in front of the fifty-foot-tall obelisk monument to Nathanael Greene. Looking north from where they sat, just up Bull Street, they could see Savannah's distinctive city hall building. Its original copper-domed roof had been gilded in the late 1980s with 23-karat gold leaf sheets. The dome glistened in the afternoon sunshine. A rumpled looking man was playing an off-key rendition of "Yankee Doodle" on a clarinet, of all instruments. Matt tossed a dollar bill in his open instrument case. He hoped it would be applied toward future lessons.

They had already filled Sarah in on their jaw-dropping meeting with Martha and had done their best to answer the many questions she had peppered them with.

"So let's get down to the problem at hand. How are we going to get the letter out of that?" Matt said, pointing at the imposing granite edifice that stood before them. "I mean, that's a pretty big monument, so where in that haystack do you suppose our needle is hidden?"

"*Where* is the easy part. Remember, Lafayette was here to lay the *cornerstone* for the monument. So the logical place for it to be is inside the cornerstone," Hank answered matter-of-factly.

"What do you mean, inside the cornerstone?" Matt asked.

"You've heard of the Freemasons, right?" Sarah chimed in, picking up where her father left off. "Well, the Masons presided over most of the historical cornerstone-laying ceremonies back then; they still do today, as a matter of fact. Anyway, one of their many traditions is to carve a cavity into the cornerstone. And inside the cavity certain items are placed to commemorate the time that the ceremony took place." She shooed away a pigeon that had strayed into their space, looking for bread crumbs.

Hank added, "Items such as newspapers, names of the people involved in the ceremony, coins, and other trinkets."

"I've seen cornerstones on buildings before," Matt commented, "because the polished stone usually has a date or some other marking etched into it. But I never realized that *monuments* had ceremonial cornerstones."

"You're right, in the respect that the cornerstone to this monument is not obvious. There is no stone with a date or similar marking. However, I've got some friends in town who are Masons, and I'm sure they'd be able to help us identify which is the cornerstone," Hank said.

"I still can't believe there is a surrender letter from George Washington sitting ten feet away from us," Sarah marveled at the idea.

Yet another tour group had stopped in front of Greene's monument. This one led by a large, mustached man dressed head-to-toe in seersucker. He proceeded to pass along a few tidbits about Nathanael Greene to his photo-snapping audience.

Matt thought to himself, *If only the guide knew about the letter inside, he'd have to alter his script.*

25

Present Day

Savannah, GA

S arah and Hank sat in Matt's living room, watching him pace in front of the oversized window that looked out over Monterey Square. Matt, lost in thought, was unconsciously smacking the palm of his left hand with the barrel end of his college-era aluminum baseball bat. He had barely left his window-side perch since they had arrived some thirty minutes earlier. It had been a long day full of stunning disclosures and they were tired and famished. So they had returned to Matt's third-floor apartment to regroup, get a bite to eat, and discuss their next move.

A large pizza had just been delivered. Between bites, Sarah said, "Matt, you're making me nervous pacing in front of that window. Do you really think they're out there watching us?"

"I know they are, Sarah." He swung around to face Hank and said, "Did you notice that black Escalade with the tinted windows that drove by today when we were sitting on Martha's porch?"

"No, I can't say as I did. But she does live on a pretty busy street. Let's face it, Matt, black Escalades are pretty common, especially in that part of town," Hank said, attempting reason.

"I know, but I think I remember seeing the same car outside of the Crystal when we left the other night. And the guy who shot at me was driving an SUV which could easily have been an Escalade."

"Are you serious?" Sarah said, pushing away her plate. She had lost her appetite at the terrifying thought that someone could still be following them.

"Matt, that's not doing anybody any good." Hank nodded subtly toward his daughter. "We need to be thinking clearly right now, and that's hard to do when you're scaring everybody half to death with what you *think* you saw."

"Fine, then how do you explain this?" He walked into the kitchen and returned with a copy of that day's *Savannah Morning News*. He flipped open the paper and read aloud, "The National Park Service reports that vandals have desecrated the grave of Catharine Littlefield Greene."

He paused and looked up at Hank and Sarah before continuing. "Major General Nathanael Greene, of Revolutionary War fame, purchased the property at Cumberland Island on August 11, 1783. He died of sunstroke three years later and left the property to his wife, Catharine." He skipped ahead, "Catharine died in 1814, and the stone on her aboveground vault reads: 'She professed great talents and exalted virtues,' blah, blah, blah."

He scanned the article silently until he found what he was looking for. "Here it is. 'Late Wednesday evening, vandals unearthed Catharine Greene's grave, located in an abandoned, slightly overgrown cemetery located a little northeast of Dungeness. The old four-story main house once belonged to the Carnegie Estate. Park Ranger Anna Pruitt cannot be sure of what the looters found or took with them, but was appalled to find bones scattered around the gravesite.'"

"Oh my Lord," Hank gasped at the thought of Caty's remains being treated with such disrespect.

"Unfortunately, that's not all. Listen to this." Matt forged ahead as if he were presenting a case before a jury. "'In a separate incident, the Georgia Ports Authority reported vandalism on the old Mulberry Grove Plantation. Evidently looters wielding metal detectors and a small backhoe snuck onto the property and dug around Nathanael Greene's old home site, presumably looking for slave tags, which reportedly can fetch more than $20,000 on the open market.'"

He stopped reading and said, "Slave tags, my ass; we all know exactly what they were looking for: Washington's surrender letter."

"But how; why?" Sarah said, trying to make sense of the new information.

"There's only one explanation: because they followed us to Mulberry Grove. Somehow they must have overheard us talking about Cumberland Island," Matt concluded.

"I'm afraid you're probably right, Matt," Hank agreed. "Which means someone is deadly serious about finding this letter."

"And desperate enough to risk desecrating historic gravesites and trespassing on deserted plantation land owned by the government," Sarah added, looking anxious.

"Which means we better hurry up and retrieve the letter from Greene's monument before they figure it out for themselves," Hank said. Then he added, "Assuming, of course, that the letter is actually in the monument."

"It's got to be in there, Hank. But you're right about one thing, we need to act fast," Matt said.

He tossed aside the newspaper. "So does anyone have any ideas for how we're going to remove the letter from inside the monument without being detected?" He picked up a piece of pizza, folded the slice lengthwise, a habit he brought with him from the North, and disposed of half of it in a single bite. It wasn't quite New York–style pizza, but it would have to do.

"Look, guys, we can't just sneak around in the middle of the night, desecrating a fifty-foot-tall monument to exhume a letter that we *think* is inside. And besides, Johnson Square is in the middle of Savannah, with tourists around every corner. We'd never get away with it," Sarah said.

"First of all, we're not going to desecrate anything. After we remove the cornerstone and find the cylinder with the letter inside, we're going to put the stone back where it was, so the monument will look better than new. But you're right, it won't be easy, given where it's located," Matt admitted.

"If we get caught, we could go to jail," Sarah countered. She got up and took a nervous look out the window, alongside Matt.

He put down his bat and gently took her by the shoulders. He turned her around to face him, "Nobody's going to jail, Sarah, we just have to be careful not to…"

At that moment, Hank started to laugh. He didn't stop until he looked up and saw both Sarah and Matt looking at him as if he'd lost his mind.

"Care to tell us what you find so funny, Dad?" she said, somewhat annoyed, thinking her father was making fun of her.

Her father held up his hands and replied, "Oh, Sarah, don't be so sensitive. I'm laughing because of something Matt said. It's so simple and so obvious that it just might work." But he didn't elaborate. He just sat there thinking through the idea still taking shape in his mind.

Finally, Matt had had enough and said, "Hank, what the hell are you talking about?"

"Matt, when you said that we'll put the stone back so the monument will look better than new, it reminded me of some locals who had petitioned the city council a few years back. They wanted the monuments in town cleaned because they had gotten so covered in dirt and grime over the years. They had made some headway, but then the economy went south and the town no longer had the money available to fund the effort. So the idea died on the vine," Hank explained.

Still not seeing where her father was going, Sarah said, "What does that have to do with us?"

Her father continued, "Then there was something you said, Sarah, the part about us not being able to sneak around in the middle of the night. Well, you're absolutely right; we wouldn't get away with that. But here's the beautiful thing, we won't have to sneak around in the wee hours of the night. We can do our little excavation project in broad daylight!"

"All right Hank, time to speak English. What the hell are you talking about?" Matt demanded.

"Don't you see; it's brilliant in its simplicity. All we have to do is volunteer ourselves to clean Greene's monument! We set up scaffolding around the edifice, the same kind that's used to clean the sides of buildings. Then we wrap it in a black tarp so that nobody can see what we are doing. We can rationalize the presence of the black tarp by saying that it is needed to protect passersby from getting harmed by debris from the spray of our power washers. And the power washers will provide ample noise so that we can hide the actual excavation work we'll be doing, once we determine the exact location of the cornerstone. Nobody will ever suspect that we are doing anything other than removing grime from an old monument," he concluded with a flourish.

Matt smiled widely, finally able to share in Hank's excitement. "My God, Hank, you're right, that *is* perfect!"

"I have to admit, Dad, it is a clever solution," Sarah admitted, "but there are still a lot of details to work out. Not the least of which is how to remove the cornerstone without toppling over a fifty-foot-tall monument."

"You're right, Sarah, we have a lot of details to work out," Matt concurred. "For starters, we have to figure out how to get permitting from the town, and then we have to find a contractor we can trust to help us with the extraction."

"And don't forget the small matter of who is going to pay for all of this. Our little archaeological dig is going to cost a pretty penny," added Hank.

Matt's cell phone began to vibrate in his pocket. He pulled it out.

"Oh, hey, James," he said, while silently mouthing *It's James Fox* to Sarah. "What's going on?"

"Sorry for calling so late, but I figured you'd want to hear this," Fox said, and then paused momentarily before continuing. "I hate to admit it, but you guys were right."

"What do you mean? Right about what?" Matt asked. He had all but forgotten about the journal, amid the excitement of discovering the potential whereabouts of the letter itself.

"You were right about the intern, Matt," Fox said.

"Really?" he said, sitting down on the couch.

"Are you ready for this? He's the nephew of William Emerson's campaign manager, Chuck Conrad. When we confronted him he admitted that he had called his uncle. And he told him about your discovery of the journal. Evidently the kid worked on the campaign last spring. He felt that, given Emerson's obvious connection to Washington, his uncle should know about the letter. Needless to say, we dismissed him immediately."

"Un-fucking-believable. So it was Conrad's henchmen who stole the journal from my apartment."

"It's the only explanation. And frankly, Matt, this whole thing just got a lot scarier. We're not talking about some random burglary anymore; we're talking about Watergate, for crying out loud. You need to be careful, because obviously these guys mean business. Clearly they're willing to go to extremes to get their man elected," he said.

"The stakes definitely just got a little higher, that's for sure, James. But you don't even know the half of it." He got up, threw his empty soda can into the trash, and paced around the room as he talked.

"Not sure I'm following you. Did something else happen?" James asked with concern.

"You could say that. We made a discovery today that makes Caty's journal look like table scraps in comparison."

"OK, you've got my attention."

"What if I told you we're pretty sure we know the location of the surrender letter itself." As he shared the day's events with Fox, Matt found himself looking out the window again. He was searching for anything or anyone that might look suspicious. Paranoia, he had a feeling, was going to be his companion from now on.

When he finished, Fox had not responded. "You still there, James?"

"Yeah, I'm here. I'm just trying to absorb everything. This is all so unbelievable, Matt. Do you realize the historical significance of a find like this?" he said excitedly. "First the journal with Caty's bombshell revelation, and now the actual surrender letter? The ramifications of this are huge! History books will have to be rewritten. Hell, the book I wrote about Washington will need to be rewritten."

"How do you feel about that, James? I mean, would the revelation of this letter be a good thing or a bad thing?" Matt asked cautiously.

"It's neither good nor bad. It just is," Fox said.

Then he realized what Matt had really been asking. "If you're wondering whether I have a problem revealing the letter to the world, I don't. I'm a historian Matt, which means I'm in the camp that believes if it happened then people should know about it. If it changes opinions about the man, which I'm sure it will for some, that's out of my control. Personally, I think it reveals the human side of Washington, which is all too often lost amid the glorification of his image."

He paused for a moment and then said, "I also think you guys need to *really* watch your backsides now. If the Emerson campaign was willing to steal the journal, I'd hate to think of how far it'd go to prevent the actual letter from surfacing, especially with an election hanging in the balance."

"We'll be careful, but nothing is going to stop me from finding this letter, James. And when I do, I'm going to call a big press conference. Then sit back and enjoy watching Emerson's handlers scramble." Matt was still pissed off that the man with the scar on his cheek had gotten the better of him, apparently at the orders of Chuck Conrad, Emerson's campaign manager. He looked forward to delivering a little retribution; he didn't know when or how, but he knew he would get his chance.

"But Matt, you'll never be able to prove that they stole the journal," Fox warned.

"I won't have to. The revelation of the letter alone will cause enough of a distraction that it may cost them the race. At the least, I'll have the satisfaction of watching them run around trying to explain why their campaign's icon tried to surrender to the British."

"Just be careful not to get too emotional about this, Matt," Fox counseled.

"Too late, this thing got personal the minute they broke into my apartment. But I appreciate the advice. And don't worry—I know the historical significance of the letter far outweighs my petty thoughts of payback," Matt said. "I also owe you an apology. I accused the society of being behind all this when the truth is, you've been nothing but helpful. I suppose there was no way for me to guess that a man running for president of the United States was the one behind all this, but that doesn't excuse my behavior toward you."

"That's ancient history as far as I'm concerned. I probably would have thought the same thing had I been in your shoes. I'm just excited to be a part of all of this. It's not often you get the chance to make history, or at least rewrite a little bit of it. So what can I do to help?" he asked. "The society has connections and resources that I'm sure could be made available to you. All you have to do is say the word and I'll see what I can do."

"I may take you up on that. Let us think through our next steps here and we'll get back to you. Thanks again," he said, and hung up.

———

After Matt had filled them in on the details of the call, they sat quietly, thinking through their next move. Sarah finally broke the silence and said, "Well, I can think of an organization that could help us with our monument cleaning project."

"Who's that?" Hank asked.

Matt had picked up his bat again and resumed his vigilant watch out the window. He was always pacing and watching, she thought. Like a caged animal.

"The Society of the Cincinnati, of course," she said. "Matt just told us that Director Fox offered his help, and they have a chapter right here in Savannah. They're the perfect cover organization to provide credibility with the town. And they probably even have some connections to help us secure the required permitting. Maybe they'll even provide the funding. After all, their stated mission is to preserve and protect Revolutionary War history."

Matt was amazed at how Sarah could move from a scared little girl to a clearheaded thinker from one moment to the next. He smiled in spite of himself and responded, "Sure makes sense to me. What do you think, Hank?"

"I'm not sure we have a choice. I guess it's time for you to show off your sales skills. You'll need to convince Mr. Fox to join in on our nefarious little scheme," Hank said with a smile.

After a few more minutes of discussion, Matt called Director James Fox back. He quickly brought him up to speed on their monument-cleaning scheme. He told him that, while they thought their covert operation could work, they simply didn't have the resources to make it happen. They'd need the help of the society to pull it off.

Fox had some questions but he told Matt that he thought the idea was sound. Before committing the resources of the society, however, he would need to get approval from his boss. His boss was a man by the name of Charles Metcalf, who was the president general of the society. He promised that he'd speak with Metcalf first thing in the morning.

Matt hung up and took one final look out the window. He wondered if there was any way Emerson's cronies could know the whereabouts of the letter. He didn't think that was possible, given that they had only learned about it that afternoon from Martha Sampson. And Martha was the only person in the world who knew about Lafayette's possession of the cylinder at the time of the dedication ceremony of Greene's monument, back in 1825.

He should have been comforted by the thought that they were the only ones who knew Martha Sampson's family secret. But given the stakes, it only made him more nervous.

26

Present Day

Washington, D.C.

C harles Metcalf's dermatitis-ridden hands were raw from repeated washings. He attempted to keep them hidden from
view, under his desk or stuffed inside his pants pockets, but with
only limited success, for he had an equal compulsion to check
the time on his wristwatch every few minutes. He had many of
the classic symptoms of obsessive-compulsive disorder and had
battled the affliction for as far back as he could remember.

The cycle of maddening repetition was his daily companion.
He would brush his teeth exactly twenty times up and twenty
times down. And if he lost count, he would have to start over
again. He would constantly rearrange his desk so that all items
were placed at right angles to one another at all times. He had an
intense fear of germs and never shook hands, and when entering
his multimillion-dollar penthouse apartment, the smell of bleach
and ammonia from continual cleaning was overpowering.

While his many compulsions would have driven a lesser person insane long ago, Metcalf knew that they were his friends.
They kept his mind preoccupied from the paranoid and sometimes violent thoughts that forced their way into his brain like an

invading army. It was a battle he waged daily. A battle he did not always win.

He had done things and, in fact, continued to do things for which he was not proud. He was disgusted at his sexual desires, but he knew that the high-priced escorts that he favored provided him with an outlet for his many fetishes and dark perversions. He had never been married and had very few close friends in his life. He had been picked on mercilessly in the Brooklyn public schools he had attended in his youth. His odd behavior and his equally odd looks had made him an easy target. Even his parents wanted nothing to do with him. His mother used to hit him with an electrical cord hoping to beat the strange behavior out of him, and his father simply ignored him. He had endured much in his life, and he carried the psychological scars to prove it.

As a teenager, he had flirted with the notion of suicide, but was able to find other outlets to channel his dark and angry thoughts. He set things on fire. He cut his arms and legs with a razor blade. And he built traps to catch and torture small animals, most notably the family cat. As he matured though, he became skilled at hiding his compulsive behavior, so that most people merely thought he was a bit quirky or eccentric. But what really allowed him to function in mainstream society was his extremely high intelligence. It was this intelligence, coupled with a compulsive love for numbers, that enabled him to be successful in the business world. So successful, that he had earned millions in the financial markets as the founder and sole owner of Metcalf & Company, a multibillion-dollar hedge fund company.

He had been granted membership into the Society of the Cincinnati years earlier when, by chance, he discovered that one of his long-lost descendants had been a colonel, of no great fame, in the Continental Army. He had joined the society then, and had recently lobbied for the president general's job. The only reason he had done so was because the position provided him with privileged access to the personal fortunes of its many blue blood members. Being elected to the position had been a monumental achievement for Metcalf, even though he knew his appointment had been heavily influenced by the size of his bank account. Still, he took great pride in presiding over the type of people who had once shunned him. If only they knew the tormented soul and twisted mind that lay buried beneath the expensive suits.

As president general, he was the society's most senior officer. He presided over its standing committee, board of directors, and executive committee and coordinated the management of the society's affairs with the executive director. The reality was, however, that Director Fox ran the day-to-day operations. This arrangement suited Metcalf just fine, as it allowed him to focus most of his attentions on his hedge fund company, and the only thing that truly made him happy—making money.

As Director Fox entered his boss's office, he noted how different it was from his own. While his was littered with personal mementos, Metcalf's was as sterile as an operating room. He knew better than to extend his hand in greeting, as he was quite familiar with his boss's aversion to physical contact. He sat down in the seat facing the large oak-paneled desk.

"Sorry to interrupt, I know you're very busy, but something's come up that I need to talk to you about," Fox began. He was amazed at how his boss could work all day without ever taking off his suit jacket.

Metcalf was meticulously dressed as usual. He wore a hand-made, Brioni single-breasted suit that cost more than five thousand dollars to craft. The made-to-measure, obsidian-colored suit was offset by a stiffly starched, white oxford shirt and cobalt-blue Armani silk tie. Fox had often wondered just how many black suits one man could own. Unfortunately, the most talented

tailor in the world could not make up for the fact that Charles
Metcalf was not a handsome man. His heavily gelled, jet-black
hair was combed over and forward. It was a futile attempt to hide
a receding hairline that crept backward along a cranium that was
two sizes too large for his rail-thin frame.

"I'm quite busy, Mr. Fox, can this wait until later?" Metcalf
said, without looking up.

"Actually, it's a bit time sensitive, sir, but it should only take
a few minutes."

Fox didn't call very many people "sir," but somehow he
couldn't help himself around Metcalf. If he were completely
honest, he'd admit to being intimidated by the man. Maybe even
a little scared of him. There was something about the man's eyes
that made the hair on the back of Fox's neck stand on end. They
were lifeless, yet mesmerizing at the same time. He thought that
if the grim reaper were to take a human form, Metcalf would be
him. Metcalf stared at him, his penetrating black eyes seeming to
bore a hole through the middle of the director's forehead.

"Well, Mr. Fox, what is it?"

"Oh, sorry, well, I'm not exactly sure where to begin," he
said, a little flustered. "You see, there's been a discovery of sorts
in Savannah, Georgia." He went on to tell the story about Matt
and Sarah's discovery of the journal and the subsequent theft of
the journal from Matt's apartment. Finally, he shared their theory regarding the survival and current location of Washington's
surrender letter. He also revealed the Baylor University intern's
connection to Emerson's campaign manager, as well as the campaign's alleged role in the theft.

"So you believe the Emerson campaign stole the journal?"
Metcalf asked. Fox thought he detected a trace of anger in his
voice.

"I do," he said, squirming uncomfortably in his chair. He felt
like a schoolboy in the principal's office.

Metcalf stopped to check his watch again. Fox wasn't sure if this was one of his boss's unusual eccentricities or whether he was truly pressed for time. So he forged ahead and said, "I also think we should help the folks in Savannah attempt to exhume the letter from Greene's monument. The society certainly has the resources to help offset the costs. And, if the letter is actually found, we can offer up our document preservation lab to analyze it. As well as take the necessary steps to preserve it properly." The words tumbled out of his mouth quickly and awkwardly.

After a few moments of uncomfortable silence, Metcalf said coolly, "I'll agree to the society's involvement on one condition. That the letter be brought directly here if it is found. I don't want some novices running around with a document that holds such historical significance. That letter belongs here." He quickly added with a little less intensity, "For preservation purposes, of course."

"I'm sure they'll have no problem agreeing to those terms, sir," Fox said, somewhat surprised that his boss seemed so readily amenable to the idea. "And I'll travel to Savannah myself to oversee the efforts." He got up quickly from his chair, anxious to vacate Metcalf's oppressive presence.

"Good. Then you have the full resources of the society at your disposal. I want you to keep me up to date on developments as they happen. And, Mr. Fox," the tone of his voice stopped Fox in his tracks, "I want you to personally escort that document back here immediately after it is exhumed, understood?" It was an order, not a question.

Metcalf walked Director Fox out and closed the door. He opened and closed it again. Then he repeated the cycle three more times until it sounded just right.

The demons were once again kept at bay.

27

Present Day

Savannah, GA

The last tour of the day had exited the historic building. The "extraction team," as Matt had jokingly dubbed them, had congregated in the first-floor sitting room of the Harper Fowlkes House. With all the period furniture around him, Matt felt like an oversized kid trapped inside a museum display. In attendance were Sarah and Hank Gordon. And representing the Society of the Cincinnati were Sissy Hightower and Director James Fox, who had flown in from Washington, D.C., earlier that afternoon.

Matt began, "Sissy, what's the status with the permitting? Any issues with the city of Savannah that are going to hold us up?"

He couldn't help but notice that Sissy had outdone herself again with yet another colorful outfit. He thought to himself that her closet must look like a Kandinsky painting, splashed with every color in the palette.

"No problems so far, Matt. In fact, just the opposite. The city was thrilled that the society stepped up and offered to clean Greene's monument," she said, in her singsong voice.

"That's great, Sissy. So how long until we receive approval for the permit?" Matt asked, shifting gingerly on the one-hundred-year-old settee.

"I expected to pick it up today but it wasn't ready. And if it's not ready by tomorrow then I'm going to raise hell with Tommy Jenkins down in city hall. I'm very close to his mother, you know. Believe me, he doesn't want to cross either one of us. Don't worry, I'll have the permit by the end of day tomorrow," she said with an assured smile. Her head pivoted left and right, challenging anyone who doubted her resolve.

"That's why you're on the team, Sissy. I knew you'd play dirty if the situation required it," Matt said with a wink. He turned to his left and said, "So, Hank is the power washing company ready to go?"

"Patrick O'Leary, an old acquaintance who runs the company, assures me that he's ready and waiting for us to pull the trigger. He told me they plan to construct the scaffolding, wrap it in black netting, and set up perimeter fencing to keep onlookers safely back at least twenty feet from the edifice. And before you ask, yes, he can be trusted. I taught all four of his sons in high school and, believe me, they were a handful. A couple of them had a run-in with the law and faced some time in juvenile detention. But I vouched for them and was able to help keep them from being prosecuted. Their old man is an ex-con who ran a gang in his youth. He evidently went to prison on manslaughter charges years ago. But he's been a model citizen ever since, and he's always been cordial to me. I think he considers what I did for his boys a debt that he can never repay. Anyway, they'll work on the opposite side of the monument and stay out of our way while we work on the extraction. And most importantly, their machinery will provide plenty of noise to cover our activity."

Hank had also been in contact with some old friends in town who were Masons. They had helped him identify exactly where the cornerstone was located on the monument. They had even gone so far as to provide him with photocopies of the original architectural blueprints from noted architect William Strickland, who had been commissioned to design and build the fifty-foot-tall monument.

Matt turned to Sarah and said, "And last, but certainly not least, have we secured an engineering firm?"

"We owe a big thanks to James for his help with that one," she said with a nod to Fox. "Evidently the society has used this particular firm in the past. They have all the necessary technology that will allow us to remove the cornerstone safely and efficiently."

Matt had been stealing glances at Sarah since the meeting started. But now that it was her turn to talk, he took the opportunity to take a long look her way. He was transfixed by a mole on the curve of her neck that he hadn't noticed before. He was aware of his increasing feelings for her, beyond just the physical, and as much as he tried, he couldn't seem to shake them. The dependable defense mechanisms that he had successfully deployed since his divorce, to prevent him from getting close to other women, weren't working. He couldn't understand why, and it was unsettling.

Director Fox jumped in and said, "The laser technology that they employ is amazing, state of the art all the way. It makes precision cuts that will allow them to remove the cornerstone from the edifice as easily as if they were slicing the corner piece out of a layered birthday cake. Obviously, they'll first construct a supporting frame to ensure the integrity and stability of the monument, before beginning their laser surgery."

"Sounds like just what we need. So how long will all this take?" asked Hank.

"Not long, according to the head engineer. If all goes well, a day, maybe two tops, including setup," replied Fox.

"Well, guys," Matt said, looking around the room, "I think we're set to go. Assuming we receive the permit from the town, it looks like we can begin our covert operation the day after tomorrow. By the end of the week, either we'll have a document in our hands that will change American history, or we'll have wasted a lot of time and money." The room fell quiet as Matt's proclamation came out more ominously than he had intended.

"It's going to be there, Matt," Sarah chimed in optimistically, breaking the awkward silence.

"I think it will be there, too," Hank agreed. "The only question is whether or not Whitney's invention will prove to be as impenetrable as Caty described in her journal. If it wasn't, then I'm afraid the letter may have turned to pulp after all this time."

"Whitney was a brilliant engineer, and the fact that the cylinder's been sealed inside five tons of granite can't hurt either," Fox noted with a smile.

He paused before reminding everyone of Metcalf's one condition. "Now, I know it's going to be maddening to wait, but just to confirm, in case anyone is tempted to open the canister on site. We agreed to wait until we get it back to the society's headquarters. Our state-of-the-art manuscript room is the safest place to ensure the integrity of the document. Assuming it has survived all these years."

"Agreed, James, but you know me. I'll be tempted to crack it open the minute I get my hands on it, so Sarah better carry it with her," Matt said, only half joking.

"Speaking of which," Sarah said, "I checked the Amtrak schedule. The last train of the day leaves Savannah at seven thirty p.m. and arrives in Washington, D.C., the following morning at eight. Matt and I thought it best to avoid the airport. That way we don't have to try to explain a suspicious metal tube at airport security."

"Just as well. Union Station is right in the middle of D.C. It's just a short cab ride away from the society's headquarters near Dupont Circle," Fox said. "I'll take care of booking seats for us once we have the canister in hand. I guess that leaves Hank and Sissy here to oversee the resealing of the monument and the completion of the cleaning."

Sissy, who looked like a schoolgirl who had just been assigned the seat next to her crush, said excitedly, "We can handle it. It will be just like old times, Hank; you and me spending all this time together." She gave him an exaggerated wink that hinted at rekindling their high school romance from more than fifty years earlier. Hank's face turned a shade of crimson.

Matt came to his rescue by changing the subject. He turned to Fox and said, "It's a little ironic, don't you think?"

"Sorry?" Fox answered.

"That the society is once again funding the search for Washington's surrender letter, just as it did twice before. The first time in 1793, when Larz Anderson's great-grandfather Richard Clough Anderson visited Caty Greene at Mulberry Grove at the request of Henry Knox. And the second time, when Larz himself came to Savannah in 1901."

"Maybe the third time will be the charm," Fox offered with a smile.

28

March 21, 1825
Savannah, GA

*A*s part of his celebratory tour of the United States, Lafayette had dedicated monuments in most every state he had visited. The laying of the cornerstone for these monuments, traditionally a ceremonial stone placed in the corner of the structure, became the event around which the general public could celebrate Lafayette's visit to their city. Freemasons were almost always the organization chosen to dedicate and symbolically level the cornerstone for these commemorative monuments. And this was once again to be the case for the monument to be erected in Nathanael Greene's honor in Savannah's Johnson Square.

By ten o'clock in the morning of the final day of Lafayette's stay in Savannah, an impressive processional had made its way through the sandy streets. The route took them from his boardinghouse lodgings to Johnson Square, where the day's ceremony was to take place. When Lafayette arrived, his honorary military escort split into two columns and marched around either side of the park. As he approached the park entrance, Lafayette was greeted by more than five hundred schoolchildren dressed in their finest clothing. The children proceeded to toss fresh-cut flowers at his feet as he made his way toward the wooden platform that had been erected at the excavated site of Greene's monument.

The ceremonies began with a military band playing a patriotic anthem, followed by an address from the chairman of the monument committee. Lafayette did not hear a word of it. He was lost in his own thoughts as he nervously felt for the metal canister. It weighed heavily in the front pocket of his overcoat. He had come a long way in his life.

His journey had taken him from his days as a young and fearless revolutionary fighting side by side with his adopted American brethren, to an exile from his own country during the French Revolution, to the old and doting grandfather that he now was. He thought his achievements had long been forgotten to history. But his spirits had been lifted by the adoring citizens in every city he had visited during his celebratory tour of America. Now, the day had arrived that he had been anticipating for so long.

It had been twenty-five years since he had received the package containing the odd-looking canister from Caty Greene, the wife of the man for whom hundreds of people had gathered in and around Johnson Square that day to honor. If only they knew. An absurd thought crossed his mind: What if he were to stand up, remove the letter written by Washington from the canister, and read it aloud in place of his prepared speech. Would they still want to celebrate and honor Nathanael Greene? Would they still revere Washington?

But Lafayette pushed these thoughts from his mind as quickly as they had entered. He had made up his mind long ago never to share the letter with anyone. He was determined to lay it to rest with the man who had made the decision to seize it in the first place. He did not think any less of his friend Nathanael Greene, for he knew him to be an honorable man who must have had his reasons for holding on to the letter. And he certainly thought no less of George Washington, the man whom he would always love as if he were his own father.

Having participated in many cornerstone-laying ceremonies, Lafayette was fully aware of the Freemason tradition of carving a cavity into the cornerstone for the placement of common artifacts. For Greene's monument, the list of memorials to be deposited included current paper currency and coins; medallions to honor Washington, Greene, and Lafayette; and copies of the Savannah Republican and Georgia local newspapers.

An odd-looking canister that contained a surrender letter written by George Washington during the darkest days of the Revolutionary War was not on any list. But it would nevertheless find its way into the cornerstone's cavity that day.

As the speeches concluded, the memorials were deposited and the cornerstone was lowered down into place. General Lafayette then descended from the wooden platform to perform one of the final rituals of the ceremony, which consisted of striking the stone three times with a mallet. Before giving way to the high priest to give the benediction upon the cornerstone, Lafayette reached into his jacket pocket.

He discreetly withdrew the canister and placed it gently inside the cavity with the rest of the artifacts. Eyes moist with the memories of his many long-lost revolutionary friends, as well as his own inevitable mortality, Lafayette watched as a large stone slab was then lowered down over the top of the cornerstone. The ritualistic ceremony was over.

Washington's surrender letter was sealed inside for eternity. Or so he thought.

29

Present Day

Savannah, GA

I t was just like any other late September morning in Savannah, Georgia, with one small exception. What happened today could alter the face of American history. Matt had to keep reminding himself of the potential implications of finding a surrender letter from the Father of the Country entombed inside Greene's monument.

For some, the letter would be seen as a sign of weakness, and Washington would go from patriot to pariah, irrevocably falling from divine status. Others would be more sympathetic and empathize with the incredible burden he had to bear as commander in chief of the Continental Army. Still others would flat out not believe the letter to be true, no matter how much authentication could prove otherwise.

All of these things paled in comparison to what Matt knew in his heart would be the single biggest consequence of the letter's revelation. The impact it could have on the outcome of the presidential election. It was this thought that had not allowed him to sleep the prior evening. It was this thought that had his head on a swivel all afternoon, scanning the sidewalks and parked cars, looking for anyone or anything that looked suspicious. His nerves were already on edge, but now that they were so close to finding the letter, he was jumpier than ever.

As he scanned the perimeter of the park, Matt's eyes fell upon a black Escalade SUV parked along the southwest corner of the square. Without thinking, he grabbed a three-foot piece of scaffolding pipe and began slowly walking toward the car. About halfway there, the driver's side tinted window powered down. Matt could see a man in dark sunglasses looking directly at him. As he got closer, he saw the distinctive scar that he had been hoping to see on the man's left cheek. *Son of a bitch*, Matt thought to himself.

As if controlled by an unseen force, Matt began running toward the car. Revenge was on his mind. Just as he started running, the man extended a beefy arm out the window and, with his thumb and forefinger, made like he was shooting Matt between the eyes. Startled, Matt hesitated for just a second. Then, he broke into a full sprint. The man smiled arrogantly and stepped on the gas. By the time Matt reached the vacated parking space, the car was already halfway down the block. All he could do was swear under his breath in frustration.

After many hours of preparation, the engineering team had finished making its final measurements. They were ready to cut into Greene's monument. Hank draped his arm around Matt's shoulders and gave a fatherly squeeze, "Well, son, the moment of truth has arrived. Are you prepared for what we might find today?"

"You read my mind, Hank. I was just thinking about all the different ways people are going to react to this." Matt looked skyward. It was a crystal clear day with a high blue sky.

"I know it can be overwhelming. But you've got to remember that you're just the messenger, not the interpreter. When it comes to historical events, you have to let people decide for themselves what to make of them," Hank counseled. The workers had just finished wrapping the structure to hide the operation from public view.

"But this was a historical event that technically never happened. So are we doing the right thing by searching for the letter? Maybe we should just leave it alone. Clearly Lafayette put it here because he didn't want anybody to find it, right?" Matt questioned. He was relieved to be verbalizing the thoughts that had been tormenting him the past few days.

"Before you make conclusions about what Lafayette wanted, let me ask you this, why didn't he simply burn the letter? That would have ensured that no one would have ever seen it." Hank had to raise his voice to a near shout now that the laser cutters had begun to make their first incisions. "But he didn't burn it, he placed it intact into this monument," he said, pointing toward the structure that stood proudly before them. "Because in his heart, I think he knew it was too significant to be destroyed."

Sarah was standing just off to the side watching Matt talk to her father. There was something about his easy manner and the way that people seemed to gravitate to him, her father included, that was incredibly appealing to her. He was good looking, that was obvious, but it was his effortless charm that made liking him so natural. As if on cue, he glanced over and smiled at her. She felt her insides jump. Deep down, she knew she was falling for him.

Since they could do nothing now but watch the experts begin the excavation, she joined in on the discussion. "I agree with you Dad," she said, "and while there's no way we'll ever know the reason he didn't destroy the letter, I think a case could be made that Lafayette put it in the monument knowing that it *would* be found one day. And when that day came, the country would be ready to handle it."

"So do you think our country is ready to handle it, Sarah?" Matt asked "Because I can think of one guy in particular who would prefer the letter to stay right where it is."

"I think most Americans will handle it just fine. And as for Emerson, as far as I'm concerned, he made his bed and now he's got to sleep in it. He made a choice to run for president, not on his own achievements and ideals, but on the coattails of Washington. If his character is damaged because Washington's image gets tarnished and he loses some votes in the process, then he's got nobody to blame but himself," she said, with a little more passion than usual.

"And it doesn't hurt that you think he's a blowhard, right?" Matt kidded, leaning in to give her a playful shove.

"No, I guess it doesn't," she said with a coy smile, enjoying being in close proximity to him. "But my view wouldn't change if the candidate that I supported were in the same position."

———

It was late in the afternoon when the head engineer and contractor notified everyone that they were getting close. It had been a frustrating day of stops and starts. Every cut had been followed by the placement of shims and wedges to create gaps to continue cutting, and to properly stabilize the structure with support rods to prevent it from toppling over.

Director Fox had been busy monitoring the progress of the engineering team. He finally made his way over to where Matt was standing. "We're ready Matt," he said, his excitement showing through his normally professional bearing. "I can't believe that we're standing on the precipice of such a discovery. Just imagine—the last person to touch that canister was the Marquis de Lafayette. It's just incredible!" he shouted.

Matt appreciated Fox's enthusiasm. He had grown to like the director and felt foolish for having ever doubted his sincerity. "Come on, let's go," Matt said and slapped him on the shoulder as they disappeared behind the protective black netting.

The cornerstone had been pulled about halfway out of the monument. It was almost as if they were playing a game of Jenga®. Everyone was waiting for the sucker who would pull out the one loose block that would topple the rest of the structure. Matt prayed that was not going to be him. Fox handed him a black metal flashlight and gave him a nod of encouragement.

"Watch your step," Hank said, as Matt maneuvered around the supporting rods and crawled onto the wooden platform that had been constructed to provide access to the cornerstone.

He took one last look back at the search team assembled around him. He couldn't help but marvel at just how far they had come in such a short period of time. "Well, here goes nothing," he said. It wasn't exactly a quote worthy of Neil Armstrong, but what the hell, he thought, it pretty much summed it up.

The black tarp and the setting sun made it quite dark inside the scaffolding. When Matt first peered into the cornerstone cavity, he couldn't see much of anything. He noticed that it had also gotten eerily quiet—not just because the power washers and laser cutters, which had been operating nonstop all day, had ceased their constant drone, but because everybody seemed to be holding their collective breath. He switched on the flashlight and directed the beam inside the cavity. His heart was beating like a jackhammer against his rib cage.

Unable to control herself, Sarah blurted out, "What do you see?"

The flashlight provided enough light so that Matt could see clearly down into the cavity. He spotted some old coins and a pulpy clump of what might have been old currency or perhaps newspapers. He also saw what appeared to be a commemorative medallion to Lafayette among some other unidentifiable trinkets. He recited these discoveries aloud one by one. The beam of his flashlight moved haphazardly around the abyss, like a prison searchlight scanning the grounds for an escaped convict. Finally, Matt's play-by-play description ended abruptly.

"That's it?" asked Fox. "You mean it's not there?"

"Lafayette didn't put the canister in there after all?" Sarah uttered dejectedly.

"Damn, Martha Sampson was wrong," echoed Hank, in disappointment.

Matt turned his head slightly and winked. "Not exactly, Hank. I'm just sticking to Martha's rule about storytelling..." he said, and a broad smile creased his face as he continued, "...that a good story unfolds slowly."

He removed his hand from inside the cavity and turned around to face the assembled group. He thrust his arm triumphantly in the air, looking very much like the Statue of Liberty with a five o'clock shadow. Only it wasn't a torch in his right hand. It was Whitney's clever little invention.

Stunned silence was followed by whoops of joy as Matt scampered off the scaffolding. The first to greet him was Sarah. She threw her arms around him and squealed like a kid on Christmas morning. The rest of the group quickly formed an impromptu circle around them. They hugged, whooped, and jumped up and down like a football team during a pregame cheer. When the spontaneous eruption of relief and joy subsided, they looked in awe at the incredible little canister that Whitney had designed for Caty Greene more than two centuries before.

Matt handed it first to Sarah, who had tears in her eyes. He pulled her close and said, "Incredible isn't it?" But she couldn't speak. The cylinder was in remarkably fine shape, save for some rusty surface residue that left marks on everyone's hands as it was passed around.

The canister finally made its way back to Matt. He said, "We did it guys. Thanks to all of your hard work, we actually found it." He felt a kinship to the people surrounding him. People he hadn't even met until a few short weeks ago. It had truly been a team effort and Matt was supremely proud of how they had banded together. Remarkably, they had somehow found this incredible artifact that had been hidden from the world for almost two hundred years.

Hank brought the group back to reality when he said, "I think you guys have a train to catch."

They made their way out from behind the cover of the scaffolding and noticed that the sun had set. They didn't have much time to catch the 7:30 train. Matt looked back at Director Fox, "You coming, James?"

"Go on ahead. I'll catch up to you." He waved them on.

Then he took out his cell phone and dialed Charles Metcalf's number.

30

Present Day

Washington, D.C.

Anderson House was located less than two miles northwest of the White House, in the fashionable Dupont Circle neighborhood of Washington, D.C. The stately Beaux Arts mansion served as the headquarters for the Society of the Cincinnati. If the turn of the twentieth century fifty-room mansion were to be constructed today, it would cost well over twenty million dollars to build. Matt and Sarah had no time, however, to take in the majestic carved wood walls, gilded papier-mâché ceilings, and intricate marble floors that had taken the finest craftsmen countless hours to construct.

Upon arriving, they made their way downstairs to the lower level where the society's archives were located. Tucked away in a far corner was a small lab where the society undertook conservation treatments. Nicknamed the clean room, it was here that rare book and manuscript collections were sent to be preserved and stabilized. Surprisingly, there was no sign of President General Metcalf, even though Fox had alerted him to their arrival at Union Station some forty-five minutes earlier.

Over the years, Director Fox had acquainted himself with many of the society's preservation techniques, so he was confident that he could remove the document safely from the canister. He was well aware from past experience that paper documents that had been folded or rolled and stored for many years had a tendency to resist opening. Sometimes these documents were so stiff and brittle that they would crack or break if handled incorrectly. But he also knew that if he tried to ask Matt and Sarah to wait a minute longer, he would have a mutiny on his hands.

Matt placed Whitney's device on the metal worktable and waited anxiously while Fox prepared a special solution. The solution would hopefully make it easier to unscrew the top of the canister from the base. They had already attempted to remove the cap a few minutes earlier, but it became apparent that the two-hundred-year-old threaded mechanism was frozen shut.

"Wouldn't a can of WD-40 be a hell of a lot faster?" Matt said, only half joking. He was already on edge and now he was running low on patience.

"OK, Matt, if you'll hold the canister steady," Fox said, ignoring Matt's eagerness, "I'll apply the lubricant to the area of friction."

Fox covered the seal with the solution and let it sit for a minute. Then he took the canister in his hands and attempted to turn it once again. Ever so gently, he twisted but the seal remained frozen in place.

After Fox applied a second round of lubricant, Matt asked, "Do you mind if I give it a try?"

"Not at all, but be careful. While the metal may seem structurally sound, the last thing we'd want to do is to squeeze too hard and have it disintegrate in your hands. That would severely damage the letter," Fox warned. "Just twist this way while directing your pressure here at the seam."

Matt took hold of the canister very carefully. He began to turn the top in the opposite direction from the bottom, as if he were trying to open a stuck jar of pickles. "You know, when my mom couldn't open things, she'd bang the top end on the counter to loosen it up. It never failed to work."

"No, Matt," Sarah shouted, unsure of whether he was joking or serious.

"Just throwing out ideas," Matt offered with a sheepish grin.

Smiling, he handed over the canister to Sarah and asked, "You want to give it a try?"

She took hold of the device and gave it a firm twist. Remarkably, she felt the top give way and thought she heard a slight hissing sound. The lubricant must have finally worked its way into the seam. At long last, Whitney's impenetrable seal was broken.

Then, Sarah's sudden euphoria turned to dread. She looked around nervously, like she had just opened Pandora's box. "Now what do I do?" She was holding the canister at arm's length, away from her body, nervous that she might somehow damage it.

"Now we need to very carefully extract the document," Fox said, as he carefully reclaimed the cylinder from Sarah's hands.

"Aren't you going to put on white gloves or something first?" Matt asked.

"White gloves make for dramatic television, but it's actually been proven that wearing them dulls your sense of touch. They actually increase the potential for physically damaging fragile material, especially ultrathin or brittle papers," Fox replied.

Matt and Sarah crowded around Director Fox. They peered inside the canister, like expectant parents. A rolled up document was clearly visible inside the opening, but they had no way of determining its condition. Fox very gently turned the canister so that it was angled slightly downward. He delicately shook it back and forth until the top end of a document began to appear. He continued jiggling, until more than half of the document was unsheathed. Then, with extreme care, he wrapped his right hand gently around the circumference of the single sheet of paper. Finally, he removed it the rest of the way. For the first time in close to two hundred years, Washington's letter was visible in the light of day.

He handed the canister over to Matt and gently placed the still rolled up letter on the table in front of him. The three of them exhaled in unison. The first thing Fox noticed was that the paper relaxed a bit on its own. The fact that it unfurled notice-ably was a very good sign. It meant that it was not as stiff and brittle as they had originally feared.

"OK, Matt, I want you to put your fingertips very gently on the top ends of this side of the document while I unroll it toward me," Fox instructed.

Now it was Matt's turn to be nervous. He was about to place his hands on a document signed by George Washington. Not exactly an everyday occurrence for him. His heart was pumping and he could feel the adrenaline coursing through his body. He drew in a deep breath and exhaled slowly to calm his nerves.

After a quick glance at a pensive-looking Sarah, he placed the index and middle finger of his left hand on one side of the document. Then he did the same on the opposite corner, with his right hand. It reminded him of playing a game called Ouija, as a kid. In that game, the players would lightly place their fingers on a pointer and wait for the spirits to spell out the answer to their questions. He wondered what questions were about to be answered, and if Washington's spirit was somehow present. He shook these thoughts from his head and refocused on the task at hand. "Ready," he said.

Ever so slowly, Fox began to unroll the document. He prom-ised himself that if he felt any tension or brittleness whatsoever, he would stop and wait for the help of experts. But remarkably, the document was supple to the touch. So he continued unrolling. Then, the first words began to come into view. More specifically, a date appeared: *February 17, 1778.* He locked eyes with Matt and then Sarah. It was almost as if they were sharing a religious experience.

Not a word was spoken as he continued to unfurl the document. The next words that came into view were *To Sir William Howe.*

Sarah gasped, "Oh my God, it's true."

Now with little fear that he would damage the letter, Fox unrolled it fully and placed his fingers on the bottom corners of the document to hold it in place. The two men had the letter pinned to the table between them. The Ouija board was about to give up its secrets.

Matt thought that Washington's flowing cursive was the most beautiful thing he had ever laid eyes on. He was the first to speak after each of them had silently finished reading the short note to General William Howe, commander of the British Army. "Very formal and brief, but there is absolutely no doubt that Washington was extending an olive branch to the British," he said.

"He was definitely serious about his offer of reconciliation," said Sarah. "The second sentence here," she pointed to the line on the page, "he says '*willing to discuss terms of a negotiated surrender of the Continental Army.*' And later on, he emphasizes again that he is '*ready to act in good faith to peacefully end this bloody conflict.*'"

"It also appears that he wanted to do this without the involvement of Congress. He states plainly that he would prefer that these '*negotiations take place in secret,*' right here toward the end of the letter," Fox noted.

"I know my emotions, as usual, are getting the best of me, but I can't help but be a little disappointed in him. Surrender is bad enough, but acting without the consent of Congress is treasonous," Matt said.

"I grant you that it's shocking to see the word *surrender* in a letter written by Washington. And this is certainly going to cause many to view him in a new light. But still, we have to remember the context in which this was written. He didn't have much of an army left. He had lost the support of many in his own government. And let's not forget that the British had a seemingly insurmountable force that was getting stronger by the day," Fox said.

"And at that time Congress was like a den of vipers. So he probably believed he was acting in the best interests of the country. Personally, I think the formality of the words he uses reveals a man extremely torn by the decision he had to make. You can almost feel his pain in having to pen this letter," Sarah said sympathetically.

"Say what you want, but surrender is surrender, and that changes everything I once believed about him," Matt said, not hiding his disappointment in Washington's decision.

"There's no question this is going to be debated and analyzed for years to come," Fox said.

After staring in awe for a few more minutes, Fox and Matt began to carefully release the document. Slowly they let its shape memory return it to the rolled up position in which it had spent the last two centuries.

It was then that the door to the clean room opened. Charles Metcalf strode into the room, flanked by two beefy security guards that Fox did not recognize.

"Good morning, Mr. Fox," he said, without extending his hand. "And this must be the quite persistent Matt and Sarah." He had yet to remove his hands from his pants pockets. Sarah felt an involuntary shiver go down her spine at the sight of the peculiar little man, dressed completely in black.

"I trust everything is in order, Director Fox, and that you've gotten the letter here safely?" he said in a clipped voice.

"It's right here," Fox said, pointing to the artifacts on the table in front of him, "and it's in remarkably good shape given its age. It's truly an incredible find; one that will open up an exciting and vigorous new debate about our country's Founding Father."

Metcalf had made his way around to Fox's side of the table to get a closer look. "Yes, well that debate may have to wait a little while longer," he said as he quickly snatched up the document.

He took a step back from the table, revealing his crimson, chafed hands for the first time. They stood out in stark contrast against the yellowed letter he held firmly in his grasp.

Matt had always prided himself on his good instincts, especially when it came to anticipating danger. When Metcalf entered the room, his instincts told him that this guy was trouble. It wasn't just his bogeyman appearance and emotionless voice; it was something much deeper than that. Matt thought to himself, *this guy is rotten to the core.*

So when Metcalf snatched up the letter, Matt reacted immediately. He moved quickly forward and said, "What the hell do you think you're doing." But he didn't get more than two steps before being knocked to the ground by a blow delivered to the back of his head by one of Metcalf's henchmen; then a knee planted firmly in the small of his back, to make sure he stayed pinned to the ground.

Sarah screamed. Fox made a move to help, but was stopped in his tracks by security guard number two, who held a Sig Sauer handgun pointed directly at his forehead. Everything happened so fast and unexpectedly that Sarah felt as if she were somehow dreaming. She closed her eyes and opened them again to make sure it was all really happening. It was.

"All right, the show's over," Metcalf exclaimed, in as close to a raised voice as he ever allowed. He turned to his two guards and said, "Get them out of here. Bring them to my office upstairs and wait for me there. I'll join you in a few minutes."

"What the hell are you doing, Metcalf?" Fox blurted out in anger, as he was hustled into the hallway.

"Why, isn't it obvious, Director Fox? I'm cleaning up someone else's mess. And making a potential problem go away," he said.

With a dismissive wave of his hand, his hired guns cleared the room.

31

A Few Days Earlier

A few days earlier, Metcalf placed an urgent phone call to Chuck Conrad. He had placed the call right after Director Fox informed him of the discovery of Caty Greene's journal and the subsequent theft of the journal by Conrad's people. Metcalf was surprised to hear about Conrad's involvement, and he loathed surprises. He hadn't been able to reach Conrad the first time he called him, so he tried again when he got home that evening.

Conrad was in the middle of yet another meeting at the Richmond, Virginia, campaign field office when his phone buzzed. His caller ID alerted him that Metcalf was on the line. He had ignored him earlier and thought it best not to do so again, so he excused himself from the room to take the call.

He had been introduced to Metcalf six months earlier by a mutual friend. The two had begun a conversation that eventually resulted in a secret proposal by Metcalf. It outlined a plan for how the two men could make a lot of money together. Conrad had hesitated at first, but the prospect of being paid a king's ransom for some simple arm-twisting of his boss, had ultimately swayed him. There was only one thing he craved more than power, and that was money. He had made his deal with the devil and he would have to tolerate Metcalf for the foreseeable future.

"Conrad here," he growled.

"We need to talk, are you alone?" Metcalf said.

"Hang on a second." Conrad found an empty office and closed the door. "I am now."

Metcalf was calling from his five-thousand-square-foot luxury condominium on K Street. His four-bedroom, four-bathroom penthouse apartment had walls of glass and a huge wraparound terrace that overlooked the Potomac River. It provided phenomenal views for entertaining, but in the three years he had lived there, he had yet to entertain once. A wall had been removed between two of the bedrooms and the expanded space had been converted into a mini trading floor. It housed state-of-the-art technology to track financial markets around the world, as well as videoconferencing capabilities to communicate with his offices in Manhattan. He only required four hours of sleep a night, so when he was home, the majority of his time was spent in his personal trading room. There, he devised and executed investment strategies designed to maximize returns on his billion-dollar hedge fund.

"I understand we've got a problem. A problem that you evidently didn't see fit to share with me," he said.

"We've got lots of problems, Metcalf. Which one are you talking about?" Conrad said, making no attempt to hide his dislike for the man on the other end of the line.

"Don't toy with me, Mr. Conrad. You know better than to do that," Metcalf replied stonily. "Whether you like it or not, we're in bed together now. So why don't you tell me everything you know about the journal you stole from Savannah."

He knew his knowledge of the journal would take Conrad by surprise and he reveled in turning the tables on him. He placed a premium on having information, especially insider information. It always gave him the upper hand.

"How the hell did you find out about that?" Conrad said, trying to hide his surprise. "Never mind, I guess my pinhead nephew couldn't keep his mouth shut. It really wasn't that big of a deal, Charles. I discovered a potential problem and dealt with it." He stalked animatedly around the room and talked in a near shout. He was the emotional opposite of Metcalf.

"You didn't make anything go away. You've created problems you don't even know about," Metcalf said, as if lecturing a child. As he talked, he rechecked to make sure that the three deadbolts on his front door were locked. The demons were surfacing again.

"Like what?" Conrad said. He did not like being patronized. "I've got the journal; problem solved."

"Do you have the letter, too?"

"What letter?" he said, a pit forming in his stomach.

"The *surrender* letter, you idiot. The one thing that, if made public, could cost us the election," Metcalf hissed. "Evidently those people in Savannah were not deterred by your little theft. They kept digging and digging until they discovered the resting place of Washington's misguided correspondence. And now they are only days away from finding it."

"What are you talking about? How can that be? I've read the journal and there's nothing in there that even hints at the location of the letter," he said, the first signs of concern creeping into his voice.

"Evidently you were unaware that the descendants of southern plantation slaves like to tell stories," he said. He then shared what Director Fox had told him about Martha Sampson's great-grandmother's sighting of the canister with Lafayette, prior to the dedication of Nathanael Greene's monument.

"Well I'll be damned, what are the chances of that? But do you really think the letter could have survived all these years, inside a statue?" he said in disbelief.

"It doesn't matter what I believe, it only matters that *they* believe the letter has survived. And it just so happens, they'll be cutting into the monument later this week in an attempt to exhume it."

"We can't let that happen," Conrad sputtered. Outright panic now replaced his disbelief.

"No, *we* can't. Which is why *I* will be handling this problem from here on out. Do I make myself clear?" He needed to ensure that the chain of command was understood.

After a long pause, Conrad muttered, "Understood," in a deflated tone. "So what's your plan?"

"First, tell me where the journal is now."

"I've got it in my briefcase."

"Good, have it couriered to my office immediately."

"All right, but what about the letter?"

"The letter will be hand delivered directly to me after it is found, by the director of the society, James Fox," he said. He went on to tell him about his agreement to fund the extraction operation. And that the document would be brought back to the society's facilities under the guise of preservation. "Much easier than breaking and entering, don't you think?" he said smugly.

"So they're just going to hand it over to you?" Conrad countered.

"They know nothing of my involvement with you, or our," he paused to find the right words, "shared financial interests. They believe only that the society has graciously offered their facilities to assist in the authentication and preservation of this historically significant document. When they arrive at our headquarters in D.C., I'll thank them for their efforts and send them on their way, minus the letter, of course."

"What about Fox?"

"Let me worry about Director Fox, you just get me that journal. Once the letter arrives at my doorstep, I'll have all the evidence that Washington's letter ever existed safely locked away. Leaving you to focus on getting that fool elected president," he said.

"So how is our investment strategy progressing anyway?" Conrad changed the subject to one that was close to both men's hearts—money. Emerson knew nothing of the arrangement with Metcalf because Conrad hadn't told him, and wouldn't, until after the election.

"Let's just say Metcalf & Company has taken a very large and highly leveraged position in Fannie Mae and Freddie Mac. And based on the latest polls showing Emerson in the lead, I'm going to keep buying up preferred stock in the two government-sponsored companies until there is nothing left to buy. Once Emerson is elected and we execute our plan, our hedge fund should be worth close to a billion dollars. And your stake will make you an extremely wealthy man."

"And if we lose the election?" Conrad asked, without thinking.

"Then we'll both be ruined."

The line went dead.

That had been three days ago. But now that Metcalf had the letter safely in his hands, he was confident that there was very little chance of financial ruin for either man.

32

Present Day

Washington, D.C.

They were sitting anxiously in Charles Metcalf's cold, stark office on the second floor of the society's headquarters. The two built-by-steroids security thugs stood guard silently. Director James Fox sat with slumped shoulders, trying to make sense of what had just transpired. Meanwhile, Sarah applied pressure to the back of Matt's head with a handful of tissues. She had finally managed to stem the bleeding. They hadn't hit Matt hard enough to give him a concussion. But the blow had left him a dangerous combination of woozy, embarrassed, and angry. He had had enough. His home had been violated, he'd been shot at, and now he had been physically assaulted; he silently renewed his vow that, eventually, someone was going to pay.

"Nice guy you work for there, James. You want to tell us what the hell he's doing?" Matt glared at Fox. He winced in pain, as he felt around the angry knot that was forming on the back of his head.

"I'm as confused as you are; honestly, I have no idea what he's up to," Fox said.

"Come on, James, he's your boss, you work for the fucking guy. You're going to need to do better than that."

"I wish I could," he said, imploring Matt to believe him. "He's been here for less than six months and he doesn't spend a lot of time at the office. I hardly know anything about him. I have no idea why he'd want to steal Washington's letter."

"Stop it, Matt. James was as blindsided by this as we were. You can't honestly believe he had a hand in any of this?" Sarah said, defending the director.

"I don't know what to believe anymore. All I know is, my head hurts like hell and the letter is gone. That's the second time something's been taken from me and it's starting to piss me off."

The door opened and the dark shadow of a man slipped into the office. The temperature in the room seemed to dip a couple of degrees. Fox pointed at Metcalf from his seated position and said, "Do you really believe we're going to just stand by and let you steal the letter?"

"Yes, Mr. Fox, that's precisely what you're going to do. These two," he said, pointing at Matt and Sarah, "are going to go home to Savannah and return to their innocuous lives. And you are going to resume your job of running the day-to-day affairs of the society," he paused, "as if nothing ever happened."

"What makes you think that I'm not going to go straight to the police?" Fox asked incredulously.

"And tell them what? That you illegally broke into a monument in Savannah? After which you removed, or rather, *stole* a two-hundred-year-old letter? And not just any letter. A *surrender* letter, from George Washington no less, written during the Revolutionary War?" he said, painting quite an unbelievable scenario, albeit one that had actually happened.

Fox was at a loss for words, so Metcalf continued, "No, Mr. Fox, you will not go to the police. You will forget about all of this. You have no evidence that these documents ever existed, and you would look quite foolish trying to make a case that they ever did. You'll just have to take comfort in the fact that they are safe, safely hidden from the world, just as they were before you disturbed them."

Fox knew Metcalf was right; they didn't have the evidence to prove any wrongdoing.

Sarah spoke up, "Wait a minute. You just said 'these documents,' and 'they' will remain safely hidden from the world. You have the journal, too?" She had picked up on the apparent slip of the tongue by Metcalf.

Metcalf's eyes flashed with anger and seemed to darken a shade. "Quite perceptive Miss Gordon," he said.

"Are you concerned that the revelation of Washington's surrender letter will harm the reputation of the society? Is that what all this is about?" she said, searching for an explanation for all this madness.

"Hardly," he replied, with a dismissive shake of his head. He was losing interest in continuing the conversation.

Matt, who had remained quiet until then, jumped in and said, "This has nothing to do with the society, does it, Metcalf?" He went on, "You could care less about the society's reputation; this has to do with getting Emerson elected, doesn't it?" He was slowly piecing together a different hypothesis for Metcalf's motive. "That's what you meant downstairs when you said that you were cleaning up someone else's mess. Conrad had the journal stolen but you didn't find out about it until Fox clued you in. You had to clean up Conrad's mess. You only offered the help of the society to exhume the letter so you could get your hands on that as well. And now that you have both the journal and the letter, the potential problem you mentioned has been dealt with. Is that about right?"

For the first time since he had met Metcalf, Fox actually thought he saw the trace of a smile on the strange-looking man.

But it was the kind that would make a child cower behind his mother's skirt.

Metcalf replied slowly and evenly, "Even if everything you said were true, it wouldn't change a thing. You have nothing to show for all your troubles, and you can prove nothing."

Matt ignored him. Switching gears, he said, "Why is getting Emerson elected so important? That's the question we should be asking, isn't it?"

The impromptu inquisition had gone far enough, so Metcalf ended it. "I think we're done here. Gentlemen, please see them out."

Before the two goons could usher them out of the office, Matt yelled over his shoulder, "You may have won round one, Metcalf, but I promise you, payback's gonna be a bitch."

The door to Metcalf's office slammed shut.

33

Present Day

Washington, D.C.

M att desperately needed a jolt of caffeine to clear his head. They walked a few blocks from the society's headquarters to the nearest Starbucks. Each of them sat silently, replaying events from that morning, still trying to comprehend everything that had happened. As the caffeine began to kick in, the throbbing in Matt's head finally began to subside. Abruptly, he got up and took out his cell phone.

"Who were you calling?" Sarah asked, when Matt returned to the table.

"An old Wall Street buddy. I asked him to do some digging into Metcalf's hedge fund."

"To what end?" Fox asked.

"Clearly Metcalf is in bed with the Emerson campaign. And if my hunch is correct, this has to have something to do with money. It usually does. Someone once said to follow the money if you want to solve the crime. Well, we know Metcalf is the crook, now we just have to connect the money trail back to Conrad or Emerson, or both," he explained.

"You mean like campaign financing or something?" Sarah said, trying to get inside Matt's head.

"Maybe, or maybe something bigger, I'm not sure. But we've got to start somewhere."

"I don't know what to say to you guys, other than I'm sorry for the mess that my involvement has caused," Fox said, looking truly devastated.

"Don't be ridiculous, James, you had nothing to do with what happened today," Sarah replied.

"Not directly, but I feel like I should have sensed that Metcalf was up to something, especially when he insisted on my bringing the letter back to the society's headquarters."

"There's no way you could have known, James. No one could have ever guessed the crazy shit that went down this morning. And I'm sorry I jumped down your throat back in Metcalf's office. If you haven't noticed by now, my emotions tend to get the best of me," Matt apologized.

"You don't have to apologize to me; you're the one who got smacked in the head. How are you feeling by the way?" he asked.

"I'm fine; just a nasty bump is all. Although with a nurse like her," he said, smiling at Sarah, "it's amazing I'm even able to stand up." In stressful situations, Matt always turned to humor to break the tension.

"Very funny, next time maybe I'll let you bleed to death," she said, giving Matt a playful slap on his arm. She was glad to see Matt's sense of humor had returned. "Seriously, though, you guys, what do we do now? We've got to get that letter back."

"I like your gumption, Professor," Matt teased. "Got any ideas?"

"Not really." Then she looked suddenly panicked and said, "You don't think that goon would have really shot us, do you?" The rational side of her brain had stepped in to question the sanity of her earlier suggestion of pursuing the letter.

"He looked pretty comfortable with a gun in his hand, that's for sure. But I don't think we'll know just how far these guys are willing to go until we figure out the true nature of Metcalf's relationship to Emerson," Matt said.

"All I know is that I'd rather not have a gun pointed at my head again," Fox said, without a trace of humor in his voice.

"Let's hope it doesn't come to that. But if you don't want to pursue this any further, we'd completely understand, James," Matt offered.

"No way, Matt, I want this letter back just as badly as you do. This is personal now for me, too." Fox sat up straighter in his chair, as if to prove his resolve.

"Good, well we're all in this together then. So now we need to figure out our next move." They each returned to their coffees and silently mulled over ideas for how to get the letter back.

After a few minutes, Fox spoke up. "There's one person I could call. He's a mentor of mine and he might be able to help us brainstorm some ideas."

"Who's that?" asked Matt.

"His name is Buzz Penberthy, and he was the president general of the society before Metcalf. The two men couldn't be more opposite, though. Buzz is a former naval pilot who served with distinction in Vietnam and also in Desert Storm before retiring with the rank of colonel. He's the guy who hired me into my current position. He's a clear-thinking, no-nonsense guy and he knows the society inside and out. Maybe he'll have some ideas to help us figure out our next move," Fox said, before draining the last of his coffee.

"Sounds like my kind of guy. Does he live here in D.C.?" Matt asked, pushing his sandy-blond mop of hair out of his eyes.

"Not anymore. He lives on a farm out in Fredericksburg, Virginia. But I'm sure he'll be willing to talk to us," he said.

"And he can be trusted with the full, crazy story?" Sarah inquired.

"I'd trust him with my life."

"We don't have any better ideas, so I say we give Colonel Penberthy a call. At least it's a start," Matt said.

Fox took out his cell phone and dialed Penberthy's number.

"He invited us down to his farmhouse. I think he gets a little lonely on the farm all by himself. He lost his wife a couple of years ago to cancer and his kids are all grown," Fox said. "I hope you guys don't mind, it's only an hour's drive."

"Not at all. After this morning, I'd prefer to get away from here anyway," Sarah exclaimed.

"Sounds like a road trip," Matt said.

34

Present Day

Fredericksburg, VA

B uzz Penberthy's thirty-five-acre farm was an oasis of country living set amid the creeping sprawl of suburbia. He and
his wife had purchased the iconic landmark property five years
earlier. It was to be their dream retirement home one day, with
plenty of room to board horses and entertain their grandchil-
dren. God had other plans, however, as Buzz's wife, Adele, had
succumbed to pancreatic cancer just three years later. She had
truly been the love of his life, and after forty-five years of marriage, he still woke up every morning expecting to see her smiling
face. After her death, he had taken a leave of absence from his
duties as president general of the society. Eventually he retired
altogether, unable to rekindle the passion he once had for the
job. The board of directors had subsequently filled the vacancy
he had left, with Charles Metcalf.

The property was a postcard of country charm. It was
anchored by a simple, white clapboard four-bedroom farmhouse with original wide pine floors and recently updated
kitchen. Both the living room and dining room had oversized
fireplaces, and a stately porch wrapped around three sides of

the home. But the signature structure on the property was a huge red dairy barn with an attached fifty-foot-tall white grain silo. Buzz had invested a significant amount of sweat equity into these two buildings over the past couple of years, replacing siding, fortifying stalls, and even painting the silo from top to bottom by himself. The latter had taken him all summer and had required more than fifty gallons of paint. But Buzz didn't mind the physical labor required by the circa-1814 farmhouse property; it provided him temporary solace from the still painful loss of his beloved partner.

It was late afternoon by the time Matt, Sarah, and James passed through the brick front entry posts. The wrought iron gate had been left open for them and they noticed an oval wooden sign hanging from a limb of a sturdy cherry tree. The words BINGO FIELD had been neatly hand painted in bold black letters.

Buzz was waiting for them on the front porch. They got out of the car and stretched their legs. Buzz waved and made his way down the steps. He shook Director Fox's outstretched hand firmly. "Welcome to the country, James," he said. Fox could feel the calluses on Buzz's palm—a testament to the many hours of self-inflicted hard labor.

Most people would be surprised to know that Buzz Penberthy was almost sixty-eight years old. He looked at least ten years younger. The only clue to his senior status was his steel-gray hair. But he kept it trimmed high and tight, in the same military buzz cut he had worn since he had entered the navy, almost fifty years earlier. He had lost little, if any muscle tone, due in large part to the physical demands of keeping a thirty-five-acre farm in tip-top shape. And his lean frame was kept that way by early morning jogs, which, on good days, could stretch to five miles or more. But the pronounced dimple on his chin and the friendly twinkle in his soft blue eyes belied his military bearing. They made him appear more like the doting grandfather that he was, rather than the fiercely intense fighter pilot that he had once been.

He gave them the nickel tour of the first floor. It had been tastefully decorated by his late wife, right down to the nineteenth-century period furniture acquired from local antique stores. They sat down at a chunky kitchen table that looked like it had been made from a tree felled by Paul Bunyan.

"I've been wondering about the name Bingo Field on the sign outside," Matt said. "Is there a story behind that name?"

Buzz smiled and replied, "Son, there's a story for just about everything attached to this farm. Bingo Field is what we pilots call land-based runways that carrier-based aircraft could divert to in case of an emergency. When I first walked this property with Addy, it reminded me of an open field that I once had to make an emergency landing in during the Vietnam War.

"I was returning from a bombing run when my aircraft was shredded by shrapnel," he recounted. "I lost all power and my ejection seat failed. I had to find a spot to crash-land or I was toast. I was losing altitude fast and there was no place to set her down. All I could see below me was miles and miles of continuous thick green jungle. I had maybe thirty seconds left until I'd have to say a prayer and ditch her. Then, incredibly, out of nowhere, like Moses parting the Red Sea, a field opened up right in front of me. I wouldn't exactly call it a land-based runway, but that goddamned field saved my life."

"Anyway, when we bought this farm, it brought back the memory of that day, and I knew we had found our new home." He paused before he could continue. "Addy and I had found our safe haven, our Bingo Field." Buzz never used to be an emotional man, but ever since he lost his wife to cancer, he'd find himself tearing up at the most inopportune times.

"Enough about that," he said, clearing his throat and regaining his composure. "You didn't come here to listen to my boring old war stories. James, you sounded pretty upset on the phone. What's so serious that you were willing to drive all the way out here to talk about?" Buzz asked.

"Well, it's a long story, Buzz, and it's best if you hear it from start to finish. So if you don't mind, we'll start from the beginning."

"I've got no place to be, James. Fire when ready."

Director Fox began to tell his old boss the story about the surrender letter. With help from Matt and Sarah, they recounted all of the events of the past weeks. They started with Matt's discovery of Caty Greene's journal inside the atlas from the Bull Street Library. Thirty minutes later, they finally finished telling the tale of incredible events that had led them to Penberthy's country kitchen that afternoon. Laying it out in a linear fashion made them realize just how crazy it all sounded. But remarkably, it had all happened.

"I knew that son of a bitch was no good," Buzz growled, referring to Metcalf. "I never understood why the society hired him anyway. It was clear to me he wasn't just an odd duck; he was a sneaky little bastard. I guess your story proves my instincts were right." He took a pocketknife from his pocket and removed some dirt from beneath a fingernail, as if the dirt were the manifestation of Metcalf himself.

Buzz shook his head in disgust, "One of the only times I met with him was after the board had already made the decision to hire him. I thought I'd help him get acquainted to his new job by outlining the expectations of the president general and by answering any questions he might have had. Anyway, I tried discussing the responsibilities and duties of the job but all he seemed interested in talking about were the names of the biggest donors to the society. I guess I shouldn't have been surprised, those Wall Street guys are always all about the money." The blade of his pocketknife snapped shut loudly.

"You may not be that far off, Buzz. Matt believes we may be able to tie Metcalf to the Emerson campaign if we follow the money. He's got a friend trying to dig for a possible financial link between the two as we speak," offered Sarah.

"Good idea, money definitely makes this guy's world go around." Changing gears, he asked, "So what's your next move?"

"Well, our goal is to get the letter and the journal back. We just haven't figured out how yet," Fox said.

"You're sure Metcalf has the journal, too?" Buzz inquired. All three nodded in the affirmative.

"Positive," Matt said. "Sarah was smart enough to catch him in a slip of the tongue that tipped us off that he has the journal in his possession, too. That's why we think Metcalf is somehow connected to the Emerson campaign. Because we know that it was Conrad who was alerted to the fact that the journal existed in the first place. We just assumed that Conrad was the one who took it, but now it appears that Metcalf has it. Either way, these two are somehow in bed together."

"If he's got the documents," said Buzz, turning back to Director Fox, "there's a good chance that they're in the private safe in the president general's office." He continued to open and close the blade of his pocketknife as he spoke.

"That would make sense, although there is a chance he could have moved them to a new location by now," Fox said. He glanced out the large bay window and noticed the sun dipping slowly behind the big red dairy barn.

"I doubt it, James," Matt jumped in. "Why take the risk of moving the documents when they are safely locked away in a building that's constructed like Fort Knox and has around-the-clock security? He'll probably get around to moving them at some point, though. So we better act fast." Matt pushed away from the table and began to pace.

Sarah smiled to herself because she had wondered how long it would take Matt to get up from his chair. She had come to expect a certain level of intensity from him. Not an edgy intensity, but more like a boyish enthusiasm that she found endearing. She took in his strong, athletic build as he stalked around the room. Something stirred inside her and she felt a flush rise in her cheeks. She looked away before anyone noticed.

"So this safe that you're talking about, it's in your old office?" Matt asked Buzz. "The same office Metcalf occupies today?" He had made his way across the room and stood by the antique double-well copper sink.

"That's right. But I know what you're thinking, Matt, and it's not going to be that easy. I'm sure the first thing he did was create a new combination code. It's the first thing I did when I took over, and I'm just an old warhorse, not a slick hedge fund manager," Buzz said with a chuckle. The chuckle ended in a raspy cough, the residue of too many years of smoking Marlboro's in his younger days.

"Well, at least we know where it is. Now all we have to do is find a way to open it," Matt said, always the optimist.

"And let's not forget the small matter of getting in and out of Metcalf's office undetected. Which might be a challenge considering the two oversized gentlemen we had the pleasure of meeting earlier today," Sarah said, injecting a sobering dose of reality into the plan.

"Well, it appears we have our work cut out for us, folks," Buzz said. "I don't know about you, but I think better on a full stomach. I hope you don't mind, but I went to the market after you called, James, and picked up a few steaks for us to grill. I had a feeling we might be here awhile." Buzz hadn't had any company on the farm since his daughter and grandkids visited three weeks earlier. He would never let it show, but he'd be disappointed if his guests didn't stick around for dinner.

"I've never turned down a steak in my life, Buzz, and I don't plan on starting now," Matt said, flashing his trademark grin. "But at least let me help with the cooking. Just point me in the general direction of the grill and I'll fire it up."

"Sounds good, Matt. I'm sure everyone will appreciate your cooking over mine anyway. My wife used to say that I never met a chicken breast that I didn't char. Personally, I always thought a charcoal crust brought out the flavor," Buzz said with a laugh, clearly happy they had decided to stay. He got up quickly to help Matt prepare the meal, before they could change their minds.

After feasting on a home-cooked meal, they returned to the task at hand. They had to come up with a plan to retrieve the stolen journal and letter from Metcalf's office safe.

They had already run through a number of ideas but had come up empty. Then Matt remembered something. "It just might work," he said, more to himself than to the others, as he was still thinking through the idea in his head.

"What might work, Matt?" Fox said, as he helped clear the dishes from the table.

"Well, there is this guy in Savannah that I know, a locksmith who has helped me out in the past. One time, a few years back, I bought a rusty old antique house safe. It was locked and of course nobody knew the combination. I bought it anyway, on the off chance that if I could get it opened I might find something valuable inside. I found a locksmith in town who claimed to be able to open any safe. So I thought, what the hell, and tried him out. And let me tell you— Bradley, that's his name—was amazing. He didn't use any tools. He simply picked the safe by the use of sight, touch, and sound," Matt explained, standing up to demonstrate how it was done.

"He told me that he feels for what he calls contact points, or areas on the dial where he can feel slight resistance. And sure enough, he spun the dial a few times, rocked it back and forth, and in less than a minute he had the first number of the combination. And in less than fifteen minutes he'd figured out all three numbers and the safe was open. Pretty incredible when you think there's got to be millions of possible options."

"That's pretty impressive. But picking an old house safe in Savannah is a little different than picking a state-of-the-art safe in the Anderson House," Sarah said skeptically.

"I'm telling you, this guy can pick any safe," he said confidently. "He even won an international safecracking competition one time."

"They have that?" Fox asked, surprised.

"According to him, they hold the competition every year in Las Vegas. The winner gets ten grand or something. If he can win a competition like that, then why can't he open the safe in Metcalf's office? All we have to do is sneak him in there and twenty minutes later he'll have it opened," Matt said. His excitement was contagious.

"You think he'll do it? I mean, technically, he'd be breaking the law," Sarah said tentatively, but she was slowly starting to come around to the idea.

"Once I explain to him what Metcalf has done, I'm pretty sure he'll be up for it. Besides, he told me a few stories about his past that led me to believe that he has an unconventional side to him. We'd have to fly him up here, of course, and pay his fees and expenses. But at this point, what other choice do we have?"

"If you think this guy can do it, then we might actually be able to make this work. Metcalf's secretary used to work for me, so I'm sure I can come up with some excuse to get your safecracker past her," Buzz said. "As long as you," he continued, and pointed at Fox, "can get Metcalf out of his office."

Matt was up and out of his seat again. "It's late, but locksmiths are supposed to be available 24/7, right? So what do you think, should I give him a call?" He looked at Sarah.

She didn't hesitate long before she answered, "It's risky, but I don't think we have a choice. Not if we're ever going to get those documents back. And the sooner we act, the less time we give Metcalf to move them out of Anderson House."

That was enough for Matt; he walked outside to get better cell reception. About fifteen minutes later, he returned with a smile on his face. "He'll do it," he said. "It wasn't a layup, but I convinced him that it wasn't really stealing. It was more like returning what was stolen from the good guys. Plus, I doubled his fees," he added.

Buzz moved on to the next task at hand, "Assuming we get the documents back, have you guys decided what you're going to do after that?" The room fell silent.

"Well, not exactly," Fox admitted. "We were kind of focused on the first step."

"Well, my guess is that Mr. Metcalf won't be happy when he discovers he's been had. And you can bet he'll want those documents back. Particularly after the lengths he went to steal them in the first place. So, as we say in the military, we'll need a contingency plan for when he counterattacks, because he will."

"I agree, Buzz, those documents will be like a hot potato until we go public with them. So the sooner we do that the better. That's our out; we'll have to go to the press with our discovery as soon as possible. Once the cat's out of the bag and the world knows about Washington's letter, Metcalf will have no reason to chase after us anymore," Matt reasoned.

"Folks, it's already dark outside and we've still got a long night ahead of us to come up with a plan of action. Why don't you just stay here tonight. We can use the farm as our command center and coordinate our efforts from here," Buzz said, sounding like a flight commander drawing up a top secret mission for his squadron. "I've got plenty of beds."

There were no objections, so he said, "It's settled then. I'll go put a pot of coffee on. It looks like it's going to be a long night."

As retired Colonel Penberthy rummaged about in the kitchen, he seemed to have an extra hop in his step. It was "go time" once again for the navy man and he was feeling a rush. A feeling he thought had long since disappeared from his life.

"I need to take a walk to clear my head before we dive back in. Do you want to join me, Sarah?" Matt asked.

"I'd love to," she said.

He opened the front door and they were greeted by the unseasonably warm and humid evening, the by-product of an Indian summer that had gripped the mid-Atlantic over the past week. Together they made their way outside.

35

Present Day

Charlotte, NC

The campaign of William Washington Emerson had been pumping out rhetoric like an uncapped oil well. With Election Day fast approaching, the "Emerson for President" political spin machine was in overdrive, refuting accusations from its opponent as fast as it created them against him. Press releases, letters, and e-mails flew out like ruffled grouse flushed from the tall grass. Emerson had actually pulled slightly ahead in the most recent CNN poll, for the first time since the race had begun. Chuck Conrad, Emerson's campaign manager, wasn't about to let that slow down the frenetic pace that had been one of the keys to success for the campaign. Conrad was the master strategist behind the incredibly thorough and motivated network of field offices around the country: offices staffed mostly with conservative young volunteers eager for a change in Washington. He was appreciative and amazed at the dedication, passion, and countless hours his minions of volunteers had given to the campaign. But he kept pushing them for even more, with no intention of letting up until Bill Emerson was elected president.

Emerson's feet ached. He was tired after yet another long day of campaigning and he relished the chance to relax in his deluxe two-bedroom suite on the twenty-second floor of the Hilton Hotel in downtown Charlotte. He sat in an overstuffed chair in the connecting sitting room. One hand cradled a scotch on the rocks and the other rubbed his sockless feet. Chuck Conrad walked into the room to join him.

"Dammit, that blister's come back again. I think I need new shoes, Chuck. Those wingtips are too damn tight," complained Big Bill.

"How's the voice? You sound a little hoarse. You know, you should probably be drinking herbal tea, not Johnny Walker Black on the rocks," Chuck said.

"Fuck that, my body needs the scotch more than my voice needs the tea," he said.

"Yeah, well, we still got a long way to go, partner, so you need to take care of yourself. Nobody's going to vote for a guy limping around like an old man with big bags under his eyes," Conrad teased.

"You know, you don't look so hot yourself," he said.

"That's because I've got a lot going on right now. Between interview requests, preparing for debates, lining up speeches, and keeping you looking pretty, it's no wonder I look like shit," he said.

"Hey, speaking of pretty, who was that staffer you introduced me to today?"

"Don't even go there, Bill. One, she's married. Two, you're married, for a second time. Three, we don't need anything upsetting the applecart right now."

"I was just asking, Chuck. Damn, man, you need to lighten up. We're kicking ass; some polls even show us leading the race now, right?"

"We're doing great, and it's my job to make sure nothing gets in the way of our continued success. That's why you saw me talking to J. J. Stanton earlier today," he said. Conrad had decided that it was time to tell Bill about the discovery of the journal.

"I meant to ask you about that. Are you adding him to our security team?"

"You could say that. I hired Stanton preemptively, so to speak, to remove a potential obstacle for us," Conrad said, somewhat vaguely.

"What kind of obstacle?" Bill said, holding his icy glass against the stinging blister on his foot. He hoped it would provide some temporary relief.

"The kind that can cause me and you headaches," said Conrad. Over the next few minutes, Chuck laid out the events that had occurred in Savannah, from the journal's discovery to the alleged existence of the surrender letter from Washington to his authorizing Stanton to steal it.

Ever since he had received the phone call from his nephew, Conrad's mind had been preoccupied. He had worked through a myriad of potential scenarios, trying to determine how big a threat Caty Greene's journal posed to the Emerson campaign. If the journal were to become public, he had reasoned, her claims regarding a surrender letter from Washington would almost certainly become national news. Not only because he was the country's original Founding Father, but because the Emerson campaign had explicitly linked its conservative values with those of the revered Washington—right down to plastering his image on the campaign bus. The revelation would undoubtedly make some feel that Washington was really just a chickenshit who wanted to surrender rather than fight for his country. Not exactly the imagery Conrad had in mind when he had recommended to Big Bill that the campaign hijack Washington's patriotic persona to promote their righteous agenda.

He had concluded that if the journal became public, the liberal press would descend like flies on an open wound. They'd ask

Emerson all sorts of inane questions about his forbearer, which would be distracting to the campaign, at the very least. It could even create enough of a public relations circus to cost him a half point in the polls. And in a deadlocked race, that could be the difference between winning and losing. Conrad knew from his experience as a litigator that their Democratic opponent would not let the opportunity slip by without at least attempting to seed some doubt in the minds of the electorate. He could envision the placards at Democratic rallies that would read "Surrender Emerson!" That's exactly what he would do, if the situation were reversed. He also knew that strange events and accusations, no matter how far-fetched, had caused candidates to lose votes in the past. The birther conspiracy that had been concocted in a previous election was proof that it didn't take much to seed doubt and cost critical votes.

The American public had proven themselves to be fickle in the past, so Conrad had come to a quick decision. To preserve Big Bill's chances of ever sitting in the Oval Office, he needed to put a lid on the story, and quickly. There simply was no room for a misstep this late in the election. That's when he had scrolled through his contact list until he found the name Stanton Security and called J. J. Stanton to make the problem go away.

"Jesus Christ, Chuck, you actually had Stanton break into somebody's house?!" Big Bill said. He got up from his chair, ice rattling noisily in his glass tumbler. "That was a hell of a risk, don't you think?"

"I take a lot of risks, Bill, calculated ones. That's what I do and I'm damned good at it. And in case you've forgotten, my risks have saved your ass plenty of times in the past," Conrad said, pointing at Emerson emphatically with his index finger.

"Yeah, but this time you broke the law, Chuck." He stood up so his back was to Conrad. He stared out of the large picture window, looking down at the lights of downtown Charlotte far below him. He dared not look his campaign manager in the eye, because when Conrad got angry like this, he scared the hell out of him.

"It's too late to take the high road now, Bill, especially after all the shit you've pulled over the years. You know damn well that I've broken the law for you in the past. And you know that I'll break it again if it means protecting our chances of winning the election. We're in this thing to win, at all costs. So save me the righteous indignation," he finished, as if lecturing an idealistic student. He could only see Emerson's blurry reflection in the window, so he couldn't make out how Bill had reacted to his dressing down.

Bill knew his objection sounded hollow. He was well aware of Conrad's reputation for playing dirty. He had been accused of strong-arm tactics, or worse, many times in the past, especially when feeling threatened. During his senatorial campaign, one of Bill's junior staffer's had turned up dead. This occurred shortly after Conrad found out that the staffer was planning to go public with damaging dirt on Emerson. The police attributed it to an "overdose." But some believed the death to be a little too coincidental, especially since the staffer had not been known to use drugs.

The two men remained silent, letting their emotions settle. Conrad knew he had probably come on too strong, but at the moment he didn't care. He had painstakingly crafted a campaign from nothing and put it on the path toward victory. It was his idea to leverage Washington's squeaky-clean image to their advantage. And lest anyone forget, it was *he* who had taken an overweight, spoiled rich kid with a reputation for less-than-intellectual pursuits and turned him into the Republican nominee for president of the United States. Chuck felt entitled to the White House; he had earned it. *You're damn right I broke the law*, he thought to himself. *And I'll do it again if necessary.*

Bill finally broke the silence. "You really think anyone would have cared about something written in a two-hundred-year-old journal?"

"Not under normal circumstances. But when the person is George Washington and the journal in question claims that he offered to surrender to the British, then yes, I think people would have cared. Especially when we've got his mug plastered on everything related to this campaign. The press would have had a field day given your lineage. And that could have easily cost us the election. Let me make myself clear, I don't want the word *surrender* and Bill Emerson ever mentioned in the same sentence!"

"You really think it could have cost us the election?"

"Stranger rumors have sunk candidates in the past. Don't ever underestimate the damage that a controversial claim can inflict, no matter how remote. I wasn't going to let that scenario play out, so I made the problem go away. Preemptive damage control, if you will," he said smugly.

"So where's the book now?" Bill asked. He returned to his seat and resumed massaging his calloused feet.

"It's safely locked away." Conrad didn't mention the fact that he had sent it to Charles Metcalf in Washington. Bill had no knowledge of their illicit partnership. Conrad would have to tell Bill one day, but today was not that day. He removed his necktie and tossed it across the back of the chair, glad to have that conversation out of the way.

Emerson looked up with panic in his eyes and said, "You don't think it's possible that the surrender letter could have survived all these years, do you?"

"I think that's highly doubtful, but we're not taking any chances. Stanton's team has returned to Savannah to keep an eye on the folks who found the journal, just in case they're tempted to stir up any more trouble." Again Conrad only told Bill the sparsest of details. He held back that the letter had probably already been discovered and was back in D.C. by now.

"Got to hand it to you, Chuck, you see things most people wouldn't see."

"Like I've always told you, Bill," he replied, considering the man who represented his ticket to the White House, "your charm and my balls are going to take us far."

An unsettling Cheshire grin crept across Conrad's face.

36

Present Day

Fredericksburg, VA

The heavy, early fall air was filled with the sound of crickets, singing out as if they knew their days were numbered. Matt and Sarah walked slowly in the direction of the dairy barn, enjoying a brief respite from the frantic pace of the last few days. The outline of the large silo rose ominously in front of them in the early evening dusk, like a solitary sentry standing watch over Bingo Field. The smell of sweet hay, fresh-cut grass, and manure assaulted their senses. It reminded them that this place was real and that the journey that had brought them there had not been a dream.

"I still can't believe that this is all really happening," Sarah said. She pulled a piece of hay out of a bound bale stacked next to the barn and twisted it anxiously between two fingers. Her body was tense with nervous energy. "If you hadn't called me to ask my opinion on Caty's journal, I'd probably be preparing a lesson plan for my students right now or quietly researching my next book."

"Is that what you'd rather be doing?" he asked.

After a brief pause, she stopped and looked up at him. "No," she replied, "it's not that. I'm just not used to all of this—breaking into monuments, being held at gunpoint, and hiring safecrackers. It's quite a change from being curled up on my couch with a mug of herbal tea, grading term papers."

She went quiet for a moment before continuing, "This experience has made me realize just how ordinary my life has been up to now. It's been one planned move after another. After I graduated from college, I had already decided to go to grad school. Then the book happened, then teaching. My life has been so boring and predictable," she paused again, "until you came along."

They stopped walking. Sarah's green eyes glistened in the reflection of the spotlight that shone down on them from the corner of the dairy barn. They stood there, like two actors sharing a scene at center stage.

Matt smiled and said, "I know this has been a whirlwind, and it's not like I'm used to this kind of lifestyle either. But I have to admit, I feel more alive than I have in years. The thrill of discovery, the historical intrigue, and even the danger that we've experienced together is so real, so tangible. It's everything that Wall Street wasn't to me. So I wouldn't change a thing that's happened. Especially the thing that got it all started," he said, "making that first call to you."

He reached out his hand and pushed back a strand of hair that had blown across Sarah's face. The wind had picked up and a gust rustled the leaves on the trees surrounding the paddock. A rumble of thunder signaled an imminent storm. But neither Sarah nor Matt seemed to notice. She leaned into his palm as it brushed against her cheek. His hand slipped behind her neck and he pulled her toward him. Her full lips parted in anticipation as he leaned down to kiss her. Their mouths met. A flash of lightning lit up the night sky, as if ignited by their sexual tension. They held their first kiss a long time, oblivious to the tempest that was building around them. The first big drops of rain splashed on their faces and broke the spell. They reluctantly pulled back from one another.

"I've wanted to do that for a very long time," he said.

She smiled and replied, "And I've wanted you to do that for a very long time."

Then, all at once, the rain started to come down hard. Matt saw a small shed under construction about twenty yards to their right. Hand in hand, they made a run for it. Laughing and screaming, they crashed through the front door. It appeared to be an old loafing shed that Buzz must have been in the midst of converting into a small guest cottage. It was near completion but still had some tarps and tools lying about. They were dripping wet, but safe from the deluge that was coming down outside.

The electrical work had not yet been completed so it was dark inside the shed. There was barely enough light to see, but every thirty seconds, a flash of lightning would light up the inside of their little bungalow. It was as if paparazzi were camped outside, trying to catch the two lovers on film. Matt stripped off his shirt and shook it out.

"You should take that off," he said, motioning to her top with a mischievous grin. "You wouldn't want to catch a cold."

She hesitated just for a moment, then unbuttoned her shirt and slipped it off. Their hands were on each other in an instant, groping like a couple of overheated teenagers in the backseat of a Buick. Thunder shook their makeshift shelter. They stumbled their way across the room to a newly installed couch. They pulled and tugged at each other's clothes, until there was nothing left to remove. Then their hurried pace slowed and they took their time exploring each other's bodies, not wanting to rush through what each of them had been anticipating for some time.

Sarah trembled slightly at Matt's touch. He slowly kissed his way across her breasts, then along her soft, flat belly. When at last he worked his way downward, she thrust her hips up to meet his mouth. Her nails dug into his shoulders and she came quickly. They shifted positions and she climbed on top of him. As he entered her, she ran her hands across his chest and muscular arms. He propelled her up and down. She willingly gave in to him, rocking like a small boat, in perfect rhythm on the swells of the powerful ocean that churned beneath her. She leaned forward and her hair fell across his face. The rain hammered against the roof of the shed. Another clap of thunder rumbled above them. They were one in the ecstasy of the moment. It was perfect.

Afterward, lying naked, with her head on his chest and her leg draped languidly across his, she said, "I'm glad you made that call to me too, Matt."

His thumb gently traced the curve of her jaw. Her hair smelled like a mixture of honey and wildflowers. "To be honest, the only reason I called was because the online article I read included a really cute head shot of you," he kidded.

Sarah twisted her body around, and propped herself up on one elbow. She smiled and said, "You mean it wasn't my academic credentials that led you to choose me?"

"You have academic credentials?" he countered sarcastically. He expected to get an elbow in the ribs for his comment. He did.

They lay there quietly for some time, enjoying the warmth of each other's bodies. Sarah suddenly turned serious. "Matt," she said tentatively, "what just happened doesn't normally happen to me. Actually, it never happens to me. I've only had three serious relationships in my life, and the last one didn't end well. But your spontaneity is so contagious that I find myself doing things I normally wouldn't do. Wait; that came out wrong," she stammered. "Don't get me wrong, I wanted to do what we just did. God knows, I could use more spontaneity in my life," she paused because she hated when she rambled, which she always did when she was nervous. So she finished quickly, "I just don't want to get hurt again, that's all."

The rain was letting up and the choir of crickets had begun to return from their forced intermission. Matt said quietly, "Sarah, the morning when we first met, when you walked into that little breakfast joint, something sort of gave way inside me. It's hard to explain," he stopped, searching for the right words, "but after my divorce, I pretty much gave up on relationships. I just figured I wasn't very good at them. Over time I built up a kind of protective wall around myself. I kept everyone at arm's length."

He could feel her heart beating quickly against his chest. He wondered if she could feel his. "I know it sounds corny, Sarah, but there was a goodness that radiated from you that just felt so right to me. And for the first time in a long time, I let somebody get behind the wall. So the last thing I would ever do is hurt you." His voice caught in his throat as he spoke with more feeling than he had anticipated.

Sarah felt for his face and she kissed him long and hard. Matt wasn't sure if the moistness on her cheeks was from the rain or her tears. It didn't really matter. He held on to her tightly. They lay there quietly, listening to the low rolling sounds of thunder fade slowly into the distance. The rain had finally stopped. The storm was over. But neither of them wanted to let go of the moment.

———

They reappeared in Buzz's kitchen looking a bit disheveled, a noticeable flush in their cheeks. "Sorry guys," Matt said, trying unsuccessfully to restore order to his ruffled mop, "we got caught in the downpour and took shelter in a converted shed. The one that looks like it's in the middle of being made into a guesthouse."

"Ah, my first guests in the dacha. I'm building that for my grandkids so they can have sleepovers away from the adults. Glad it came in, uh, handy," Buzz said, hiding a smirk after exchanging a quick glance with Director Fox.

"Yeah, well, anyway, where's that coffee you were brewing?" Matt said, quickly changing the subject. He grabbed a cup and joined the group sitting around the kitchen table.

"We were just discussing the point you made earlier. Assuming we're able to steal the documents back, we'll need to move fast with a plan to go public with Washington's letter. Because the more we wait around, the more opportunity we give Metcalf and his hired guns to strike back," Fox said, already halfway through his second cup of coffee.

"No doubt about it, that letter is a threat to us until we go public with it," replied Matt.

"Exactly what do you mean by threat?" Sarah said, concerned. The glow that had radiated from her face just moments earlier dissipated all at once.

"He means we need to plan very carefully so we can stay two steps ahead of Mr. Metcalf," Buzz said reassuringly, reaching over and patting the back of Sarah's hand.

"That's right, so let's start by talking about *how* we should go public with the documents," Matt said. He looked over at Sarah for guidance. She had a hell of a lot more experience with the press than he did. He also knew if he kept her mind busy, then she wouldn't have time to worry so much.

"Well," she said, after some consideration, "I think we should go to the most reputable news outlets we can find. We should try to orchestrate a very public press conference, to ensure maximum press coverage. That way the genie will be out of the bottle and Metcalf will call off his dogs."

"Sarah, we've both published books," Fox said. "Our publishing reps must know a few good reporters in New York."

"You read my mind, James. I was just thinking the same thing," Sarah replied. "I think we should make some calls first thing in the morning and see if we can't drum up some help.

I'm sure we can find an in somewhere—the publishing world is pretty close-knit."

"Perfect, and while you guys do that, I'll take on organizing the press conference. I'm assuming we'll want to hold it in Savannah to lend authenticity to the story, right?" Matt asked.

"Definitely," replied Sarah. "Right in front of Greene's monument in Johnson Square would be the perfect spot, if that's even possible."

"Anything is possible," Matt said with a confident wink.

"And I'll take care of Metcalf," said Buzz, the twinkle in his blue eyes replaced by a cold, hard stare. "I've still got a few friends on the society's board of directors, and I think they'll be very interested in hearing about the recent activities of our president general."

"Just be careful, Buzz. Clearly he's not a guy to be messed with," Fox cautioned.

"Neither am I, James," he said. Nobody doubted him for a second. The ex-military man avowed, "We're going to bring the fight to Mr. Metcalf, fast and hard, and on multiple fronts. He's not going to know what hit him."

"What time are you picking up our safecracker from Reagan National Airport tomorrow, Matt?" Fox asked, happy to be shifting the conversation away from Metcalf.

"I should be there and back by noon at the latest," he said.

"Well then, that gives us the rest of tonight and most of the day tomorrow to devise a plan to steal the documents back from the safe in Metcalf's office. And to develop the details of our plan to go public with the press," Fox said, leaning back and stretching his back.

"Do you think that's enough time?" Sarah asked, stifling a yawn. It had been a long and eventful day.

"We don't have a choice. Metcalf could move the documents out of Anderson House at any time. We have to move now,"

Matt said, without a trace of exhaustion. On the contrary, he appeared to be picking up steam.

"All right then, let's get down to business," Buzz said. "Who's got an idea for how to get into Metcalf's office without being detected?"

—

The next day was a blur of activity. As promised, Matt was back from the airport by noon with Bradley the locksmith in tow. They briefed him on his role in the planned theft and decided to spend one more night at the farmhouse. They would set out first thing the next morning to deploy the first part of their offensive, stealing the journal and the surrender letter back from the president general's office in Anderson House. They were ready. But they also understood that, even if Bradley could successfully crack the safe, there was no guarantee that Metcalf hadn't already moved the documents to a new location.

And if he had, their hopes of ever recovering the priceless artifacts would be gone forever.

37

Present Day

Pittsburgh, PA

E merson's campaign caravan arrived in Pennsylvania to canvas the Keystone State for the next six days. It was the final opportunity to convince voters that its candidate was the right man for the job. Pennsylvania's twenty electoral votes were up for grabs, making it the largest of the remaining battleground geographies.

Conrad and Emerson were dressed in tuxedos, headed to a black-tie fund-raising affair in downtown Pittsburgh. Emerson looked like an overstuffed penguin as he fidgeted in the backseat of the Suburban. The bulletproof car was being driven by a secret service detail who had been assigned to Big Bill after he was named the Republican nominee for president the prior June.

The two men sat side by side in the backseat. The Steel City's skyline could be seen in the distance through the vehicle's tinted windows. They had just crossed over the Fort Pitt Bridge, a double-decker arched structure that spanned the Monongahela River near its confluence with the Allegheny River. Bill ran a finger underneath his collar. The tight-fitting starched color had his neck in a choke hold.

"Goddammit, Chuck, I think I've gotten fatter. I barely fit into this fucking thing anymore," Bill barked at Conrad.

Thankfully, Chuck's phone rang, saving him from an uncomfortable conversation with his boss. He had grown weary of Big Bill's emotional rants, which had increased in frequency over the past couple of weeks. But now that the finish line was in sight, he had held his tongue more often than not. He dutifully played the role of therapist, coaxing Emerson like a reticent child toward Election Day—and the ultimate prize, the White House. After seeing that the call was from Charles Metcalf, his first impulse was to let it go to voice mail. He'd rather listen to Big Bill bitch and moan about his expanding girth than be patronized by the cold son of a bitch waiting on the other end of the line. But he knew that given the recent events in Savannah, there was no avoiding the call.

"Conrad," he grunted.

"I've got the document," Metcalf said, bypassing any greeting.

"They actually found it?" Conrad replied in amazement.

"Right where they thought it would be, in the cornerstone of Greene's monument. Director Fox and his two friends from Savannah delivered it right to my doorstep. Of course, they thought they were bringing it here to be authenticated. So they were a bit disappointed when they left empty-handed."

"They went to a hell of a lot of trouble to find the letter; they really just left without a fight?" Conrad asked. He had to hold up a hand to quiet an agitated Emerson. Big Bill had been assured by Conrad that there was no way the actual surrender letter could still exist, so he was apoplectic when he realized that Conrad had been lying to him.

"They really didn't have a choice, considering I have the letter as well as the journal that you couriered to me. They had nothing left to prove that Washington ever even considered surrendering to the British. And just to be safe, I also removed Larz Anderson's journal from the archives here at the society."

"What about your man Fox, is he going to be a problem?"

"Mr. Fox reports to me, and if he wants to keep his job then he'll forget all about the surrender letter. I don't think he'll be willing to risk his scholarly reputation on a scandalous claim against our first president. Especially considering that he doesn't have a shred of evidence to back up the claim. No, you have my guarantee that this is over. You can return your undivided attention to getting that Texas-sized buffoon elected president."

Conrad changed the subject. "Our Washington strategy continues to be received favorably by the crowds. So based on what you just told me, I don't see any risk in continuing to borrow from the Founding Father's patriotic image right up until Election Day."

"By all means, if that's what it takes to get the American public to trust Emerson, carry on with the greatest of confidence. I can assure you that the letter is securely locked away in my safe. So Washington will remain as beloved as ever by the flag-waving American public you seem to be so fond of."

After Conrad hung up, Big Bill launched a barrage of fiery questions. It took the rest of the drive into town to calm him down. By the time they arrived at the fund-raising event, Conrad had convinced him that everything was under control. The surrender letter was no longer going to be a problem.

If Emerson had noticed the worried look on his campaign manager's face however, he may not have felt so assured.

38

Present Day

Washington, D.C.

Director Fox returned to work at Anderson House. It had been two days since Metcalf's shocking double cross. To anyone who might have passed by his open door that morning, it appeared as though he was at his desk working like any other day. But he wasn't working. In fact, he could barely think straight.

Buzz should have called by now, but he hadn't. And this had Fox's insides churning. He silently chided himself for drinking too much coffee on the commute back into D.C. from Fredericksburg. He was about to check in to see if the operation had been aborted, when his cell phone chirped. He answered on the first ring.

"Fox here," he said anxiously.

"It's Buzz, we're across the street. Set the plan in motion, we're sending Hank over there now. Be sure to hit redial on your phone when Metcalf is with you so we know it's clear to come over." He spoke in a clipped military tone.

They had flown Hank to D.C. at the last minute, after finally agreeing on a viable plan for getting Metcalf to vacate his office so that Bradley could get inside to steal the documents. Because security was heaviest after hours, they decided to strike during regular office hours. They had no intention of dealing with alarm systems, motion sensors, and armed guards.

The problem was that during the day, Metcalf never left his office. Not even to take lunch. Matt had finally come up with the solution to have Hank pose as a wealthy new member interested in donating a large sum of money to the society. He would show up at Anderson House unannounced and ask for a tour of the museum. And, most importantly, he would insist that President General Metcalf be his guide.

Matt's reasoning was that Metcalf couldn't resist the entice-ment of money. And this would draw him out of his office like a rat to cheese. Fox had to convince Metcalf to come down-stairs and spend at least thirty minutes with Hank. That should be enough time for Bradley, their safecracker, to get inside the office, break into the safe, and get out again. After Buzz had described the wall safe model to him, Bradley estimated that he would only need twenty minutes, maybe less, to get the job done. They hoped he wasn't being overconfident.

Fox made his way down the hall to Metcalf's office. He approached the president general's assistant, who was sitting at her desk directly outside his office. "Good morning, Joan," he said, "is he in? I have an unexpected visitor downstairs who would like to meet the president general." He hoped she didn't notice his frayed nerves. It felt to him like his whole body was shaking.

"Good morning, James. He's in. Let me tell him you're here," she replied warmly. Joan Ross had been at the society for more than twenty years. She had been the executive assistant to the office of the president general for fifteen of those years. She had worked for Buzz prior to Metcalf and for three other presi-dent general's prior to Buzz's tenure. Even though she was one of the kindest people Fox had ever met, he thought even she must dislike the man sequestered behind the closed door directly in front of her desk. She was very professional, however, and would never let on even if she despised the man.

Metcalf always kept his door locked, so Fox had to wait until the frail little specter emerged from his inner sanctum. "Well, I see you finally decided to return to work," he scoffed, a sour look on his face, as he referred to Fox's absence for the past two days.

"I had a forty-eight-hour stomach bug, but I'm feeling better today," Fox lied.

"I'm sure you are," Metcalf said with a smirk. "So what is it you want?"

"There's a new member here who has paid an unexpected visit to D.C. and he'd like to meet you. He's downstairs right now." He motioned toward the stairwell at the end of the hall and added, "I told him I'd see if you could spare a few minutes."

"What on earth made you think that I would want to do that?" Metcalf asked, dumbfounded by the absurdity of the request.

Fox stole a glance over to Joan, who looked away quickly so as not to show her embarrassment. He said, "He owns an industrial refrigeration company and he's considering making a large donation to the society as a thank you for his membership. Not the most exotic of industries, I'll admit, but he is evidently quite wealthy. He's also quite enthusiastic about being a member of our organization. I wouldn't have bothered you if this was just any member, but this guy is what you might call a heavy hitter." Matt had told him to lay it on thick because the more money that Metcalf could sniff out, the more likely he would be to make an effort.

"What's his name?" Metcalf asked skeptically, but Fox could tell that his interest had been piqued. The hook was set, now all he had to do was reel him in.

"His name is Toby Morton." Hank had insisted on using the name of Martha Sampson's father, the man to whom the journal

had belonged so many years before. They decided it was a harmless twist of irony, so they let Hank have his fun.

"Never heard of him. In the refrigeration business you say?"
he asked.

"International refrigeration; evidently they manufacture in
China and ship all over the world," Fox said, knowing it was
time to tug on the line a bit. Matt had coached him that to close
the deal he should threaten to walk away. Sharks didn't like their
chum taken out from under their noses. "I can see you're very
busy, so I'll just tell him maybe some other time." He turned to
leave, but inside he was dying, because he knew that if Metcalf
didn't stop him, their entire plan was finished before it even
began.

He hadn't taken more than a step or two when Metcalf cleared
his throat, "Hold on a minute, Director Fox, I guess I can spare a
few minutes." Turning to Joan, he said, "I'll be back shortly."

Fox exhaled so loudly that he thought he had given himself away, but Metcalf wasn't paying any attention. The two men
started to make their way downstairs to greet Toby, a.k.a. Hank.
Fox discreetly reached into his pants pocket and pulled out his
cell phone. He hit the redial button and hung up after three rings,
the prearranged signal that Metcalf had vacated his office.

Five minutes later, Buzz and Bradley made their way across
the street and into Anderson House. After climbing the steep
staircase to the second floor, they approached Joan's desk.

"Well, hello there, gorgeous," Buzz said loudly, startling Joan
as she typed at her computer.

"Buzz!" she exclaimed, and got up and gave her old boss a
warm embrace. "What are you doing here?"

"I was in town with my nephew here," he motioned to
Bradley, "and I just had to stop by and say hello to one of my
favorite people." Buzz released Joan from a mini bear hug.
"Bradley, say hello to one of the finest people you'll ever meet."

Introductions and small talk were dispatched with quickly. Buzz talked Joan into joining him in the kitchen for a cup of coffee, under the pretense of getting caught up. Bradley said that he would join them after visiting the bathroom. Buzz told him the way, and then escorted Joan toward the opposite end of the hall.

Bradley waited for them to disappear around the corner and then quickly returned to Metcalf's office. Fox had warned him that the door would be locked. But that proved to be only a minor roadblock. He had it picked in less than thirty seconds. Inside, he found the safe right where Buzz told him it would be. So far, so good. He put a pair of sweatbands on around his wrists and started the stopwatch function on his watch. He had fifteen minutes at most to open the safe and get the hell out of there.

Downstairs, Hank was doing his best to keep Metcalf talking. He had studied up a bit on the fundamentals of the refrigeration industry, enough to be believable. But he spent the majority of his time dropping hints as to the extent of his wealth.

Hank said, "Enough about me, Mr. Metcalf, please tell me how I can help you. I told the very capable Mr. Fox here that in appreciation for granting me membership, I'm contemplating making a gift to the society. Perhaps even a sizable one."

"I'm sure that could be arranged. How sizable a gift did you have in mind?" Metcalf inquired. The shark had officially picked up the scent.

"Well, before we get down to brass tacks, why don't you show me around a bit. I'd like to get acquainted with the place." Hank stalled. He was trying his best to assume a nasal midwestern tone, to hide his natural southern drawl.

Fox seized the opportunity to keep the ruse going. "Absolutely, let's start right over here," he said, walking to his left.

Metcalf looked down at his watch and hesitated for a moment. Fox was afraid he might be thinking about begging off.

He seemed to reconsider, however, and followed the two men into the formal reception room. Known as the Key Room, it was named after a Greek key motif inlaid in white marble on the floor.

Back upstairs, Bradley had already secured one number of the combination and was working on number two. Without the aid of an earpiece or an electronic listening device, the wiry fingers of his right hand spun the dial, feeling for the imperceptible tremors in his fingertips. If he found an area of slight resistance, it would signal to him that he had found another number. It took him about four more minutes to determine the second number. He knew that finding the last number would simply be a process of elimination. It was just a matter of time now before he opened the safe. But time was running short—shorter than even he anticipated.

Metcalf's patience for entertaining his unexpected guest had run out, so he abruptly excused himself. Fox knew that he needed to delay him for at least five more minutes, so he called after his boss. Metcalf kept on walking, ignoring Fox as if he were a mongrel dog sniffing at his pant leg. Desperate to stop him from leaving, Fox reached out and grabbed Metcalf's elbow.

The quirky little man jerked away violently and almost tripped over backward, as if he had just been scalded with a branding iron. "What are you doing?" he spat. He massaged his arm as if to soothe some phantom pain.

"Sorry, sir," Fox stammered, "but we're not done giving Mr. Morton his tour." He fumbled for something, anything, to say that would keep Metcalf occupied for just a few more precious minutes. "I mean, we don't want to jeopardize that potential sizable donation he mentioned, do we?"

"Mr. Fox, I don't care about his donation. The only reason I came down here was to see if he might have potential as an investor in my hedge fund. Unfortunately, I've made the determination that he is not. So I'm done here." He once again turned and walked away.

"But, sir, I really must insist that you," but Fox didn't have the chance to finish his sentence. Metcalf spun around and gave him a look that made the words dry up and stick to the roof of his mouth like peanut butter.

"And don't *ever* touch me again," Metcalf seethed, a bony finger pointed in Fox's face. He held his gaze an extra beat, then left for the third and final time. Fox hoped that he had given Bradley enough time.

Bradley had the final number. After coolly entering the last part of the combination, he stood up straight and took a deep breath. This was his favorite part of the job. He grabbed the safe's lever and swung the thick steel door open. His face was a mixture of pride and relief. Only sixteen minutes, and that included the time he and Buzz had spent talking to Metcalf's assistant. He knew that what he had just done would have taken another locksmith at least two or three hours to accomplish, and with a lot more tools.

His euphoria was short-lived, however. The handle on the office door had started to turn. Someone was coming. In one motion he pushed the safe door closed and crouched behind Metcalf's large desk. A split second later the office door swung open.

Metcalf thought he heard a noise inside his office. But when he opened the door, there was nobody there. He closed the door behind him and walked toward his desk.

Bradley was sweating profusely. He tried to calm his breathing so as not to give himself away, which seemed futile at this point. He was trapped. He would be discovered in a matter of seconds. He said a quick prayer and readied to spring from his crouched position to make a run for the door.

Then the demons came. They spread out from the spot on Metcalf's elbow where Fox had touched him a few moments earlier and began to claw up his arm. He knew that the only thing that would restore order to his tormented mind now was a thorough cleansing with soap and water. But he had to hurry. He could feel the bad thoughts taking over. He left the office abruptly and headed straight for the men's bathroom.

Bradley was confused when he heard the office door open and close once more. Unsure of what to do, he tentatively peered around the edge of the desk. To his surprise and relief, he saw that the office was empty. He was alone again. Without hesitation, he stood up and reopened the safe door. His nerves were shot and he was on borrowed time. So he grabbed the entire contents of the safe and stuffed it all into the leather flight bag Buzz had given him earlier. He was out of the office less than thirty seconds later. He had just closed Metcalf's office door behind him and was headed around the corner when he collided head on into the President General himself.

"Hey, who are you?" Metcalf said accusingly, "You're not supposed to be here." He was completely flustered, trying to disentangle himself from Bradley. He had been touched again and it was almost too much to bear. The demons had begun to reappear.

"Excuse me, I was looking for the bathroom and must have taken a wrong turn," Bradley lied, moving on quickly without stopping to look back. Metcalf started to call out to him, but the urge to return to the sanctity of his office and restore order in his tormented mind, took precedence.

Bradley quickly found Buzz in the kitchen and gave him the thumbs-up and an anxious jerk of the head. Buzz received the unspoken message loud and clear. The two men said an abbreviated good-bye to Joan and then made a hasty retreat. They fought the urge to break into a run. Hank and Fox were waiting at the bottom of the stairs, and the four men exited the building together. They double-timed it down the wide, granite front steps. Sarah and Matt were waiting in Fox's and Buzz's cars, respectively. They scrambled into the vehicles and were under way before the car doors slammed shut.

"Did you get it?" Matt shouted at Bradley, who was breathing heavily in the backseat.

"I didn't have time to pick and choose, so I just grabbed everything," Bradley said, still slightly out of breath.

"What do you mean you took everything?" Matt pivoted his head around.

"Hey, I didn't exactly have time to put my feet up and read the paper, if you know what I mean," he said, annoyed at the grilling.

"Shit, I'm sorry, Bradley; I didn't mean to question you. But are you really not sure if the letter and the journal are in there?" Matt asked anxiously, gripping the steering wheel even harder.

"Well, I did see that metal cylinder you described to me," he said.

"Really?" Matt and Buzz said in unison.

"Yeah, it's in there but I'm not sure about the journal. There were a few books. And like I said, I just grabbed them all. Here you go," he said, and passed the flight bag forward to Buzz, riding shotgun.

Like a bad surveillance tail, Sarah was following very close behind Matt's car. They were about a half mile from the southbound on-ramp to the highway that would take them back to Bingo Field. Sarah and Fox, however, would split off and head in the opposite direction, continuing straight to the airport. They had to fly to New York to meet with some press contacts that Sarah's publishing company had arranged for them.

Buzz zipped open the bag and dug in. In short order, he pulled out Whitney's metal cylinder. He checked to make sure the document was still inside; it was. He dug a little further. Finally, Buzz held up the small leather-bound book with the faded gold inlay design on the cover. Matt let out a loud and relieved yelp. They had pulled it off!

Buzz grabbed Matt's phone from the console and dialed Sarah. After Buzz shared the good news, Matt rolled down his window and thrust a jubilant fist in the air. Sarah blew him an exaggerated kiss in return. A few minutes later, the two cars peeled off in opposite directions. The first part of the battle plan had been executed.

It was time to initiate phase two: a war that would be fought on three separate fronts.

39

Present Day

Washington, D.C.

It took him longer than usual to beat back the dark thoughts. He had been touched, twice, in the span of a few minutes. And that had set his world spinning off its axis. After returning to his office, he struggled to regain control of his warped mind. He arranged and rearranged his desk until everything was placed just right. He meticulously searched his five-thousand-dollar Italian suit, top to bottom, in search of a piece of lint or a stray hair. He found none, but it kept his mind occupied and safe from the shadow creatures that had been closing in. Finally, he slathered his hands with sanitizer yet one more time, grimacing in pain as the alcohol burned his already chafed skin. When he could finally breathe normally again, his analytical mind was freed up to replay the events of that morning. Something began to gnaw at him. He picked up his phone and dialed his assistant, Joan.

"I'd like you to search the member database for a man named Toby Morton. Evidently he was recently admitted to the society. And do it quickly," he ordered.

A few minutes later, she called back. She informed him that there was nobody by that name in the database. He slammed the phone down and quickly made his way outside to her work desk.

"Are you sure? I told you he was a *new* member. Perhaps there's a separate list for that."

Joan replied professionally, "There's only one directory and there is nobody in it listed by that name. The database was just updated last week." She handed him the computer printout so he could see for himself. "Toby Morton is not a member of the Society of the Cincinnati."

"But that can't be. Director Fox took me downstairs to meet a man named Toby Morton. He owned a refrigeration business and he wanted to make a large donation," he recited the facts of his meeting, as if stating them made them true. He scanned the printout but could not find the name. A shadow fell over his face, like a curtain after the closing act. He said, "Tell Mr. Fox I'd like to see him in my office, *immediately*."

"I'm afraid that's impossible, sir. Director Fox left the building with Buzz Penberthy close to an hour ago, and he hasn't returned," she said matter-of-factly.

"Buzz Penberthy, my predecessor?" Metcalf said, in confusion.

"Yes, he was in town this morning with his nephew and they stopped by to say hello. They left in quite a hurry. Maybe that's why you missed them."

Metcalf's brilliant mind was spinning like a Rubik's cube. When all at once the puzzle began to click into place, he said, "This nephew—was he tall and lanky, with his hair tied back in a ponytail?" He knew the answer to his question even before Joan's reply.

"Yes, that's him. So you met him?" she asked.

"No, not exactly," he muttered over his shoulder. He returned to his office and slammed the door shut behind him. He didn't have time to make sure it was shut just right. Demons be damned, he thought. He raced over to the wall safe and quickly entered the combination. He swung open the door; it was empty. His legs nearly gave way beneath him. Not only were the Washington-related documents gone, everything was gone. He was losing control of the situation.

He fell into his chair. Perspiration beaded on his brow, and Charles Metcalf was not a man who sweated. He picked up his phone, and the sight of his red hands revolted him. The first call was to his security team. He ordered them to go directly to an address in Fredericksburg, listed in the member directory as the home of former president general Buzz Penberthy. They were instructed to use all means necessary to retrieve the contents of the safe.

The second call that he had to make was going to be much more unpleasant.

———

The Emerson campaign was in high gear with barely a month to go before the election. Press appearances, speeches, and glad-handing kept Big Bill busy from sunup to sundown. He was exhausted. But no matter how spent he felt on the inside, he never let it show in front of potential voters. He had a unique talent to morph from a fat, spoiled man-child to a vibrant, charming candidate the moment he walked onto a stage or stepped in front of a camera. It was a gift, one that had carried him to the precipice of the office of president of the United States.

Emerson was in full showman mode. He stood at the podium, entertaining a luncheon audience made up largely of undecided voters. His campaign was about to wrap up its Pennsylvania swing before heading to Ohio. There, he would repeat the process all over again. Different state, same spin. The methodical approach devised by Conrad was tedious, but it had worked. The three latest polls all had Emerson leading by a point.

Conrad was picking at his rubbery chicken when his phone rang. He excused himself and walked outside the banquet hall in search of privacy.

"Conrad," he answered abruptly, as usual.

"We've got a problem," Metcalf said, wasting no time, "a very big problem."

Metcalf brought Conrad up to speed on the theft of the Washington documents from his office safe. He also revealed that the stolen contents included copies of the legal documents that connected Conrad to Metcalf's hedge fund.

"Jesus Christ!" Conrad seethed, barely able to control the level of his voice. A few heads in the lobby turned in his direction. "The Washington-related documents are bad enough. But now I can be tied to your Fannie Mae and Freddie Mac scheme!"

"Not *my* scheme, *our* scheme, Conrad," Metcalf replied icily. "We're in this thing together, right up until the end."

"You said you were going to control this, so what the fuck happened?!" Conrad made his way outside the building. He sneered back at the disapproving stares from a gaggle of old ladies who had overheard him drop the f-bomb. It took a monumental effort not to reach out and wring their scrawny busybody necks.

"I had it under control, until something unforeseen happened. Not to worry, though," Metcalf said. He was trying hard to maintain a false air of calm amid the volcanic eruption that was Chuck Conrad. "I've got my men heading to Penberthy's house as we speak."

"You deal with Penberthy and Fox and all the rest of your society cronies, but I'm going to get those documents back. My guess is they're headed back to Savannah. So the minute I hang up with you, I'm telling my men to get back down there and clean up your mess," Conrad said.

"I'm sure that won't be necessary, I'll deal with it before they get that far."

"Tell you what, Metcalf, you call me after your guys come up empty in Fredericksburg. Savannah is where this thing is going to go down, and I'm going to handle it. You had your chance and fucked it up. This is my election, my ass, and my operation now. Stay the hell out of my way," he yelled into the phone.

After a brief silence, Metcalf relented, "Have it your way. Just keep me informed of any developments."

"Don't worry, I'll make sure this gets handled the right way this time," Conrad promised, right before hanging up.

———

Fifteen thousand feet in the air, Buzz's 1965 Piper Comanche six-seater was making two hundred miles an hour. At that speed, they would make the trip, from a private airstrip just outside of Fredericksburg to Savannah, in just over two and a half hours. Buzz no longer flew F-4 Phantoms as he had in the service, but he still enjoyed the thrill of being at the controls of his pride and joy. Matt was seated in the copilot seat and Hank and Bradley were just behind them, in the first row of seats. Everyone but Bradley, who had fallen fast asleep shortly after takeoff, was wearing headsets with attached microphones. It allowed them to communicate above the engine noise.

"Touchdown in approximately ninety minutes," Buzz announced.

Matt looked at his watch, "Sarah and Fox should be boarding the plane to New York by now."

"So where is this 'safe house' that you mentioned located?" Hank asked, his usually buoyant voice sounding scratchy through the bulky headset. "You said we'll need to hole up there until we can arrange the press conference."

"There's a woman who works for me at the store named Christina, and I talked her into letting us invade her apartment," Matt said. "It will be cozy, but her roommate is out of town, which is probably the only reason she agreed. That, and I told her I'd give her a little extra in her paycheck this week." Matt was amazed at the vast array of buttons and switches on the instrument panel in front of him. He wondered how the hell anyone could know which button controlled which function. His already healthy respect for Buzz ratcheted up another notch.

"That's very nice of her," Hank said. "I'm looking forward to meeting this young woman."

"Yeah, well, temper your enthusiasm Hank, she's an acquired taste."

———

Metcalf's security team arrived at Buzz's farmhouse less than an hour after receiving a very anxious phone call from their boss. They drove up the drive slowly. They were on high alert, ready to respond if anyone tried to flee from the scene. But the place was deserted. After canvassing the house and grounds, they found no signs of life. And, more importantly, no sign of the documents Metcalf had described. They called to tell him the bad news. Metcalf in turn, phoned Conrad to let him know that they had come up empty.

Conrad was not surprised. In fact, he had already dispatched his men to Savannah.

40

Present Day

Savannah, GA

C hristina watched impatiently as the men emerged from the small plane. Matt had asked her to pick them up at an out-of-the-way airstrip. She would never admit to her boss that she got lost twice trying to find it, but it did make her more ornery than usual. A fact she would happily share with him. Bradley had arranged for his own ride, so Matt and Hank said their good-byes to the locksmith and hurried over to where Christina had parked. Matt was surprised when he saw his '66 Chevy pickup in the lot, instead of Christina's fifteen-year-old Volkswagen Jetta beater. Matt also noticed that she had parked his baby in a tow-away zone, probably on purpose.

"Hey, that's my truck! Let me guess, your shit box broke down again," Matt said. He was irritated that she hadn't asked permission to borrow his truck. But this wasn't the first time. Whenever her car was on the fritz, which was more often than not, she'd find the extra set of keys that he kept on a nail in the shop and borrow his truck, sometimes asking, most times not.

"Yup, and you owe me gas money. It was on empty and I had to put twenty bucks in it." She turned to address Hank, "And who are you?"

Hank replied formally, "I'm Hank Gordon; it's a pleasure to meet you, Christina." He moved around the front of the truck to extend his hand in greeting, but she had already disappeared behind the wheel.

Hank raised his eyebrows at Matt, who said simply, "I told you she was an acquired taste." The two men tossed their bags into the bed of the truck and climbed in. It would be a snug ride home, as they sat three across on the vinyl front bench seat.

Leaving the small airfield, Matt noticed Buzz had already begun refueling his plane. He would be turning right around to make the trip back to D.C. Once there, he would attempt to organize an emergency meeting of the society's board of directors. His goal was the immediate ouster of Charles Metcalf as president general. Matt wished him a silent "good luck."

Christina turned on the radio to a hard rock station that Matt was unfamiliar with and said, "So what's with this cloak-and-dagger shit anyway? Why did you ask me to pick you up at this Podunk airport, and why do you want to crash at my apartment?" Although there was a trace of concern mixed in with her annoyance.

"Sorry I was so cryptic on the phone, but we've found something important that some people would prefer we would un-find," he said. He turned down the head-banging music and told her an abridged version of the events of the past few weeks.

"Holy shit, boss, you're knee deep in it this time." Then she slammed on the brakes. Hank and Matt nearly went through the windshield as the truck came to a complete stop in the middle of the road. "Wait. What if the guys with the guns find out you're staying at my apartment? They'll kill me for being your accomplice or something." She was hysterical.

"Calm down, Christina, and for chrissakes, start driving before someone rear-ends us," Matt said as he glanced out the back window, praying that an eighteen-wheeler wasn't bearing down on them. But luckily they were on a country road traveled by very few cars. "They don't even know you exist, so they're certainly not going to come snooping around your apartment."

"How do you know they're not following us right now? You just said yourself you thought they had followed you before." She ground the truck into gear and sped down the road.

"Don't be ridiculous." Even so, he cast a sidelong glance at the passenger's side mirror. "We'll be out of your hair by the day after tomorrow. Two nights, Christina, that's all I'm asking, OK?"

She was grim faced and had the truck's oversized steering wheel in a death grip. "Fine," she said, "but if I die, I'm going to kill you."

"If you die, you'll be dead," he corrected.

"So then I'll haunt you for the rest of your miserable life."

Just then, Matt's cell phone rang. Mercifully, it allowed him to escape the wrath of Christina, at least for a few minutes. It was his Wall Street contact calling him back with some information on Metcalf and Company.

Five minutes later, he hung up and turned to Hank. "Can you hand me the flight bag?"

Hank handed him Buzz's well-worn bag that presently held the entire contents of Metcalf's safe. Matt pulled out Metcalf's personal files and began to sift through them for the first time. As he did, he uttered a few "I'll be damned" and a couple "sons of bitches" before he returned everything back into the bag.

"So what did you find?" Hank asked.

"I believe I've found our smoking gun, Hank. The connection we've been looking for between Metcalf and the Emerson campaign." But he didn't elaborate.

Instead, he turned and stared silently out the passenger's side window. In spite of the head-banging music that had returned with a vengeance, he remained deep in thought all the way back to Savannah.

A plan was beginning to take shape in his mind.

———

They arrived in one piece at the small row house that Christina and her roommate rented on the outskirts of Savannah. Matt was pleasantly surprised at how homey it looked inside. Definitely funky, but it worked in a weird way. Kind of like Martha Stewart meets Marilyn Manson. He even took notice, with some pride, of the presence of a few antique pieces that she had bought from the store using her employee discount.

"What?" she said defensively, when she noticed Matt inspecting the premises.

"Nothing, it's just nicer than I expected, that's all," he muttered.

"You're a real charmer, Matt, you know that," she said. She turned to Hank, "Are you hungry, I've got some homemade guacamole."

"That would be lovely, Christina, I'm famished," he replied pleasantly, and the two of them disappeared into the kitchen.

Hank and Matt spent what was left of the day trying to make headway with the bureaucrats down at city hall. They had to convince the city fathers to let them stage a press conference in historic Johnson Square in less than two days time. They were making very little progress when Sissy called and informed them, matter-of-factly, that she had arranged a meeting with the mayor himself for the next morning. Once again, the quirky little lady with the Technicolor wardrobe had come through.

Hank was reminded of the stories his father used to tell him about the political machine that ruled Savannah from the 1930s to the 1950s. A man called Boss Bouhan sat atop the established hierarchy. And through vote tampering, payoffs, and handpicked appointees, he gained control of city hall and most of the politicians in it. Boss Bouhan, he thought, had nothing on Sissy Hightower. When Sissy wanted something done, her sheer will made it happen.

However, before Hank hung up, Matt overheard him sheepishly agree to dinner plans with her for the following week. Apparently, obtaining a meeting with the mayor had some strings attached. Matt stifled a chuckle.

With that part of the plan set in motion, he contemplated calling Buzz to see what success he had had in arranging an emergency meeting of the society's board of directors. Buzz was convinced that if the board heard his firsthand account of the events of the past few days, then Metcalf would be summarily fired. He had made it his mission to bring the fight directly to Metcalf, and that's exactly what he intended to do. But he decided to leave Buzz alone for the time being, as he probably had his hands full. As if on cue, his phone rang. He felt his heart beat a little faster when he saw that it was Sarah calling, and not just because he was anxious to find out how her meetings went.

"Hey, gorgeous," he said playfully.

"Hey, yourself."

"So how did it go, did you get us booked on the late-night interview circuit?" Matt teased.

"No, but you better not be camera shy," she said. "Because you're going to be interviewed by CNN!" she shouted into the phone, unable to hide her excitement. She went on to tell him that representatives of both the *New York Times* and CNN would be in Savannah the next morning to authenticate the documents.

If they checked out to their satisfaction, then Washington's sur-render letter would be the lead story the following day.

This was all thanks to Sarah's Manhattan-based publishing house. They had a high-level contact at CNN and pulled some strings to arrange a meeting with David Becker, one of the top investigative reporters at the *New York Times*. Becker had won the Pulitzer Prize a few years back for a series of articles written about the events leading up to the financial crisis of 2008.

"That's fantastic, Sarah. Tell them we're ready. Sissy said we can use the Harper Fowlkes House to conduct the authentication."

"Great! Any progress with city hall?"

"Actually, yes, thanks again to Sissy." He went on to tell her about the meeting with the mayor arranged for the next day.

Matt continued, "Since both meetings are at about the same time, I'll send Hank to meet up with you guys at the Harper Fowlkes House, with the documents in tow. I'll head over to city hall with Sissy. I need to explain to the mayor why we want to hold a press conference in one of his town's most prominent squares." He took off his shoes and stretched out on a scratchy zebra-print couch that took up most of Christina's living room.

"Can you believe that this is all really coming together?" she said in amazement.

"I know; we might actually pull it off."

After a brief pause, she said, "Are you sure we're doing the right thing by telling the world about Washington's surrender letter?" the anxiety clear in her voice, "I mean this man is an American icon, a hero to our country. Are you prepared for the potential backlash that might come our way?"

"Sarah, we didn't write the letter, George Washington did. If we're made pariahs, than I'm OK with that, because I think it would be a worse crime to sit on the letter and not share it with the American public. As your dad said, you can't rewrite history but you can learn from it. I'm hoping that the American people are mature enough to learn from it."

"All I'm saying is that we need to be prepared for anything. This is big news on a lot of levels, if you know what I mean," she said, in a thinly veiled reference to the impact the revelation could have on the race for the presidency.

"I know. Speaking of which, I want you to be careful, OK?" he said, genuinely concerned. "The bad guys are still out there somewhere, so watch your back. Metcalf and Emerson probably both have people looking for us."

41

Present Day

Savannah, GA

Sarah and Fox arrived with *New York Times* reporter David Becker at the Harper Fowlkes House a little before noon. Hank was waiting for them along with the representative from CNN, who had arrived just a few minutes earlier. He gave his daughter a big hug and introductions were made all around.

"It's good to be home, Dad," Sarah said, embracing her father.

"I know exactly what you mean, sweetheart. Come on, let's head back into Sissy's office so we can get started."

As Hank guided everybody to the back of the house, he turned to Becker, "Your authenticator arrived about twenty minutes ago. He's in the office getting set up. He looks familiar to me, is it possible I've seen him before?"

"Thomas Reece is one of the leading document and signature authenticators in the world. He's been on Fox News and the History Channel, so you may have seen him there. Plus, he was recently featured in the *New York Times*. But his celebrity isn't the reason we chose him. Thomas knows George Washington's signature and writing style better than anyone alive. In fact, he's done a lot of work with the FBI tracking down professional forgers. These crooks make millions selling fake historical documents 'signed' by Washington, Lincoln, Jefferson, and others to amateur collectors who don't know any better."

They filed into Sissy's cramped office and spread out in a semicircle around the desk. They looked like first-year residents getting ready to observe the head surgeon perform a new medical procedure. Once they were all settled, Hank reached into the leather satchel and removed Caty's journal. He handed it across the desk to Reece.

After examining the book for a few minutes, Reece spoke up. "I understand that you've already had a local authenticator look at this, and I must say that I agree with her conclusion that this appears to be authentic. The leather cover and paper are definitely of the time period."

As he spoke, he was looking through what appeared to be a magnifying device shaped like a small flashlight. "Before coming down here," he continued, "I found some writing samples of Miss Greene's from a museum collection that had been digitized and made available online."

He glanced up briefly to make sure his audience was following along. "Right now I'm comparing these samples with your journal and, oh yes," he paused, leaning forward so he could place his eye even closer to the scope, "the writing has a choppy flow to it, and her *n*'s and *r*'s are quite distinctive." He put his instrument down on the desk and said with finality, "This journal is most definitely in the hand of Catharine Greene. It's authentic."

"What's that instrument you're using that allows you to compare the writing samples?" interrupted the CNN representative, clearly new to the document authentication process.

"It's a digital microscope that gives me magnification of up to two hundred power and lets me manipulate the light to provide the best resolution possible. I can also take pictures of the document and upload them wirelessly to my laptop. That allows me to make side-by-side comparisons to previously authenticated writings, which is the analysis I just performed," he explained. The CNN representative was scribbling away furiously in her notebook.

"One down and one to go," Becker said. Then cutting to the chase, he continued, "While I appreciate the fact that the journal is a fascinating piece of history, there's still no story without an authentic surrender letter from Washington."

"Quite right," Hank said. He reached into his bag one more time and pulled out the cylinder containing the letter and handed it to Sarah.

The air seemed to leave the room all at once as she removed the top of Whitney's device and carefully pulled out the rolled-up letter. Everyone was in awe to be in such close proximity to a document written by Washington himself, let alone an alleged surrender letter. She placed it gingerly on the desk.

The only one not in awe was Reece, who had handled hundreds of Washington documents over the years. He slowly unfurled the letter. Then he placed small weights at both ends to hold the letter flat to the table. Everyone remained completely silent as Reece worked.

"I'm going to start with Washington's signature, since it is so distinctive," he said. "The nice thing about his signature is that it's very neat and readable and it didn't change over the years. Some signatures of notable public figures changed as they matured and got older, but Washington's didn't. Not only did it stay the same throughout his life, but it also never fell apart, meaning he never got lazy with it, he always finished every letter in his last name.

"I've seen some very good forgeries over the years," Reece continued, "and one of the biggest 'tells' in a forged document can be found in the letters *G* and *W*. Washington often signed his letters G. Washington and did not spell out his first name. In an authentic Washington signature, the *G* and *W* connect in a very unique way. The two letters lay down on their side in quite a pronounced manner. In a forgery, you can detect a hesitation between the *G* and the *W* as opposed to a free-flowing, connected line." He continued, as he stared intently through his digital microscope, "But that's not the case here; these letters are correct, the size is right, and the flow is perfect."

"So it's real?" asked the CNN advance person, seemingly surprised that her trip might not have been a waste of time after all.

"Now I'm going to move on from the signature to the rest of the document," he said, ignoring the premature question from the overeager press rep.

Reece didn't talk for three or four minutes. The anxiety in the room had peaked and everyone was on edge. Finally, he continued his running dialogue as if he had never stopped. "The paper is late eighteenth century. The scattered toning and foxing is right and you can even see the original fold marks. The body of the letter is definitely in the same hand as the signature, which is very important, given the controversial subject matter.

"I'll be damned." He stopped, looked up at Becker, and said, "When you put all the evidence together, there is no denying that this is an authentic letter written and signed by George Washington in the year 1778."

"Holy shit," Becker blurted out, "you're sure?" He knew that this was like asking Einstein if his formula was correct. But a good reporter always confirmed information from his sources, especially when the information was this explosive.

"It's real," Reece said, "and in my thirty years of doing this, it's the most historically significant document I've ever had the privilege to hold in my hands." He stared back at the letter in near reverence before looking over at Sarah and Hank. "It's been an honor for me to authenticate this for you. Congratulations, this is one hell of a find."

"Thank you, Mr. Reece, but we already knew it was real," Sarah replied honestly. "But thanks to you, now they do, too," she motioned to the members of the press in the room.

"So how much is something like this worth?" asked the woman from CNN.

"That's nearly impossible to say. Historically speaking, it's priceless. But for comparison purposes, an average letter written and signed by George Washington with good subject matter can go for sixty thousand dollars or more. But clearly, the subject matter contained in this letter is far from average. The best comparison I can come up with is a letter written by Robert E. Lee to his brother, in which he resigned his U.S. Army commission to take up arms with the Confederacy. I believe that letter went at auction for around $600,000. My best guess is that if your letter were to ever go up for auction, it could fetch ten, maybe twenty times that because of its historical significance. There would be plenty of interested buyers both here in America as well as in Britain, so frankly, the sky's the limit."

"Well, I've got what I came to hear," Becker announced. He turned to Sarah, "I've got a lot of work to do in the next few hours if I'm going to make deadline for tomorrow's paper. I'll call your cell if I need more background or any additional quotes from you or Matt." He turned and hurried out the door.

The CNN representative had been speaking on her cell phone with Anderson Cooper's team back at the office. She cupped her hand over the phone and said, "We're in. Anderson will want the first interview with Matt right after the press conference. I'll confirm with you later today." Then she followed Becker out the door.

On the way out to Hank's car, Matt called from the mayor's office. He had come clean with the mayor and revealed to him that their monument-washing scheme was just a cover-up to secretly extract Washington's surrender letter. The mayor had not taken the news well. In fact, he had threatened to throw them all in jail for defacing city property.

It had taken all of Matt's charm and selling skills, and the better part of an hour, to convince the mayor that they had left the monument in better condition than they had found it, and that the discovery could be a potential boon to Savannah's tourism industry. Thousands of people, he reasoned, would be interested in seeing where the document was found and hearing the story of its discovery. New tours could be created, money could be made, and so on. This had gotten the mayor's attention, but what had really swayed him was when Matt had delicately pointed out that it would be very embarrassing if it were to come out that the mayor's office had been duped and the incredible historical document was uncovered without his knowledge or consent.

Matt knew he had him. Before agreeing to grant them the permit to hold the press conference in Johnson Square the next day, however, the mayor had insisted on viewing the documents personally. So Matt called Hank and asked him to hurry over to city hall with the journal and Washington's letter.

Overhearing her father's conversation, Sarah said, "You and Director Fox go on ahead; I need to stop by my house. I'll cab it home and meet you back at Christina's later on this afternoon."

"I don't think that's a good idea, Sarah. It's still not safe. There are a lot of bad guys who want what we've got," Hank said, his brow furrowed with concern. "I think you should stay with us."

"Dad, I'm the only girl on this team and I've been wearing the same outfit for the last few days. I need a change of clothes. And besides, I need to check on my cat."

Her father still didn't like leaving Sarah alone and told her so.

"Hey, I'm the one who's usually the chicken," she smiled reassuringly at her father. "Besides you guys have the documents, not me. If anybody should be worried, it's you two."

Hank looked at Fox, who wisely looked away, knowing better than to get in the middle of a father-daughter spat. Hank turned back to Sarah and relented, "All right, but be careful and don't take any longer than you have to. We'll see you at Christina's in two hours tops, OK?"

"OK, Dad, and good luck with the mayor." She affectionately squeezed her father's arm before heading off in the opposite direction. She couldn't wait for a nice hot shower in the familiar surroundings of her own house.

42

Present Day

Savannah, GA

A Pedicab came around the corner. What the hell, Sarah thought, it was a nice day and she hadn't ridden in one of those in years. She flagged down the college-aged driver and climbed into the rickshaw seat affixed behind the bicycle. As they made their way past Forsyth Park towards her home, Sarah could see the Confederate War Memorial standing proudly in the center of the park. A bronze soldier in Confederate uniform stood alone atop the monument's sandstone base, facing north, of course, toward his enemy. So many monuments, she thought, so many battles. What other secrets have been lost to history?

She spotted a man sleeping in a hammock haphazardly strung between two trees. She yawned. It reminded her of how exhausted she was; it had been a very long week. Ten minutes later she was dropped off in the alleyway that ran behind her house. She paid the driver and made her way along the tiny driveway and up the wooden staircase to the back door of her rental home.

When she had left Savannah to go to Washington, D.C., she thought she'd only be gone for one night. Then Metcalf stole the letter, and her life had taken a host of unexpected turns that had kept her on the road for five. She hoped the automatic cat feeder hadn't run out of food. She pulled open the screen and unlocked the back door.

It was stuffy inside, so she left the heavy back door open to let some fresh air in. At the sound of the screen door slamming shut, the cat appeared from around the corner, probably having been disturbed from an early-afternoon slumber. The tabby's normal ritual was to follow the sun around the house, sleeping wherever its rays warmed a spot on the floor. The cat leapt into her owner's arms and purred sleepily as Sarah scanned the kitchen. The flowers on the windowsill needed some water, but other than that the house seemed no worse for the wear.

Suddenly, the cat's ears perked up and her furry head pivoted around in the direction of the back door. The cat hissed and sprung from Sarah's arms, sensing imminent danger. Sarah screamed reflexively when she saw an enormous man silhouetted by the sun, filling up the entire frame of the screen door. He kicked the flimsy screen door so violently that it was removed from its hinges. She froze for just a second and then bolted in the opposite direction.

Sarah scrambled out of the kitchen and through the center hallway. She reached the front door and frantically tried to unlock the security dead bolt, desperately trying to escape the intruder. The house shook as the man's large footfalls closed the gap between them. Finally, she managed to get the front door open; her escape was only seconds away.

An enormous hand landed above her head, and the door slammed shut. She was trapped. Terrified, she tugged at the knob and managed to force the door open just a crack. It was no use, the behemoth was simply too strong, and the door slammed shut once more. She screamed. But her scream became a whimper when the intruder forced his full weight against her body, pinning her to the door and choking off her air supply.

The terrifyingly long knife had a serrated blade and it appeared out of nowhere. She began to cough and cry at the same time. For the first time, he spoke. "You scream again and I'll slit your throat."

Her head was pinned face-first to the door. She could feel blood oozing from her chin, the result of being slammed up against a nail that had been protruding a half inch out of the door, probably leftover from holding up a holiday decoration the prior Christmas. Slowly, he turned her around while making sure she never lost sight of the blade in his hand.

She finally took in her assailant's full size. He was impossibly large.

"What do you want?" she stammered, even though she already knew the answer. This had to be one of Metcalf's or Conrad's men.

"I want a lot of things," he said. A perverted smile appeared as he gave her a lascivious once-over from head to toe. His left forearm held her shoulder firmly against the door while his right hand held the knife close to her throat. She imagined kneeing him in the balls as she had seen brave women do in the movies, but the knife was so big and sharp that she couldn't muster the nerve. Her mind raced to come up with another way out.

As if reading her thoughts, he inched the blade even closer to her throat. "Now, are you going to tell me where the documents are or are we going to have to do this the hard way?" His breath was sour and smelled of garlic and cigarettes. She said nothing and tried to avoid looking him in the eye. In a flash, he took the tip of his knife blade and sliced the top button off her shirt, exposing the tops of her breasts.

"You're a good looking woman, Sarah. I'm kind of hoping you *don't* tell me where they are, because then I could have some real fun slicing these clothes off your fine body."

"Don't!" she shouted. Tears began to well up again in her eyes.

"If you don't play nice, then I'm going to have to play dirty," he said. He slid his left hand down to her breast and gave her nipple a hard squeeze through her shirt.

"Stop it, you pig," she spat out in anger. She shot up one hand and swiped his thick paw away while tugging her shirt closed with her other hand.

The man laughed a cold laugh and said, "Now that's the spirit. I like some fight in a bitch, it's more fun that way." The smile disappeared and was replaced by a hard look that made her body begin to shake uncontrollably. "Now Sarah, I'm only going to ask you this one more time before the real fun begins. Where, are, the, documents," he paused between each word for effect.

Sarah's resolve finally caved and she blurted out, "My, my friends," she stuttered, "they have them at a house here in town; it's not far from here." She desperately hoped Matt would know what to do when they showed up. "I'll take you there."

"There, now, that wasn't so hard, was it? But we don't need to hurry over there right away, do we?" he said. Instead of releasing her, he sliced another button from her shirt and smothered his mouth against hers.

Oh God, this can't be happening, she thought, as she squirmed to escape his awful embrace. Just then, a loud voice boomed out from the kitchen behind them, "Let her go, Anthony, right now."

The giant released her and spun around, ready to pounce. But he relaxed when he saw that the voice belonged to his superior, J. J. Stanton, the former marine and the owner of Stanton Security, the firm who employed him.

"What the fuck are you doing?" Stanton said, clearly pissed at his subordinate.

"Just having a little fun, boss."

"Let her go, we don't have time for that shit. Did you find out where the documents are?"

"Yeah, they're being kept at a house here in town, and she's going to lead us there, aren't you, honey?"

He grabbed Sarah forcefully by the hair and pushed her toward the back door. On the way out, he pulled her close so that Stanton couldn't hear him. He whispered in her ear, "Don't worry, we're still going have our fun, you can count on it."

———

Fifteen minutes later, they pulled up in front of Christina's tiny rental house. Stanton got out from behind the wheel and went right to the front door. He rang the bell nonchalantly, as if he were selling encyclopedias.

Christina opened the door cautiously. "Can I help you?" she asked. Her instincts told her that something wasn't right. Hank also came to the door and stood slightly behind her in the foyer.

"Yes, you can, Christina," Stanton said. Sarah had told him Christina's name on the way over.

"How the hell do you know my name?" She shifted her stance, and made ready to slam the door in his face.

"I wouldn't do that if I were you," he said calmly, as if reading her mind. He motioned to the car behind him. The back passenger door of the tinted-window Escalade opened and Sarah emerged, followed closely by a giant of a man. Sarah looked terrified, maybe even hurt.

Hank immediately noticed the blood on his daughter's chin, and her torn shirt, but it was the fear on her face that made him shout out, "Sarah!" He pushed his way past Christina, desperate to come to the aid of his only child. But halfway to the car he stopped in his tracks.

"That's far enough, pops," Anthony said. He revealed the .45 revolver he had planted firmly in Sarah's ribs.

"I'm OK, Dad," she said in a shaky voice, "they just want the documents and then they promised to let me go."

Stanton, still standing outside the front door, said, "That's right, the faster someone goes inside and gets the documents, the faster we'll be on our way. Nobody needs to get hurt."

Christina looked over at Hank, who nodded quickly for her to go get them. She turned to go, but Stanton said, "If you don't mind, I think I'll tag along, Christina." He opened the door and was standing beside her before she had time to react. "Move," he commanded.

He followed her into the living room where Director Fox was standing, gripping the leather flight bag in his hands indecisively. He was clearly torn about what to do. Stanton could see the wheels turning inside Fox's head. "Don't try to be a hero, son," he recommended. Then he lifted back his jacket to show a very large handgun holstered beneath his armpit. "Just toss it on over here, nice and easy."

Fox hesitated for just a second before tossing the bag into the waiting arms of the ex-marine. He unzipped the top of the bag and took a few moments to take inventory. The surrender letter, the journal, and the legal documents, which Conrad had told him were a top priority to recover, were all accounted for.

"Now, if you two will kindly stay right where you are, we'll be leaving," he said, backing out of the room.

Hank was standing on the front lawn, still trying to assess the condition of his daughter, when Stanton returned. "You've got what you came for, now let my daughter go," he said angrily. "Come on, Sarah, walk on over to me."

Stanton made his way around to the driver's side of the car and tossed the bag into the front seat. Anthony hadn't loosened his grip on Sarah since they had arrived. He looked over at his boss for direction, with an expression on his face that seemed to ask, *you want me to let her walk?*

Stanton thought for a moment and then said, "Just to make sure nobody gets any crazy ideas, like trying to follow us or something stupid like that, we're going to take Sarah with us. Don't worry, we won't harm her, we'll just drop her off on our way out of town."

Sarah saw the hideous smirk reappear on Anthony's pock-marked face as it dawned on him that he'd have the opportunity to make good on the promise he had whispered in her ear back at her house. The evil look on his face struck Sarah like a body blow. She knew that if these men took her with them, bad things were going to happen to her. She snapped.

She thrust her elbow with all her might into Anthony's side. His grip loosened for just a moment. Hank ran toward her and was able to wrestle the large man's arm from his daughter. Anthony lashed out with his free arm and pushed Hank hard. He fell backward to the ground. Sarah turned quickly and clawed at Anthony's face, drawing blood. That's when she looked up and saw Stanton's gun pointed directly at her father's forehead.

"Get in the car now, Sarah, or I swear I'll put a bullet in his head." Anthony was now seething with anger. He grabbed Sarah and tossed her like a rag doll into the backseat. This time she didn't resist.

Stanton, his gun still leveled at Hank, looked over at Fox and Christina. They hadn't moved from the doorway, frozen in fear. He said calmly but forcefully, "If you call the police, Sarah will die." He turned and hurried into the driver's seat.

The large V-8 engine roared to life. He stepped on the accelerator and they were gone.

43

Present Day

Savannah, GA

Christina was the first to spring into action. The look on Sarah's face was one that she knew all too well. It was a look of defeat, a look that was resigned to the horror that she now faced. Christina could empathize because she had been a victim of abuse, by her own father no less. And after she ran away and escaped the hell that was her childhood home, there was still more bad treatment by other men, until one day she had finally had enough and changed the trajectory of her life, vowing never to let another man take away her dignity again.

She ran into the house, grabbed the keys to her balky Jetta, and was back outside in seconds. Fox was helping Hank up from where he still lay sprawled out after being knocked to the ground. He was physically fine but clearly distraught. "Come on, we can follow them in my car," she yelled, in an all-out sprint to the driveway.

Fox and Hank hurried over to the beat-up car, but turned when they heard the sound of a large engine as it raced by Christina's house at top speed. Hank, who only caught a glimpse of the blue vehicle as it thundered by, looked over at Christina and said, "Was that Matt's truck?"

———

Earlier that afternoon, Hank and Fox had left their show-and-tell session with the mayor, leather flight bag in hand. They had left Matt and Sissy downtown to finalize the details of the press conference for the next morning. Even though they had to jump through a lot of hoops, it had all been worth it, because the city had granted them a permit to hold their press conference in Johnson Square. After the meeting had adjourned, Matt drove Sissy back to her office at the Harper Fowlkes House and was making his way back to Christina's place to meet up with the rest of the team.

He felt a little nervous driving his conspicuous vintage truck around Savannah. Especially when he realized that his only line of defense, if confronted, was his trusty baseball bat, currently wedged behind the vinyl front bench seat. He prayed it wouldn't come to that, because bringing a bat to a gunfight was not good odds.

He was only a couple of blocks away from Christina's when he noticed a commotion ahead on the tiny lawn in front of her house. He was confused at first, but when he saw a person being forced into the backseat of a car that raced off seconds later, he knew that something had gone terribly wrong. He stepped on the gas. His mind was racing and panic began to creep up his spine. He couldn't be absolutely sure, but he thought that the person being tossed into the back seat was a woman. Was it Sarah? As he raced by the house, he caught a glimpse of Hank and Fox on the front lawn and Christina hurrying toward her car.

"Oh God," he said out loud, as the reality struck him like a body blow. Sarah was the only one unaccounted for; she was the one who had been forced into that car. He floored it to close the gap on the Escalade. Was it the same Escalade that he had seen right after the journal was stolen from his apartment? It had to be, he thought. His mind was racing as fast as his truck's engine. So these must be Conrad's men, not Metcalf's, or more likely they were working together to find the documents, because they were so damaging to both men, financially and politically. The documents! They must also have the flight bag! His only thought had been to rescue Sarah, but clearly they must have taken the documents as well.

He was less than a block behind the Escalade now, but he had been spotted. The Escalade picked up speed and started to widen the gap between them. Even though his truck had a large engine, it was no match for the much more modern, fuel-injected V-8 of the Escalade. Thirty seconds later the gap had widened back up to two blocks. Matt knew his time was running short.

A flurry of options raced through his head. "Think Matt!" he screamed aloud. He took a deep breath and tried to slow down his mind. *You're never going to outrace them*, he thought to himself, *so you're going to have to outsmart them. You need to anticipate where they are going and beat them there. That's the only way you're ever going to get Sarah back. Where are they going?* He suddenly knew. They had to be headed for the interstate!

His one advantage was his local knowledge. These guys weren't from around here, that much he could count on, so they would most likely take the predictable route to the highway. They were probably using a GPS system, which rarely made use of shortcuts or alternate routes. That would provide him an edge. Hopefully it would be enough.

Stanton had spotted Matt's truck five minutes earlier and knew exactly who was following them. He recognized the distinctive truck from when he had followed Matt and stolen the journal from his apartment. "Son of a bitch, we've got company," he said, looking in his rearview mirror.

Anthony and Sarah turned their heads in unison to look out the back window. Their reactions couldn't have been more different. A scowl appeared on Anthony's face, while Sarah's spirits were instantly lifted. Anthony must have noticed, because he snarled, "Don't get happy, bitch, he'll never catch us." But it didn't matter to Sarah, she knew Matt would never give up, and she clung desperately to that hope. It was the only hope she had.

Stanton's dim-witted sidekick looked back again to monitor the progress of their pursuer, but Matt was gone. "Where'd he go boss?" he asked, in confusion.

"I don't know," he answered in a clipped tone with a trace of worry.

"Maybe he gave up and went home," Anthony mocked. "Sorry, sweetheart." He put a hand on her leg and slipped it under her skirt. "Guess they figure you're just not worth it." The evil grin had returned.

But Sarah's resolve had returned. She pushed his hand away, "If you touch me again, I swear I'll rip your eyes out."

"We'll see about that," he said simply.

Matt made the turn onto a road that cut diagonally across town, whereas the kidnappers had taken a more squared-off route. His only hope now was that the time he saved by taking the more direct route would be enough to head them off before they reached the entry to the highway, because he knew that if they reached the interstate ahead of him, he'd never be able to catch them. He pushed this thought from his mind. And he pushed the accelerator to the floor.

"On-ramp's just up ahead," said Stanton, mostly to himself. He could see the entrance sign less than five hundred yards away. He began to relax ever so slightly. That's when he looked to his left and saw a flash of blue barreling through the intersection, heading directly toward them.

Matt knew he was getting close to where the shortcut would meet up with the main road. Then, as he approached the intersection, he saw them up ahead, directly in front of him. The next few moments were a blur as his rage took over. He didn't have time to think, only react.

He shot through the intersection and made a beeline for the driver's side door. He knew that Sarah was going to take quite a jolt but he had no choice. His only hope was to disable the Escalade and pray that the car's side air bags deployed, which would help soften the impact on Sarah.

The half-ton truck shot across the intersection like a missile, and scored a direct hit against the driver's side panel. The sound of metal on metal was deafening. Matt's seat belt strained mightily upon impact, and his head took a nasty blow, courtesy of the oversized steering wheel. A gash opened up on his forehead instantly. The good news was that he was conscious, and miraculously didn't have a concussion. The other good news was that his truck was in much better condition than the Escalade, whose front end was now a crumpled mess. They definitely don't make them like they used to, Matt thought.

He extricated himself from his truck, but not before grabbing the baseball bat from behind the seat. He had no idea of the condition of the assailants but was taking no chances. As he approached the vehicle, the first thing he noticed through the blown-out driver's side window was that all the air bags had deployed. He breathed a sigh of relief. The next thing he noticed made him smile.

Running down the man's left cheek was a ragged scar, a scar that Matt recognized instantly. The driver was a bit woozy and was feebly attempting to open his door. He wasn't moving very fast and was all tangled up in the air bag. Matt didn't care, he moved in quickly and coldcocked him through the shattered window. The man was knocked out instantly. Matt's fist hurt like hell, but it was worth it. Payback always felt good.

He was desperate to find Sarah, but the back passenger door had absorbed some of the impact so it was jammed shut. He quickly made his way around to the other passenger side. As he came around the back of the car, the door flung open and a giant of a man emerged. He was clearly dazed, and, like Matt, bleeding from his head. He held a gun in his hand and, after quickly gaining his bearings, pointed it directly at Matt.

Matt braced for the blast he knew was about to come. Then, unexpectedly, the man cried out in pain. Sarah had lashed out from her prone position on the backseat and kicked him hard in the thigh. His gun lowered for just an instant, which was the only opening Matt needed. He took one quick stride forward and let loose, as if taking a hack at a hanging curveball. The aluminum bat found its mark. Anthony's elbow shattered with a sickening crack. The gun skittered across the asphalt. Remarkably, though, the giant didn't go down. He did, however, let loose a howl that sounded more animal than human. And the crazed look in his eyes let Matt know that he wasn't finished yet.

He lunged, but Matt was ready for him. This time he took dead aim at the man's kneecap, and when he connected, Anthony crumpled to the ground, writhing in pain. Matt kicked the gun further out of arm's reach and bent down to look inside the car, afraid of what he might find.

Sarah, expecting to have to defend herself against her assailant again, nearly kicked him in the face. "Whoa," Matt said as he flinched, "it's OK, Sarah; it's me." He reached a hand inside the car. She tentatively took it.

He eased her out gently, not knowing what injuries she might have suffered in the wreck. But to his great relief, she looked to be in one piece. She had a few scrapes on her face from the air bags that had deployed, and probably some bruises that wouldn't appear until the next day. But, all in all, she was in remarkably good shape. Finally understanding that she was out of harm's way, she let her guard down and collapsed into Matt's arms. Tears streamed down her face, reflecting the relief, fear, and joy that she felt, all at once. Matt held on to her tightly.

A car skidded to a stop behind them. It was Christina. Hank was out of the car in an instant and rushed over to check on his daughter. Christina stalked over to Anthony, whom she had noticed writhing in pain on the ground. She promptly kicked him hard in the nuts. The big man would definitely not be going anywhere for a while, Matt thought to himself.

She looked over at Matt as if nothing had happened, and said, "I'm proud of you, boss. You did good here today."

"Yeah, thanks, so did you." He was uncertain how to respond to a compliment from his usually temperamental employee.

A white panel van came screeching to a halt behind them, kicking up dirt and gravel in the process. Matt immediately thought the worst, but then he saw Hank rush over and greet a familiar-looking man emerging from the van.

When Matt approached, Hank said, "You remember Patrick O'Leary and his boys." Three of his four beefy-looking sons had materialized.

"I was desperate when they took Sarah, so I called Patrick from the car, figuring we might need some extra help. Thanks for getting here so fast," he said, nodding in appreciation of the speed in which the O'Leary clan had mobilized.

"When you told me they had your daughter, I knew we had to act fast. You took care of my boys once, so I'm more than happy to repay that debt today," O'Leary said.

Suddenly, Sarah screamed and the next few minutes played out as if in slow motion.

Matt turned to see Stanton stalking around the front of the crumpled Escalade, gun extended. He had somehow managed to slip out of the driver's side window, unnoticed in all of the commotion. Without hesitating, Stanton fired off two quick rounds.

The first shot went just wide of Matt's right shoulder and obliterated the front windshield of O'Leary's van. The men scattered in all directions. The next shot threw one of O'Leary's sons backward about five feet. Blood from a gaping wound immediately began turning his white T-shirt crimson.

Stanton turned his gun on Matt once again. He was not going to miss this time. The last thing Matt saw before the gun went off was the scar, which looked more menacing in the hot glare of the sun. He heard the blast and, for the second time in the span of a few minutes, Matt thought for sure he was going to die.

But instead, it was Stanton who tumbled over backward, his gun clattering across the hood of the Escalade. At first Matt was confused, and then he looked to his right, where Christina had been keeping watch over an immobilized Anthony. In her hand was Anthony's gun, still smoking from the round she had just discharged; the one that had dropped Stanton in his tracks. She held the weapon in two hands. It was extended and locked in front of her, the perfect shooter's position.

Matt hurried over. She hadn't moved and the gun was still extended out in front of her. She started to shake ever so slightly. He gently pressed down on her hands.

"It's OK, it's over now," he said in a soothing a voice.

Finally, she lowered the gun to her side. "I remembered he had a gun because he showed it to me earlier at my house, when they came for the documents," she said, in a daze. "I figured you probably missed it." Matt wondered if she was going into shock.

"I was going to go check and see. That's when he came around the front of the car firing. I saw the other gun on the ground over there," she nodded to the spot where Matt had kicked Anthony's gun aside earlier, "and I just reacted."

Matt, still startled at the fierce resolve and fearlessness that Christina had just displayed, said, "You did the right thing, you saved our lives. You saved my life." He smiled appreciatively and she nodded tentatively back at him. Matt took that as a good sign. Maybe she was going to be all right after all.

"So would now be a good time to talk about that raise?" she said, eyebrows raised. She took a quick glance down at the loaded pistol she still held in her hand and smiled ever so slightly. She was definitely going to be all right, Matt thought.

Patrick O'Leary had already manhandled the hobbled Anthony to his feet and was ushering him roughly toward the open back doors of the van. The two uninjured O'Leary sons were in the midst of carrying Stanton there as well. He appeared to be breathing, but if the third O'Leary boy didn't make it, Matt was sure that Stanton wouldn't either. But as he glanced behind him, he could see that the boy was conscious and talking to Hank, who was holding a compress to his shoulder. Evidently the bullet passed right on through and missed any major arteries. It appeared as though he would survive and most likely recover.

Patrick approached Hank and said, "We need to get out of here before the cops show up. I'm assuming you don't want to have to explain all this, right?"

"I'm so sorry, Patrick," Hank said. "This is all my fault. Your son was shot because I called you here today."

"You don't need to apologize, Hank. This comes with the territory. I know that better than anyone, and so do my boys. Sean is going to be fine. We'll get him stitched up and now he'll have a little war story to tell, right?" he said with a half-smile that looked more like a grimace.

"What about them?" Matt said, motioning to the back of the van.

"They won't be bothering you, or anyone else, again. That I can promise you," Patrick said with a cold, hard look. He turned and headed for the van. Matt caught Hank's eye. He knew he was wondering the same thing: What was going to happen to the two men in the back of the van? Both of them knew the answer, but neither man spoke of it.

Fox had already retrieved the leather bag from the front seat of the disabled Escalade, and he and Hank climbed quickly into Christina's car. Sarah joined Matt in the truck, which was leaking oil, but still roadworthy.

They left the scene of the accident as quickly as they had arrived. Patrick was right; there was no way they wanted to explain to the police what had just happened. It would take too much energy and too much time, neither of which they had a surplus of at the moment.

44

Present Day

Savannah, GA

They had reconvened back at Christina's place for the evening. Some were more battered and bruised than others, but everyone was exhausted. Christina prepared some hot tea and tended to Sarah's minor cuts and bruises with some bandages and an ice compress. Matt was grateful for her help. She had acted without hesitation throughout the day, so when she looked his way, he mouthed the words *thank you* and gave her an appreciative smile.

Sarah went to lie down on Christina's bed. Hank and Fox were busy in the kitchen, mustering something for dinner. Christina walked over and sat down next to Matt on the couch.

"How are you doing, boss?" She used a rubber band to tie her purple hair back in a ponytail.

"I'm good. A little sore, but I'll live. You OK?" he asked, wondering how she was handling the aftereffects of the shooting.

She was quiet for a while, lost in her own thoughts. Then she said, "The only thing my piece-of-shit father ever taught me how to do was shoot a gun. I guess it came in handy today."

"Hey, you'll get no argument from me on that score. If you hadn't done what you did, I wouldn't be sitting here right now."

They sat quietly for a few more moments, each of them processing the events of the day.

"It feels weird, you know, shooting another person. It's not a good feeling, but that creep had it coming, don't you think?" she asked hesitantly.

"Absolutely," Matt said, without missing a beat.

"The look on Sarah's face, you know, when they took her away in that car today," she paused, "let's just say that I don't like seeing women in those kinds of situations." She looked down briefly, trying to compose herself.

When she looked up, her eyes were moist. "Men who treat women like that deserve to..." But she stopped short of finishing her thought, and her bottom lip quivered ever so slightly.

Matt reached over and took her hand, "I just want you to know," he said, "I appreciate everything you did today; we all do. You're a good person, Christina, and you should be damned proud of the woman you've become."

She gave his hand a squeeze in return. But she was uncomfortable in these situations. Even though Matt was the only man she had ever really trusted, gestures of gratitude and appreciation were still new emotions to her. So she pushed up from the couch to go outside and grab a smoke. Halfway to the front door, she stopped and pulled something from her front pants pocket. "Oh yeah," she said, turning back around, "I took this off the driver before they loaded him into the van." She tossed a cell phone across the room. Matt snatched it out of the air with one hand.

"I thought it might come in handy," she said, and disappeared outside.

Matt shook his head in amazement at the enigma that was Christina. He flipped the phone over, debating what to do with it. Out of curiosity, he ran through the listing of previous calls. There was one number listed more than any other. And it was the last call made right before Sarah had been kidnapped.

Matt yelled into the kitchen, "Hey, does anybody know what state the area code 512 is from?"

Fox stuck his head out of the kitchen. "Austin, Texas," he said. "Remember when you asked me to look into that intern who turned out to be Conrad's nephew? Well, the kid was from Austin, so I made a lot of calls to that area code when I was checking into his background. It's 512, for sure."

"Thanks, James." He looked back down at the number on the glowing screen, deliberating his next move. *Could it be?* he thought to himself. There was only one way to find out. Sitting alone in the living room he hit redial and put the phone up to his ear.

On the second ring a gruff voice picked up, "Conrad," it said, and continued without waiting for a response. "Where the fuck have you been, Stanton? You should have checked in hours ago. Did you get the documents?"

Once Matt had confirmed that the area code was Austin, Texas, he knew that the men they had confronted that afternoon had to have been sent by Conrad. But he didn't expect the campaign manager himself to pick up the phone. He was so surprised he almost hung up, but the urge to confront his nemesis won out.

"Yeah, we've got the documents," he said.

There was silence for what seemed like minutes.

"Who the fuck is this?" Conrad growled, but with considerably less confidence in his voice this time.

Matt thought to himself, *What the hell, I'm all-in now.* "This is Matt Hawkins, you son of a bitch. The guy whose apartment you broke into." He let that revelation sink in before adding, "And like I said, we've got the documents, and I mean *all* the

documents." He stressed the word *all*, referring to his possession of the legal contracts that detailed the arrangement between
Conrad and Metcalf, and their illicit hedge fund scheme.

"That's impossible," Conrad stammered. "I talked to J. J. earlier today and he assured me that," he stopped suddenly. "How
did you get Stanton's phone?"

"Let's just say that we relieved Mr. Stanton of his cell phone.
We relieved him of a very large handgun, too."

"Jesus Christ," Conrad muttered. He exhaled deeply into the
phone. "Do you have any idea who you're fucking with?" His
anger had bubbled over, but he quickly checked himself. He knew
that he had to tread carefully because Matt held all the cards.

As always, Chuck Conrad's mind was churning, thinking
through all the possible options that would allow him to control the damage. He finally landed on a tactic that he'd often
deployed. He would reclaim the upper hand by preying on his
opponent's fears.

"Listen, Matt, you're a smart guy, so you must know that
you're in way over your head, right? I mean, this is the big time
here. You don't want to complicate your life any further, do you?"

Conrad took Matt's silence as a sign to continue. Gaining
confidence, he said, "Here's what I'm going to do for you, son.
I'm going to give you the chance to walk away from all this and
get your life back again. That sounds good, doesn't it? So let me
explain to you what I want you to do," he began to say.

"Stop," Matt cut him off mid-sentence. "You really are a
pompous ass, aren't you?"

"Excuse me?" replied Conrad. The intimidating campaign
manager was not used to being chastised.

"You've got nothing, don't you understand that? No journal.
No surrender letter. And, oh yeah, you also seem to have misplaced a few interesting legal contracts related to your involvement in a certain hedge fund scheme. And still, you have the balls

to try to dictate to me how this is all going to go down?" Matt asked incredulously.

"Listen, you little prick, I'll ruin you."

"No, *you* listen, because I'm going to be the one dictating terms here, *not* you," Matt was still seething over how Sarah had been treated.

He was having trouble keeping his emotions in check, but these next few minutes were going to be critical for Matt. He knew he had to get Conrad and Metcalf out of their lives forever. The easy thing to do would be to publicly expose the hedge fund documents they had found in Metcalf's safe. But he had already ruled that out as an option, because they had all agreed that they wanted the next day's press conference to be all about their remarkable historical discovery, and not tainted by some present-day hedge fund scandal involving the campaign manager of the Republican nominee for president—and perhaps even Emerson himself.

But at the same time, he knew that these bastards would not rest until they had those hedge fund contracts back in their possession, which meant they would probably send more men down to Savannah. God knows he couldn't subject Sarah, or anyone else for that matter, to a life of constantly looking over their shoulders, especially given what they had all just been through. He needed a solution that would give him leverage without having to make the Conrad-Metcalf connection public.

When he had first discovered the legal contracts between the two men, a plan had begun to take shape that could potentially give him the out he had been looking for. Now it was time to execute that plan. It was a simple and elegant solution, but in order for it to work, everything would have to go just right.

So he said, "Here's what you're going to do," and he spent the next several minutes telling Chuck Conrad exactly how it was going to go down.

45

Present Day

Savannah, GA

The story started on page one and continued on page seven of the *New York Times*. Becker had written a factual and fair accounting of Washington's surrender letter. As promised, he had not editorialized or drawn hasty conclusions regarding Washington's character. Instead, he detailed the dire conditions at Valley Forge during the 1778 winter encampment and left it up to the reader to interpret the commander in chief's motives.

Clearly they had chosen the right man to break the news. But the story still centered on the irrefutable fact that George Washington had made a surrender overture to the commander of the British troops, General William Howe. Reading it in black and white, in the venerable *New York Times* no less, made them all realize that what they had discovered was *very* big news indeed.

Large red type scrolled across the bottom of the television screen that read, "Secret Washington letter discovered. Wanted to surrender to the British at Valley Forge. Treasonous?" The talking heads on CNN laid out the details of the discovery, mentioning Savannah a number of times. They went on to promote an exclusive interview, to air later that day, with the people who discovered the letter. They also promised a roundtable discussion with a panel of historians they had lined up. No doubt, they would pick apart every last detail of Washington's life in an attempt to explain the writing of the letter.

———

A large crowd had assembled in Johnson Square. The press conference had begun. The mayor was making his introductory speech from a hastily constructed podium, going out of his way to mention the integral role his office had played in enabling the discovery.

Matt scanned the crowd. Among the dozens of members of the press, both local and national, he saw a number of friends and acquaintances, including Martha Sampson, who had a front row seat, courtesy of Hank. She was dressed in her Sunday best and Matt knew that this day probably meant more to her than most. He caught her eye and gave her a nod, which she returned. He glanced over and noticed the Greene monument's freshly scrubbed surface gleaming in the late morning sun; he smiled to himself.

Hank and Fox were seated to his left behind the mayor on the podium. Sarah was seated directly to his right. Hank leaned over and, with a touch of irony, whispered, "I think the last time there were this many people in Johnson Square was two hundred years ago, when Lafayette dedicated this monument," he paused, "right before placing Washington's letter inside."

A chill went up Matt's spine as he thought of how the letter had come full circle.

He reached over and gave Sarah's hand a squeeze. He was glad to have her next to him to share in this moment. She flashed him a smile and his heart leapt. He hadn't felt this way about anyone in a very long time, and he hoped that the feeling was mutual. Even though the depth of his feelings scared him, the thought of how empty his life had been before he had met Sarah scared him even more. He vowed to try his damnedest not to screw this one up.

The mayor was winding down and he turned to Matt, introducing him as the man who discovered the letter. Matt stepped up to the microphone, but the enormity of the moment suddenly hit him and he became very nervous and uncertain about where to begin. His eyes fell on Martha Sampson, who was staring intently at him. It was almost as though she could read his thoughts. Her voice suddenly resonated in his head and he recalled her words, "A good story isn't rushed."

Calm washed over him and his nerves disappeared. He began, "A wise woman once told me that the key to storytelling is that a good one unfolds slowly," he glanced at Martha, who was beaming with pride. "So I hope you all don't mind, but I'm going to start at the beginning, because I've got a hell of a story to tell."

———

The press conference was picked up by every major news outlet, and Matt became famous overnight. All in all, the coverage had been fair and measured, but only time would tell how the American public would treat Washington's legacy.

46

That Same Day

Central Texas

They had been campaigning for three weeks nonstop. Unexpectedly, Conrad recommended that they return to Emerson's Texas ranch for an impromptu couple of days of R&R, before gearing up for the final four weeks of the race. Big Bill had not complained. They left Ohio and flew back to Blackjack Ranch the night before the press conference in Savannah.

Conrad had made the spur of the moment change of plans after Matt Hawkins made it clear in their conversation that there was no way to stop the news from getting out. He had tried but failed to keep both the journal and surrender letter under wraps. Conrad hated to fail, but he was also a realist. So once again, he had taken decisive action.

It was a calculated move to sequester Emerson on his secluded two-thousand-acre ranch. At least it would keep the candidate far away from probing reporters sticking microphones in his fleshy face looking for comments on the discovery. Conrad knew that when the news broke it was going to be a cluster fuck, and he wanted to keep them well clear of the maelstrom when it hit. He hoped lying low would limit the damage. They would stay holed up for a couple of days in central Texas until the initial news cycle ran its course. Then the campaign would issue a carefully worded statement. Under no circumstances was Conrad going to let Emerson appear on camera. He had to distance his candidate from the Washington letter controversy, at all costs.

Big Bill had arisen early, if only to avoid his second wife, who was quickly becoming as much of a pain in the ass as his first wife. His initial attraction to her, which was based in large part on a beautiful pair of silicone-enhanced boobs, had begun to wane. Emerson had always been a sucker for a big set of knockers, but the novelty of wife number two's had long since worn off. He hadn't realized just how much of a fitness nut she was when he married her, but experience told him he better vacate the bedroom quickly. If she woke up before him, she would only nag him to join her in their fully equipped gym for an hour of aerobic exercise, something Big Bill loathed.

He quietly pulled on his robe and tiptoed out of the bedroom. He emerged undetected onto the expansive patio that led to the kidney-shaped swimming pool. The over-the-top pool was equipped with a cascading waterfall that had cost him six figures to install. He slipped out of his robe and dove into the pool, completely naked. It was his favorite way to start the day, and a routine that he did not look forward to giving up, should he someday reside in the White House.

As a freshman in high school, Big Bill had actually been a member of the school's swim team and hadn't been half bad. But that was close to forty years and well over a hundred pounds ago. So after a few laps, he climbed out, threw his robe back on, and withdrew a long stogie from one of the pockets. He lit it and reclined on one of the many chaise lounges scattered around the deck.

He breathed in the early morning air that somehow seemed crisper at eighteen hundred feet, despite the thick acrid smoke emanating from his enormous Presidente cigar. He scanned the horizon and decided that he hadn't felt this good in weeks. He only had a month to go in the marathon campaign and then the race would be over, one way or the other. Although he still wasn't sure which outcome he'd prefer.

He heard the slider open from the main house behind him. Panicked that his wife had hunted him down, he turned quickly. He was relieved to see Chuck Conrad approaching, even though he looked more serious than usual. Emerson didn't want to have his good mood dampened, so he held up his hand and said, "Unless you have good news to share, Chuck, I don't want to hear it."

Chuck pulled up a nearby chaise and sat down with a heavy sigh. "Sorry, chief, but this one can't wait," he said ominously.

"Aw shit, Chuck," Big Bill whined.

"Listen," Conrad said, forging ahead, "you remember that journal from Savannah?"

"You mean the one you *stole*?" Emerson couldn't resist taking a dig at his campaign manager.

"Yeah, that one," he said irritably. "Anyway, there's a problem. They stole it back."

"What?" Bill sat upright in his lounge chair so that the two men's knees were almost touching. "What do you mean they stole it back?"

"Bill, you've got to stop interrupting me, OK? Just hear me out, because it gets worse, a lot worse," he said. "Those pains in the ass from Savannah now have both the journal and the actual surrender letter," he paused briefly, "and they're going public with them today."

"Oh Jesus," Bill groaned. He tossed the cigar aside and massaged his temples with his thick knuckles. His perfect morning had just gone to shit. His head began to throb instantly. "What does 'going public' mean exactly?" He could feel his blood pressure starting to rise, which reminded him that he had forgotten to take his hypertension pills.

"They're holding a press conference later this morning in Savannah," Conrad declared. He placed a copy of the *New York Times* on Emerson's knees. "But the news is already out," he said as he pointed to the front-page article. "Read it."

Big Bill spent the next few minutes skimming the article, swearing aloud as he read.

"The liberal press is going to crucify me, Chuck," he was up out of his seat and pacing in front of the pool. He wished he could dive in again, and that the cool blue water would wash away all his problems. "I've got Washington's goddamned face on everything connected to this campaign; I think I even saw his mug on the fucking toilet paper!"

Conrad remained quiet, knowing he had to let Bill vent.

Now on a roll, Bill continued, "They're going to ask me how I feel about my namesake surrendering. They're probably going to want to know if I think what he did was an act of sedition. What do I say to that, for Christ's sake?"

He continued his one-way dialogue. "If I say yes, then I condemn my *ancestor*," he said, making exaggerated quotes with his fingers. "And if I say no, then I come off supporting his decision to usurp Congress and surrender to the goddamned British!" He was now red in the face and very animated. "I'm going to be made to look like a fool, Chuck."

Finally, Conrad had had enough. "Calm down, Bill, and sit down," he demanded. "That's exactly why I brought you here last night, to prevent the press from getting to you. You will not make any comments. Do you understand? We will issue a statement when the time is right; maybe tomorrow after the dust has had a chance to settle a little bit, OK?" He waited for Bill to look him in the eye and acknowledge him, like a parent would do with a misbehaving child.

Reluctantly, Emerson looked up, "OK, but this is a fucking mess, Chuck. You were supposed to have this under control." He looked away when he saw anger flash in Conrad's eyes.

"I've got work to do," was all Conrad said, before stalking back inside the ostentatious, custom-built lodge.

———

The press set up a makeshift camp outside the gates of Blackjack Ranch. But Big Bill was more than two miles up the private drive, safely holed up inside his massive home. Since they couldn't interview him directly, the press found anyone even remotely connected to the candidate to comment on the letter. They interviewed his high school history teacher, former associates from both the business world and the U.S. Senate, even his ex-wife. It was a feeding frenzy and Big Bill's silence only made them hungry for more.

His opponent, the Democratic nominee for president, had graciously made himself available for interviews. He seemed to use the word *surrender* as often as possible when referencing Emerson in his talking points. The only statement from the Republican side came from a right-wing fringe element, which issued a press release claiming the surrender letter discovery to be a hoax. They accused the Democrats of fabricating the whole thing, calling it a desperate and unpatriotic attempt by supporters of the opposition to gain points in the polls by disparaging the great name of George Washington.

As the day progressed and the coverage did not abate, Emerson began to question the strategy of remaining mum on the matter while everyone else in the world offered up opinions. He went to find Conrad and tell him that it was time to break their silence. After searching a good portion of the compound, however, his campaign manager was nowhere to be found. Finally, he ran into one of his senior staffers. "Where the hell is Chuck?" he asked irritably. "I can't find him anywhere!"

"Oh, sorry, sir, he asked me to tell you he had to leave town for a while. He said he had some very important business to take care of and wouldn't be back until late tonight," the staffer relayed the message nervously, knowing it would not be well received by his boss.

"Very important business—what the hell could be more important than this?" he shouted, pointing emphatically at the sixty-inch flat screen television mounted above the mammoth stone fireplace. It was still tuned to CNN, which hadn't given the story a rest all afternoon.

Unbeknownst to Big Bill, at that precise moment, Chuck Conrad was seated on a friend's private jet. He was making an unscheduled and unpublicized trip to Savannah, Georgia. He had some personal business to attend to, and if all went according to plan, he would be back before the night was over.

47

Present Day

Savannah, GA

S avannah's city hall sat proudly atop Yamacraw Bluff. The Renaissance Revival structure overlooked the Savannah River to the north, with an unobstructed view, to the south, of Johnson Square—the site where Matt had dropped the surrender letter bombshell earlier in the day. Normally used as the council chambers, the room just down the hall from the mayor's office had been set aside for interviews. Most of the throng of reporters had finally had their fill and departed. Sarah went looking for Matt and spotted him near the building's signature dolphin fountain. He was having a serious conversation with *New York Times* reporter David Becker. Becker had stuck around after the press conference to ask a few more questions for a follow-up piece he was going to file for the next day's edition.

Sarah approached the two men. "Hey Matt, my father, Director Fox, and I were thinking about going over to the Crystal for a celebratory dinner. Are you game? And, Mr. Becker, you're more than welcome to join us."

Matt stole a quick glance over at Becker before responding, "That sounds great, Sarah. I'll join up with you guys a little bit later." He hesitated before adding, "I've got something I need to take care of first."

Sarah found his cagey response a bit odd, but chalked it up to a long day of nonstop interviews. "No problem, come join us when you can." She stood on her tiptoes and gave him a peck on the cheek. "You did a great job today, we're all really proud of you."

"Thanks," he gave her hand a squeeze, "so did you."

She smiled and turned away. When she glanced back over her shoulder, she noticed that the two men had immediately resumed their serious discussion.

———

About an hour later with the sun dipping over the horizon, Matt sat by himself in a back booth of a twenty-four-hour diner on Abercorn Street, about eight miles south of historic downtown Savannah. His booth had an unobstructed view of the front door. After trying unsuccessfully to talk him into ordering the special of the day, chicken-fried steak, the large black waitress kindly refilled his coffee and left him alone. He was fidgety, and not just because he had consumed too much caffeine.

His final meeting of the day was late and Matt began to worry that he wouldn't show. He glanced at his watch for probably the twentieth time in the last ten minutes. Finally, the front door swung open and a man walked in. Matt had seen him on television and downloaded his image from the Internet so many times that he had memorized his face. He was wearing a baseball cap and a leather jacket, an outfit that was way too heavy for the warm October evening. Clearly, he wished to keep their meeting discreet. The man scanned the inside of the diner looking for Matt, which didn't take long since there was only a smattering of blue-collar patrons scattered about. Matt nodded in subtle acknowledgment when their eyes met, but it wasn't necessary, the man recognized Matt's now-famous face instantly. He made his way to the back of the diner and slid into the booth.

"Mr. Conrad, I was beginning to wonder if you were going to show," Matt said cordially, although his voice was hoarse from the strain of talking to the press all day.

"I'm not sure I had much of a choice." Then, as was his style, he got right to the point, "You stole something of mine that I'd like back."

Matt replied with an ironic smile, "You have to admit, that sounds a little strange coming from the man who authorized the theft of Caty Greene's journal from my house not too long ago."

"Let's cut the crap. I'm a very busy man who woke up today in the middle of a shit storm, thanks to you. You said on the phone you wanted to cut some kind of deal, so hurry up and make your offer. I'm in no mood to dick around."

Once again, Chuck Conrad was on the offensive. "I'm this close," he continued, putting up his thumb and index finger, "to picking up the phone and calling my associates and having them pay you another visit. Maybe I'll just take back what you stole from me," he said with a cold stare.

Matt stared back, unflinching. He knew that Conrad was coming on strong because aggression was the only leverage he had left. He knew that, because he had seen enough Wall Street sharks do the same thing; it was called the art of the bluff. But Matt was about to call that bluff.

"Well, you might have a little trouble reaching your *associates*." He reached into his pocket and tossed Stanton's cell phone across the table. "They're somewhat indisposed at the moment."

The two men stared at each other like gunfighters in an old western movie. Matt was no longer intimidated. In fact, he started to see Conrad as more pathetic than scary. Conrad, realizing he was running out of cards to play, finally relented, "So how do you want to work this?"

The front door jingled again. Matt looked up and saw that the second man he had invited to the diner that evening had just shown up. He looked around nervously, like a ferret just emerging from its hole. He also looked like he had never set foot inside a greasy spoon in his life. Matt waited patiently until he looked his way, and then waved him over.

Conrad turned and saw whom Matt was gesturing at. "What the fuck is he doing here?" He snapped his head back around to face Matt, a wild look in his eye.

Matt ignored him and greeted his other guest. "Mr. Metcalf, please have a seat next to Chuck Conrad. I believe you two know each other," he said with a smile, clearly enjoying holding the equivalent of a full house in poker.

Metcalf looked like he'd rather receive a sharp stick in the eye than touch any surface in the diner, let alone sit on the heavily stained vinyl seat of the corner booth. But eventually he did, carefully arranging himself so as to come into contact with as few surfaces as possible. His hands, however, never emerged from inside his trench coat pockets.

Neither of Matt's guests greeted the other. Metcalf's impossibly small shoulders twitched nervously, and his eyes shifted briefly to his right just once—the only acknowledgment he gave of Conrad's presence at the table. He still had not spoken a word.

"Glad you could take the time from your busy schedule to join us," Matt said. Still Metcalf said nothing. He just cleared his throat loudly, yet another of his many odd quirks.

"OK, the gang's all here, son. So I'm going to ask you again, what do you want?" Conrad's patience was wearing thin.

Now that Metcalf had arrived, it was time to get down to business. Matt didn't want to spend any more time with these lowlifes than he had to, so he began, "Here's the deal. It's no secret that I've got something of yours that, if I decided to take to the authorities, could result in both of you ending up in jail," he paused to make sure he had the men's undivided attention.

He did, so he continued, "Let me start by saying, I have no intention of doing that, and I will *never* do that, as long as you agree to the terms that I'm about to lay out."

Conrad butted in, again trying to seize control of the dialogue, "If this is about money, I'm sure something can be arranged." He shut his mouth when he saw the look on Matt's face. "Sorry, go ahead," he said, in a rare show of contriteness.

"Here are my terms for staying silent about your insider hedge fund scheme. One, if your boy Emerson is elected president," he stared directly at Conrad, "then one of the very first things he is going to do is announce that he will never support the privatization of Fannie Mae and Freddie Mac. Your administration must never pursue privatization.

"Two," he said, turning his attention to Charles Metcalf, "while it's true that unraveling your Fannie Mae scheme will no doubt deal a significant blow to your portfolio, we both know it will by no means ruin you. You will still be a wealthy man and you are going to put some of that wealth to good use. You are going to make a significant donation to the Society of the Cincinnati to establish and maintain a scholarship fund to help deserving African American kids attend college. This scholarship will be one of the largest of its kind, and it will be established in the name of Martha Sampson, the woman whose family was the keeper of Caty Greene's journal for over a century." Matt had added this condition at the last minute, believing it would be a fitting tribute to Martha and her father, Toby Morton.

"And three," he held up three fingers on his right hand, "you will both stay away from me and all my friends who were associated with exposing to the public the journal and Washington's surrender letter. You will not attempt to harm or disrupt our lives in any way." He concluded, "If any of these three conditions are not met, then our deal will be considered null and void. And the incriminating illegal contract between the two of you will be made public."

Metcalf, who had sat stonily silent, finally spoke up. "Do you know who you are talking to? People like you are nothing more than an insignificant nuisance to someone like me. I have the resources to destroy you if I choose to do so. So don't you dare try to dictate terms," he said, his voice dripping with condescension.

Matt struggled to remain calm. "It's true you have a lot more resources than I do, but I've got the one thing that can bring you down. So you better think long and hard about my offer."

Metcalf leaned forward, and through gritted teeth said, "And what makes you think I won't just have someone put a bullet in your head." His reptilian eyes darted about rapidly, making him look like a snake eyeing where to sink its venomous teeth into its prey.

Matt wanted nothing more than to reach across the table and wring the little freak's neck. Instead, he took a deep breath and stuck to the plan. He responded, "That would be unfortunate, because it's been arranged that if anything were to happen to me, your highly illegal contracts will automatically be released to the press."

"Hah!" Metcalf spat out. "You're bluffing."

"Am I?" Matt said. He nodded to a man sitting at the counter sipping coffee. Both Metcalf and Conrad turned around to see whom Matt had signaled.

David Becker got up from his stool and approached their booth. He calmly set two business cards down on the table.

Matt spoke with more confidence now, "This is David Becker, the man who broke the story on Washington's letter in this morning's *New York Times*. Mr. Metcalf, you may remember him as the reporter who won the Pulitzer Prize a few years ago for a series of articles on the financial crisis of 2008. He is very well versed in securities law and takes great pride in exposing criminal activity, particularly crimes of a financial nature." He turned the floor over to Becker.

"As Matt has already told you gentlemen, my name is David Becker, and I work as an investigative reporter for the *New York Times*." He continued as Matt had scripted for him, "My paper is in the possession of a sealed envelope, the contents of which I have been authorized to publish should anything untoward happen to Matt or any of his associates. You need to be assured that I will do just that." Without waiting for a reply, Becker turned and walked out of the diner.

The two men were stunned into silence. Matt went for the close, "Do we have a deal, gentlemen?"

Conrad had already made up his mind. The damage to Emerson's campaign had been done, but at least he could escape with his reputation intact. He knew that if the contract with Metcalf were ever made public, then, at a minimum, he would never be able to practice law again. It was time to cut his losses, so he held up his hands in defeat and said simply, "You win."

"I'll take that as a yes," Matt said quickly. "Mr. Metcalf?" He waited for a response from the grim reaper. Metcalf refused to speak but he finally did nod his head, just once, in agreement.

"Excellent," Matt said. He slid out of the booth, anxious to vacate the premises before either man changed his mind. "Hopefully, I'll never have the pleasure again."

Matt threw a ten-dollar bill down on the table, more than enough to settle the bill, and followed the path Becker had taken moments earlier out the front door. He would have loved to have heard the conversation between the odd couple he left sitting side by side at the table.

But then again, he thought, maybe not.

48

Present Day

Savannah, GA

M att marveled at just how much had happened in his life in such a short period of time. Had it only been a few weeks ago that he had visited the Bull Street Library and returned home with a box of atlases? He wondered what his ex-wife had thought when she had seen his face plastered all over the news, or his old colleagues on Wall Street. Then it occurred to him that he really didn't care. He had made a new life for himself in Savannah. And because of that, he had been in the right place at the right time, and had been given the privilege of discovering Caty Greene's journal. And that had, in turn, set off the extraordinary chain of events that culminated in the press conference earlier that day.

He shook his head in wonder as he came through the back entrance of the Crystal Beer Parlor. He headed straight for the bar, where he saw Sarah and Hank along with the rest of the group of friends and family who had all, in one way or another, played a part in the discovery of Washington's letter.

The popular saloon was packed as usual. Through the crowd, Matt could see Buzz, who had flown back into town that afternoon from D.C., hoisting a bottle of Budweiser. He was sandwiched between Sissy Hightower, who was bending Hank's ear, and Director Fox, whom Matt still felt a little bit ashamed about, for having once doubted his loyalties. Christina was also there, apparently in the middle of ordering a round of drinks, as she was shouting instructions to the bartender. No one had seen Matt yet, and he hesitated for just a moment. He smiled at how this unlikely group of amateurs had somehow banded together to uncover a centuries-old mystery. And when his eyes landed on Sarah, laughing at a joke that Buzz had just told, he smiled wider still. He felt at home for the first time in a long time.

Sarah looked up and saw Matt halfway across the bar with that trademark crooked grin on his face. She leapt out of her bar stool and snaked her way across the crowded room. She was being pulled toward him by some unseen magnetic force, as if her entire being were nothing more than scattered steel shavings that could only be made whole again by meeting up with him.

"Hello, handsome," she said, arriving at his side.

Prior to meeting Matt, Sarah knew that her life had been predictably safe, and if she were honest with herself, even boring. It wasn't until being immersed in the harrowing, yet strangely exhilarating encounters of the last few weeks, that she had realized just how much so. It had been baptism by fire, but the experience had forced her to appreciate that life was not just to be read about in books, it was to be lived. And she vowed to herself to do just that from now on. Spontaneity had never been one of her strengths, but the new Sarah was determined to change that, so she threw her arms around Matt's neck and planted a passionate kiss on his lips.

"Wow, what did I do to deserve that?" he said happily, taken off guard by Sarah's spontaneous and very public show of affection.

"Sometimes there doesn't have to be a reason," she said with a mischievous smile. "Come on." She led him by the hand toward the bar to join their friends in celebration.

After another round of drinks, food became the next order of business. They all squeezed into a single booth and ordered burgers, meatloaf, chicken and other stick-to-your-ribs entrees from the Crystal's oversized menus. Matt looked across the table at Buzz. "So how did it go in Washington?" he asked. He had to raise his voice to be heard above the din in the restaurant. "Did the board take any action against Metcalf?"

Buzz filled them in on the emergency meeting of the Board of Directors of the Society of the Cincinnati. Apparently after Buzz had shared the details surrounding Metcalf's involvement in the theft of the surrender letter it hadn't taken long for the board to reach a unanimous decision. They removed Metcalf from his position as president general, effective immediately.

"Well, he certainly earned his dismissal," said a disgusted Sissy.

"That he did," Fox seconded, before offering a toast, "good riddance to the phantom!" They all raised their glasses in a hearty cheer, laughing at the amusing toast from the usually restrained director.

A reflective silence followed. Everyone seemed to be replaying recent events in their minds. Sarah finally spoke up and voiced what the others were most likely thinking, "Is anyone else worried that Metcalf and Conrad might be still be a little upset with us? I mean, they hired hit men to track us down once before. Do we really think they're just going to go away quietly, without retaliation, after what we did to them?"

Heads nodded around the table amid murmurs of agreement. Matt broke in, "Charles Metcalf will never bother us again, that I can promise you. And neither will Chuck Conrad, for that

matter." There were confused looks as everyone was taken aback
by Matt's definitive proclamation.

A thought occurred to Hank, "Does this have anything to
do with those documents you found in Metcalf's safe?" He was
referring to the contract that Matt had reviewed in the car ride
home from the private airstrip. "You never did share them with
me, but I remember you saying that those files helped you connect Metcalf to Conrad. I believe you called it our smoking gun."

"It does," Matt acknowledged, "and the reason I didn't share
them with you or anyone else, for that matter, was because I
figured you'd all be safer if you didn't know about what I had
found."

"You used those files to blackmail them, didn't you?" Hank
stated matter-of-factly, as he began to piece together Matt's plan.

"Let's just say I put them to good use," Matt replied with a
sly smile.

He knew he owed it to the group to fill in the rest of the
story, so, after a swig of beer, he started in, "When Bradley, our
safecracker, ran out of time and had to grab all of the contents
of Metcalf's safe, we received an unexpected bonus. Amongst
his personal files were some legal contracts between him and
Conrad.

"Evidently Metcalf had cooked up a hedge fund scheme that
involved buying up all the outstanding shares of preferred stock
in Fannie Mae and Freddie Mac. Those are two government-
sponsored companies that currently own or back about half of
all outstanding home loans in the country. Turns out that these
enterprises have become quite profitable over the last couple of
years, and there has been talk on Capitol Hill of privatizing them.
Not many investment firms are willing to invest in Fannie and
Freddie because there is simply too much risk. Primarily because
there is no guarantee that the government will ever privatize the
two companies. And if they don't, whatever shares you hold in

the companies would be essentially worthless, especially if they choose to liquidate them, which has also been discussed," he explained.

Matt paused to make sure everyone was following. He had plenty of experience in and around the world of investments but he knew that the financial markets were baffling to most people. Everyone seemed to still be tracking with him, so he pressed on. "But Metcalf is a very smart *and* a very devious guy, so he came up with a brilliant idea to eliminate all the risk associated with such a speculative investment strategy. You see, he wasn't going to invest millions of dollars on the *chance* that the two enterprises were going to be privatized; he needed a *guarantee* that they would be privatized. And that required a man on the inside."

"Emerson?" Sissy guessed.

"No, but the next best thing," he said.

"Conrad," Sarah said.

"Exactly. This is where Chuck Conrad entered into the plan. Conrad promised Metcalf that one of the first things Emerson would do as president would be to push for the privatization of the two government companies. That would pretty much guarantee that Metcalf's investment scheme would pay off handsomely, to the tune of hundreds of millions of dollars," Matt explained.

"And what was Mr. Conrad to be paid for his troubles?" asked Hank.

"The contract stipulated that Chuck Conrad owned ten percent of the fund. So if all went well, he would have walked away with a hundred million, minimum."

"Whew," Sissy whistled, "that's a lot of moolah."

"And you would never have been able to connect Metcalf to Conrad if that contract hadn't fallen into our hands?" Hank asked.

"Probably not. My Wall Street friend helped me connect some of the dots, but I still needed the smoking gun. It's only because our safecracker ran out of time and had to empty all of the contents of Metcalf's safe into Buzz's flight bag that we found the contracts," he said. "And that gave me the leverage I needed to cut a deal."

Sarah put a hand to her mouth and said, "Oh my God, that's why you were late tonight." The risk Matt had taken had suddenly dawned on her. "You met with the two of them, didn't you? That's what you and David Becker were talking about at the press conference." She was clearly not happy with Matt's reckless decision.

"It's OK, Sarah," Matt said, taking hold of her hand. "I met with them in a very public 24-hour diner just outside of town. I was never in danger. And yes, Becker agreed to come with me. Metcalf and Conrad had to know that if they ever bothered any of us again," he said looking around the table, "that every detail about their scheme would be published and their respective careers would be finished. David Becker was my trump card."

Sarah pulled her hand away. "You've seen what these men can do, Matt. *I've* seen firsthand what they're capable of, in case you've forgotten," her voice quivered slightly as she spoke. "You should have told us; you should have told *me*." She was hurt and angry, and Matt realized she had a right to be. He knew he'd be furious with her if she had pulled a stunt like this.

"You're right, I should have told you, and I'm sorry. But you have to believe that I did what I did to protect you—to protect all of us—from ever having to worry about these guys again. Coming into possession of these contracts gave us the perfect out, so I took advantage of the opportunity. And it worked," he said. Then he made an attempt at humor to try to thaw the chill between them. "And if it's any consolation, when I left the two of them sitting alone together at the diner, they looked like poster children for blind dates gone bad." Matt grinned tentatively, hoping he was a step closer to getting out of the doghouse.

Just a hint of a smile appeared at the corners of Sarah's mouth. She knew she couldn't stay mad at him. Deep down, she had to admit that she was relieved more than anyone that Conrad and Metcalf were out of their lives forever. Even so, she smacked Matt on the arm. "No more secrets, all right?" she said seriously.

"I promise," he said. And he meant it.

"Nice job, boss, looks like you might have finally grown a pair of balls," Christina couldn't help but throw a barb Matt's way.

Not to be outdone, Matt countered, "I've always had a pair, Christina; you just never noticed because you were too busy admiring your own."

Epilogue

9 Months Later

The grand ballroom of Anderson House, the Society of the Cincinnati's headquarters, had been chosen to house the *Decision at Valley Forge* interactive exhibit about to be opened to the public. The exhibit would tell the story of Washington's role as commander in chief of the Continental Army, the battles he won and lost, and the many strategic decisions he made along the way. It would also detail the conditions at Valley Forge and the state of his army at the time of the writing of the surrender letter. The letter itself would be showcased in a specially designed, state-of-the-art case, similar to the one used to display the Constitution at the National Archives Building. The case that had been installed was airtight, temperature controlled, and filled with inert helium gas to help preserve the fragile document. It also came equipped with special glass that would allow visitors to view the document while keeping out harmful light.

A separate section of the exhibit had been created to tell the story of Catharine "Caty" Littlefield Greene and her remarkable life, to provide an understanding of the Revolutionary War from the unique perspective of a general's wife. And, of course, her incredibly revealing journal would be prominently featured. The exhibit would recount its more than two-century journey from

Mulberry Grove Plantation to the Bull Street Library, where Matt had discovered it hidden inside the oversized atlas. The final piece of the interactive exhibit would be from the point of view of African American slaves, to help people understand the lives they led during the revolutionary time period. This unique perspective would feature a living history section, giving visitors the opportunity to hear the taped reminiscences of Martha Sampson. She would offer recollections and stories of past events, as told to her by her father, one of the last people to be born into slavery during the Civil War, including her family's almost 150-year relationship with the journal itself.

It was this final piece of the exhibit that had brought Martha Sampson to Anderson House on this day. Matt and Sarah had escorted her from her home in Savannah to Washington, D.C., on Buzz's Piper Comanche airplane. Matt had affectionately dubbed the plane Air Buzz, for the many trips it had made to and from Savannah over the past nine months. As for Buzz, he had been busier than ever. He had accepted an offer from the board to take over as interim president general of the society until a permanent replacement could be found. He seemed so energized by the preparations for the exhibit, however, that Matt wondered if he wouldn't choose to stay on indefinitely.

They had all been a little nervous about taking a ninety-year-old woman up in Buzz's little plane, but Martha had been surprisingly excited by the trip. So much so that she had peppered Buzz nonstop with questions throughout the course of the flight. Upon arriving at Anderson House, she had been given a VIP tour of the exhibit and had become very emotional upon viewing the journal for the first time since she was just a little girl, thus completing the Morton family's long association with the little leather-covered book. Tears streamed down her face when she toured the section of the exhibit devoted to African American slaves that prominently featured her ancestors. She couldn't stop thanking Matt for all he, Hank, and Sarah had done to preserve the memory of her family. And she was stunned when Matt had revealed to her that a large scholarship had been established in her name to send deserving young African American scholars to college.

Indeed, Charles Metcalf had lived up to his end of the bargain. In return for Matt's silence, he made a sizable donation to establish and maintain a college scholarship program in the name of Martha Sampson. As expected, the hedge fund that he had created with Chuck Conrad had imploded when the insider scheme fell apart, making his entire investment worthless. Fannie Mae and Freddie Mac were not privatized; in fact, the latest talk on Capitol Hill was that they would be dissolved. But as Matt had predicted, the man they had nicknamed the grim reaper was far from penniless, as his primary hedge fund was still doing well. He had moved back to Manhattan after he was unceremoniously removed from his position as president general of the society. There, he had purchased a brownstone on the Upper East Side and completely gutted it, installing the latest air-filtering technology. He had spent less and less time out in public, choosing to live most of his days in the completely germfree, controlled environment of his reclusive home. Rumor had it that ironically the brownstone had once been a funeral home.

William Washington Emerson, also known as Big Bill, lost a very close election. It was so close in fact that the votes in Ohio had to be recounted twice. But when it was all said and done, the verdict had not changed. The jury was still out, however, on what effect the revelation of the surrender letter had on the outcome of the election. The fact was that Emerson had been slightly ahead when the announcement had been made, and ended up losing by a hair. Political pundits debated the letter's effect for many weeks after the election, some believing it had cost him the presidency. Others were not so sure, and thought that Ohio was going to vote Democrat regardless. But there was no debating that the Emerson campaign had tried to distance its candidate from the negative publicity surrounding the surrender letter. In the final weeks of the campaign, it had removed all traces of Washington's image from the campaign materials. Unfortunately, it had proven to be too little, too late.

Only time would tell how Washington's legacy would ultimately be treated in the court of public opinion. In the months after the announcement, there had been those who had called for the stripping of his name from popular monuments and bridges. Some others even asserted that his face should no longer grace the one-dollar bill. But most Americans seemed to take the news in stride. For some, it was because the event had happened too long ago to care; for others, it was because the letter was never delivered, which made the whole thing seem irrelevant; and still others who could empathize with his controversial decision. And while most Americans' lives would remain unchanged by the revelation of the letter, Matt knew for certain that at least some people's lives would never be the same.

One of those people was Chuck Conrad. Things had gone from bad to worse for the would-be chief of staff since the prior November. During the days following the election, he had made quite a spectacle of himself. He loudly claimed voter fraud and conspiracy against the Emerson campaign, as he desperately clung to his fading dream of one day roaming the halls of the White House. For a short time, he was the darling of the political talk shows, but soon even they grew weary of his increasingly hollow-sounding cries of injustice. And when they too finally moved on, Conrad was left without a soapbox, without a job, and without the power he so craved. He felt irrelevant and fell into a deep depression. He began to drink heavily to escape his misery. One evening, after leaving a Dallas men's club, a very intoxicated Conrad was pulled over and charged with DUI. A newspaper photographer arrived at the scene and took a less-than-flattering picture of him that ended up on the front page of the *Dallas Morning News*. It was subsequently picked up by news outlets around the country. He hadn't been seen in public since.

Big Bill, on the other hand, was secretly relieved that he had lost the election. He had never really aspired to be the leader of the free world and was decidedly more comfortable in more leisurely pursuits. Unfortunately, one of those pursuits had been a young Mexican housekeeper on his ranch—a tryst that had subsequently led wife number two to file for divorce. It would cost Big Bill another chunk of his shrinking fortune, but he was glad to be rid of her. He had put on an additional twenty pounds since the election but didn't seem to care. He spent his days happily hunting exotic game, shooting skeet, and riding ATVs on his two-thousand-acre ranch. Big Bill still knew how to throw a party and he entertained often, so he always had an audience for his larger-than-life stories. He was happier than he had been in years. And he swam naked whenever he wanted to.

Hank had been busy back in Savannah, where he had started a foundation dedicated to reclaiming the property where Mulberry Grove had once stood. The plan was to turn it into an educational center to preserve the incredible history of the plantation. He hoped to build a state-of-the-art cultural attraction where people could learn about life on a southern plantation during the late eighteenth century. Visitors would be told how Eli Whitney invented the cotton gin while staying as a guest at Mulberry Grove. They would hear the incredible stories of Caty Greene, Nathanael Greene, Anthony Wayne, and the many other famous people who had at one time or another graced the grounds of the old plantation; headlined, of course, by George Washington himself. Hank had increasingly been sighted around town with Sissy Hightower, and Sarah hadn't seen her father so happy since before her mother's death, more than a decade earlier.

Sarah, she had been busy writing a book in collaboration with Director Fox. They hoped to present a picture of what might have happened if Washington's surrender letter had actually been delivered to British general William Howe as intended. It had already required two trips to England to interview historians and to research British archival materials to get an accurate perspective on how the British might have reacted to an American offer of surrender. Director Fox was also busier than ever. Not only was he collaborating on the book with Sarah, but he had also been put in charge of managing the highly anticipated grand opening of the *Decision at Valley Forge* exhibit. It was estimated that more than one hundred thousand visitors would enter through the doors of Anderson House during the exhibit's first month alone. Fox had been working around the clock making all the necessary preparations.

As for Matt, his life had initially been a whirlwind of interviews, speeches, and appearances. He had enjoyed the notoriety at first, but was glad when things had settled down somewhat so that he could get back to tending to his store and life in Savannah. Business was great, as the shop had become a popular stop for tourists looking to meet the man who had discovered the famous letter. Matt didn't mind, as long as they were respectful of his time—and especially if they actually made a purchase. Christina had again brought up the idea of charging people admission if they didn't buy anything, and although tempted, Matt had yet to act on her suggestion. While she no longer complained about the lack of customers, Christina still found creative ways to be a pain in Matt's ass. But in the end, as much as the two of them sparred, they knew that theirs was a special friendship. They would always be there for one another.

The lawful owner of Washington's surrender letter was still in question, and the case would probably be tied up in the courts for some time. In the meantime, however, an agreement had been

worked out that provided the Society of the Cincinnati temporary custody, for the purposes of displaying the priceless historical artifacts for the world to see. The society had made Matt a
generous offer for Caty Greene's journal, for which there had
been no dispute of ownership. Matt had accepted their six-figure
offer, knowing that the journal's rightful place was alongside the
letter, but he had yet to decide what to do with the money. He
knew that he would be donating some of it to Hank's efforts
to revive Mulberry Grove, and he'd probably use some of it to
continue his slow but steady shabby-to-chic renovation on the
nineteenth-century Savannah mansion that he called home.

And while the money was nice, he knew that he had been
given a gift of far greater value as a result of his journey of discovery. He had been given a second chance. The defensive wall
he had built around his heart had come down, removed brick by
brick by Sarah Gordon. Over the past nine months, the initial
attraction that had flared up during those harried days of discovery had blossomed naturally and effortlessly into something
deeper and more substantive. He knew with certainty that his
life had changed forever, not because of his newfound celebrity,
but because of his shared future with Sarah. He was finally truly
happy.

And the trademark crooked grin, which seemed to never
leave his face these days, proved it.

####

Author's Note

While the story of a surrender letter written by George Washington is entirely fictional, the historical places, dates, people, and organizations are factual.

❖ Catharine "Caty" Littlefield Greene was close friends or acquaintances with a remarkable number of Revolutionary War figures, including Benjamin Franklin, Henry Knox, Alexander Hamilton, "Mad" Anthony Wayne, Benjamin Lincoln, the Marquis de Lafayette, and, of course, George and Martha Washington.

❖ Caty Greene lived on Mulberry Grove Plantation from 1786 until 1800 when she was forced to sell the plantation at auction due to her diminished financial means. She moved to Cumberland Island and built a new home, called Dungeness, where she lived until her death in September 1814. Her simple grave can still be found today in an abandoned cemetery a little northeast of where her home once stood on the island.

❖ George Washington did, in fact, visit Caty upon two separate occasions over a three-day period during his presidential tour of the South in May 1791. During his second visit, the two met alone for more than three hours. It is not known what they discussed.

❖ Less than a year after Washington's visit, Caty presented her indemnification case before Congress and was awarded the sum of $47,000 paid out in two installments of $23,500 each. The checks were signed by Secretary of the Treasury Alexander Hamilton, and personally approved by President Washington.

❖ Eli Whitney was a guest at Mulberry Grove from the latter part of 1792 through the first half of 1793. It was during this time that he invented what would come to be known as the cotton gin, the invention that would dramatically change the economy of the South.

❖ The Society of the Cincinnati is a real organization founded by Revolutionary War officers in 1783. George Washington was its very first president. Controversy swirled around the society in the early post-revolutionary years, as there were charges of conspiracy by some people against the newly formed government, and fears of a military coup. Among those opposed to the formation of the society were most notably Benjamin Franklin and Thomas Jefferson. It remains today the country's oldest private patriotic organization and is headquartered in Washington, D.C., at Anderson House.

❖ Asa Bird Gardiner was a member of the Rhode Island Society of the Cincinnati. In 1901, Gardiner traveled on behalf of the Rhode Island Society to Savannah, Georgia, to locate the misplaced remains of General Nathanael Greene.

❖ Greene's remains were in fact "lost" for more than one hundred years until they were found by Gardiner's search team alongside his oldest son, George Washington Greene, in the Graham-Mossman vault (where they had been all along), which is located today in the historic Colonial Park Cemetery in Savannah. They were subsequently reburied, along with his son's remains, in the base of the monument erected in his honor in Johnson Square.

❖ The Harper Fowlkes House in Savannah is the headquarters of the Georgia Society of the Cincinnati. Although it functions primarily as a museum today, the Georgia society members still meet regularly in the meticulously kept 1842 Greek Revival mansion.

❖ The Marquis de Lafayette was a close friend of both Nathanael and Caty Greene. The reason for Lafayette's visit to Savannah in 1825, during his celebratory tour of the United States, was to lay the cornerstone for Greene's monument in Johnson Square. He stayed for two nights at the Owens-Thomas House, then an elegant lodging house run by the widowed Mary Maxwell.

❖ Lafayette was a Mason and the ceremonial cornerstone-laying ceremony for Greene's monument was presided over by Masons. In addition to newspapers and currency of the day, items placed inside the cavity of the cornerstone included medallions of Washington, Greene, Franklin, and Lafayette. Presumably they still remain buried inside the obelisk monument.

❖ The neoclassically designed Bull Street Library, located just south of Forsyth Park, still stands proudly as the oldest library in Savannah. The Robin Hood mural that covers the entire south wall of the children's section is a sight to see. The library conducts periodic book sales.

❖ The Crystal Beer Parlor has been a favorite watering hole of Savannahians for decades. It opened as a restaurant in 1933 and was rumored to be a speakeasy during the days of Prohibition. While ownership has changed hands a number of times over the years, the building and interior have retained enough of their original design that it remains true to its colorful roots.

❖ The Mulberry Grove property where Caty and Nathanael Greene's Federal-style plantation house once stood is now owned by the Georgia Ports Authority. Unfortunately, the site has been fenced off and largely forgotten. Remnants of the brick front steps are all that is left of the once stately mansion where so many incredible historical events took place.

❖ The Savannah River still meanders its way past the deserted ruins. The old sandy drive that Washington and Caty once traversed, while overgrown, is still visible. And it is still lined on either side, as it has been for more than two hundred and thirty years, by massive oaks dripping with Spanish moss.

❖ The rest has been lost to history, and left for our imaginations to conjure.

MATT HAWKINS RETURNS IN TED RICHARDSON'S NEXT NOVEL.

ABOLITION OF EVIL

They are the richest family in America that nobody has ever heard of, with a net worth of over $100 billion. Their privately held company has been quietly bankrolling politicians, influencing elections, and shaping public opinion for over thirty years. Hidden behind a sophisticated network of grassroots advocacy groups, think tanks, and well-heeled lobbyists, they are on the verge of achieving their lifelong goal—a return to the Gilded Age of their forefathers, when the United States was controlled by a handful of powerful families. But the potential revelation of a centuries-old family secret threatens to sabotage their subversive plans.

Savannah antiques store owner Matt Hawkins discovers lost field notes written by Meriwether Lewis during the historic Lewis and Clark Expedition. They contain a curious claim of a seemingly impossible discovery in northwest Montana. Hawkins follows a trail of clues, from the Spanish Conquistadors to a legendary tribe of invincible black Indians to the hallowed halls of Thomas Jefferson's Monticello. His pursuit of the truth leads him out of the past and headlong into the center of a modern-day conspiracy—whose outcome will determine the fate of America's democracy.

Please turn this page for a preview.

AN EXCERPT FROM THE FORTHCOMING

Abolition of Evil

By Ted Richardson

Available in 2015

1

June 1973

Blackfeet Indian Reservation, Montana

The two Indian teens raced side by side, their dirt bikes kicking up rocks and leaving a swirl of dust in their wake. The bigger boy, Tommy, yelled in youthful exuberance as he accelerated past his best friend. His shoulder-length jet-black hair shimmered in the early summer sun. His bright white teeth stood out in stark contrast against his dark skin, made darker by a fresh smattering of mud.

Despite the fact that he was a year older than Tommy, Leonard was barely half his size. The two boys made an odd pairing but they had been inseparable since elementary school. Leonard pushed the throttle on his secondhand 1964 Honda 90 Trail bike to its limit to catch up with his friend. The max speed on the speedometer was listed at 60 mph but Leonard had never been able to get the well-used 87cc pushrod engine much over forty-five, and even that required a stiff tailwind.

The trail bikes were favored by most hunters and fishermen on the res, because they could handle rough terrain and climb just about anything. More importantly, they were lightweight, so they wouldn't get stuck in the mud. They had reached the foothills on the western edge of the reservation, so Tommy shifted his bike into low gear and began to climb. It didn't take long, however, for the smaller Leonard to overtake his man-child best friend— one of the rare occasions when Tommy's size proved to be a disadvantage. Leonard grinned and thrust his fist into the air as he crested Ghost Ridge first.

The two boys paused to take in the picturesque view. Behind them, to the east, they could see for miles as the sweetgrass of Montana's Great Plains went on seemingly forever. To the west, directly in front of them, the Rocky Mountain front rose up rapidly and majestically—its many peaks still blanketed in white from the record snows of the past winter. Just to the north, straddling the border of Glacier National Park and the Blackfeet Reservation, stood an isolated block of Proterozoic rock known as Chief Mountain. It was the tallest of all the peaks at an elevation of over 9,000 feet. It was also one of the most sacred sites to the Blackfeet. Spiritual sweetgrass ceremonies had been held at its base for generations.

The old-timers claimed that the small ridge the boys had just ascended was haunted by the spirits of a mythical tribe; thus the name Ghost Ridge. Tommy used to be fascinated by the story as a little boy, but had come to believe it was just another bullshit Indian legend that the tribe elders always seemed to be trying to pass along to his generation. He'd been out on that ridge plenty of times and never seen or felt anything. *Ghosts my ass*, he thought, and reached into his shirt pocket for his lighter. He sparked up a fat joint he had rolled earlier that morning and took a long hit before passing it over to Leonard.

They sat straddling their idling bikes, silently taking in the scenery and getting slowly stoned. Getting high had become a daily ritual for the two boys. Life on the res was isolated and filled with hardship, and they had a difficult time envisioning a future with much promise. Tommy began to feel a familiar wave of depression creep in around the edges of his psyche. Not today, he thought. He breathed in deeply, revved his engine, and took off. He was alive again as he barreled down the western slope of Ghost Ridge, hollering at the top his lungs.

The heavy snows of winter had given way to an unseasonably warm spring, causing serious flooding the previous month. As the boys reached the base of the opposite side of the ridge they could see the significant erosion that the last round of flooding had caused. Tommy pointed to a few new caverns carved in the side of the hill by the powerful runoff. The gaping crevices hadn't been there the last time the two boys had traveled out this way.

The sun was getting lower on the horizon and a glimmer from something on the ground caught Tommy's eye. He steered his bike in that direction. As he got closer, he saw an odd-shaped piece of metal sticking out from between two rocks. He killed the engine, engaged the kickstand with the heel of his boot, and dismounted. He had to roll away a few loose stones to free up what appeared to be a metal helmet of some kind.

"What the hell is that?" Leonard asked, as he rolled to a stop ten feet behind Tommy.

"Hell if I know, but it looks old," Tommy answered slowly.

He inspected the helmet in his hands. It was oval-shaped and came to a point on top. The brim that ran around the entire base of the helmet was curved downward, almost like the top half of a duck's bill. It had a number of dings and dents, but considering its age, it seemed to be pretty intact.

Leonard walked up from behind Tommy and grabbed the helmet out of his hands, "Where do you think it came from?" he asked, turning it over to peer inside.

Tommy pointed toward the mountains and said, "Looks like the runoff from the spring thaw must have carried it here. Hell if I know from where, though." He looked back at Leonard who had the helmet perched on his head and a shit-eating grin plastered on his face.

"What do you think, pretty badass, right?" His eyes were still slightly glazed over from the pot and the helmet was too big for his head. He looked ridiculous.

"Yeah, a real warrior, bro," Tommy deadpanned. They both burst out laughing.

Tommy took a step forward to grab the helmet off his friend's head, but Leonard was too quick. He darted out of the way. "Give it back, Lenny!" he shouted, and started to give chase.

Leonard looked back over his shoulder. He could feel Tommy bearing down on him. He knew it wouldn't be long before his more athletic sidekick caught up and tackled him, so he quickly tossed the helmet back over his shoulder. Tommy caught it in midair, but in the process, his toe caught on a large stone. He stumbled and fell. Leonard flopped to the ground nearby in a fit of uncontrollable, stoned laughter.

A few minutes later, Tommy got up. "Come on, Lenny, it's getting late. We better head back before the sun goes down."

He lashed the helmet to his rear cargo rack and turned his bike in the southeasterly direction of home. The boys were especially quiet on the long ride out of the foothills. Their adventurous day was quickly fading into a memory, replaced by the depressing reality of their everyday lives that lay just a few miles ahead.

———

A few weeks later, a stranger arrived at the double-wide trailer that Tommy shared with his mother and two older sisters. His father had fled the scene shortly after Tommy was born. Tommy was home alone when an older white guy with neatly trimmed gray hair emerged from a shiny, new Cadillac.

"Yeah?" Tommy said warily, pushing the door halfway open.

Tommy could tell by his accent that the man was from somewhere else. He told Tommy that he had seen the boys' picture in the newspaper and was interested in purchasing the old helmet. A couple of weeks earlier, the local paper had run a story about Tommy and Lenny's discovery. The story had been picked up by a couple of larger circulation newspapers in the nearby towns of Missoula and Great Falls.

Tommy didn't have much need for a funny-looking old helmet, and some quick cash sounded good. Weed and beer didn't come cheap. The man made an offer but Tommy smelled a bigger payday. He thought he could squeeze more out of the dude, so he looked him square in the eye and asked for double. The man hesitated just long enough for Tommy to fear that he might have blown his opportunity. But then he reached into his pocket and pulled out a wad of cash. The exchange was made quickly. Tommy stuffed the cash in his jeans pocket and watched from the doorway as the Cadillac disappeared from view.

That was the last he ever saw of the man or the funny-looking helmet again.

2

Present Day

Savannah, Georgia

The plump middle-aged woman kept stealing glances at Matt as she browsed through a table full of architectural fragments. Matt had purchased the pieces at a local auction a couple of months earlier. The restoration of old homes in Savannah was a never-ending endeavor, so period door knobs, window frames, fireplace mantles, staircase finials, and the like were always in demand. Plus, Matt had a weakness for the beauty and craftsmanship that went into nineteenth-century homebuilding. That's why he never passed up the opportunity to salvage a piece of Savannah's glorious past.

Matt smiled at the woman as she stole yet another glance at him. Finally she got up the nerve to approach him and said, "Aren't you the guy who found Washington's surrender letter?" He guessed she must have hailed from Chicago because the word *the* sounded more like 'da' and the word *guy* sounded more like 'gay'.

Matt was more than prepared for the question. He had heard it a thousand times over the past eighteen months. He had become quite famous ever since he had unearthed a surrender letter written by George Washington during the Revolutionary War. For a time, Matt had enjoyed all the attention as he traveled the media circuit, appeared on talk shows, and gave countless interviews. The American public was fascinated by the story, and Matt's effortless charm and athletic good looks had earned him a legion of fans.

He patiently explained to the plump woman and her equally round husband that he indeed was "dat gay", but of course that was something they already knew. They hadn't ended up in his 6,800 square foot shop by accident. The only reason they came to Hawkins Antiques, located inside of a circa-1860's converted mansion, was to meet the famous Matt Hawkins. They hadn't a clue about antiques and couldn't tell the difference between Regency and Victorian styles if their lives depended on it. But Matt always made time to talk, so he did his best to patiently answer their questions.

He finally had a chance to extricate himself when his cell phone began to chirp. His good friend, James Fox, the executive director of the Society of the Cincinnati, was calling. Matt walked outside to take the call.

The Society of the Cincinnati was the nation's oldest patriotic organization. It was founded in 1783 by officers of the Continental Army. The society's stated purpose was "to promote knowledge and appreciation of the achievement of American independence." For the past year, Anderson House, the society's headquarters in Washington D.C., had housed the now-famous George Washington surrender letter exhibit, which had been viewed by tens of thousands of curious Americans.

After catching up for a few minutes, Fox came around to the reason for his call. "Matt, something remarkable was donated to the society a couple of weeks ago. One of our members bequeathed a rolltop desk that was used by William Clark when he was the superintendant of Indian Affairs back in the 1830s," he explained.

"You mean William Clark, of Lewis and Clark fame?" Matt replied. Matt was an amateur history buff and had always been fascinated by the 1804 expedition that was the brainchild of Thomas Jefferson.

"One and the same," Fox said excitedly.

"Wow, James, nice score," Matt said enthusiastically. As he talked, he walked across the street from his shop and into the beautiful confines of Monterey Square. Monterey was just one of twenty-two beautifully landscaped squares located throughout the historic section of Savannah. He found an unoccupied bench and sat down.

"Thanks, but I haven't even told you the best part yet. Inside the desk, we discovered something even more remarkable— a cache of never-before-seen field notes, written by Meriwether Lewis, during the final months of the Lewis and Clark Expedition!"

"What?" Matt nearly shouted. "How is that even possible? I mean, how come nobody ever found them before?"

"Well, the gentleman who willed the rolltop desk to the society was ninety-seven years old when he died. The desk had been left untouched in his attic for more than fifty years. Nobody even knew it was up there except for the old man, and he had suffered from dementia for years. According to his will it had been passed down to him by his grandfather who had acquired it shortly after Captain Clark's death in the 1838."

"And Meriwether Lewis's notes were just sitting right inside the desk all these years?" Matt asked, still in disbelief.

"Well, they weren't exactly sitting out in the open. In fact they were pretty well hidden. When the society received the desk, it was in rough shape. It was filthy and the drawers were stuffed with all kinds of old papers and other junk. As our curator was cleaning and preparing it for display, he came across a clump of wadded-up old newspapers in the back of a bottom drawer.

Out of curiosity he began to read some of the headlines. You can imagine his shock when, as he unraveled the bundle, he discovered hand written field notes from perhaps America's most famous explorer."

"Are you sure they're real?"

"One hundred percent," Fox replied without hesitation. "We hired a highly experienced authenticator. He has no doubt they were written by Meriwether Lewis."

"They must be worth a fortune!" Matt said excitedly. "So when are you going public with your find? The Lewis and Clark buffs are going to go crazy over this."

Fox paused before continuing, "Actually it's funny you mentioned the word crazy, Matt, because that's the reason I'm calling."

"Sorry, James, but you've lost me now."

"Well, here's the thing. The notes were written in a somewhat rambling nature. You could even say that they were incoherent in parts. You see, Lewis tells an unbelievable story about being captured by a tribe of Indians. More remarkably, he describes them as looking a lot like Toby, Captain Clark's black slave who accompanied them on the expedition," Fox explained, his tone turning more serious.

"Wait a minute, James," Matt interrupted, "I've read a lot about the Lewis and Clark Expedition and I don't remember reading anything in the history books about Lewis being captured, let alone by a tribe of black Indians!"

"That's because there was never any mention of it in Lewis and Clark's official correspondence. Believe me, we made a trip to the American Philosophical Society in Philadelphia and read copies of the original journals cover to cover, just to make absolutely certain," Fox related. "Like I said, it's an unbelievable story, and by unbelievable I don't mean remarkable, I mean we're not sure if we believe it."

"I guess I see now why you haven't gone public with your find," Matt replied. "So when did Lewis say this mysterious capture happened?"

"He claims it occurred toward the end of the expedition, in July 1806. That would have been shortly after he and Captain Clark split up so they could explore more territory. Clark went south and Lewis headed north. Along the way, Lewis explored the Marias River, not too far from the present-day Blackfeet Indian Reservation near Glacier National Park, in Montana. Evidently he was on one of his many famous solo walks, when he was surprised and captured."

"So what happened next? Were they friendly? How did he say he escaped?" Matt's questions came in rapid succession.

"Whoa, slow down, Matt. I know you've probably got a hundred questions and I've still got a lot more to tell you" he paused, "but I'd rather discuss the next part of the story in person. Buzz and I want to fly down to Savannah in Buzz's plane tomorrow afternoon—are you available?"

"Believe me, James, even if I had box seats at Fenway, I'd give them away for this."

————

Matt sat at a back booth at the Crystal Beer Parlor waiting for Fox and Buzz to arrive. The Crystal was a favorite eatery and bar among local Savannahians, and had been for more than seventy-five years. Matt had discovered it shortly after arriving in Savannah from New York City. His ex-wife had never understood what Matt saw in the old tavern—just one of many incompatibilities that had resulted in their divorce a decade earlier.

At the moment however, Matt's mind was on a more recent woman in his life, Sarah Gordon. He had met Sarah during their harried search for Washington's surrender letter. The two had begun a whirlwind romance which Matt thought had the makings of something special. But then Sarah accepted an offer to be an adjunct professor from a prestigious university in England. She was only half way through her one year commitment, and the distance had already taken a toll on their nascent relationship.

Fox and Buzz's arrival snapped Matt out of his melancholy. After ordering a round of beers, Matt couldn't wait any longer, "All right, guys," he said. "I've been pacing around like a mad man ever since you called. So what's the rest of the story?"

"Sorry for the intrigue, Matt," Buzz began, "we're just not sure what to make of all this."

Buzz Penberthy was president general of the Society of the Cincinnati, and James Fox's boss. At sixty-nine years old, he was nearly twice Matt's age. Although by looking at him you'd never know it. And despite their age difference, the two had become close friends.

"As you may know," he continued, "Meriwether Lewis was thought to have been saddled with both depression and alcoholism—and he was even rumored to have contracted a bad case of syphilis on the expedition. So before taking his field notes at face value, we need to make sure these aren't just the demented ramblings of a man with a sore pecker and a bad hangover."

"Like I said to you on the phone," Fox said, ignoring his boss's off-color comment, "Lewis makes some pretty incredible claims, and being captured by a tribe of black Indians is only the first one."

Matt raised his eyebrows, "What do you mean, only the first one?"

"It's what he describes next that really made us question the truth behind his story," Fox continued. "Lewis claims that the black tribe's mannerisms, customs, and style of building were unlike any Indian tribe he had ever encountered. He even goes so far as to say that some of the words seemed more European in origin than Indian."

"Come on guys, that's impossible," Matt said. "I mean, no Europeans had ever made it that far into the interior of America by that time, right?"

"That's what the history books tell us," Fox agreed. "But there's more. Lewis also claims that during his short captivity he was taken to what he describes as a 'religious shrine'. And sitting atop the shrine was this," Fox said. He pulled out a photocopy of a crude sketch that Lewis had hastily drawn in his field notes. He slid it across the table to Matt.

"This looks like a Conquistador helmet!" Matt blurted out.

"Yup, there's no mistaking it," Buzz interjected, "that is definitely the distinctively shaped helmet that de Soto, Coronado and other Spanish Conquistadors made famous."

"Wow, that's incredible," Matt offered.

"Actually, more like *impossible*," Buzz offered. "The problem is that Spanish Conquistadors never made it any farther north than Colorado, which is more than a thousand miles *south* of where Lewis claims he saw this helmet."

"You guys aren't screwing with me, right?" Matt looked across the table with raised eyebrows. The two men shook their heads from side to side.

"So let me get this straight," Matt continued, with more than a touch of skepticism, "we've got authentic field notes written by Meriwether Lewis."

"That's right," confirmed Buzz.

"And these field notes describe his capture by a mysterious, European-sounding tribe of black Indians."

"Right again."

"And these Black Indians apparently worshipped a Spanish Conquistador helmet, even though the Spanish never made it anywhere close to Montana" he concluded.

"That about sums it up," Buzz said with an ironic smile.

"I'm beginning to think your theory about this being the ramblings of a sick man is probably true. Maybe the pressure of two years in the wilderness finally got to our fearless captain, or maybe he was tripping after eating a bad mushroom," Matt said, only half-joking.

"We thought so, too," Fox said, "Until we found something that may actually lend credibility to Lewis's wild claims." He reached into a manila folder and pulled out a copy of an old newspaper clipping.

"We did a little research to see if there had ever been any findings of Spanish Conquistador antiquities that far north. The only reference we could find was this single newspaper article," Fox explained. "It appeared in the *Great Falls Tribune* in 1973." He handed it over to Matt.

The black-and-white photograph in the article was grainy but Matt could easily make out the grinning faces of two teenage Indian boys. The next thing he noticed nearly took his breath away. The larger of the two boys held a helmet in his hands, a helmet that matched Meriwether Lewis's sketch to a tee.

"Holy shit," Matt said, amazed.

"I'll second that," Buzz replied dryly.

Matt quickly scanned the short article. "It says the boys found the helmet out in the western hills of the Blackfeet Reservation, but it doesn't say much else. So what ever happened to it?"

"That's where the mystery deepens," Buzz's tone became more serious. "We looked and looked, but there are no other references to the boys' discovery—anywhere."

"There are lots of unanswered questions, Matt," Fox interjected, "which is why we came here today. Like you, we first believed Lewis's claims too preposterous to be true, but when we found this picture in the newspaper, it changed everything."

"I agree, so where do I come in?" Matt asked.

Buzz answered, "Before we go public with our discovery of Lewis's field notes, we need to do our homework. That means following up on this lead." He pointed an index finger at the article lying on the table. "Since we came up empty searching the Internet for additional information, I think it's time to do a little boots-on-the-ground recon."

Buzz was an ex-navy fighter pilot, and even though he had long since retired, military jargon was still part of his lexicon. He continued, "We found out that one of the Indian boys in the photo is long since dead, but the other one, Tommy Running Crane, is still alive and still living on the Blackfeet Reservation in Browning, Montana." Buzz smiled, and the familiar twinkle returned to his steel-blue eyes. Then he added, "So, what do you say, Matt, you up for a trip to Montana?"

Buzz knew Matt couldn't resist a good historical mystery so he wasn't surprised a bit when his impulsive younger friend didn't hesitate for a second.

"I was due a vacation anyway, Buzz. Count me in."

A fter more than twenty-five years as a business professional,
Ted Richardson parlayed his fascination with American
history and his love of a good mystery into producing his first
novel, *Imposters of Patriotism*. He lives in the Atlanta area with his
wife and two daughters.

Visit him on Facebook at

www.facebook.com/AuthorTedRichardson

DATE DUE

MAR 2 8 2015	
APR 1 3 2015	
	PRINTED IN U.S.A.

CPSIA information can be obtained at www.ICGtesting.com
Printed in the USA
LVOW05s1915290714

396578LV00007B/903/P

AUG - - 2014